Zed

Zed

Elizabeth McClung

Arsenal Pulp Press

VANCOUVER

ZED
Copyright © 2005 by Elizabeth McClung

ARSENAL PULP PRESS
341 Water Street, Suite 200
Vancouver, BC
Canada V6B 1B8
arsenalpulp.com

The publisher gratefully acknowledges the support of the Canada Council for the Arts and the British Columbia Arts Council for its publishing program, and the Government of Canada through the Book Publishing Industry Development Program for its publishing activities.

This is a work of fiction. Any resemblance of characters to persons either living or deceased is purely coincidental.

Front cover photograph by Luis Jacob
Design by Shyla Elan Seller

Printed and bound in Canada

Library and Archives Canada Cataloguing in Publication

McClung, Elizabeth, 1970-
    Zed / Elizabeth McClung.

ISBN 1-55152-197-0

    I. Title.
PS8625.C58Z3 2005   C813'.6   C2005-903991-4

ISBN-13 978-155152-197-8

Chapter 1

HER NAME? ZED. AGE? Eleven, twelve, maybe thirteen – it wasn't like she was getting three square a day and multivitamins. She was small, four-foot nothing: thin, grubby, but with a thrust to her chin which told you, as you saw her beetling down the hall towards you – *best step aside*. Most people were fairly certain Zed was female. Her soft features and long lashes were contrasted by grey uniform coveralls, slick and shiny from constant wear. The hair was the deciding factor, because it fell, wildly uneven, to shoulder length. Once a year, Zed assaulted it with her knife, hacking it back above her ears. She had a habit of tilting her head down and staring up at people from under her bangs. She just showed up one day – no relations, no history. No one knew much about her, and those who did never passed it on. People didn't gossip about her, at least not more than once, because if she caught them she'd stick her knife point somewhere soft on them and ask, "Got anything more to say, Chuckles?" which, invariably, they didn't.

Yes, she fit right in with the Tower.

THE TOWER, AN UNPAINTED concrete tenement block twenty storeys high with basements and sub-basements below. Twenty storeys of long hallways with ancient whitewash and carpets laid down from the war. Which war that might be was a subject of heated hallway controversy. At each end of the hall ran concrete stairs, unpainted and unventilated, winding back and forth, up and down. They were cob-webbed, grimed, half-lit, urine-scented, and suspiciously sticky. Still, a majority of the tenants used them, unless they were suicidal enough, or drunk, or stoned or oblivious enough to take the elevators. Not that anyone had died ... yet. But both elevators did have a tendency to groan a little. One of them, when going to the top floors, would shake and stop before letting out a moan of tearing metal. Then, without warning, it would drop a few inches and you prayed and clutched each other. The lights would go out and it'd drop a bit more. But after a while the lights would flick on and the elevator would start again, shrieking as it shuddered up the shaft. So when the doors did open, you didn't mind so much that it had missed the 17th floor by over two feet and you had to climb up to get out. In the Tower, this elevator was known as "Lucky," or "the good'n."

The other elevator, "Jimmy," was named after the inaugural suicide of the building, a mythic figure who had jumped into the empty shaft and now resided in the elevator that occupied it. This was why, some of the time, the elevator would take you where you wanted to go without a fuss. It was also why, at other times, it would close the doors and send you up and up, say, to maybe floor 18 and then right down, to the 4th floor: up to 17, down to 11, up to 16, down to 2, all the while never obeying a single pushed button including the emergency stop and never once opening the doors. Once aboard, the only way out was if someone on the outside pushed the elevator button. Then, like a diabolic amusement ride, one passenger would be let out for another to come in before it started all over again. Everyone avoided "Jimmy" after the unfortunate incident when a 2 a.m. drunk was stuck inside for over an hour, screaming his lungs out.

At one time the Tower may have had a real name, like "Highland

Heights" or "Viewside Towers," but that was back before the downtown drifted away, leaving the empty lots and shells of buildings behind like trash after a picnic.

If you had a choice, you lived somewhere else. Otherwise, welcome home.

ON THIS MORNING ZED stood before the main entrance, those two great sunken glass doors, and looked up. The top of the building was wrapped in a shroud of early morning mist. A crescendo of yowls had drawn Zed's attention upwards and now, accelerating toward her through the mist, came a writhing, wailing bundle of cat, its claws extended. Watching the way the air rippled its fur, Zed recognized the cat as Valerie's, "Val" of the 19th floor. Zed saw the cat often as it waited, curled on Val's doorstep. This was because Val lived within the grip of two moods: the first sent her roaming the halls, aggressively horny, in search of a screaming fuck; the other left her curled on the floor in a three-day crying jag petting a cat desperately trying to escape.

While the earth is patient, gravity is not. The cat accelerated, the ground remained.

Zed, no stranger to bloodstains, edged backwards, stepping out of the splash radius.

The cat hit with a wet thud, its head twisted back, mouth gaping. The flight was over. Zed shrugged. She'd check that out later, but now, with the building just waking up, it was time to do the rounds. Time to get to business.

Hammer, the building's security guard, with his bulging forehead of bone and flat top, leaned against the door. He looked down at the colourful addition to the sidewalk. "Cat," he rumbled with his stick-on-gravel voice. Zed nodded. "Outside building." Zed nodded again. "Not my jurisdiction," he said, with a low coughing sound. Zed looked at Hammer's throat, wondering if the volume of words had choked him. It was when he turned that she saw the quake of his shoulders. Hammer was laughing. Zed followed him as he returned to his concrete room, its 180-degree slit holes built just like a real bunker.

Hammer handed her a dog-eared paperback mystery. "Done," he told her. "Mafia book." Zed put the book into her satchel, a heavy, green sack with a shoulder strap. Hammer watched her, his stubby grey hair matching his pressed shirt.

"Mafia," Zed confirmed. Speaking as little as possible became a habit when talking to Hammer.

"Mystery," he shrugged. He rubbed his nose and looked at her. "Good kid." He leaned forward and indicated with one finger that she should do likewise. "Afternoon," he said softly. "The power." He drew a finger across his throat.

Then he leaned back with the start of a smile. "Info," he nodded. "Two books."

She held up one finger.

He shook his head.

"So the power's off overnight?"

"Maybe."

"Off overnight, two, if it lasts until dark, one."

Hammer grunted, agreeing. His gaze drifted past her and Zed turned to see the first of the can-men coming into the lobby, ready for the day's search for all things metal.

"Out," Hammer barked at Zed, but she was already gone.

Zed had slipped through a dusty-grey steel door and now stood at one of the junctions of the inter-hallways. These hallways, snaking in and around the main floor, were the alternate highways connecting the elevators with the outside, the storage rooms to the water tanks, and the garbage bins to the parking garages.

She stood, extending her senses. She absorbed the plinks of warming metal doors and the stench of dried piss and vomit. Where to head first? She felt the hairs on her cheek catch a puff of air and the smell of sour bile and turned cheese caught in her nostrils. Someone was in the garbage bins and she wanted to see who.

One of the prebuilt luxuries of the Tower was the garbage chute system: four hatches for each floor into which bags of garbage disappeared. But like any magic trick, there was a functional underbelly: four industrial garbage bins sitting in a square on ground level under four matching holes in the concrete ceiling. Every few seconds, like expectant subway tunnels, a deep rattling would grow from one of the openings. This indicated that a bounding, hurling, and hopefully-bagged mass of garbage was approaching. After a loud metallic twang, a high-spinning, high-speed sack of previous personal property would arrive. Of course, not all bags or all trajectories are equal. The occasional bag of garbage exploding right out of the hole like a shrapnel grenade just added to the excitement, not to mention the smell.

Zed's nose, when she stood on tiptoe, only just reached the lip of the bins. Who'd be digging this early? "Dan?" Was that a rattle she heard in the back bins?

"Dan!" Nothing but another series of rattles.

"*Rat!*" she finally bellowed. A brown head popped up from the farthest bin.

"Damn it, girl," he said. "Don't you know not to bother me at work? I tell you, I have had about fucking enough...." But whatever he had enough of was silenced as a bag of garbage flew out from above, clipping him on the head. He and the garbage dropped from view.

Zed waited. She assumed he'd recover from the "freefaller," the silent but deadly bag of garbage and the main hazard to dumpster diving. Zed wasn't in a rescuing mood.

She heard a low moan and a rustling sound. Then silence. Then more rustling. "Get up, you cabbage-fucker!" she told the back dumpsters. "Hump the hampers later. I've got things to do."

A hand shot triumphantly into the air holding a piece of metal. "Fork," a rasping voice declared. Rat's body followed his arm upright and he hoisted a burlap sack onto his shoulder.

"Hup!" Rat called as he somersaulted into the next bin. With a swimming slither he poked his head over the edge, pushing the fork into Zed's face. "Fucking treasure from fucking heaven." They both considered the treasure with its two bent tines. "Spoons oftener," Rat added, "but forks better."

"So what ya got?" Zed looked up at a face grimed so brown it was like poured gravy. Rat's beard and hair were a mare's nest of rotting garbage, bits of recent meals and wandering maggots.

"Fork!" Rat smiled his black stumps.

"Know that, what else ya got, Dan?"

"I like that, when you call me Dan, not Rat like them others. Fuckers. Treat me like an animal, like some fucking animal!" His spittle flew in all directions, some hitting Zed on the forehead. She decided not to wipe it off just then.

"Just like yesterday," Rat declared. "I'm out in the morning scrounging a new dump from some townie car in that lot across the street, like there's no garbage pickup for the fucking townies, and there's a newbie who didn't know who's King Rat on this pile." Rat nodded slowly and pointed to his chest so Zed would not misunderstand to whom he was referring. "So I'm showing this newbie the way of the world and all, and just as I'm administering a final ear bite, for good measure you know, cuz you can't really get at their ears till they're already down, and what do I see? A fucking gawk shop from a townie doing a drive-by with the kiddies. Those little porkers, faces up at the window like I'm a wildlife fucking safari. I tell you, those townies, those fucking, fucking townies...." Rat's eyes were bulging and his words choked into a growl.

"Ain't I a human being?" Zed nodded. "Ain't I a stand up citizen? Do I drink in the morning? Am I some sex nutter, a panter, or some kind of druggie?" He pointed his fork at Zed. "Am I?"

"You don't shoot up?" Rat was well-known for his periodic heroin abuse, putting heroic quantities into his veins. Strangely, all it seemed to do was make Rat more ... well, more Rat.

"Well, a bit of horse now and then, what's that?"

"And grass?"

"Well, who doesn't take a puff now and then, end of a hard day?" He stared at Zed, the whites of his eyes standing stark against the rest of his face.

"A real stand-up," she assured him. "So what you got, eh?"

Rat blinked a few times, scratched his head; a maggot fell out. "Picked it up this morning...." He rummaged through his bag, then held out a toaster oven, dented and doorless.

Zed looked it over. "Got a door?"

He searched the bag further, pulled one out, and handed it over. "What you got today?"

Zed gave him a coy glance. "Cookies."

"Cookies! Fresh cookies!" Rat bounced up and down, singing the word "cookies." "How many you got?" he asked, thrusting his face towards her.

As intimidating as it was having Rat thrust himself upon you, Zed didn't get to be Zed by being pushed around. "Six."

"Six, just six." It came out as a whine. "That's not enough. Ten or no toaster."

"Seven and you throw in the fork."

"I thought you only had six, you fucker!" Rat yelled. Zed raised an eyebrow and turned to go.

"I'm sorry," he cringed. "I'm sorry." His eyes flicked from side to side before settling on her. "Nine."

"Eight, or I'm outta here."

Rat handed over the fork, and Zed eased two wrapped waxpaper packages out of her bag and handed them to Rat. Rat danced off into the underground parkade singing his cookie song. Zed kept her hand on the satchel, covering the other four individually wrapped cookies until he had gone.

With the toaster under one arm and the fork and door stowed in the satchel, the next stop was Gears', the local fixer, builder, and all-around gearhead of the building. At this time of day he was most likely at his workshop in the sub-parkade. Walking down the short corridor to outside, Zed walked around to the main entrance. She passed two human bottom feeders fighting over the cat carcass, entered the lobby, gave Hammer's eyes peering from the cement slit a wave, and then into the stairwell. This particular stairwell was the living and hiding place of Eric, one of the building's "panters." Eric was the least restrained of the panters and attacked anyone or anything smaller than himself, trying for a poke. Zed was reasonably sure that he was out this morning. Reasonably. Still, beyond the knife in her pocket, the pin hidden round her ear, the steel in her boots, and the spiked kneepads, Zed had her defences.

Descending a level, Zed walked across the parking lot dotted with abandoned vehicles, flat tires, and cracked glass. She walked up to a large sliding door marked B-1 and gave three sharp raps.

When the door opened, the first thing that spilled out was the musical scream of a husky alto, accompanied by guitar and bass. The second was a cloud of sweet-smelling smoke and then came Gears, with dilated eyes and a smile from Alpha Centari. Gears was a massive man, six-foot-four with long, blond Nordic hair and an upper body to match. He waved her in, then disappeared through the curtain of car bumpers, swaying gently above car batteries, copper tubing, and any and all assorted pieces of metal. The woman's voice shrunk from shriek to sub-vocal. Gears reappeared.

"Listening to *Ferron*: Now that lady, she knows where the wild is at." He looked down at Zed through one eye and gave her the peace sign. "But I guess the question is," he tilted his head, "where are you at?"

Zed held up the toaster and door.

"Aha. You wish that the blind could see and the lame could walk. I know about that, I. When I was in California, I was at this 'school'" – Gears' hands made air quotations – "for helping those behind get ahead, teaching to empower, but I tell you..."

Zed let her eyes drift. Whenever Gears went off into one of his stories, it was best to find something else to do until it came to its conclusion. She examined the stack of hubcaps next to her. Gears had quite a few and Rat found some too, but Zed never traded for them. She could never think of their practical use.

"...so I asked him, are we teaching to succeed or teaching to fail and that's when we both decided it was time for me to look at new opportunities. So I hear you." Gears took the toaster and the door. Zed took out a hand-rolled paper and gave it to him. "The requisite offering, beautiful," Gears said, taking the joint and putting it on a workbench. "Tomorrow, all ready." He turned and disappeared behind the curtain of bumpers. Zed let herself out.

NEXT STOP, COUNTESSA.

For Martin Luther King it was Mobile, Alabama; Calcutta had Mother Teresa, and in the Tower there was Countessa. Countessa gained followers not by her morality, but rather by this simple formula: where people are poor and desperate, those who give hope become important. And Countessa sold hope: personalized, divided into half-hour segments, and mixed with a little old-fashioned listening. Countessa was old school, sometimes very old school. She did palms and dreams, runes and divinations, astrology, the cards, tea leaves, and white magic. If you wanted to see the future, the dead, or the unspoken past, and were willing to pay the price, you went to Countessa.

Zed stopped in the gloom outside the glass bead curtain which served Countessa for a door. In the same way no one had seen Countessa's original door, no one had ever seen the lights around Countessa's doorway shine. Zed smiled. Those who sell secrets are in the business to buy information, and Zed was in the mood to sell.

"Come in, little friend." Countessa's rich contralto cut through Zed's thoughts.

As Zed pushed the beads aside and groped for the chair in the single candlelight, she dearly wished she knew how Countessa always figured out it was her.

"Powerful visions," Countessa told her, "visions of you down with the animals, covered in rats."

"Yeah, I've been to see Rat, but I think that vision might have come off the security cam or maybe smelling some of the Rat's stench still on me."

"There are many kinds of visions," Countessa conceded. "Yet you have something for me."

"Another pigeon," Zed joked about the one she had supplied, no questions asked, last year.

Countessa didn't respond to jokes. Her hands, the only part of her seen by anyone, sat in the light, folded on the table.

"All right, I'm selling info, but straight pure dope," Zed told her. "Price, ten candles."

"Candles, girl? What use are candles but lights in the darkness?"

Zed's heart sank; perhaps she had nothing to trade after all. But Zed didn't scrape a living by giving freebies or folding up and blowing away. She could bluff with the best.

After a minute Countessa asked, "Individual or collective, specific or general?"

Well, Zed definitely wasn't going to answer those questions. "If you can use the info, then give me the ten. Use it once and it's five. Anything else and it's on the house. You call it, no?"

Countessa's hands withdrew into the darkness, leaving Zed staring at the candle's flame. She calculated how much she could make if she ever got a look at the Countessa's face, or better yet, learned her history. But that was all info pipe dreams. The next time she looked at the table, Countessa's hands were back with ten stubby candles lined up.

"Power outage this afternoon. Last till dark, minimum."

"Mmm ... candles indeed." There was a soft chuckle. "I should have read the bones, but never mind." Her rings glittered as Countessa pushed all ten candles across the table.

Zed packed them away with a smile. Nothing is as fun as winning.

"Be wary, little one," the Countessa said suddenly. "I do see things, and for you I see a long road. Be wary of your enemies and friends both."

Zed packed the last candle away, then looked up grinning. "What? Friends, enemies? I'm a free trader. I got neither."

Countessa pulled her hands back into the darkness. "Never mind then, I say only what I see. Water's at the door. And tell Jenny to come in."

Zed shook her head, rose and went to the door. Stooping, she picked up a gallon jug of water with each hand.

"Later," she told Countessa and then she was gone, leaving only the tinkling of the glass beads in her wake.

JENNY, A POCK-FACED WOMAN with nibbled ears and a bobbing parakeet on her shoulder, waited in the hall.

"In." Zed hooked her thumb toward the door. "She told me."

Jenny's face lit up. "She always knows."

"Yeah, yeah, she always knows."

Zed worked up the stairs to the 7th floor, set the containers down in front of 712, and knocked.

A tiny, grey-haired sprite of a woman opened the door. "Hello? Hello? Who's come a-knocking on my door?" Her Welsh-Irish singsong died out as she spotted Zed. "Ah! It's my ray a' sunshine come, and look at all that water you've been carrying.

"Ach!" Ivy threw up her hands. "And where are my manners? Come in, come in, and bring all that lovely water with you, why don't ya. We'll have a cuppa. Not that I mind a little carrying, but with my water gone and my bones all aching...."

Zed put the two gallons of water on the kitchen counter. Ivy grabbed the bottles as she bustled around the kitchen making tea.

"Been seeing that Professor fellow today?" Ivy asked. Zed shook her head. Ivy laughed. "I wore on him yesterday, let me tell you. Aye, down in the mail room I was, looking through my good little mail slot when that tall rod of a man, him reading all the time, mind, comes round the corner, calm as you please and walks right on top of me. Well what do you think a' that? Not a word he said, not a word a-tall.

"I told him then. Up his eye I looks, 'An egghead you are, to be sure, but you've got no sense. No sense!'" Ivy gave a laugh. "I rounded him off, him and his book. I tells him, 'You may have your learning, but I'll tell you what I learned, me with no mother or father, is to treat people right.'" Ivy shook her head and gave another laugh. "But him, I respect him, mind, I do, he got smarts. But that poor Valerie, with her cat smashed up like the fine china and her already a bit twp." Ivy tapped her forehead with a forefinger.

"I've seen it before," she told Zed. "I can tell by that look in the eye. In my day, back in the valleys, used to see it growing in the women, them whose husbands never came out of the mines. One lass, a friend 'o mine, she was, and her husband, they were all set to move down to the city, work in the town like, when the news came he'd been killed in the mines. O' that knocked that on its head, to be sure, gone doolally within a week she had. Sad, that."

The water whistled and Ivy went, making the tea: a bit of water in the pot, a vigorous swill, then out it goes with good boiling water to replace it. "Here, have a cuppa and some Welsh cakes. Cuppa never hurt no one." Ivy poured and they sat drinking their tea.

"So where are you off to?" Ivy asked.

"Luc."

"Luc." Ivy threw up her hands. "O' Luc, o' that Luc, he's a sly one, mind, him with his suit and glances and the things he's done round here, the books I could write on him, I tell you." Ivy pointed a finger at Zed. "You keep shy of that one, but if you do deal with him, put it to him like he was one of the city folk, or he'll be all over you, him being so slick."

Ivy laughed at herself. "O' I'm a bad one, talking up a man like that behind him so."

Zed had finished her tea and Welsh cakes. The deal done, she stood to go.

"Up, down, up, down, you're like one of them Mexican jumping beans." Ivy laughed while she wrapped up Welsh cakes in wax paper. "Take these, take these." She pushed them at Zed.

As Zed packed them away, Ivy's hand touched her cheek. "Aye, you're all right, you're all right."

For no reason Zed could think of, certainly for no *good* reason, she found herself holding out two of her candles to Ivy. "Keep these close."

"What's this?" Ivy studied the candles. "What's this? What do you be knowing?"

Zed didn't respond, simply put the candles in Ivy's palm and slipped out.

Next stop: Luc's. His corner office was on the eleventh floor, right in the middle of the building or, as he put it, "where heaven and hell meet."

At the eighth floor she paused, the light tripping of footsteps on the stairs above making her look up. Soon, the sandy-haired, flushed baby face of the Father appeared, framed by his friendly red sweater and black slacks. "Jesus, Joseph, and Mary!" he cried out in an unfamiliar tone as he looked down at her. "What's with the wee ones? Never in Mass and never at service, tsk!" He bounded down the stairs to join her.

"'Lo, Father. Something wrong with your throat?"

"No, nothing is wrong with my throat, thank you very much." He gave her a puppy-dog look. "I will take that as a fervent rejection of my attempts at being Irish."

"You sound all normal now, Father."

"Yes, and may I remind you for the three millionth and last time that I am not a Catholic. I am a Methodist with a slant towards self-determinist interdenominationalism. So again, not a priest, not a Father. Why don't you just try calling me Gary."

Zed looked at the Father's face; late thirties but still with youthful exuberance. Why couldn't he understand that here, names were who you are, not who you wanted to be?

"Where ya going, Father?"

"Zed, I thought I just explained. Hey, Zed, how would you like it if I called you … Chris, for example?"

"No. I'm Zed."

"Yes, but I could call you Chris, couldn't I?"

"But I'm Zed."

The Father looked at Zed's determined face and sighed, "Yes, you're Zed and I'm … whatever."

"Father," Zed reminded him.

"Father," he agreed.

"Who ya seeing today?" Zed asked again because for some inexplicable reason the Father gave away info for free.

He cocked his head and regarded her before speaking. "Burl, Sandi, and Valerie."

Zed thought a moment, "Drink, drugs, and depression."

"Recovering alcoholic, glue addiction, and … depression," Father corrected.

"I got info for trade," she told him.

"What's it get me?"

"Time. Effort."

"Okay," Father agreed. "I'll owe you one, what is it?"

"You owe me six already!"

"Hey, I'm good for it. Didn't I get those books for you?"

"Yeah, *Christian books*, which don't trade."

"Seven all right? I owe you seven, so tell me already."

"Burl didn't cash his welfare check till day before yesterday."

"Wonderful, wonderful. He made it three days!" Father's face lit with triumph. "Drunk now?"

"Singing!" she assured him.

Father frowned as he did the calculations. "I think maybe tomorrow morn will incline his heart to repentance." He gave Zed a wink. "I feel strong about Burl; he's going to beat it. Soon, soon he'll pass that corner and have it beat."

Zed gave a one-shoulder shrug. "Yeah, whatever." She edged past him on the stairwell.

"Off to Sandi then," Father told her. "Stay clean, stay safe, and keep to the right, my child. It always pays in the end."

"What does it pay?" Zed asked.

"Oh no," said the Father, shaking a finger at Zed as he started off down the stairs. "I'm not falling for that one again." His feet pitter-pattered downward. "I owe you." He called back up.

"I know!" She yelled down the stairwell, "Seven!" There was no response. Zed sighed. Typical.

LUC'S OFFICE WAS ON THE building's front right corner, the door guarded by Luc's two henchmen: Stu and Barry. Zed pushed her way through the crowd of the stoned, the waiting, and the bored in order to reach the door.

"Hey, Barry," she called, taking the mystery paperback from her satchel. "Wanna book?"

Barry turned and inspired in Zed's mind the word he inspired in all who looked upon him: crooked. It wasn't just the one shoulder higher than the other, nor was it the strangely bent nose or the leaning teeth of his leery smile. No, there was something more, or perhaps less, about him which said that there was more muskrat to Barry than just his wispy moustache. He reached out and plucked Hammer's cast-off book from Zed.

Barry's fingers rubbed the book up and down while he fixed his eyes on Zed. "Used," he told her finally, "piece of crap, one cigarette."

"Okay." Barry smiled, whistling in and out between his teeth as he handed her the cig. She tucked it behind her ear and strolled past him to see Luc.

Luc was leaning back at his desk, listening to Steve, one of the Tower's many heroin addicts. "Just a little smack, man, anything," Steve pleaded, his hands twining around each other like coiled snakes.

Luc gave him a beautiful white smile, opening his large hands in compassion. "You know I would do anything for a gentleman such as yourself, but I have" – he touched his white Panama hat – "what shall we call them ... overheads. My friend, you have to work with me. What have you got, CDs, DVDs, cigs, a TV, what?"

Steve was almost crying, his ravaged cheeks twitching. "Man, I got nothing, all six of us just got a mattress, I got nothing."

"Then it looks like we are at an impasse, my friend."

"A what?"

"Well, as you have nothing to offer...." Luc drifted off and looked at the junkie writhing on the chair with a smile. "But," he said slowly, "if you were willing to be a bit beholden, I might be able to help you."

Steve leaned toward Luc eagerly. "All right, man! What's the stuff, where do I get it? You want me to do a pick-up, right? That the deal?"

"Um, no. Let me spell it out to you. I have decided, for no reason whatsoever, to give you some of my product. Not because I like you, not because I owe you, and not because I care. That okay with you?"

"For nothing?" Steve looked at Luc and then around the room. "You're going to give me some H for nothing?"

Luc just gave him the beatific smile.

Zed looked at Steve, who was so close to losing it he didn't know if he was up or down. She remembered when Steve moved in three months ago. He had looked a lot younger then. Sometimes he'd play his guitar in the lobby. He'd given her a Megadeth t-shirt. It was a good t-shirt.

"Give me some H," Zed said, pulling the cigarette from behind her ear and two packs more from her satchel.

Luc looked over at her, surprised. His eyes crinkled, and Zed couldn't tell if he was amused or annoyed. "Of course."

He swept the cigarettes off the table and pulled out a small bag of white powder. He looked at the bag and at Zed, put it back and took out a slightly larger bag of powder and pushed it across the desk. Zed pushed it in front of Steve. "Take it and get out."

Steve looked from the bag to Luc and back. He reached out for the bag. "Sorry, man."

"Come back anytime," Luc told him with sincere warmth. Steve fled through the door.

"Get over here." Luc nodded at a chair beside him.

Zed sat down.

"You queered my deal," he said sternly. "In front of me." He repeated it: "In front of me."

"Old debts," Zed said.

Luc leaned back in his leather chair, smoothed the front of his silk shirt, and cocked an eyebrow at Zed. "What are you here for?"

"I need a joint."

Luc clucked his tongue. "So young, so many habits."

Stu cleared his throat. They both looked to the door. "Boss, Howard is here to make an appointment."

"My child, do you mind?" Luc asked her. "It's not as if I have anything to hide, but some of my clients find it ... discomfiting to have a young female listening to their sexual arrangements." He frowned, thinking. "On the other hand, a few might find it quite stimulating." He fished a card out of the desk. "Hmm, Howard ... definitely discomfiting. Off you go then."

Zed rolled her eyes and hopped out of the chair. Outside the door, Howard, an overweight middle-aged man from the 9th floor, was nervously wiping his glasses. She pointed with her thumb. "In."

He scurried by, smelling of sweat and onions.

"Hey, that's my job," Stu protested, before going back to combing his blond hair.

Zed amused herself by watching Barry trying to sell the mystery paperback to one of the potheads in the hall.

"How much is it?" asked the pothead holding the book in his hand.

"Six cigs," said Barry. Then, as the pothead looked up, "No, I meant ten, yeah, ten." He looked into the pothead's face, which was losing interest. "No, no, eight, yeah, eight." His eyes twitched and danced.

"Fuck, Barry, make up your mind."

"Eight, yeah, eight."

The pothead slowly shook his head and handed it back, then turned and slouched forward to his group.

"You want it, it's five," Barry shouted, blinking and twitching.

"Hey, Barry, what time is it?" Zed called out. She loved doing this.

Barry abandoned the pothead and squinted at her. "Why do you want to know?"

"What time is it?"

"How much will you pay, three cigs, what?"

Zed laughed. Barry didn't even have a watch.

The door opened and Zed heard Luc say, "She will be with you tomorrow at two o'clock, friend," as Howard left.

Zed re-entered.

Luc was putting a thin stack of bills into his desk drawer. "Stu!"

"Yes, Boss?"

"Please go chat up Mr. Andrews on the 13th. His payment is delayed."

Stu smiled. "Sure thing, Boss."

Zed was looking at the drawer closing on the money. "What do you do with all the money?" she asked.

Luc looked at her askance. "Now that, my darling, is a truly rude question."

Zed waited with an equally rude expression on her face.

Luc gave a little shrug. "Truth? It just disappears."

Zed kept waiting.

Luc held up his hands. "No, it is the truth, a little here, a little there, a little missionary work like Steve, and soon enough, it is all gone. But," he held up a finger and took a noble pose, "I do not do this for the money, not old Luc. I do it for the same reason I live up here, cuz I love the people."

"Like the Father does?"

Luc shook his head. "Ah ... no, not exactly the same. See, I love the people just as they are, not like old high and mighty. He never really seems happy, does he? Always working against what people are. Me, I'm happy. You're happy. Everybody's happy."

"'Cept Val," Zed reminded. "Father's visiting her."

Luc perked up. "Going round to see Valerie, eh?"

"Shit!" Zed kicked herself for letting it slip out. "So what's that info worth to you?"

"Sorry," Luc grinned. "If it's laid, it's played. Val and Father ... that could change things." He stood and went to the wall and pulled on two handles hanging near the ceiling. Two blackboards dropped down, one filled with a checkerboard pattern and the other with columns.

"What's that?"

"That, my little pixie?" Luc answered distantly as he moved about adjusting the numbers in the columns. "The current tote on dear Valerie. To the left," he waved at the checkerboard, "the pool on her, and here," he ran a finger across the columns, "the odds on means and method."

"Means and methods of what?"

"Why, her suicide, dear one, her imminent suicide. Poor Valerie." He looked down in sombre reflection. "Never a very well person," he said, tapping his head with his forefinger at the word "well." "Seems that most days her life just isn't worth living and now, on top of it all ... the loss of poor kitty." He pulled a sad face. "She just can't cope with the world anymore. Time to unite with old fluffy."

"You sure?"

"Oh, yes." He bared his straight razor teeth. "Oh, yes."

"When?"

"Don't know, child," Luc said. "That's why it's called gambling." He laughed. "I'm betting heavily on tonight. But not if the good Father changes that. I really must have a chat with him."

"No!" Zed cried. "Not a beating."

"My child, I am speaking literally. I just want to talk." He pantomimed talking with his hands, then frowned at her. "My, you sure are flighty, what's wired you up?" He considered her. "Speed? Doubtful. Sugar? Perhaps. Caffeine? Almost certainly." He pointed a finger at her. "You've just come from that Welsh woman."

"You're not as impressive as Countessa."

Luc sniffed as if responding was beneath him. "So, am I a drop-in centre now? Lay a bet, do business, or be gone."

"A joint?"

"Clean forgot." He rolled the boards back up and sat down at his desk. He took a single joint from a drawer and placed it on the table. "What do you have today?"

"Info, worth more than that," she nodded toward the joint. "Worth two and a sawbuck."

"Sawbuck? A sawbuck? Since when are you calling twenties a sawbuck?"

Zed shrugged. "BB called it that. So, you in or out?"

"Neither. Why don't you just tell me and I'll pay you what it's worth."

Zed smiled.

"Fine, in. But one joint and a five, or 'fin' if you want to persist in slang."

Zed mouthed 'fin' a few times. "Naw, but how's this, two joints and I tell you the 'what,' then we deal for the when, how, and why."

Luc sighed. "Fine."

Zed coughed and extended a hand.

Luc opened the desk, added another joint to the one on the top, and pushed them over. "A little trust would be nice."

They both laughed.

"Power outage, whole building," Zed said.

Luc sat up even straighter. "When?"

"Thirty bucks."

"I thought it was twenty?"

"That was the package deal," Zed told him. "Separate it and it's more."

"Figures." Luc pulled out a roll and peeled off a twenty and a ten.

"This afternoon, maybe all night. Hammer knows."

Luc smiled. "Thank you, my dear, cheap at twice the price." Zed muttered a curse while Luc sang out, "Barry!"

Barry shambled in.

"Barry, find the Father, keep him distracted until the lights go out, then help him lose his way."

"The lights?"

"Just do it."

Barry shrugged, and after a glare at Zed, slid off down the hall.

Luc opened a drawer and removed a stack of bills, then rose from the chair and went to the rack by the door to put on his steel-blue silk jacket. "I'm kicking you out," he told Zed. "I have to go speak to the power man. By the by," he told Zed, "if you want to see the show, be here by six o'clock. The matinee: Valerie crying; main feature: the final act!"

Zed nodded, picked up her joints, and traipsed off.

Chapter 2

Zed's day was broken into five sections: Dealers (morning), Norms (midday), Slackers (late afternoon), Punters (night), and Animals (beyond midnight). Zed slept through Norms, while the building examined, compared, and gossiped over the doings of the previous night and the delivery of the morning mail. Zed had a hidey-hole, a padlocked room in the first basement, crammed with rotting and decrepit furniture: fridges without doors, collapsed tables, and sofas *sans* arms, backs, or cushions. Within the piled jumble, Zed had created a little nook for sleeping and storing, connected by tunnels just her size.

Over the years, Zed had covered the bits of exposed concrete with pictures from magazines. There were pictures of ships on the sea (the idea of a whole structure moving from place to place appealed to her) and pictures of fruit trees (the Father had told her that food appeared regularly on trees for free, beyond belief). Once, she had traded for a couple plants. She even gave them water. Beyond a rank smell, they had produced nothing. Above the blanket on which she slept was a picture of a buffalo. Zed figured any animal that large would be a useful ally.

Beside her bed was the large wooden box holding her basic trading and living supplies. The box had a false bottom, and today, before going to sleep, Zed lit her candle and pulled the top shelf out exposing her emergency supplies: two cartons of cigarettes, some cocaine, three leather-bound books, a box of candles, two bottles of whiskey, and $1,624. Zed pulled out the box of candles, replaced the top layer, lay down and slept.

Around 4:30 p.m., the start of Slackers, Zed roused herself, collected the candles, and headed up to the second floor, or "Brat Alley."

The route was so familiar, so routine, Zed did not register the darkness of the stairwell until the metal door clicked shut behind her. She'd mis-timed it; the power had already gone.

Survival instincts took over. Zed slid sideways, away from the silhouette she presented as she entered, and stopped to listen. At first she could hear nothing but the blood in her ears. Then she felt it, a soft movement of the hairs on her arm: a quiet steady breathing coming from her left. Her hand crept to her pocket. The breather was coming closer in a slow, searching, zig-zag pattern. Groping with her foot, she found the first stair, eased herself up on it, and slipped the switchblade out of her pocket.

Had she made a noise when she transferred her weight to the stair? The sound of breathing was gone. Where was the breather, and why had he stopped breathing? With an explosive gasp, a heavy panting started moving right toward her. She felt for the cold comfort of the steel button on the switchblade. There was a lovely swish as the click of the blade opening filled the stairwell. She moved the knife so the blade pointed down, her hand at shoulder height in a defensive crouch.

At the click the breather had stopped, but now, in a soft shuffle, he rushed her and within a pounding heartbeat a hand pulled her head forward, fingers gripping her hair. Instinctively she brought up her arm, raking the blade across the exposed forearm. With a grunt her hair was released and she was off, up the stairs, six steps up to the landing, turn and six more, up and up to safety. From below, bouncing up the dark well, a plaintive voice shouted, "Fuck!"

At the door of the second floor, she inspected her knife in the dim reflected daylight. Kneeling, she wiped the knife on the carpet, cleaning the blood off the fore-edge before closing the blade. Rising and continuing down "Brat Alley," Zed could see Ellen and Teresa sitting in the hallway on their folding lawn-chairs. Empty wine bottles cluttered their feet while they passed a bottle of red between them. Their children, Charles and Christina, sat on the floor. The two mothers were local success stories, getting multiple cheques for child support.

"Zed, who'd you run into?" Ellen had noticed Zed tucking her knife into her pocket.

Zed shrugged. "Too dark to tell. Norman, Quince maybe?"

Teresa took a hit off the bottle and offered it to Zed, who shook her head, so Teresa passed it back to Ellen. "Quince, the little girl man, yeah, he caught Christina the other day."

Zed looked at Christina who sat in an old blue jumper and picked idly at the floor.

Teresa shrugged. "A little petting and he whacked himself off, nothing heavy." Teresa sat up a bit and looked at Zed with interest. "Whatcha got today?"

Zed showed a packet of Ivy's Welsh cakes. "You?"

"Condoms." Ellen said. "Social worker came by to talk about 'Planned Parenthood'." She and Teresa cackled.

Zed waited. Ellen thought some more. "Got some batteries."

Zed considered a moment, then nodded. Ellen staggered off and returned with some C batteries. "They dead?" Zed asked.

Ellen shook her head. "Naw, I got the social worker to bring them for my vibrator, told her it was my solution to abstinence."

The exchange made, Ellen unwrapped the cakes and split them with Teresa. With the crumbs flying, Zed's stomach started to comment, so she unwrapped the single cake she had kept aside. As she looked down at her hand, she noticed Charles: he had lifted his head from the leg of

Ellen's chair and fixed his eyes on her cake. His mouth opened and his little hand extended.

Zed's brow furrowed and, slightly insulted, she stuffed the cake into her mouth. Charles' eyes fell and he began to sniffle. Ellen looked down briefly, then ignored him. Zed stepped over him to get to the stairwell. Children at best confused her, but more often, like this, sickened her. How could they stand to be so dependent? For Charles to hold out his hand with nothing to trade, it was beyond understanding. She took out her box of candles and proceeded up each floor, making deals with those who wanted a little light.

By the time she staggered to Luc's door, she was heavily laden with CDs, DVDs, some loose cigarettes, a broken Walkman, three pens, and two tins of canned ham. Unlike the rest of the building, Luc's doorway shone with brilliance. A sea of faces talked and waited at the edge of the light. Peeping in, Zed saw a couple of kerosene lamps blazing away.

"Hey Luc," Zed walked over to her customary chair. She pulled out a DVD. "You want *Awesome Threesomes IV*?"

He shook his head. "I do not. I've seen it and found it lacking. It does not deserve the good name of the Awesomes."

Zed shrugged and put it away. Luc turned his smile toward her. "Want to see today's distraction? Take a look out the window."

Zed rose and pulled back the curtain, letting in the shadowy grey of evening. She could see the lights of downtown starting up in the distance. In other parts of the city, people rushed into and out of downtown. In the bright sun of afternoon, and now, in the first wan of light, the downtown looked deceptively close; you could see past the boarded-up hospital, past the crumbling warehouses and empty lots to where windows shone. You could hear the murmur of cars and people talking. It was an unpleasant reminder of where you were. Much better was the black of night when the Tower was the world and the life, and you were more than some schmuck waiting for a monthly cheque and a delivery of booze. Zed turned her gaze down, and noticed several new blotches in front of the building. She was about to question Luc when a grey yowling blur flew past the window followed by the cackle of drunken laughter. Zed watched the cat until it hit the ground. Turning from the window, she found Luc watching her.

"Seems that this morning released the creative impulse of every cat hater in this building. And one goldfish hater," Luc added in afterthought.

Drunken cries of "Meow, meow, splat!" echoed from above, followed by guffaws of laughter.

"Stu!" Luc called. Stu walked in, sporting a new leather jacket with studs.

"Yo!"

"Enough with the yo's!" Luc told him. "You're a lackey, not a fifties hoodlum." He took a breath as Stu uncomfortably straightened his jacket. "Deal with them." He jerked his thumb upward.

Stu nodded.

"Those peepholes ready at Valerie's?"

Stu moved closer to the desk. "Yeah, Boss, I did them this morning after I got rid of Val's cat for you."

Within a split second, Luc had stood, reached out, and grabbed Stu's larynx. The skin around Luc's eyes tightened as he pulled Stu in close, speaking above the gurgle in a calm, conversational tone. "Regretful, isn't it, about Valerie's kitty-cat?" He lifted his hand until Stu hung gasping, a hooked fish, on his tiptoes. "So sad because no one knew who did it." He emphasized that point. "And here I sit, all refined and suave, just enjoying the twilight with Zed," he said, giving a nod in her direction, "and you have to cause this verbal indiscretion." He shook his head, like a sad father disappointed over the acts of a particularly wayward child. Bringing Stu into eye-to-eye range, Luc told him, "I think it is time for us to have that chat."

Stu squeaked out, "No, Boss!" before Luc's other hand joined the fun. Together they squeezed and squeezed until Stu's face turned a kind of ochre-purple all over, except for the whites of the bulging eyes. Stu thrashed about suitably.

"What are you going to do with him?" Zed asked.

Luc's brow was lined, intent on his work. "Make him an ex-minion, of course."

"Won't you go to jail?"

Luc's head turned toward her as he laughed. Stu's head hung off his loosened hand, a strand of drool falling from Stu's quivering lips. "My dear, the police are my friends. They like me. Verily, you should see my merit badge collection. Why just last week I helped them catch a burglar in this very building."

"But wasn't that just Dirty Irv? And wasn't he stealing to buy smack from you?"

Stu's eyes rolled upward as he passed out, hanging limp in Luc's hands. Luc dropped him with a withering look – "They're no fun when they're not wriggling," he commented to himself. "Seems like they don't even struggle anymore." He turned to face Zed. "As to Dirty Irv, I couldn't comment on his motives – I certainly don't comprehend the criminal mind."

"But I thought Irv already owed you for smack?"

"Really, child, this is so tiresome. Are there no other subjects to occupy a growing mind?" Luc straightened his shirt and sat back down.

Zed lapsed into silence. Luc checked his watch. "Five minutes to showtime. Sure you wouldn't like to share a peephole with me?"

"Naw." Zed stood and went to the door. Before leaving she turned and asked, "What are the odds on overdose?"

"Two to three."

She dug a wrinkled bill out of her pocket and unfolded it. "Put a ten on." She handed him the bill. He nodded, opened a book on his desk, and made a notation. Something brushed Zed's leg, making her start. She looked down. It was only Stu crawling out, one hand clutching his throat. Zed looked up and met Luc's eyes watching, full of cheery delight. With a nod, Zed turned and humped her overflowing bag to the stairwell. From there she descended to her hidey-hole and flopped down for the night.

THE NEXT MORNING AS SHE started her rounds, Zed avoided the guard bunker as much as possible. The power was just coming back and she didn't want to meet Hammer's smirk; she hated owing people.

She met Rat in the concrete foyer that connected the hallway to the collective garbage. He was crouched over a mattress someone had dragged down and abandoned during the night.

"Mine," he sang out as he saw Zed. "Mine, mine, mine!" He stuck out his tongue at her and laughed. Zed sighed.

"What you got?" Zed asked.

"Mattress," he said pointing. "I got me a fucking beautiful mattress, and I didn't even have to scrap for it. You want a mattress? Where do you sleep?"

She ignored the question. "Turn it over." He complied, crouching on one side and flipping it over. It raised a plume of dust and Rat sneezed, the snot flying from his nose. He wiped his hand across his nose and got all but two long strands that dangled from his wiry nose hair.

"What?" he said to Zed, who was mesmerized by the bobbing of the two white strands as they jiggled and swung with the slightest movement. "What?" He felt his nose and, quickly dropping on all fours, he pressed his face into the mattress and slid it along. "Ha!" he proclaimed, sitting back. He looked up at Zed, but she was gazing past him at the end of the mattress. He turned to look.

The lower end of the mattress had a gigantic reddish-brown stain. The centre of the stain was almost black and out from this centre, strange elliptical rings of lighter-coloured ochre spread out. "Hmm, blood," Rat said, passive and bored. He turned back to Zed. "Slight stain. I'll give you a good deal."

Zed looked it over. "Anything else?"

Rat shook his head.

"Not today," she told him. He shrugged and busied himself with loading the mattress on his back. Then, with a little grunt for goodbye, he staggered off into the hallway, humming happily to himself.

Zed watched him go and then followed him into the hall. Two quick turns and she connected up to one of the underground stairwells. At the doorway to the underground she heard a shuffling behind her and, turning, saw the timid pale face of Quince watching her. "Boo!" she shouted and watched him scamper back into the shadows. She wrinkled her nose and laughed before disappearing into the parkade.

She gave Gears' door her rat-a-tat and waited. Gears opened the door, letting out a delicious aroma of cooking which made Zed's mouth water. Gears went to his side counter where the toaster oven sat, still dented, but with a new cord and a door. "What's on?" Zed asked, trying to stop salivating.

"Stew," Gears said, eyeballing her. "Old family recipe."

"Trade you a canned ham for a bowl," Zed offered, pulling out the tin.

Gears shook his head. "It's not ready yet. All things in their time," he told her, handing her the oven. "But it is cool to see that society has not closed your mind with the fear of the different." His hands made a billboard in front of him: "New and Improved – Lap It Up." He turned to another imaginary billboard, "Different – Run and Hide."

Zed watched, bored. "Whatever."

"That's it," Gears said pointing to her. "You are who you are. No pretences, no pretending. The world is appearance and reality, and in this nuthouse you are, like, the only patient." Giving her another peace sign, he told her, "Don't let 'em catch you."

She gave him a little salute and left. She had a long climb up to the 14th floor where the Professor dwelled. She occupied her time trying to figure out what to do with the canned ham.

At the 14th floor, she found the door space blocked by a stained grey sweatshirt. Zed took a step back. It was one of the building's zombies. This zombie was a woman, her hair stringy, unwashed. Her eyes were dilated and wide, sunken deep above the jutting cheekbone. The skin on the face was pulled tight, making the head an animated skull. Zombies had gone over the edge of drug use long ago. Zed let the door go and it hit the zombie in the face. There wasn't even a flicker of pain, just a continued shuffling. The zombie moved past and started down the stairs. Zombies were so slow that Zed would probably have to pass her again later.

She gave 1406 a knock and waited. Behind the door, a rustling, then a thin dry voice called out, "Wherefore, wherefore? My lost Lenore?" Some more sounds of movement and the door opened. A head popped out, angular and balding with black wispy hair, perched atop a long tall frame.

"*Nevermore!*" he screamed.

Zed didn't jump back, but only because she'd been expecting something like this. She opened her mouth to speak, but before she could say a word, he did it again.

"*Nevermore!*"

They glared at each other.

Zed reached into her bag.

The Professor opened his mouth, revealing a row of black teeth, threatening.

Zed ripped out the toaster and held it above her head, shoving it into his face.

"*Neverm –*" The Professor blinked twice, long and slow, before pronouncing,

> I'm a little toaster,
> Ugly, short and cracked
> I toast the one side golden
> I toast the other black.

"Yeah, yeah," Zed muttered, pushing past him into the dim apartment. "Hello to you, too."

She started for the kitchen, threading her way carefully along the narrow passage banded on both sides by bookcases. Books also were stacked on boxes, on chairs, on each other, up to the ceiling in some parts. She made it to the kitchen and, removing a book called *Sheep Raising* by the TV vet, she put the toaster oven down and plugged it in. After staring out the door for several seconds, the Professor retreated back to his chair and picked up his book. Zed paused to peek at the title: *I Hear Voices* by Paul Ableman. She thought this might not be the best choice for the Professor. She went over to the corner by the door where the Professor kept his trading items. After sorting through the box of books, she pulled out a thick mystery as well as a true crime book on the Boston Strangler. She poked around some more and added a thick historical novel by Penman. She also checked the box of miscellany and found a small magnifying glass with a brass handle.

Zed stood in front of the Professor and cleared her throat. He looked up, startled. "Bad mice," he muttered, "always ransacking the doll's house."

She showed him the books and the magnifying glass. "OK?"

"OK? OK, abbreviation for Oklahoma, Oklahoma is OK, state motto, OK is Indian Territory, Mr. Andrew Jackson, Battle of New Orleans, Don't shoot till you see the whites of their eyes," he told her.

Zed sighed.

"British River, French Territory, Napoleon. Why is everyone in history short?" he asked himself.

Zed let herself out. She could still hear the Professor as she closed the door. "Lack of vitamin C? Rickets? Little Dorrit?"

Zed tucked the books away and headed downstairs to pay off Hammer. By the 7th floor the stairwell was so congested Zed was pushing through armpits.

"What's on?" she asked the nearest head.

"Countessa's got a prophecy coming down."

Zed's rule about free entertainment was the same as her rule about anything free – grab it while it's going. She followed the crowd as they crammed themselves into the hallway of the 5th floor. Zed continued to wriggle forward, squeezing around legs until she was stopped by familiar black wingtips.

"Whatcha doing here?" she demanded of the Father.

"I'm a spy in the enemy's camp."

Zed stood on her tiptoes, but was still too far away. Now that she'd stopped, everyone piled in, closing the openings. She was polishing up for a fight when the Father grabbed her around the chest, giving her a boost. Over the rows of heads she could just see the bead curtain covering Countessa's dark doorway before the Father dropped her with an "Ompf."

More people had packed the hall, foot to foot, shoulder to shoulder. Zed defended her space with knees and elbows.

"Ow! That's not very sociable," the Father told her.

"Then stop crowding me."

His retort was lost in the collective cry that went up as every hallway light simultaneously went out. After a minute, bathed in the red glow of the exit signs, the murmur died away.

Countessa's strong contralto cut through the last of the whispers. "The Bones speak."

The hall grew still. Zed could hear murmurs, then only collective wheezing and breathing, until at last just the sound of one stuffed nose, behind her left shoulder.

"I see a house." The Countessa gave weight to each word. "A house where Death lives. The death that was, and is, and is to be."

"Last night's news," a critic called out, "which lost me a tenner, thanks very much."

Countessa didn't even falter. "The Bones speak. I see a man in black, a man not of fire or steel or air and he brings death by three. The suicide was the gateway and even now we stand in the halls of death.

"The Bones speak. I see those of innocence die, death eating those who know no death."

The crowd murmured appreciatively. They loved this cryptic stuff.

"The first of three I see in dark and water, which even now turns light. The second dead rests in another's death, but the third is stranger still. I see death, and a body underground, yet there is no death."

There was a silence before she spoke again.

"It is finished. The Bones have spoken."

And with that the lights came on, the fluorescent tubes flickering to brightness and everyone peering through half-blind eyes.

As entertainment went, Zed figured it was a whole sight better than last night's: Bottomless Joe's drunken rendition of the eighteen verses of "My Sweet, Sweet Colleen" of which he could only remember the words to six and a half.

The crowd was moving out and Zed had enough room to look up at the Father, who had been muttering non-stop the last minute. "Always with the bloody bones. Good thing she hasn't a supply of doves or who knows what we might have seen."

Zed was denied further observations by a shout from the stairwell.

"A body!"

A ripple of questions spread down the hall and then back to the speaker, who stood in the doorway shouting, "Body of a boy, dead, main floor, powermen found it in the water tank!" Then with a pounding of footsteps he was gone, back down the stairs.

For a moment, everyone looked at their neighbour, most thinking about the quickest way downstairs. Then the hallway erupted. People pushed, fought, and scratched to get into the stairs. A few clung to Countessa's doorway, calling questions into the dark. Another small clump stood still, waiting it out.

Zed was torn. Really, really torn. On the one hand, how often do you get a chance to see a body up close? Not more than once or twice a month, and murders less than a third of that. And this body was fresh! But Father was staying. Some of the others in the hall were glaring at those hanging round Countessa's door. That meant there could be a fight, right?

Zed's decision was made for her when a voice called out, "Odd about the boy, you know, so quick-like."

This statement of doubt caused a hiss to rise from the crowd around Countessa's silent door.

"Odd," the voice continued, "cuz a suspicious mind would think you might have already known about it. That you knew before your little show."

The believers' voices grew loud in shouting that down.

"Odd," it finished, "cuz a really suspicious mind would think you might have put it there."

Shouts of "Take that back!" and "Shithead!" came from the crowd at Countessa's door as they swirled out to meet the clumped sceptics, shouting and shoving.

Zed was moving out of the line of fire thinking, *All right, a fight!* when Countessa's voice boomed out. "Do the Bones lie? Do the Bones lie, Jimmy?"

Jimmy, a short, freckled-headed muscle man, stepped out of the crowd. "Bones!" He gave a short barking laugh. "What do bones know? Some chicken, some dog, they tell you something?"

"They tell me something, Jimmy," Countessa said. "Dogs? They tell me about a dog and a potting shed. What do you know about that, Jimmy? A dog, a clothesline, and a potting shed."

Jimmy's mocking smile had gone and he stared at the doorway in horror.

"The Bones tell me things, Jimmy. They tell me you didn't use enough lime. What's that smell in the potting shed?" A low chuckle came out of the dark doorway.

"*Shut up!*" Jimmy's finger kept pointing at the door. "You just shut the fuck up!"

"The Bones tell me things, Jimmy. What's that...? They want to tell me something about a fire? A fire in the old barn?"

"Shut up! Oh God, just shut up!"

"I didn't know horses could scream, did you, Jimmy?"

"Oh God, oh God." Jimmy was white and trembling all over.

"How do these things start?"

Jimmy erupted, leaping toward the door, spittle flying. "You bitch! You bitch!" he choked out. "Just shut the fuck up!"

The believers stopped him from reaching Countessa's door. As he threw himself against the arms holding him back, Countessa's voice came again. "The Bones see you, Jimmy. They see you in a fire, in the past, in the future, choking, choking."

Jimmy slid to the floor, the passion drained out of him. "You fucking bitch," he mumbled, "you fucking bitch." His friends came and helped him to his feet, dragging him away.

As the sceptics retreated into the stairwell, Countessa's mocking voice called out, "Remember me, won't you, Jimmy." Then her voice turned cold and hard. "Remember me when you are in flames, when you are dying for air, when you lie gasping, remember me and my *lying bones*!"

Chapter 3

THE LOBBY WAS AS PACKED as stripper night in the freak tent. People crammed into every nook, even climbing the walls to get a better view; people who died in the Tower tended to look dead long before they finally kicked off, so the chance to see a young, fresh body was something of a special occasion.

Zed was working her way through others' knees, a laborious process accompanied by outraged or ribald comments from those who participated in her progress. She wished now that she had stuck closer to the Father. He was somehow able to part a crowd with an authoritative gaze.

A murmur swept over the people and everyone turned to see the two attendants bringing in the stretcher. The attendants, knowing that resuscitation was hopeless, were making an entrance. Smiling broadly, they started waving as the crowd broke into spontaneous applause and whistles. Something was finally gonna happen.

With the attendants already here, Zed knew she only had a few moments to get up front if she wanted to see them loading the body. She fought on, knowing in her heart it was hopeless when, like a cool, clear breeze, she heard a familiar voice over by the elevator. "My, what delightful congress." Zed could see Luc's white Panama hat floating through the crowd. She wiggled and pushed until she burst past the crowd into the respectful space that had appeared around Luc and his entourage.

Unfortunately, her thrust was greater than the mass and she flew across the space like a cork out of cheap champagne. She bounced off the leg of crooked-faced Barry. His eyes widened while his hand crept down to rub the impact spot. "You … you touched me." Zed looked up from her sprawl at his feet. "One cig … two cig … four cig," he muttered in quick little breaths, calculating damage costs before crying out again. "You touched me!"

"Control, Barry, control," Luc told him as Zed picked herself up. "We make appearances, we don't become them."

Zed moved in behind Luc as he walked to the water tank; the two henchmen followed. Barry kicked her calves every step. The crowd parted, letting Luc pass.

By the time they reached the front, the attendants were pulling the body from the water tank. As they placed the corpse down and pulled the red straps tight, Zed got herself a nice close look. She immediately recognized the lolling head and glassy stare: it was Charles and he was looking the same as always, except for the breathing, of course.

As the attendants draped a white blanket over the body, covering the face, there rose two simultaneous moans. The first came from those who read books entitled *Final Wishes: Jessie's Farewell* and loved sucking the delicious, heart-wrenching emotion from life. The second and louder moan came from the majority, those who had not gotten a good look at the body and now realized they probably never would.

Zed, however, had uttered not a sound. Her eyes focused on the patch of blanket where Charles' breast would be. For in transfer, before the attendants had pulled Charles' shirt down from where it had bunched up at his neck, Zed had seen a hole, a triangular hole as big as her fist, which had been cut out of Charles' breast.

Ellen stood next to the tank, the Father smoothing her hair and murmuring to her as she cried on his shoulder. Barry, having left his master's side, stood beside Ellen, occasionally giving her back a stiff pat before scanning the crowd with a glower.

Zed looked from Ellen to Barry, then asked Luc in disbelief, "She slept with *him*?"

Luc shook his head sadly. "We truly are living in the last days."

Zed nodded and watched as Barry slid his hand down her back in a show of sympathy. The hand continued, however, and as it neared Ellen's posterior, Barry's face took on a more distracted look. After a long pause and a twitch of the hips from Ellen, Barry shook off his sexual daze and returned hand and face to their appropriate positions.

With Charles strapped, wrapped, and ready to roll, the attendants started bucking the gurney though the crowd. Everyone pressed in, trying to get an eyeful, slowing progress to a crawl.

"Okay, that's it," yelled one of the attendants, "this is our fuckin' body and if one more fuckin' cocksucker lays a motherlovin' finger on it then I guarantee you, this won't be the only thing I take to the morgue today!"

Unfortunately, this only brought cheers of colourful language from the fans. And in the pause, someone, in a whisk quicker than the eye, whipped the white blanket off, exposing Charles in all his semi-rigor mortis glory.

After that, things started to get ugly.

A COUPLE MINUTES LATER, with clenched jaws and sore hands, the attendants slotted the gurney into the back of the ambulance and crawled into the cab.

"More like a fucking lockdown ward every time we come," one attendant muttered.

"A-fuckin' right!" His partner hit the siren and pulled away from the cheering crowd which covered the sidewalk and had started pounding on the walls of the vehicle. The ambulance was chased for a block and a half by the alky, Brandy Bob (BB to friends) who banged on the back screaming, "*Meeeeeeeeee! Take meeeeeeeeeee!*"

As BB staggered back to the Tower, the crowd broke up, people trickling inside or clumping up to talk.

Zed turned to find Luc looking down at her with two bills in his hand. "Overdose at 8:12."

She pocketed the bills.

"Out of professional curiosity…?" Luc waited.

"No power – no hot water. No hot water – no wine, bath, and razor."

"Mmmm."

"So why'd they send the white box 'stead of the black one?" Zed asked.

"Seems some cretin called in a body 'drowning' instead of 'drowned'." They walked back to where the Father stood with Ellen. "So they sent the ambulance and stretcher instead of the body bag and hearse. Mmmm, please excuse. Time to be the caregiver." Luc continued in a louder voice, "Ellen, oh dear Ellen." He strode up and somehow slipped his arm between her body and the Father's, separating the two. "The loss, the pain." He gently pulled the loose hairs off her brow and gave it a kiss. She opened her mouth. "I know you can't talk about it now," Luc said, forestalling her by placing a hand on her mouth. "I'm just here to help you through, to hold your hand." He dropped his hand to hers and gave it a pat. "Now what you need," he told her in a *sotto* whisper, "are two of these." He extracted a small pillbox from his jacket and opened it, exposing the red pills inside. "Better make it four," he told her, looking her over, "and wash them down with this." He handed her a fifth of whiskey with a wink. "When you wake up, and you need to talk, remember … we're all here for you." He helped her eyes turn toward the Father. "As for me, I shall be searching, seeking, and catching whichever nasty did this to your dear … offspring."

Ellen, whose eyes had lit up on seeing the pills, grabbed six. Luc gave an elegant shrug as if to say, "Aren't we all friends here?" Clutching the small whiskey bottle, Ellen shoved her way through the crowd and up the stairs.

Luc closed the pill case and was lightly brushing the dust off his arm when a hand grabbed his shoulder.

"Hello? Have you got a brain?" the Father hissed, his face inches from Luc's. "An overdose is not the solution to grieving."

"Please," Luc said, removing the Father's hand. "First, no one dies in this building without my say-so." He remembered the crowd. "Present death excluded, of course. Second, I think I know Ellen's chemical tolerance better than you and can state that without some serious mixing and matching, Ellen is immune from overdose. Now, we both know she hasn't got the readies to gulp; she's stony and if she had them, she's already used them. I love Ellen, but I will not hide the fact that she is, shall we say, not a long-term thinker, momentary pleasures and all."

The fire in the Father's eye had not died down any, and he opened his mouth to speak his mind when Luc murmured, "It gives little comfort to those here to see us at odds." The Father looked around at the faces of his faithful. "I am sure," Luc continued, "neither of us wants to test the limits of our flock, at least not yet. You are ever welcome in my office, however."

"I'd rather sup with the devil," the Father retorted.

"I'll see if that can be arranged." Luc touched the rim of his hat. "Till then...." He turned his back and walked to the elevator, Barry sidling up behind and joining him.

"The Lord blesses us by the strength of our enemies," the Father muttered to himself, watching Luc depart. "God must really like me."

"What?" Zed asked.

"Nothing, child." He looked down at her with a tight face. "Just trying to keep both my perspective and my temper." He turned to the stairs. "I'd better make sure Ellen's still breathing, all of Luc's assurances notwithstanding."

Zed watched him go till she felt a feather-touch on her shoulder and a voice in her ear. "Aye, nothing like a death to bring out the hunger, isn't it?"

Zed turned with a gleam in her eye towards Ivy's smiling face. "Hungry? Want some canned ham?"

"What a dear," Ivy said, "a dear for offering me a lovely ham."

Zed frowned, about to stop that idea right there.

"You keep it." Ivy touched Zed's cheek. "You're but skin'n' bones. Me body's peckish, sure enough, it's telling me, 'not dead yet, are you, though they're dragging out another one?' I've seen plenty go and always the same, that hunger, that dreadful hunger. You having it?"

"No."

"Oh, all cut up on losing your playmate are you?"

Zed gave a short laugh.

"Well it's neither here nor there. Will you be joining me for a cuppa after that fine drama?"

"Sure."

Zed accompanied Ivy to the elevator and after much waiting and not a small amount of squeezing, they made it up to Ivy's.

"Just a moment, love." Ivy opened the door and headed right for the tea kettle. "Take out those biscuits, why don't you."

Zed dutifully pulled the battered tin off the counter and opened it on the table.

"That poor Ellen," Ivy commented, "losing her only child."

"Sure," Zed agreed.

Ivy poured the tea and Zed pulled out the historical novel and slid it over.

"For me?" Ivy's eyes lit up. "On Wales, too. Oh, that's lovely."

She regarded Zed with warm eyes. It was an experience which made Zed itch all over. Ivy had an irritating habit of mistaking payment for gifts. She grabbed a biscuit to distract herself.

"You may mock now," Ivy said, "but family's important. In the end, they are more important than anything. Duw, the things I've done for

45

family, the places I've gone, even here...."

The sound of a roar broke from below. Zed wandered to the window and looked down. A crowd stood spread below, watching someone just to the left of the building's entrance. While she watched, the crowd's arms rose in a cheer, then died back into silence.

Zed moved toward the door.

"Leaving, love?"

Zed hesitated for a moment. "Downstairs," she said, looking at Ivy.

"I understand," Ivy said, and with that Zed was out the door, leaving Ivy and her perpetual chatter behind.

Downstairs, she slid through the clusters of people to the guardroom. Hammer was still there, staring at the CCTVs. She pushed her head in with a questioning look.

Hammer looked up, saw her, and gave a nod.

Zed pulled out the two books. "Closest I could get," she told him as he looked at the "true crime" book on the Boston Strangler. He nodded that it was OK.

"So what's going on?"

"Luc," he told her, and gestured toward the security screens. Luc stood on a box, one hand raised to the crowd. It was too bad there was no sound on the camera. Luc gestured with his hand, pointing to the building and then to the crowd. The crowd raised their arms and she could hear the roar come from the front of the building.

A weedy-looking guy wearing sandals had stopped to lean in the doorway of Hammer's guardhouse. Hammer rose silently, came up behind him, and examined the fellow's back and how much of it extended into the doorway. Then in a single move, he punched him directly in the kidneys.

The man dropped with the convulsive jerk of the kidney punched. He rolled on the floor, his scream of "Oh God!" descending into gurgles. Hammer looked pointedly at the people lounging around the doorway. They all immediately took a step away. With a self-satisfied nod, he returned to his chair.

Zed drifted to the door, working out the best way to get to Luc through the crowd. "Know anything about Charles?" she asked Hammer before leaving.

"Charles?"

"The dead kid."

Hammer pondered a moment and then looked at the people close outside. "Tonight," he promised her.

Zed gave him a thumbs-up before launching herself into the crowd, shoving and clawing her way to the hallway where she had met Rat that morning. It was empty save for Bottomless Joe, preoccupied with his glue bottle. What Zed had remembered was an offshoot emergency exit which should come out around Luc. After finding, opening, and slipping though the door she found herself in a cement cul-de-sac directly behind Luc.

"If we are pricked, do we not bleed?" Luc was asking the crowd. "And if affronted, do we not avenge?"

There was a lot of shifting and head-scratching over that one. Luc shifted tactics.

"The City," Luc gestured, "does not like us."

This was met by an immediate growl of agreement.

"The City ... wishes we would go away."

A louder growl.

"They ... leave us to rot. They don't care about us." Luc's fist punched the sky.

"If one of us dies, what happens? Nothing." He pointed inside to the water tank. "If we want justice, what do we get? Nothing!" This time some of the crowd joined in a half-second later, echoing, "Nothing."

"Well, I want blood. Blood for blood, that's justice." This got a loud and favourable reaction. "Blood for blood!"

Luc was looking fine atop his box; his white hat and blue silk suit appeared heavenly in the sunshine. On one side of him was Stu, handkerchief tied round his throat; on the other side, closest to Zed, Barry was doing his impression of a paranoid security guard.

"I, Luc, speak where the City is silent. I have a name, a blood for blood." Luc turned toward Barry. "Barry, the name of a 'little-boy-panter,' if you please."

Barry thought a second and shrugged. "Quince?"

Luc raised both hands and the crowd grew still. "The name is ... Quince." He bared his teeth. "Let us scourge this building."

With that the crowd exploded, roaring into the stairs and pouring down them. For those dwelling in the quiet darkness, the mass of footsteps was approaching thunder. Inhabitants fled into the sub-parkades, flitting from pillar to trash heap, looking for some spot to hole up.

Zed approached Luc as he stepped off the box, watching the crowd roll away. "That was quite exhilarating," he said to himself. "I should have tried this long ago. But perhaps," he mused, "these are an easy mob to sway. I must try a more demanding mob later on." Stu and Barry fell in and with Zed trailing they descended to the sub-parkade where the sound of breaking glass and screams told them that playtime had already begun.

ZED'S VIEW OF THE SUB-parkade confirmed her own axiom: the more there are, the worse they get. And for downright vicious stupidity, this mob was hard to beat. They literally attacked anything that moved, including themselves.

While Zed watched, red-haired Eric made a run for it, bounding across the tops of cars, but in mid-leap, a pair of beefy arms grabbed his ankles, bringing him down. And before his head smacked the cement a group had already formed, lining up to pound the fist and give the boot. Eric managed to scream and writhe through most of it, but eventually fell unconscious ... or comatose. While it was probably best for Eric, it sure irritated the hell out of those waiting. After a few rib-cracking kicks, the crowd threw Eric's limp form through the windshield of a nearby blue Dodge Aries.

Pete, the barrel-chested leader of the Eric subgroup, was looking for fresh meat when Stu came running over, pointing to Eric. "That Quince?" he shouted, pulling Eric's head up from where it draped over the steering wheel.

"Who's Quince?" Pete asked, looking puzzled as he led his pack off to find stragglers.

For the next twenty minutes, Zed watched as anyone who ran or looked suspicious or had pale skin or walked or moved their arms too fast or had a squint was chased, caught, and pummelled. Unfortunately, about twenty percent of the original mob squinted, ran, or otherwise attracted attention. Many didn't seem to realize their promotion to suspect until that brief flash of insight before unconsciousness. And behind every falling body ran Stu and Barry yelling, "Is this Quince?" "Is *this* Quince?" or "This better be Quince!" to which the reply was invariably, "How the fuck should I know?"

As it turned out, Quince had found a nice, dark hiding place under a car. And something told him that when a mob starts beating up people while shouting your name, it's time to stay under the car.

Sadly, while Quince's intellectual side told him to stay put, all the other sides of his brain were screaming, "*We're gonna die!* They are going to look under this car and drag us out and do things to us so bad that you can't even show them in the movies." So his brain fought it out. That lasted twenty minutes.

And then he tried to run.

Running didn't work so well.

They cut him off. They formed a circle. They closed in.

At this point Quince's brain was only able to make two thoughts: one was a long drawn out "eeeeeee" noise that rose and fell with internal volume. The other was the thought, *Hey, at least they don't have crowbars.* This was due to a dark fantasy Quince had imagined under the car about what would happen once they caught him. It involved crowbars and had to do with snapping a lot of bones in his hands. But hey, they didn't have crowbars!

The good news for Quince was that pretty much everyone in the mob had sore hands by this time. The human body has loads of hard bones, and those bones can really bruise up the hands. So Quince, coming in at the end of a whole lot of fist/flesh impact, got off easy.

Quince, lifted to shoulder height, was convinced as he was carried off to Luc that this was but a transition to a place where crowbars were readily available. He wriggled, he thrashed, he shouted: "I'm innocent! I didn't do anything! I got rights! I'm innocent! I only touched her a little! You got nothing on me! She let me do it! Let me go!"

"Hmm, wonder what we should do with you?" Luc asked, his forefinger tapping his chin.

Amongst the huffing and puffing, a cracked, throaty voice broke the silence: "Meow, meow, splat!"

As timing went, you couldn't get much better, and the crowd fell over themselves laughing.

Inevitably, with jokes and mobs, once is never enough, so the voice called again, "Meow, meow, splat," and this time a few voices joined in. With the encouragement it was repeated, and again, each time adding a few more voices. Soon the whole parkade was rocking with the sound of a hundred people shouting, "Meow, meow, splat," and the one person held aloft screaming, "What does that mean? What does that mean?"

The mob, united in purpose and community service, marched, chanting in step, toward the stairs. "Meow." Stomp. "Meow." Stomp. "Splat!" Stomp, stomp, stomp. There's something about a good group march that is just plain fun. By the time they reached the stairs everyone was bawling and stomping with enthusiasm. Only two people seemed left out; the first was Quince, still wriggling like a fish, and the second was blocking the stairs.

The Father stood, a figure in black, gripping the sides of the doorway. Had it not been for the red face, sweaty brow, heaving chest, and receding hair, he might have made an ominous figure. He'd changed from a sweater into a black suit jacket. For what he was about to do, he needed all the authority he could get.

"Stop!" The Father held up his hand.

Whatever he had imagined would happen, not being heard was probably not included. But Luc stopped and because no one sane, sober, or otherwise runs into Luc, the people behind Luc stopped. The standstill rippled back and the chant faltered until everyone had stopped and quietened down except for the drunks at the back who whispered, "Meow, meow, splat!" to each other and then killed themselves laughing.

"Enough," the Father stated. "Let that man go."

"Listen to him," Quince pleaded, which only got him a punch in the kidneys and a quick yelp.

"Look at yourselves! Murderers, is that how you see yourselves? The drugs, the booze, the sex, the stealing, the knifing, hitting, idling life away, I accept that. Man is a weak creature. But murder in cold blood? It is too much. Too much, and it stops right here."

"My, my, aren't you getting all hot under the collar," Luc said, smiling.

The Father ignored him. "Now put that man down."

Stu walked forward. "Step aside, Father, lynching party coming through."

To which the Father gave him a roundhouse that dropped Stu in his tracks.

There was a second of disbelief in which everyone said to himself, "Did he just hit someone?" Then barrel-chested Pete came forward, a grin on his face and his gang behind him. "Hell, Parson, let's rumble."

"Not Parson, Gary, just Gary ... ah, screw it." The Father advanced and the gang circled. Then, with a roar the circle closed and the Father charged Pete, fists flailing.

While the Father threw a good roundhouse he just didn't seem to understand the concept of defence. Pete sailed in a solid one to the cheek before the Father dropped him.

Two men had stepped forward to stand by the Father, one on each side, but twenty had joined to stop him. They surrounded the Father, attacking his shoulders, head, and chest. But no man faced impossible odds with greater joy. He was actually smiling. For this one moment he was not holding hands, comforting, or making dubious progress toward a bleak future, but rather mixing it up with the forces of darkness. What had they? Nothing but mere numbers. What had he? Nothing better than to stand for the good, the right, the true. And with that he started laughing.

Zed, after the shock of seeing the Father become the Fighter, watched while his two supporters were dropped, watched as the Father survived pummelling from three sides, watched knowing he was doomed. And then he laughed. His face was bleeding, one eye swelling shut, and he laughed, happy and joyful. Zed, the fighter against life and everything it sent her, felt a fierce exultation at that laugh. And before she could think it through, she had leapt forward and planted a right hook into the nose of a bent-over attacker.

After that initial punch Zed dropped into her tried and true ... low blows and fighting dirty. Within a minute, a dozen moaning men lay among the debris clutching their groins.

If only the Father can keep them off, Zed thought. Her fists were tired and so she drove a hard elbow deep into the soft flesh of the closest groin. Too bad that groin belonged to Carlotta, the ex-weightlifter female bantam. Zed heard, "None of that, my sweet," while a runaway truck seemed to connect with her head.

For that first second, the white blaze in her head overwhelmed the fact that she was flying. In the next second, the searing scrape of concrete overtook the pain in her head. By the third second, she was unconscious.

When Zed next managed to lift her head, the Father was pinned like a bug, eight hands holding him fast. Luc stood to one side, shaking his head in dismay.

"Really, old boy, swords to plowshares, turn the other cheek, no?"

"No!" The Father stared at Luc, his eye shining and turning black, his nose dripping blood.

Luc sighed. "Why do we always hurt the ones we love?" He smiled a wicked smile and then silenced the Father's retort by leaning over and giving him a full kiss on the mouth.

This surprised everyone. As Luc's lips parted from the Father's there was absolute silence. Even Quince watched in wonder. The Father, whose eyes had widened, was the first to react, spitting at Luc's feet.

Luc finished licking the Father's blood off his lips before speaking. "Well, if that's the way you're going to behave, you can forget about getting some tongue." He glanced back at the open-mouthed, staring mob. "Away with him, boys."

They stared at Luc, at the Father, and at each other. Finally they stared at Quince, who just smiled feebly at them.

"Meow, meow, splat?" a drunken voice queried.

This, finally, was something they could get their minds around. A resounding, "Fuck, *yeah!*" rose up and Quince was hoisted aloft once more. Within a minute the marching chant was back, full roar. The crowd moved past the pinioned Father and into the stairwell carrying their prize.

The Father watched them go before turning back to Luc. "Let him go. He's innocent. He only likes girls, little girls."

"Trust me, padre, we're all guilty, even you." He gave a wink. "Tempted?"

"You sad, sick man."

"Oh please, you're making me blush. Stu!"

Stu snapped to attention. "Yo!"

Luc gave him that look and mouthed, "Yo?" Stu hung his head.

"Stu, keep our friend down here until the deed is done. Now let me make this very plain. Keep him breathing, keep him healthy, but keep him out of our way." Luc raised an eyebrow. "Can you do that?"

Stu snapped out a fist and caught the Father on the jaw, the blow smashing his head against the concrete. The Father slumped to the ground, unconscious.

Luc looked at the form on the ground and back to Stu. He shook his head. "That'll do. Stay and babysit. Remember, Stu: breathing, healthy."

Zed had pulled herself to her feet and staggered over to Luc.

"Done playing? Can we go now?" Luc listened to the distant chanting. "Though with twenty floors to go, I don't think we need to hurry."

Luc insisted on riding the elevator. They left Stu with the Father and walked up to the lobby. Zed was glad the Father was unconscious. It made things uncomplicated.

"It does no good for the plebes to see me sweat," Luc told her as they boarded. "Makes them think you're ordinary." Zed was pretty sure no one considered Luc ordinary.

Zed used the ride up to feel out the contours of her new face. There was a bump growing on her left temple and her cheek felt scraped where she had landed. She smiled when she saw the blood on her hand. She hoped she'd got a scar. Scars gave you character.

"What you touching your face for?" Barry asked her. He had been watching. "You want to grow up pretty? Too late." He gave a snicker.

"I certainly wouldn't want to look like you," Zed retorted. "And what's wrong with your eye, is it infected?"

"What? What's with my eye?"

Zed put her hands up. "I'm not coming near it." There was, of course, nothing wrong with Barry's eye, but that didn't stop him from prodding it and glaring at Zed for the rest of the ride.

THE ELEVATOR SHUDDERED TO a stop close to the 19th floor and everyone climbed out. The roof access was in the stairwell and Luc had to push past the people holding their chests and sucking air, leaning against the walls.

On the roof everyone was sitting or lying down, Quince nowhere in sight. Zed ambled amongst the crowd. Coming up to a group sitting on a carpet she noticed that the carpet tended to twitch. It was Quince, and he had many uses.

Luc clapped his hands. "Showtime everybody, showtime."

People smiled and rose. Soon Quince was aloft once more, screaming, "What did I do?" over and over. It was annoying, but those holding Quince got him positioned next to the drop anyway.

"On three?" Luc offered, holding up three fingers.

Everyone rushed in, trying to get a piece of arm or at least some pant-leg to grab onto. With Barry coaching, they shuffled back until they were ten feet from the edge.

Luc raised his index finger.

"One!" came the howl and everyone rushed to the edge. Quince gave a moan.

They shuffled back into position. Luc raised a second finger, sending them rushing to the edge. "Two!"

One final, long shuffling back and a pause. Quince broke the moment by bursting into a scream. With that, everyone started screaming and like a horse out of the gate they burst forward. Quince's scream rose in both volume and octaves till it was a wailing siren. With a collective "*Three!*" they reached the edge and released. Quince flew straight out. The crowd split, everyone running and shoving at the edges, getting a look. Quince sailed on, a stone thrown into space, a human golf ball on a par one course.

Quince was silent but still his body flailed, unable to believe that a handhold could not be found in two hundred feet of air.

The beautiful moment was shattered with a "Fuckers!" One of the latecomers had pushed a little too hard, sending BB toward that ambulance he loved to chase at a speed faster than desired. BB was not amused. So now, instead of Quince taking centre stage, BB was cluttering up the vertical landscape. As BB progressed headfirst, he kept screaming, "Asshole!" He didn't seem to be taking things well.

"I certainly hope no one is trying to watch from below," Luc murmured to Zed.

Quince's landing was like a jelly doughnut dropped from a highrise: splat-acular and satisfying. Everyone burst into a cheer at the sight of the crimson starfish.

BB, silent now, hit the ground shoulder first. He bounced, his body spinning in the air, landed, bounced again and finally slid about eight feet, leaving a bloody smear behind.

Everyone murmured. BB's tasteless demise, his trails like a blood slug, had destroyed the whole mood.

Down below, the seeping blood expanded. Distant sirens rose, jolting the crowd awake. Ellen and Teresa, each with a bottle in hand, were the first to break toward the stairs, starting a general rush. People had wised up that if they could get downstairs before the hearse or ambulance, they would get to see a double feature: body bagging. Wasn't it just a grand day?

Zed turned from the edge and saw Luc standing in the shade of one of the broken cooling fans. He watched the people flow past, a contented smile on his face.

A few stayed on the roof, planning to watch the show from there. Luc, catching Barry's eye, indicated he wanted them gone. Zed crept behind the cooling unit. Barry pushed and barked, prodding old women, "Mush, you Q-tips, mush."

When the roof was cleared, Luc motioned Barry to descend with the rest. Luc paced the rooftop, rubbing his jaw.

"You see that?" Zed couldn't see who Luc was talking to. "You get a good view?"

Zed could hear Luc start to pace again. "I know you, you just hated it, didn't you? *Didn't you?*" he screamed.

She heard him stop, then with a clang he hit the other side of the cooling fan. "Well, screw you, screw you and your little dog too, because these are mine, get it? *Mine!*"

Zed peeked round the corner and saw Luc, one leg back, looking up to the sky.

"Face it," he said to no one at all. "They. Don't. Like. You." He grinned from ear to ear.

"You want them?" he asked, and in a flash his mood had changed. His face was deadly serious, jaw clamped, eyes dark and glittering. "You want them, you kill me!"

He waited a moment and then shouted it, "Kill me!"

He waited and seemed to listen and then, his face burning and bunched in hatred, he screamed with his fists above him, "*Kill me!*"

Luc stood, breathing quickly through his nose. Looking about him, he straightened himself up, hands smoothing his jacket into perfection. "That's right, then," he murmured, nodding to himself.

And with a quick, stiff walk, he went over to the rooftop door and disappeared inside.

Chapter 4

FINALLY, THE CITY SERVICES had got it right: two morgue wagons, body bags, rubber gloves, and a sturdy plastic shovel.

In the time it had taken Zed to get downstairs, the M.E. had come and gone, leaving two arguing attendants behind. Ben, white hair and pot belly, stood holding the open bag while Jim, a clean-cut twenty-something, held the shovel.

"Just keep shovelling it in, Jimbo," Ben said.

"I'm telling you, they haven't done procedure on this body," Jim said. "No pictures, nothing."

"And I keep telling you, the M.E. tagged it suicide."

"Two suicides? At the same time?" Jim shook his head.

"Maybe a lovers' pact."

"Lovers? Two men? At least twenty-five years difference?"

"Tsk, tsk. Didn't know you were such a prude, Junior. You'll see everything on this job, so get used to it."

Jim glared. "This was no damn suicide and you know it. The cops should be called in."

Ben sighed. "I like you, Swift, but you've got a lot to learn, so listen up. See this building ... this is the city's shit stack." Ben saw Zed and gave her a nod. "Heyya, Zed."

She grinned back. "New guy?"

"Tell me about it." Ben turned back to Jim. "Where was I? Shit stack, that's right, so listen, anytime a body is found in front of this building, around this building, or even in this building, they could be stabbings, gunshot wounds, tongues blue and smelling of arsenic.... I miss any?"

"Drowning," Zed offered.

"Right. Especially drowning. You find any body and I assure you, it'll be a suicide. You call in the cops and then they'll tell you it's a suicide only you won't have a job anymore cuz they don't like coming here telling people about suicides. But guess what, Jimbo? You do have a job, and it's getting this suicide off the sidewalk, so start shovelling and we'll both get outta here."

"Hey!" Jim grabbed Zed's shoulder as she stood peering into the bag. "What do you think you're doing?"

"Trading," she told him. "What ya got, Ben?"

Ben held up a bloodstained comb and a broken pipe. "Four packs."

"One for the comb. Anything else?"

Ben held a tin crucifix on a chain.

"Not much call for that," she told him.

"Good luck charm."

"Right." They both laughed. "One for the cross." Zed dug out two packs of cigs and passed them over.

"That's evidence." Jim's eyes were bulging. "Ben. Ben? What are you doing? You can't do that. That belongs to the next of kin."

Ben laughed and flicked a pack at him. "Grow up, Junior."

Zed exchanged nods with Ben before ducking back into the crowd. People were clustered at the door telling their stories and close calls: Pete, the squat, barrel-chested thug of the sub-parkade, was holding out his hairy right arm. "Had his head right there," he rasped out. His hands flexed. "That Quince, he tried to move, but I didn't let 'im." The hand

and arm were contracted, rigid, to show the onlookers the strength of the grip. Zed reached out and poked the side of the hand. It was firm all right. "Almost went over myself," he said.

Zed drifted toward the stairs, turning the comb into a black t-shirt and trading the crucifix with a metal babe for her panties. The metal babe turned the cross and chain into a headband while Zed offloaded the panties to desperate Bryan for his Zippo and a pack and a half of cigs. The Zippo worked too. Cutting loose from the crowds, she went to look up Gears.

As she opened the door to the stairwell, Stu pushed past, cracking his knuckles. The Father staggered up a few steps later: his face was a montage of red welts and grazes, a split cheek, blackening bruises, and odd green and yellow splotches. His forehead bore the bruise and bump of Stu's mighty blow.

"They kill that boy?" the Father asked, eyes grim.

She nodded. She didn't think he was in the mood for souvenirs.

He stood up straight. "I've assumed that people knew right from wrong, that they were making a choice. I don't think they are … but soon they will be." He started climbing the stairs.

Zed looked up at Father's retreating back then consulted her rules of life: #5 – *follow the action*. She scampered up after the Father.

"Choices have consequences, there are choices and there are responsibilities." The Father noticed Zed following, and smiled. "Ready to give this place a wake-up?" He opened the door to the third floor, strode to the first door on the left, and knocked.

"Wha?" An unshaven face answered. "Wha – why hello, Father," the voice slurred.

The Father pushed the door open. Empties littered the floor, couch, and counter; a fresh bottle stood open on the tabletop.

"Do you know why you keep getting drunk, Burl?" the Father asked. Burl shook his head from where he was hiding behind the front door. "It's because you keep drinking." The Father picked up the beer bottles and dropped them in the kitchen sink. "Do you want to stop getting drunk?"

Burl shifted his weight. "Well, sure I do."

"Good." The Father upended one bottle; the beer gurgled down the sink.

"Ah!" A tortured cry from Burl. The Father ignored it and opened the fridge. He started taking out bottles of beer and setting them up on the counter.

The Father gave the first bottle-top a twist. It didn't budge and the metal corners dug into his finger. "Idiot bottles. You have an opener?" Burl was staring at his hoard lined up on the counter.

"I ... uh...."

"Oh, I see one here mounted into the wall, very convenient." With a quick pull, he opened the bottle and poured the contents down the sink. "Zed, can you open? It would help things go a lot faster."

Zed pushed Burl, who was speechless, and hopped onto the counter. She started opening the bottles and passing them over to the Father.

"That's my beer!" Burl protested, and started moving forward, but he was stopped by the Father's eye.

"Burl, you are an alcoholic. Is that not so?"

"Well, I have occasional problems."

"For you, one beer is too many. Besides...." The Father stopped pouring and took a swig from a bottle. He swallowed with a grimace. "It's not as if you buy this stuff for the taste." He poured the rest of it away.

Zed thought about making an offer on the rest for selling them back to Burl later. Then she looked at the Father's face. Zed told herself, *there's a time for everything and right now, it's beer-pouring time.*

"ALL DONE," THE FATHER said, turning to Burl. "Hope to see you at tonight's prayer meeting, seven o'clock in 1205." He laid his hand on

Burl's shoulder. "It's all for the best." He gave a smile and a friendly pat before leaving Burl to stare into the sink.

Floor by floor and door by door, the Father cajoled, berated, and overwhelmed anyone who would listen, leaving behind him a wasteland of bottles, baggies, needles, and pills.

"There are some days when I just love my work," he told Zed, rapping on the door to 904 before turning the handle and pushing it open.

Inside, Howard, a middle-aged bachelor and perpetual hand wringer, lay, pants down, across the knee of Mistress Anna. Anna, resplendent in her long blonde hair, leather corset, mini, and matching gloves, raised the riding crop and gave Howard's bottom a hefty thwack.

"Ahem." The Father cleared his throat. "Howard, a word?"

Howard fell off Anna's luscious lap with a squawk and a thud. "Father?"

"Howard."

Anna rose, eye to eye with the Father in her five-inch heels. She frowned and slapped her skirt with the whip, looking Father up and down. "I've seen you. You're that priest or something, right?"

"Something, right."

"Either way, we're both pros, right? In the people biz, the pleasure biz, right? Howie has paid Luc, booked me, and so here I am. Get what I'm saying? Give us five and he's all yours, but right now I'm on the job."

"Howard, will you introduce me?" the Father asked.

"Uh...." Howard's voice dropped to a whisper. "This is the Mistress Anna."

Anna had been checking out the Father's swollen lip, his black eye, and bruising. "Priest, you sure been plastered."

"I have."

She noted his swollen knuckles. "Looks like you been in the giving mood too."

"I have."

She looked him over again. "Sure some different kind of religion."

"Thank you." The Father looked at Howard and then back at Anna. "He's mine."

"So?"

"Howard is making some changes. Isn't that right, Howard?"

Howard looked like he would just like to disappear.

Anna laughed. "Whether he wants to or not, eh? Well, I can see the way the tune plays and I'm already paid so I'll let it go. Besides, my momma always said to steer clear of chicken flicks, judges, and preacher men. Just don't make a habit of it, okay."

The Father cocked his head. "No promises."

Anna laughed. "I like you." She turned and touched the tip of her whip to Howard's cheek. "Later, Bo-Peep." Then she sashayed out the door.

The Father cut off Howard as he started to explain, "Prayer meeting, seven o'clock, 1205, be there." He strode out, Zed trailing.

"Great, just great." the Father muttered as they continued down the hall. "Now he's got faith, fear, sex, and guilt all mixed into one."

"Guilt?"

The Father stopped. "Guilt, you know, an awareness of wrongdoing, a feeling of separation from the divine."

Zed shook her head.

"Things feel wrong, bummed out."

Zed grinned. "Oh, like when you get screwed in a deal."

The Father grimaced. "Not quite. Let me give you an example: suppose you traded some heroin...."

"Like with Steve," Zed nodded.

The Father blinked at the comparison but continued. "Yeah, like Steve, and suppose he died. How would that make you feel?"

Zed thought. "I'll probably laugh, cuz only morons O.D."

The Father took a deep breath. "You know, guilt is a lot like that feeling you get when you get screwed on a deal."

Zed nodded. "Thought so. Where we going now?"

"Luc's."

"I thought you're clear of him cuz he runs a den of equality."

"Yes, something like that. Lead on, McDuff."

Zed sprinted up the stairs.

LUC'S DOOR WAS OPEN and Stu was leaning against the doorframe, his hands in the pockets of his leather jacket. The handkerchief from around his neck was gone, highlighting his five black finger bruises. Zed walked in, just avoiding a kitten struggling out of a box by the door. The box was full of furry faces and two more kittens staggered across the carpet. Barry stood in front of the desk, a kitten in his hands.

"What's with the fur?" Zed stepped over a kitten, gave Barry's leg a sharp elbow, and plopped into the chair.

"With all that vicious vandalism and animal cruelty of yesterday," Luc said, "I have decided to bring something back to the community."

"What you charging?"

"Fifty each."

"They selling?

"Like hotcakes." He looked her over. "You have a certain élan, a gleam in the eye. Have you been a busy bee?"

"Wait and see," Zed told him, smirking.

"Indeed?" Luc frowned. "Barry!"

Barry cradled a piebald kitten in his palm, his fingertips over its windpipe. The kitten's mouth opened as it struggled. Barry gave his crooked smile. At Luc's shout, he looked around, bland and innocent, as if wondering who Luc could be referring to, before taking his fingers off the kitten's windpipe.

"The merchandise. Down." Barry lowered the kitten with reluctance. He watched it stagger towards the corner, then turned and strode out of the office, relieving his frustration by pushing Cal, a lounging reefer, into the wall, who responded with a plaintive, "Chill out, man!"

"Household tip," Luc said. "Cats and paranoids don't mix." He looked up. "Well, well, if it isn't hell come a-calling."

The Father nudged one of the kittens aside with the tip of his shoe. He looked at it and then at Luc. "I'm not even going to ask."

Luc gave him an "Aren't we all just friends?" smile. "No hard feelings? Already busy with good works?"

"Luc, do me a favour, do everyone a favour and instead of being clever, just disappear, forever."

"You do have hard feelings. You don't like me anymore?"

"Deep down, I wonder if anyone likes you."

"But look," Luc said, scooping a kitten from the floor, "I've changed, I'm opening a pet shop."

The Father shook his head. "No, you've turned a way-station into a cesspool. It's time for it to stop. It needs to stop and it will stop."

Luc hung his head, his eyes peeping out under the rim of his hat. "I've been *baaaaaaaaad*," he moaned before flashing a smile. "But baby, I'm getting better every day."

The Father's jaw clenched as he turned and walked out, knocking the new joint from Cal's hand as he passed. "Man," came the complaint as Cal groped around the floor. "Everyone, just chill out!"

"He down to business this time?" Luc scratched his chin.

Zed nodded. "Even poured out that green stuff Jon Stone drinks."

"Crème de menthe." Luc had a dreamy smile.

"What you going to do?"

Luc's smile stretched across his face. "I think I'll let him win. You heard of a Pyrrhic victory?"

"No," Zed answered, in a tone that indicated she was tired of people always explaining things to her.

"It'll keep," Luc told her. "Want a cat?"

Zed looked at the kittens. Parasites. "No," she said, and hoisted her pack.

"See you at the Zombie races," Luc called as she headed out.

On the way down to see Gears, Zed fished out the broken Walkman and the joint.

The parkade was a mess, the cement covered in broken glass, plastic shards, chrome, a few bumpers, and of course, dried blood.

Zed gave Gears' door three hefty whacks, rolling the safety glass with her foot while she waited. Nothing. So far the day was a bust. She cleared a place and sat down to wait.

Adjusting to the silence, she started picking up sounds from the parkade below. *Rodents*, she thought, until she heard the singing.

She could almost make out the words from the lusty bass down below. It was irritating, just a little too soft. The chorus was louder, a long "Ooooooo" with a single repeated word. Duck? Luck?

The song climaxed in a crescendo and suddenly each word became clear.

> *Got all my shots*
> *I'm free of diseases*
> *Here's my money*
> *So stop with the teases.*
> *OOOOOOOooooooooooooo*
> *Fuck, fuck, fuck, fuck*
> *Let's fuck, fuck, fuck.*

Zed found those "fuck"s awfully familiar. "Dan?"

The song stopped dead.

"Mom?"

A rustling came from below. "You're fucking dead, Mom!"

Zed smiled. "You've been a bad boy!" she called sternly.

The rustling became agitated and came closer. "Don't say that! I'm yer boy, Ma, I'm a good boy." A crash came from the inter-stairs. "Mom?" A brown head popped up from the stairs peering this way and that like a demented gopher. Rat spied Zed. "You hear anything?"

Zed shook her head.

"Don't fuck with me!" Rat came over, hopping forward in double-steps, half-crouched. His eyeballs roved the area and settled on Zed.

"What'd you hear?" Zed asked, her face and voice puzzled and innocent.

"Nothin'," Rat muttered. "I heard nothin'." He glared at Zed. "Whatcha doing here?"

"Waiting for Gears."

"Not here. Gone all day."

"Where?"

Rat shrugged. Now, in the light, Zed could see a big black streak of grease across his forehead. "What ya doing?" she asked.

"Lookin'." He straightened up a bit and pretended that he was a lordly sightseer. "Just lookin'." He raised an imaginary monocle to his eye. "Seein' the sights."

"What you find?"

"Rear-view mirror." He pulled it out for her to see. "Pair of glasses: one lens intact, kid's shoe."

"Let me see the shoe?"

He handed it over, a nondescript white sneaker, far too small for her. She took out a canned ham from her bag. "Trade you for the mirror and sneaker."

"What you want with one shoe?"

"Why," Zed pushed him, "you want it? You want to talk up some kid, do a bit of stroking? Is that why you're down here? You trying out for the panters?"

Rat's face crinkled in disgust. "Kids! Fucking onion heads and fucking huge freaky eyes. They got creepy little hands, like some fucking insect. I hate kids!" His eyes grew wistful. "Could use a lay, nice woman, sweet smelling, soft hair. Trade you for a woman?"

"No one would sleep with you."

Rat sniffled and shuffled his feet. He rubbed his nose and nodded. "I know ... just ... you know."

Zed waited. "You want the ham?"

Rat shrugged and handed over the mirror and shoes. He took the ham and just stood there, looking down, turning the tin over in his hands.

"Rat," Zed ventured, "you ever think of ... washing?"

At that, Rat jumped back and looked up. "*Washing!*" he hissed. "That's what they all say. They can't love King Rat for Rat: they want the king, then they gotta take the rat. 'Why don't you wash a bit?' they say. They wanna make it with some pink stranger. Fuck them, fuck you!" Rat stomped off, muttering, "Fucking women always trying to change you."

Zed watched as Rat stomped and muttered his way to the stairwell, slamming the door behind. No point in hanging around here. She decided to head up to Countessa's, see if she could swap info. She packed the shoe and mirror away and crept to the stairwell door, easing it open. A check inside. Empty. She ran up the stairs, heading for floor number five.

As Zed approached the 5th floor, the stairwell grew close with a salty, musky odour and a growing haze. Pulling open the door, a cloud of pungent incense enveloped her. She staggered inside, hand clapped over nose and mouth, coughing. Two incense pots, newly mounted on the wall, belched smoke; the four on the floor chugged too. Zed wanted very much to give them a nice ringing kick, but remembered Zed's guide to living: #3 *Don't piss people off till you know the score.*

So Zed wrinkled her nose and pushed on. A couple paces later, she saw something which made her blood cold: A line of people. The line stretched the hallway, holding to the wall. A line! It was opposed to everything about the Tower. Zed surveyed this outrage of organization, a scowl on her face, hands sunk deep in the denim pockets of her overalls. Even Luc's hangers-on didn't line up.

Time for the show, Zed thought. She straightened up to a full five-foot-one, adjusted the strap to her carry-all, and started her walk: confident, even steps. She could feel the eyes on her, see them from the corners of her eyes as they stared with meek faces, hands clutching mementoes: a gilt frame, old rattle, tennis racket, pictures, a hairbrush. She walked on, steady and sure, right toward the darkness of Countessa's place. Eight feet from the door, the line of people stopped at a sawhorse topped with a blinking yellow hazard light. Behind the sawhorse stood Gears, outlined in darkness and strobed in yellow, hair pulled back in a ponytail, arms folded, watching.

Zed advanced right up to the sawhorse. "What gives? I just been down to see you."

"Pulling guard duty, little sister. I am 'The Man', can you believe it?" Gears' friendly face looked down at her, then turned to stern authority as he scanned the line before returning back to a peaceful smile. "It affirms all that I have believed about power, to be sure. These people, they outnumber me and yet they obey me. Truly, people do want to be ordered around." He gave a little laugh.

"This means I can't see Countessa?"

Gears shook his head. "Appointment and gifts only. Talking to the dead is powerful mojo, the big league."

Zed pulled out two C batteries. "I have a gift."

"Not enough and not today. Last woman gave a portable radio."

"Shit-a-brick!"

"Tell me about it."

"So what you getting?"

"For today?" Gears looked around and leaned close. "Colour TV."

Zed gave a low whistle. "Any room left to get in on this action?"

Gears winked. "Sorry sister, I'm just the muscle."

"Can I sell it, what they want?"

"Not unless you can resurrect the past."

"What?"

"Nothing. There's nothing for you here, everything about you is on top, up front, you dig? Seeing is seeing. But most people have these shadows which follow them, get it?"

Zed looked at him. "No."

Gears was about to respond when a middle-aged man in a blue V-neck emerged from the doorway. He blinked through tears, holding a black-and-white framed photo of a young beauty. He stumbled down the hall, seeing nothing.

Gears waved the next person in, a woman in a green turtleneck clutching a teddy bear. "Heady stuff, the past," he said, looking at the back of the middle-aged man as he continued down the hall.

Gears turned to Zed. "People have like two people: the people they were and the people they are. Everyone here has like, two faces."

"So who are you?" Zed asked.

"Ha, ha." Gears waved his finger. "Not yet, try again."

"Countessa?"

"Not going there, not a chance."

"Father?"

"Interesting dude, too much conviction, got booted cause he couldn't learn to play the game." Gears gave the peace sign. "Truly righteous."

"Professor?"

"Grad student who wigged out, just never stopped reading, so now he's only got a personality as long as a book."

"Barry?"

"Sister, I am not some information well for you to pump. Right now, I got to be 'the Man' and you got to be moving on, okay?"

Zed gave one last try. "Hammer?"

Gears waved her off, laughing. "See, all up front, just like I said. You want to know … find out for yourself, just ask him what he did during the war."

The war? Zed shrugged and was heading out when the mouth-watering smell of Gears' stew wafted out of Countessa's door. Zed glowered at him. "How come you're selling it to her but not to me?"

"She pays a price beyond compare," he told Zed. "Ask no questions, I'll tell no lies."

This was turning out to be Zed's worst day: first, the rate of trade with Countessa had gone out of sight; second, instead of her trading the goods and taking the cut she was getting squat; but the third and the worst was that she was out of the loop – they didn't even see her as a player anymore. She was on the outside. It seemed like everyone had changed, grown richer, more secretive.

She pulled out the broken Walkman, the batteries, and the Zippo and held them out to Gears. "Can you get me in?"

Gears examined the Walkman and flicked the Zippo, checking the flame. He took the batteries and pocketed them. "Not now," he told her. He leaned over and whispered in her ear, "Seance tonight, eleven o'clock, very hush-hush. Talking to the dead boy."

"Charles? How?"

Gears put a finger to his lips, then leaned down closer to her. "Seance is when they talk to the dead," he whispered, then stood up. "Later," he said, and gave her another wink.

"Later." Zed walked away, not sure what she had traded for, but at least she was still in the game. Too bad it was Charles, though, he had never seemed to be of much use while alive. She shrugged. Maybe death had improved him.

By now it was afternoon, its subtle warmth giving Zed's body the cue for sleep. She snuck down to her bed, lit a candle, and emptied her bag. The canned ham and the porno DVD were going to be a hard sell. The shoe, on the other hand, was a sure thing, once she found the owner. She'd check with Teresa to see if it was Christina's. She placed the objects in a careful pile by the bed, blew out the candle, and went to sleep.

ZED WOKE TO PUNTER in the early evening, about seven o'clock, when people felt their hunger hard and business was good. She loaded up and headed to the lobby.

Hammer was reading when she arrived. He gave her a nod from the book. Hammer's tongue stuck out as he read. He wet a thumb and turned the page, keeping a careful watch on the words. Zed waited. Hammer finished the chapter and put the book down.

"Mmmm." Hammer held up the mystery. "Good. Dead kids." He barked a laugh.

"So what's the news on Charles?" she asked.

Hammer looked at her and put one of his square fingers up to his nose, giving it a tap. "Seven-thirty, body." Hammer stated. "Eight-thirty, gone. Nine-thirty, body back."

"You found the body at seven-thirty this morning? You call it in?" Hammer's eyes narrowed.

"Why not?"

"Going anywhere?" He gave another barking laugh.

"So the body was moved, but returned."

He nodded.

Zed sat back and thought about this. It didn't seem to make any sense. Why move a body twice?

"Another mystery." Hammer said, tapping the cover of the one in his hand.

Zed nodded. "Hammer?" He turned his head towards her. It was like watching a turret rotate. "What did you do in the war?" she asked.

He looked at her and his eyes got hard and mean, but then they just got distant, and the smallest tweak of satisfaction appeared on his lips. "Killed," he said with a tone as close to warm as ever came from Hammer's lips. "Killed gooks."

"Gooks?"

But Hammer wasn't listening to her. His eyes and mind were distant; he squeezed his hands together, then relaxed, then again, squeezing hard and white. He laughed.

Zed slipped out, careful not to disturb Hammer from his happy place. Checking over the water tank, she came up with some new questions, like how exactly do you move a body, twice, unseen, only twenty feet from Hammer's door?

At the stairwell, Zed debated what to do. She wanted more information but Gears was out, Hammer was out, and Countessa was out. She took a deep breath and gave in to the inevitable: she would have to visit the Professor. She bounded up the stairs to fourteen and slipped through the hall door, hesitated in front of the Professor's door, hand held up to knock. Then with a quick one-two-three she rapped and stepped aside, pressing herself out of sight.

"For whom the bell tolls," someone said from behind the door as it was being opened. "Me!"

She heard the cotton of his shirt brush the doorframe. "Memoirs of an invisible man," he mourned.

She stepped inside. "Railway children?" he asked, stepping back a bit. "Anne of Green Gables?" He scrutinized her. "Little Orphan Annie."

"One day," she threatened, shaking a fist beneath his nose as she pushed past. "One day." She dug around in her bag for Rat's utensils. The Professor watched her from the doorway. "Fiery spirit," he commented before closing the door and returning to his armchair.

"Need a fork? Spoon?" She held them up.

"Forking? Spooning?" The Professor blushed. "Six and nine, ho, ho."

She checked his kitchen. He already had one of each. Well, she'd only take one book. She ran water over the utensils and put them away in the drawer. The Professor had returned to his reading. Tonight it was *Shapes in the Fire* by M.P. Shiel.

In his discards she found a mystery she'd missed, a bit thin with a split starting, but it was good enough; it disappeared into the satchel.

"Hey Prof," she called, distracting him from the reading. "What's a gook?"

"Gook? Gooks? VC. Charlie. Vietnam. French Siam." He laughed. "Never wage a land war in Asia. Alexander, O Alexander, weep on."

Zed frowned. This was not satisfactory. "Killing Gooks?" she tried.

"America, America, we're off to Vietnam. It's only a police action, sir," he said, saluting. The Professor grabbed Zed's coveralls and pulled her in close, screaming into her face, "Fire at 'em boys. Fire, fire at the bush, you've got to hit something!" He looked left, then right. "Remember, if they run, they're VC." He let go of her and sat up, talking in a moderated voice. "In Vietnam, we have a commuter war; they helicopter in, search and destroy, then helicopter back to base for hot chow. Reporting from a camp forty miles north of Hanoi, this is CBS." He stopped for a moment, then looked at her. "Wars are stupid. They always end up destroying the books." With that, the Professor picked up his book, opened it, and started reading.

Zed couldn't decide if the Prof's confusion was any better than total ignorance. She let herself out, heard the hoots and yells from down below, and swore under her breath. The Zombie races, she'd clean forgot.

The race course extended from the elevator lobby to the far stairwell. The hall was already packed with racegoers in full paraphernalia: liquor, betting slips, sunglasses. The sunglasses were considered high wit; after a few bottles, very high wit, and by race time, broken. Zed pushed through the crowd, heading for the opposite hall, trying to catch Luc in his office.

The usual gang hung by the office; the reefers, tie-dyed, grunge and rasta, the goths and slick boys in the *de rigeur* black, and the grizzled liquor veterans. The only difference was Luc's closed door.

Cal, the tie-dye reefer, recognized her. "Luc's blown," he told her, "hours ago, 'closed on account of rightousness,' he said. Whatever!"

A scream rang from behind the closed door of the stairwell. Cal ignored it, as did everyone else.

"You know when he's back?" Zed asked.

Cal shrugged. His shrug suggested, "Fuck it, I got enough for now and so what if I'm still here, hanging round Luc's door, free country ain't it, and I got to smoke somewhere." It would have been quite the shrug if Zed hadn't seen it or its equivalent twenty times a day.

"Catch you at the races," Zed said.

"Yeah. Whatever."

A whimpering shriek snuck through the stairwell door as Zed poked it open. Stu, his back to her, crouched, smoking a cig. Lying shirtless on the concrete in front of Stu was Charlie, an old bald-headed burnout. Everyone knew that Charlie had nothing left, not even pride. He'd steal anything, beg, mooch or borrow anything that could be converted into a mind-altering substance. He also had no limits on what he would ingest, hence the nickname, Bucket Charlie, human wastecan.

Stu took a long drag of the cig, brought it from his lips, and pressed it into Charlie's exposed back. The flesh under the cig sizzled as Charlie gave a shuddering moan. Leaving Charlie's body to quiver, Stu brought the cig back to his lips, fished a pack out of his pocket, and held it over Charlie's shoulder. Charlie pulled five cigs out and placed them on the pile in front of him. Zed realized that what she had taken as liver spots on Charlie were actually burns. Stu took another drag, then held the cigarette to Charlie's back again, and with a sizzle the smell of burnt flesh rose.

Zed stuck out her tongue in disgust. "How can you stand the smell?"

Stu turned, his mouth slack, his eyes pale and filmy. "What smell?" His voice was hoarse and dusky. He turned back, fished out the pack, and handed it over to Charlie.

Zed retreated from the stairwell in time to see Luc throw open his door. Zed made quick steps and drifted behind Luc, following another shriek from stairwell.

"Stu still at his 'hobby?'"

Zed nodded.

"Boys will be boys."

A reefer's head popped around the door. Luc looked at it, frowned, and shook his head. The reefer disappeared. A moment later, a moan of protest came from the hallway.

Ignoring the noise, Luc hung up his coat, pushed one of the kittens back into the box, and settled behind the desk. From a drawer, he took out a whistle and inched it over his hat until it hung round his neck, then took out the prize baggies of pills and cash before rising to pull down the tote board.

"Business calls," he said to Zed who was waiting to ask about 'Gooks.' She nodded at him. It would keep. Luc stuck his head out into the hall. "Last bets!"

As everyone rushed in, Zed slid out, wandering down to the elevator foyer. The teams had arrived, a flurry of zombies, handlers, riders, whips, and harnesses. Zed spotted Teresa in the green team's pit zone, slumped over in a lawn chair. Christina, the green's rider for tonight, was on the floor, cracking her whip on the leg of the lawn chair. Zed drifted over.

"Where's Ellen?" asked Zed.

"Greedy cow's still asleep, thanks to Luc's generosity. She guzzled it before I even saw it. Ow!" Christina had missed and hit Teresa's leg.

"You want to practice? Practice on your mount," Teresa told her.

Christina stood and went over to her zombie. Zed recognized her as the woman from the stairwell. She leaned up against the wall, her mouth open and a line of drool hanging off her lower lip. The handlers had already kitted the zombie with the light racing harness, ready to hold Christina high on her shoulders. Christina gave the woman a crack across the back. The zombie moved a few feet. Christina smiled.

A few of the serious gamblers were there, their rows of gold chains flowing across sweat-stained shirts. A hard-luck gambler named Hearts approached Christina and asked in a syrupy voice, "How you figure, dearie?" Christina ignored him, and after he looked her mount over he went to hang around the opposition.

"What's her name?" Zed asked. The zombie just stood, her eyes stuck in a thousand-yard stare.

Christina looked up. "I call her Turtle," she said, "cuz she's so slow. And her back's so thick." She gave Turtle a whack for demonstration.

The other rider was a twiggy eleven-year-old from the 16th floor named Pete. And boy, oh boy, did Zed loathe her. Pete was a grifter, a cheat, and a pain in the backside. As far as Zed could tell, Pete liked her too. Pete's forehead was bulgy on the left side and her jaw not quite true. She would only ride her mother, Bunny, an ex-floozy, ex-moll for wannabe criminals. The nickname came from Bunny's insatiable appetite of daily "fuckings" on the large leather-saddled motorbike which dominated the bedroom. But these days, with her brown teeth, limp hair, scabbed face, and fried brains, she was beyond sex; in fact, beyond almost any sensory input. Pete sat beside Bunny on the floor. Seeing Zed,

Pete bared her teeth and fixed Zed with a malicious look, her beady black eyes bulging.

A whistle sounded and Luc strode down the hallway. "Campers," he said, "it's Race Time." And with that, everyone rushed to the walls lining the racetrack, trying to find a space. After a few incidents of natural selection, the walls were lined with people, leaving a three-foot aisle running down the centre, from foyer to red ribbon finish. Late-comers and those evicted from the walls had to join the mob in the back half of the foyer, held back by Barry and Stu.

"The Trophies," Luc announced, pulling the baggies from his pocket to cheers and yells of "Gimme, gimme!" Luc dangled the baggies in front of the zombies, whose only reaction was to salivate and grunt.

"Now, last week I had some complaints that the mounts were just a little too conscious," he said, then gave Bunny a quick slap. No reaction. Turtle got a slap. No reaction. He turned and scanned the crowed with a raised eyebrow. "I trust there will be no further complaints." He waited, but there was nothing except a growing chant: "The Race! The Race! The Race!"

"Excellent." Luc slowly walked down the row of people. He dropped the baggies just past the finish line and returned to the foyer. The Zombies were in the gates. Luc scanned the crowd, looking for any trouble. Everything was clear. "Riders, mount!" Luc yelled and everyone cheered.

Teresa gave Christina a pat on the head. "Get Mummy some wine money." The handlers lifted Christina into position.

Pete had clambered crab-like up Bunny and already sat in her harness, her wild dark hair over forehead and eyes. She grinned her malevolent best at the crowd.

Luc checked the crowd again. "You," he said, pointing at a spiky-haired Ben P. who was trying to squeeze into the hallway. "Out." Ben P. slunk toward the elevator mob, besieged by jeers and catcalls. He turned before joining the crowd and gave everyone the finger.

"Today," Luc announced, "in the 11th floor invitational...." He rung out the last word as the crowd started to cheer. "Representing the

Green division, sponsored by the Closet Hydroponics Marijuana Growers Association ... Christina!" The left side of the hallway burst into applause and Christina raised her hand in salute. "And representing the Red division," Luc continued, "sponsored in part by the Association of Women Comfort Givers...." There was a high-pitched scream of support from the front of the hallway where a row of girls with painted faces and wearing short skirts and high-heeled leather boots stood. "...Pete." There was another cheer when Mistress Anna stepped forward and let out a long howl.

"Are you ready?!" Luc yelled. The crowd screamed that they were very ready. Luc's eyes scanned constantly. "Are you steady?!" The crowd responded with a continuous scream, growing in volume. Everyone was stomping in rhythm, rocking the floor, stomp, stomp, *stomp*. Luc lifted the whistle to his lips. Christina and Pete looked each other over, and tightened the grips on their whips, then looked straight ahead.

The whistle blew its hard note and the mob exploded, screaming and lunging. Only Stu and Barry's vicious jabs at lips, ears, and noses kept the mob from overwhelming the racers.

At the whistle, Christina had given Turtle two hard strikes to get her moving before settling down to a soft/hard rhythm of blows which drove Turtle forward in a rocking amble.

Pete had fallen back at the start, and with a tightly clenched fist, delivered alternating strikes of the whip, first on the left side of the ribs and then on the right. They were hard, cruel blows and Pete's black eyes glittered as they gained at every step.

Luc backed up along the route, facing the racers, making sure the crowd did not interfere. A woman in a slinky polyester dress raised her arm to throw a beer bottle when Luc's steely gaze caused her to lower it. Stu and Barry stepped back, side by side, into the start of the hallway. They stood just behind Pete and Bunny, with the leaping, throbbing mob behind.

Pete, her strikes delivered with increasing frenzy, had come abreast of Christina. Pete leaned forward, her wrist flicked, and two whip lines bled red across Turtle's face. Turtle stumbled, stiff-legged, with Christina atop, shrieking and whipping wildly. By the time Turtle was brought back into rhythm, they'd lost six feet to Bunny and Pete. The crowd was going ape, jumping and howling. "Another, another! Give her another!" they screamed at Pete. "Kill her, kill her!" they screamed at Christina.

Pete had pushed Bunny hard and Bunny's breathing was now laboured, her ribs wet with blood as each fall of the whip splattered the crowd. But Pete kept laying it on, the whip flicking from side to side in a steady flow. Under this determination Bunny continued, wheezing, legs stiffening.

Christina, seeing the gap widening, worked to bring that rhythm back: hard then soft, hard then soft. But the blows across the face had left Turtle hopelessly confused. Though she stumbled forward at first, she soon began gyrating across the hallway, first left, then right, then left again. In a sudden lunge, Turtle crashed straight toward the wall, ramming one of the only non-screaming spectators: an elderly man in a brown sweater, calmly smoking his pipe and watching the race with a cold detached eye. He did not even blink as Turtle and Christine loomed over him, then plastered him into the wall. The rider/mount/spectator sandwich shuddered along the wall before beginning a towering slide that ended in an impressive crash at the mob's feet. Christina wriggled free and stood over Turtle, who lay gasping. With clenched teeth, Christina gave Turtle a kick in the head before throwing down her whip and stalking back to her mother. The elderly gentleman sat sprawled against the wall, looking sadly into his hand at the remnants of his pipe. Meanwhile, Bunny and Pete, to the collective cheers, hisses, and boos of the crowd, lurched and lumbered across the finish line.

Luc bowed and handed the winner's baggie up to Pete, who held it two-fisted above her head, mugging it up for the crowd. She and Bunny were surrounded by the Comfort Givers, jumping in celebration.

Luc took the small baggie and worked his way back to hand it to Teresa. Christina was sitting behind the chair, pouting, ignoring everyone.

Teresa pocketed the two bills before going to help Turtle up.

Zed left the corner to stand beside Luc, who glanced down at her. "I will really have to split them up," he commented, watching Pete crawl down off her mother and start to pop pills into the waiting mouth. "But the little urchin refuses to ride anyone else." He looked longingly at Zed. "Ever think of joining the circuit?"

Zed shook her head vehemently. "It's bad business. There's no trade."

Luc raised a hand to the shocked O of his mouth. "But the fans, the little children, the mothers, everyone gets a piece of it, the winners too."

Zed nodded at the Zombies who stood motionless at the sides. "They don't trade. They're off-limits." She stated her simple rule.

"Well, aren't you Miss Goody Two Shoes," Luc said.

Zed shrugged. She didn't have a lot of guidelines, but here were three: Pay your way, trade fair, and get full payment. Those she obeyed with iron discipline.

Zed's silence seemed to anger Luc. "Well, it doesn't bother me none, child," he said fiercely. "I'd run these races every day and twice on Sundays and smile all the time if I could but get the riders."

Zed regarded Luc skeptically. "You smile all the time anyway."

"Do I?" Luc asked with a Cheshire grin. "Why, so I do." He shrugged it off. "Well, needs must when the Devil dances. Guess once a week will do then."

"What do you know about a war in Vietnam?" she asked him.

"Fantastic Black Market. But I guess you want more, no?" A wave of women clutching betting slips approached. "Luckily I am saved from active young minds by business. Come up later if you want and I might be prepared to talk ... for a little compensation." He gave her a diabolical leer as he turned to stroll into his office. The Women Comfort Givers pushed in after him.

Barry stripped the harness off Turtle and set her free for another week. Zed remembered she wanted to talk to Teresa about the shoe, but Teresa was gone. Zed headed for the stairs.

She was two floors down when she heard a baritone singing:

> *Oh, mine eyes have seen the glory of the coming of*
> *the Lord,*
> *He is trampling on the dealers and wiping out their*
> *hoards*

She looked down to see the spiky hair of the Father as he ascended, nodding to himself as he sang.

> *He has loosed the fateful lightning of his terrible swift*
> *sword.*
> *The truth is marching....*

Suddenly there was a bang and blast of air as the door behind Zed flew open, and a lanky man with a dragon tattoo on his arm burst past her. He dropped down the stairs two at a time. On the level below, he opened the door. He stopped mid-step, half through, his eyes riveted on the Father coming up the stairs. "Fuck you!" he said, arm muscles rigid as a taut rope while he looked the Father up and down. "Fuck you!" The Father ascended past, smiling and nodding. "*Fuuuuuccckkk,*" the man said, drawing out the word in boiling anger, looking up at the retreating back, "*you!*" He went into the hallway, slamming the door behind.

The Father caught sight of Zed and grinned through his swollen face. "Great, wasn't it?" he nodded towards the slammed door.

"Naw. So why'd he hate you?"

"Not I, not I, I am just the embodiment of frustrated desire."

"In English?"

"Luc's told them that I have convinced him to stop selling so now the flow of drugs, dope, and booze is stopped."

"And everyone hates you," Zed said.

"Yes, wonderful isn't it?" Behind the bruises and puffy eyes, there was a twinkle.

"But Luc just did it to mess with you."

"He may think he did, but did Pharaoh know why his heart was hardened?"

Zed let that fly by. "You gonna hole up?"

"Never. Think how many people will be suffering the effects of detox tonight, all in need of hands of loving comfort."

Zed tried to tell him. "I don't think they'll want to see you," she said.

"Worry not, my child." The Father continued up the stairs. "I float on the wings of eagles; all things are delivered into my hands."

ZED TURNED AND HURRIED down the stairs. One, nothing the Father did made sense, especially today. Two, she'd have to be on her toes cuz everyone would be flipping out right and left.

She opened the door to Brat Alley. Teresa was already sitting there, drinking a bottle of red. "You heard?" asked Teresa. "Prohibition's on. We're down to the reserves." She held up the bottle.

"Where's Ellen?"

"Sulking. When she woke up she wanted the whole bottle of red, cuz 'I'm in grief,' she said. Screw that, it's my wine, splits or nothing. So she's having a 'pity party.'" Teresa gestured towards the closed door. "*Mmm!*" she yelled, "love this wine!"

"Bitch!"

Teresa laughed and took another swig.

"Where's Christina?" Zed asked.

"Don't know," Teresa muttered. "She's high on that stupid whip. Got me on the arm, look at that!" She held out her arm to show Zed a faint red mark. "I told her to go whip someone else."

Zed held up the white sneaker. "This Christina's?"

Teresa leaned forward. "Naw," she said, looking it over. "Christina only wears pink. I dye them all with Kool Aid."

"Charles'?"

Teresa stared at the shoe. "Don't know, ask Ellen." Teresa looked down at the bottle in her lap. "Not much left!" she yelled at the door.

"Cunt!"

Zed shook her head and pushed past Teresa. She hated these domestic quarrels and solved them by walking away, quickly.

The elevator opened as she walked by; it was a good omen. She stepped inside and pressed 11. As the door slid shut, Zed noticed Gears in the corner. Behind him stood a very pale man, soft at the edges. Even his hair was pale – not blond, or white, just pale, with a white neck disappearing down a white shirt.

"What are you doing here?" Zed asked Gears. She thought he'd be at Countessa's.

"Break."

"Where ya going?" She'd never seen Gears in an elevator before, not that she was often in one.

"Where are *you* going?" he countered.

"See Luc, about Vietnam. Hey, come on, tell me what Hammer did in Vietnam?"

"Hmm." Gears was spacing.

"Hammer, Vietnam?"

"Some sort of special forces." Gears watched the numbers slowly going by, then looked back at her. "You coming tonight? Be there in like, a half-hour, okay?"

The pale man had stopped looking at the floor and gave her a few glances, then was staring.

"Who're you?" Zed asked.

"Hello?" Gears waved his hand in front of her face. "Gears, remember."

"Not you, him." She pointed.

Gears looked round then frowned at Zed. "Imaginary friends, like, reek of suburbia."

Zed rolled her eyes. For all of Gears' talk of new experiences, he could be quite dense at times.

"Just remember to be there, Countessa's place."

The elevator doors opened and she got out then looked back. Gears was gazing into space. The pale man just stared, looking at her. She gave him a wave as the doors closed.

Zed walked down to Luc's, pushing through a small crowd outside the door. The door was closed with a sign on it: "Still out of business, see you tomorrow."

"Screw these games," Tom, a thin-looking teen with a shaved head, cried. His t-shirt read, "Stoners are people too." People or not, he was pissed. "I want my stuff." He hopped up and down in anxiety.

A tall woman with a gap in her front teeth said, "Maybe he'll start selling at midnight, that's tomorrow."

"How long's that?" Tom asked.

"Hour and twenty minutes."

"Can't wait. Can't wait."

Zed was irritated by Luc's absence, but was certainly not going to hang around with this crowd. She went to the elevator and gave the button a push. Doesn't luck come in twos? After a while she figured, guess not, and took the stairs. Once the incense grew irritating, she knew she was almost there.

At the stairway door she was met by Don, a chunky no-necker wearing a black beret. Some people can wear a beret and some look like they have a leech on their head; Don was the latter. He frowned at Zed. "Special event," he said. "Only those on the list allowed in." The burners emitted a belch of smoke that poured over Don's shoulders.

"You can't just block off the whole floor. Maybe I live here."

Don shrugged. "I don't know and I don't care. Countessa tells me to keep people out so I keep people out."

When Zed couldn't get to where the action was, then the world was definitely getting out of hand. "So, who gets in?"

"People on the list."

"Fine, I'm on the list." She started forward.

Don stopped her with a hand, looking uncertain. "I dunno."

"Right! You even have a list?"

"Maybe." He pulled her back into the stairs. "What's your name?"

She looked at him, amazed. "I'm Zed. Zed. Everyone knows me."

Don gave a chuckle. "Yeah, Zed, I've heard of you. Go on in." He held the door open for her.

Sheesh! All that to get through a lousy door.

In the hallway, she met Gears. "You need some new help," she said. He shrugged and pointed her to the Countessa's door.

Zed approached Countessa's darkness, sidled up to the door-frame, and peered inside. A single candle flickered on the table.

The Countessa's voice came from within. "Join us."

The beads jingled as Zed entered. "Here, dear, by me." The soft leather of old ladies hands brought her to a chair.

Seated, she could hear the breathing of five, feel the table shimmer as they shifted, but the only thing she could see was Countessa's hands, white and cadaverous, limp in candlelight.

They waited and it was silent. Zed had never heard it this silent; in a building where someone was always screaming, banging, or muttering, this was a vacuum that made you strain your ears. Zed felt herself falling down a well of silence, losing herself, when she picked up the tap, tap, tap of approaching footsteps.

"I'm here." A man pushed among them. Zed shoved him on, heard the squeak of him sitting, and listened as his breathing slowed.

In the candlelight, Countessa's fingers slowly unfolded. As each finger rose, Zed felt she was watching a spider uncurl.

"In the days of my grandma," Countessa told them in her foreign lisp, "people would join hands around a table both to help the spirits along and to ensure there was no falsehood."

Countessa's hands were spread full on the table. "But in the time of my grandma's grandma, the dead walked the woods and mountains and we fed them from the window sills, talking through the wooden slats."

Countessa fell silent and everyone waited. *Does this mean they were supposed to join hands or not?* Zed wondered.

"I call on the dead!" Countessa boomed out. "I call their spirits to me. Come!"

There was silence.

Countessa's hands clenched to fists. "To the spirits which walk in the world within the world, I call on you to honour the binding made by my ancestors. Spirits, come! Grandma, come! Great Grandma, come! One of the blood calls you."

Countessa fell silent again. Only this time Zed could hear something, like a tickling on the edge of her mind. There was an eddy of air playing along her arms when she pinpointed the sound. It was a low whispering, a soft murmur of a hundred voices passing in a flow above her head, up at the ceiling.

"Spirits, tell me of the children, send to me the one called Charles, late of this world. Send Charles."

The whispers grew, winding around the table, rubbing past Zed, whispering, whispering, but always just out of earshot. Through the murmur one throaty croak grew, repeating over and over four syllables, louder and louder, four syllables: "He will not come. He will not come. He will not come."

"Thank you, Grandma," Countessa said, her hands disappearing from the table, "but yes, he will come."

"He will not come. He will not come. He will not come. He will not come. He will not come. He will not come."

"Charles of the Tower, Charles of the newly dead, by this talisman, I compel you; by the links to the living, I compel you; by this binding, I compel you. Speak Charles, speak." Countessa's hands held a small sneaker, one that was familiar to Zed as she had one just like it in her bag, though probably for the other foot. Well, she figured, either the value just rose or bottomed out.

The voices grated on the ears, harsh and grinding. They swirled around the room faster and faster.

"Speak, Charles!"

"*No!*" a petulant voice boomed. *Well,* Zed thought to herself, *nice to hear Charles hasn't changed.* "I want Ellen!"

"She isn't here, Charles," Countessa told him, "but she wants to know what we want to know. Who severed you from the living?"

"I don't like it here. I'm alone."

"Who did it, Charles?"

"I don't want to talk to you." The shoe in Countessa's hands twitched. "Let me go."

"Tell me, who was it?"

"*Let me go!*" The sneaker smouldered, the laces blackened, and the upper part started to curl.

"I will not let you go until you tell me what I wish to know."

"No, no, I'm not ... hey, you're here? Now I can talk to you."

"Who's there, Charles? Who are you talking to?"

The sneaker, blackened, broke into two. "Not anymore!" came the gleeful response. The whispers grew to a shout, a roaring scream that assaulted the ears, wrapping around the body. Zed pressed her palms to her ears but it was no good, they pressed in, howling.

And then ... they stopped. A few quiet whispers floated up to the ceiling before fading into nothing.

"What?" a voice asked in Zed's ringing ears. "What does it mean?"

"It means," Countessa said in a low satisfied voice, "another child is dead." And with that, the candle went out.

"Countessa?"

"Countessa, where are you?"

"She's gone." Suddenly the fluorescent tube lights in the hallway flickered with power and started to warm up, hitting the hallway with intermittent light.

Her head still ringing, Zed got to her feet and felt along the hallway. She pushed into the stairs with relief. At least here she was somewhere familiar. She leaned against the wall and felt the cold concrete on her hot cheek. Above and below, she could hear people calling out. "What was that?" The door to the floor above opened and a grizzled beard looked down. "What was that noise?" She ignored him and started up the stairs. Let the others tell. It would get around the building soon enough.

She didn't bother to look up, just noted his cracked yellow toenails. "What?" he called after her. "The noise?" But she just climbed on, one stair at a time.

At the 9th floor, Zed ran into the tail of a line, snaking up the stairs and growing thicker every step. The landing of the 11th, outside Luc's office, was chock-a-block with the waiting. Zed groaned and started shoving through. Like she needed this.

"Hey, back in line," one of the slick boys by the door told her as she elbowed past.

"Let her go," his friend in death-head makeup said. "That's Luc's chicken legs."

Zed turned with her knife out, which she jabbed an inch into his thigh, drawing blood. The death-head squealed, the sweat popping on his face, making his foundation smear.

"Fuck *you!*" Zed pulled out the knife with a twist. "Got it, asshole?" He nodded.

"If I hear anything like that again, I'll come visiting." She pushed through the hall door and left him behind.

Her glower got her past the crowd at Luc's door and once inside, she sunk into her chair.

Cal, who was still first in line, popped his head in. "Does this mean it's time, man, I mean, Luc, cuz I could use, like, a quarter of your finest, you know."

"No." Luc sat at his desk, rotating a knife up through his fingers and then back down again. "Don't know, not for another hour."

"Oh man, this is so messing with my head. First the no selling thing and now when Zed walked in, you know, I thought...."

"No, no thinking. She stays, you go." Luc looked over and Cal disappeared with a sigh.

"All goes well," Luc smiled to himself before looking Zed over. "Long face, 2:1 it's to do with that noise."

"No bet." Zed rubbed her temple. "Stupid Charles is still giving me a headache."

Luc frowned, but left it.

"Dead!" A cry came from the hallway. "Another dead."

"What? Where?" The questions came from the crowd.

"They've found another kid's body," the first voice replied.

"No, you idiot," said another voice. "The noise means another kid is dead, not that they found the body."

The crowd descended into a hubbub. Luc turned to Zed. "They found another body?"

Zed looked up, blinking. She rallied herself. "I get the answer to a single question," she bargained.

"One question ... historical?" Luc asked.

"One question, anything," Zed said firmly.

Luc looked to the crowd outside, confused from conflicting reports. "It's a deal. But only for the straight, unwatered truth."

Zed closed her eyes, remembering, "Countessa called up the dead who whispered all over and then she told Charles to come and he wouldn't and she made him come and just when he was going to say who killed him, he started to talk to someone he knew. Then the whispers became shouts! And someone asked what it meant and the Countessa said there was another dead kid and then she disappeared." Zed reopened her eyes.

Luc smiled. "That Countessa, what a showman, what presence, what moxie, predicting dead kids." He shook his head in admiration. "Did she say where the kid was?"

Zed shook her head.

He grinned. "Then we can still get in on this show." He stood up, strode to the door, and called to the crowd outside, "People! Gentlemen and Ladies! Dedicated customers, give me your ear." A sea of faces turned towards him.

"I have an announcement. While I am not a supporter of Countessa, I am willing to put my money where her mouth is. She claims that there is already a dead body somewhere in this building. Now I am offering a reward, not $50, not $100, but $200 worth of any substance for the first person who can find me this dead body." The hungry, desperate eyes at the door started calculating. Luc continued, "Before you go off bashing each other, the body needs to have been dead *before* you started looking." The crowd waited to make sure there wasn't any more. "Away," Luc said, waving his hand, "to play."

Everyone split. There followed a thundering of feet as people raced up and down the stairs.

Soon after, the sound of splintering wood came from the hallway.

"Hey, man," Ben P's thin reedy voice asked, "you seen a corpse?"

"Who the hell are – *my door*! You fucking broke my door."

"Yeah, sorry, but I really need to find that corpse, see, cuz otherwise I don't get the stash, I mean, we could go halfers but I really got to find … hey man, no, chill out man, stay back. Ow, no, put me down man, no, no, oh God!"

Luc's wall trembled when the body hit it.

"And don't ever touch my fucking door again!"

Luc and Zed emerged into the hallway in time to see Ben crawl into the stairwell. Further down, Matt and Jeff, a weightlifter and his tweedy sidekick/laugher-at-jokes, kicked in a door and glanced at each other before running through.

"This one's dead," came the rough voice.

"Naw, he's just sleeping."

"Sure?"

"Look at the drool."

The pair climbed back over the broken door into the hall. They looked to find Luc frowning at them. "Uh, let's try down a floor, or something," one said to the other. "Sure." They both took off at a run.

Luc and Zed stood listening. From the floor below came a crash and a high-pitched scream. "I am starting to see some drawbacks," Luc stated.

A stream of profanity and the sound of breaking glass came from above.

Luc looked over at Stu and Barry who were leaning against the wall enjoying the show. "Why did you not intervene?" he asked them.

Stu looked puzzled. "You want us to break down doors?"

Luc walked toward the elevator. "I think this whole episode might look better *from a distance*."

As the elevator descended, crashes, moans, obscenities, and the thud of body against body filtered in. Luc had a pained expression on his face. He looked over at Barry in time to catch him pushing something down into his jacket pocket.

"Show me!" Luc held out his hand.

"What?" Barry looked around as if Luc could be talking to anyone else. Luc continued to hold out his hand, so Barry reached into his pocket and pulled out a white kitten. "I was just saving her for later," he explained, his voice trailing off.

Luc pointed to Stu.

Barry reluctantly handed over the kitten. Stu looked at it. It sneezed. Stu quickly shoved it into the pocket of his leather jacket.

They arrived at the ground floor and walked out the front door. Zed gave a little wave to Hammer who was lounging at his doorway, fondling a billy club with an unholy grin. Across the street, they turned to look back.

From this distance, it didn't seem so bad – an occasional flash of light and the smallest murmur and tinkles. Zed noticed that many of the elderly had retreated to their balconies for safety. They looked down at Luc with accusing stares.

"Can we stop it?" Zed asked.

"Believe me, if I could, I would. Unfortunately it is a bit like pushing a big rock down a steep slope. The first couple of inches are fine, but when you are down-slope and that rock is cartwheeling towards you, cutting off treetops as it comes...." Luc turned his palms upward in a "What am I to do?" gesture.

"Hey, Boss, isn't that the Rat?" Stu pointed to a brown creature crawling from a second-floor balcony to a third.

Once on the third-floor balcony, Rat grabbed a flag, a short broom, and a jacket, tying everything to his body with a series of ropes that dangled off his belt. With a leap, he flew to the adjoining balcony, liberating two towels drying there. Stuffing them into a sack around his waist, he started climbing up to the 4th floor.

"He'll never find the body that way," Stu declared.

Zed looked over to see if Stu really was that stupid ... apparently so.

A blue-haired lady peered over the balcony on the 5th floor, watching Rat. She disappeared for a moment, returning with a book in hand which she threw at Rat's head. Rat caught the book and tucked it away. Blue-Hair withdrew. Rat reached the 4th floor, found some resin deck chairs, and dropped them over the side to pick up later. He cackled with laughter as he watched them bounce. Leaping across to the next balcony, he followed the chairs with a wooden planter, which hit the ground and splintered into a thousand pieces. Rat shrugged before leaping back to the first balcony. He stood on the railing and started to clamber up to the fifth when Blue-Hair appeared above him, pot at the ready. With a quick flick, she upended it over Rat's upturned face. His hands clutching his face, Rat's voice rose in a scream of pain as his body toppled backward off the balcony.

"Boiling water," Luc commented, watching Rat fall. "Antiquated perhaps, but still effective."

Rat landed flat on his back, still wailing and writhing. The woman up on five took the chance to throw the empty pot at him, followed by a shot to his groin with a potted plant. Zed thought about going over to help him, but after seeing Rat biting out obscenities while peering around with his bright red face, she thought again. Rat spied the chairs nearby and dragged himself to them. Up above, Blue-Hair looked down. "Fucking Q-Tip!" Rat screamed at her and with a stream of oaths and cries, he crawled toward the garbage area, dragging his chairs.

Small objects continued to rain down on Rat as more and more people came out on their balconies and followed that Tower rule about the

fallen: "Hey, you never know when I might get a chance like this again."
Everyone tried to find something small, hard, and worthless to give Rat
as a going-away present; special delivery at Mach 1. Once Rat made it to
the garbage bins, the show was over. People just looked at each other. No
one was keen to go back and brave the scavenger hunters.

"Yip, yip, *aaarrrooooooo!*" The howl came from a dancing madman
on a balcony halfway up the building.

A couple of people howled back, which only excited him further;
jumping atop the railing, a bearded mouth opened wide and screamed
out rage in defiance.

Barry nudged Stu. "Isn't that Joe? You know, anything, anytime
Joe?"

"Bottomless Joe? It looks like him, but it sure doesn't sound like
him."

Joe screamed once more.

"Uh, Boss," Stu said, sliding over to talk in Luc's ear, "isn't that your
balcony?"

Luc's head jerked in surprise. "So it would seem," he said slowly.

Joe gave another scream and proceeded to rock back and forth. "I
think he's taken some of your stash," Stu said.

Luc looked from Stu to the screaming figure that had started dancing
again and back to Stu. "Do you really think so?" He paused. "Maybe
you should go up and secure the office."

"Shit!" Barry's voice resonated with awe. It pretty much summed
up everyone's feelings as Joe yelled again and jumped feet first from the
11th-floor balcony.

Bottomless Joe dropped five floors, grabbed a balcony railing, dislo-
cating his shoulder with an echoing crack, then released it and fell the
remaining five storeys, the force pile-driving his knees into the sidewalk.
Everyone watched Joe; his arms and head hanging, each breath an animal
moan. He raised his head, bloodshot eyes glaring at Luc, levered himself
up with a rocking motion accompanied by a growing bark, crescendo-
ing to a scream as he erupted onto his feet. Joe's white bone kneecaps,

with cracks visible, showed through a bloody pulp as he lurched toward them, croaking out, "More, want more!"

"Boss," Stu said quickly with a quiver in his voice. "I don't think he knows he's just broken his knees."

"You sure?" Luc gave a tired smile.

"I think so. No one whose knees I ever broke acted like this."

Luc leaned toward Zed. "Do you think he'll stop if I tell him I'm all out?" he asked quietly.

"No."

"Me either." He stood upright and looked at Joe who was still coming, growling. "Stu! Barry! Use what you've got!"

Barry's hands flew to his pockets and whipped out a butterfly knife, then advanced, the blade dancing in the air. Stu opened his leather jacket and pulled his punch dagger from the hook. Fitting it over his fist, he advanced to stand by Barry. They approached Joe in a flurry, knives flashing.

"Don't you just hate the irony," Luc said, watching them. "This happening on the one day I'm *not* selling."

Stu ducked beside Joe's dislocated shoulder, his arm going like a piston, driving in the knife: one, two, three, before Joe knocked him back, whipping his body around to use his dead arm as a club. Barry held out longer: a slash and duck, a stab and a twist, keeping away as Joe thrashed from side to side. But it was only a few dozen seconds until Joe's good arm had caught him and picked him up, throwing him at Luc's feet. Barry's attack just couldn't work against an opponent who didn't drop, feel pain, or concern himself with defence. Joe was bleeding; a flap of his cheek skin hung down from a long cut, his sides, shoulders, and arms ran blood; yet he still limped toward them.

Stu and Barry rose, wincing, to stand by Luc. They watched Joe start across the empty road.

"Should we break an arm?" Stu asked.

"Think he'd notice?" Luc adjusted his hat. "You know, boys, I've always said that our drug dealing would catch up with us one day. Well, I think it's today."

Luc took a step forward and his hands went up under the back of his jacket, emerging with two double-edged daggers. He brought them up to chest level, his arms bent with the points down and out. Joe greeted this with a roar and took another step forward. Luc gave a little shuffle step and with a shout of "Hai!" he snaked in, his left arm flying out and delivering a cut to the shoulder. Joe turned and grabbed Luc's hand, bringing it into his mouth. Luc twisted, plunging the right-hand knife into Joe's jugular, finishing with a twist. Luc tried to step back, but the tip of his pinkie was lodged between Joe's clenched teeth. With calm disdain, Luc leaned back before delivering a whacking head-butt. His hand clear, he leapt back, pushing off from Joe's chest and recovering in a roll as Joe toppled backward.

Luc stood and dusted off his coat while Joe thrashed about. "Think he'll die now?" Barry asked, looking down at Joe.

"His neck's bleeding like a frigging hydrant," Stu said in awe.

Luc pulled out a handkerchief from his jacket and wrapped his left pinkie finger inside.

Soon Joe's thrashing subsided, his eyes glazed, and as his body relaxed, the blood turned from a spray to a trickle.

Zed looked at Luc's hand; the handkerchief was already soaked red.

As soon as Joe's body had fully relaxed, one of the scavengers scuttled forward, face full of glee.

"No!" Luc was icy. "Not this one. He's mine."

The seeker skulked back into the building.

Luc's eyes darted about under the frosty calm of his face. He shook his head. "A shambles."

"What's with the hand?" Barry asked.

Luc looked over at Barry, who immediately retreated out of arm's reach. "Joe managed to end up with just a little bit more, before he hit bottom," Luc said, then he stepped over the body and strode toward the building.

Zed hung back with Barry and Stu, trailing Luc by five safe feet. Barry seemed like warm company compared to Luc.

As they crossed the lobby, they had to step over three groaning forms. Hammer gave Zed a nod as he wiped blood from his billy club.

A voice came from the elevator. "They found it!"

The crowd parted in front of Luc, revealing a grinning woman who was bounding up and down. "They found it!" she shouted in Luc's face.

"Found what?" Luc's voice was like the sound of glass being crushed.

The woman stood petrified. "Found what?" Luc repeated, trying to press his smile into place and failing.

"The body?" she said in a whisper.

"Where?" Luc asked, his teeth emerging, his lip curled back.

"In Val's apartment, the bathtub."

An elevator had come and the four of them entered. "You," Luc called out to the woman who had been speaking. "Come."

The woman hesitantly stepped across.

Barry pushed 19.

"Get off on 11," Luc told Stu. "Check the office."

Barry slid next to Stu. "The kitty?" he asked.

Stu checked the inside of his jacket, then slowly shook his head. Barry's face fell. "Shouldn't have saved it."

"This body," Luc intoned, biting off the end of each word, "who found it?" He looked at the woman.

She struggled to speak. Luc waited. She cleared her throat. "The Father," she croaked out.

Luc's face, if it were possible, took on an even darker expression. "Oh, perfect."

The doors opened and Stu walked quickly out. He didn't look back.

The doors groaned shut again. They continued the rest of the trip in silence, except for a "plop" as another drop of blood fell from Luc's handkerchief.

Chapter 5

THE ELEVATOR LURCHED CLOSE, but not quite, to 19. Luc leapt out, and Barry scrambled after. The excited murmur of those on the floor died down as everyone dove to get out of Luc's path. One woman was a touch too slow and Luc's good hand swept up, grabbing her by the sweater. "Excuse me, please," he said as he released, bouncing her body off the wall. No one got in his way after that.

Zed then clambered out of the elevator and followed Luc, stepping on the trail of blood his wound had left. Mid-corridor, she paused, a putrid odour tickling her memory. Her stride fell short and she almost missed a drop. She gave her foot a twist on that one.

"Fucking off the toe," she heard from her left, and with a flash, the "fucking" and the odour came together. The Rat was here? But Luc was continuing, so she followed the trail.

Luc stopped before the open doorway and looked down at the oil stains on the carpet. The gurney had made them yesterday when it took Valerie away.

Luc turned to Barry. "Search the building and quiet it, calm it, and silence it. The party is *over*." Barry rubbed his shoulder and nodded. Luc turned and entered Val's.

After a search, Zed found the drop she'd seen fly off Luc as he spoke to Barry. It was on the doorjamb so she disqualified it, as it hadn't touched the floor.

Zed crept inside and peered around a settee at Luc and the Father, chest to chest in front of the bathroom door.

"This is not your place," the Father told Luc. "She can't be sold anything, addicted to anything, sold as anything. She's with God now."

Luc sighed and pinched the bridge of his nose. "As much as I'd love to enlighten you on the harvesting of body parts, I'm a bit tired tonight." He held up his hand. "Having been subject to parts redistribution myself, just let me through, eh?"

Father looked at the shortened pinkie with its blood-soaked handkerchief. "You know, in Russia they believe a bit of the Devil's tail gets you a pass out of Hell."

Luc gritted his teeth and brought a sparkle to his eye.

"Fascinating, to be sure. Remember that next time I'm in Russia. But speaking of hells and passes, aren't I here to punch yours? Ticket, that is? See, word is you've got the golden ticket and I'm the claims department." Luc tilted his head, the brim of his hat shading his eyes. "So, just give me a peek at the darling and I'll cough up the reward."

The Father crossed his arms. "She's at peace now, and she's staying that way."

Luc raised his hand. "Fine, fine, I never do this, but you do have such an impeccable character reference." He gave a nod upwards before giving the Father a wink. "Name dropper."

The Father just stood, staring.

Luc turned his uninjured hand in exasperation. Everything was so serious today. "It's easy." He sidled up to the Father. "Just tell me your pleasure, good man. Whisper it into my little ear: a fine brandy, some wine, your own private keg?" He leaned, inclining his head accommodatingly. Luc dropped his voice to a conspiratorial whisper. "Ever thought to experiment a little, a random mix of uppers and downers, mother's little helpers, and a kick from the horse? Good discount for men of the cloth."

"Out," the Father said tersely.

"But you still haven't claimed your reward," Luc protested, "to complete the holy trinity: Countessa predicts, Luc elects, and the Father collects."

"Out!"

"Abstinence. Works for me. Don't worry, padre, between us we can get this place back to the good old days. A little less of the open orgy and a bit more of the squeaking mattress and the half-closed door, no?" He gave the Father a leering wink.

The Father loosened his arm and pointed at the door. Luc touched his hat and sauntered out.

The Father waited until Luc had left, then entered the bathroom. Zed heard his grunts as he knelt by the tub. "You're safe now, child," he whispered to the body. "This day you shall be with Him in paradise." He paused a long time. "Thy will be done," he added, softest of all.

Leaving the bathroom, the Father's eyes widened as he saw Zed, but he simply passed by and took a seat in the settee by the door. Zed went to the bathroom. The carpet was soaked and squishy. She looked down at the tub. It was full of water, and Pete's distorted face was bobbing just below the waterline, a particularly distasteful apple. Her shirt was gone and there was a fist-sized chunk of flesh missing from her breast. She still had on her pants, which billowed loosely in the water. Zed gave the pockets a quick check: empty. Her eyes continued down to check on the shoes – two blue sneakers.

The walls were stained with water. Water drops discoloured the ceiling and shone on the counter top and the toilet tank.

"Quite a struggle." She turned and met the eyes of the Father; he was watching her. "She did not pass easily," he said.

Zed was unsure of what to say. "Pete was tough, didn't ask for anything," she finally offered, trying to highlight the good points of Pete's character. Truth be told, Pete didn't ask for things; she took them quite readily, and once they were in her paws, not much could get them loose. The last time they had met two weeks ago, Pete had sneaked up on her while she was dealing with Ellen, and when Zed had felt the slight tug, she turned to find Pete pulling her hand with a book in it out of the satchel. When Zed's elbows were done, Pete had a bloody nose. Then over the last week, she had caught Pete glaring at her. Not having to deal with Pete was a bit of a relief.

"Yes." The Father had risen and come into the bathroom. "She was an innocent."

Zed looked over, not sure if the Father was being sarcastic. From his tender look she assumed he wasn't.

"I've told her mother," he continued. "But whether she understood me or not.... At least there doesn't seem to be much grief."

"Why's she here?" Zed asked. By this time, they were usually packed and ready to go.

"I called the ambulance twice, but they won't pick her up. 'We don't come this late,' they said. I called the police too, but they told me they don't come out for suicides. I told the sergeant quite firmly that this was not a suicide and that a child had been drowned. The sergeant, Sergeant Wallis, I believe, only laughed and said they didn't come out for deaths due to natural causes, either." The Father gave her a tight smile. "It seems not even dead children are important enough."

"Where's the shirt?" Zed interrupted.

"Shirt?" The Father looked down at the body. "What type of person would steal from the dead?"

It seemed obvious to Zed that the answer was, "Everyone," but she decided to change the topic. "She dead long?"

"Long? I don't know. How would I know? The walls are dry, the carpet damp, how long is that?"

"Time?" Zed pantomimed looking at a watch.

The Father appeared confused, then checked his wristwatch. "One-eighteen. Why?"

"The séance," Zed said, her eyebrows furrowed in concentration, "about eleven-thirty."

"What does that mean?" he asked.

"I don't know." Zed was irritated. She needed to find someone who knew about these things. Then she remembered the Professor. "I'll be back," she told the Father.

In the hallway a few remained, most having followed Luc, hoping he'd open his office. Rat stood against the wall, his burnt face beet-red, glowing like an ember through fresh grime. He watched the door, looking worried.

"He alone?" Rat demanded from Zed.

"Why? What are you doing up here?"

"The King Rat goes where he likes," Rat responded proudly. But he quickly looked around at the hallway. "All these people, I hate it, but I gotta see the Father."

"Why?" Zed was curious. Rat had never shown an inclination toward religion of any sort.

"Gotta ask a question. That's all, just a question. But they say there's a kid in there." At the word "kid," Rat gave a shudder. "Big heads!" he muttered to himself. "Father's got to be alone."

"The kid's dead."

Rat smiled with relief and pushed past her.

Zed headed to the elevator but was stopped by Kim, who was sagging in Spandex and her peroxide ponytail. "Have you heard? Luc did it. Pete was fixing the races."

"But Pete and Bunny were winning," Zed countered.

"That's just what I heard," Kim told her. "But I saw Luc tear out the throat of Bottomless Joe with his teeth, not an hour ago." She snapped her teeth. "Right out!"

"Saw it yourself?"

"Uh-huh," Kim nodded. "Luc's one badass S.O.B."

"I'll pick no on one and yes on two," Zed told Kim, continuing to the elevator. Luc ripped Joe's throat out with his teeth? Zed couldn't get her head around how stories grew so quickly.

The elevator opened to reveal a broad back and a growing puddle in the corner. In the other corner a short man, dressed in black pants and a black turtleneck, orated to himself, "Let the dead bury the dead for they are dead, and let them have no part of the living," at which point he broke off to scratch and slap at his skin. "Off, off, get them off!" He was spinning and thrashing about the elevator, and bounced off the man pissing, who exclaimed in a hurt tone, "I said, I'm almost done!"

Zed let the doors close without entering. The man in black had gained control and peered through the closing doors. "Let their bones lie and their bodies rot."

Zed decided to take the stairs. It was only five flights down. How bad could it be?

The first landing held only two sacked-out sleepers. Zed stepped over them. From below she could hear the banging of metal, making her cautious.

On the landing to the 17th floor sat Bobo, the slab of mountain in grey coveralls. Bobo didn't get out much, for which everyone was thankful, as Bobo had loose concepts of personal health, property, or anything else that didn't immediately involve Bobo.

Bobo sat against the door rubbing his groin like petting a cat. "'Lone, lone, sooooo alone," he said, then started banging the back of his head against the door, rubbing himself in time.

Zed pulled out her knife as she crept down the stairs.

She could have sworn Bobo's eyes were closed, but before you could say, "All fucked up," Bobo was on his feet staring at her, smiling his tooth-gaped grin. "Hey, little fairy," he said, and waved her to come down.

Shit, Zed thought as she came up with several plans, none of which included going down.

"Hey, little fairy, you want to be friends? I like friends." He started pounding his crotch. "Shut up! You, shut up." He smiled up at her. "We can talk now, it's sleeping. You like Bobo?" He scratched his butt. "You want to be friends with Uncle Bobo? We can play all day."

Zed definitely didn't want to play with Uncle Bobo and wondered if she were fast enough to slip past.

Bobo slid between her and the staircase. "Come on, let's play, just the three of us."

Zed figured if Bobo was bringing a friend to the party maybe she better introduce Mr. Switchblade. Then she heard, "Now what you do scaring young Zed, Bobo?"

"No ... but, I was just...." Bobo defended himself.

"I know, Bobo," Ivy said, running a hand along his chin. "Wanting a friend, don't you? But you can't be forcing them."

"Fairies want to play." Bobo pointed to Zed.

"Well, that's one way to look at it, to be sure. Off to bed with you," Ivy said, giving Bobo's arm a slap, "or you won't be growing up big and tall."

Bobo wandered though the doorway muttering. Ivy gave Zed a nod. "I best be putting him to bed, so don't you worry, love, boys might get bigger but they're still boys."

Zed wanted to tell Ivy that she wasn't worried, that she'd never been worried, and Ivy hadn't saved her or anything so that better not be getting around, and how maybe Ivy would like a ham, just because. "Ivy...."

"Some gels need sleep too, love." Ivy winked and followed Bobo.

Shit! Aw screw it, she'd make up for it later. Zed counted her way down – 17th, 16th, 15th – when the sound of voices stopped her.

"Flip him over," a woman's voice said.

"Why do I have to flip him over?"

"Because you're always talking about what a strong man you are, so now you can prove it."

"But he's a wino, my hands will stink."

"Jesus Christ, you flip him over and I'll search him, then we'll both stink, satisfied?"

Zed had crept down enough to see the pair crouched over a body. Normally Zed couldn't care less who got rolled, but the Prof was just beyond that landing. She settled down to wait when both their heads snapped towards her. What? Was she wearing bells?

"Who's there?" the woman asked.

"Me." Zed stood still. "Zed."

"Cool." The guy rose. "I know her, she's always got a sack full of stuff."

"Shut it, numbnuts." The woman managed a smile. "Come on down." She nodded at the drunk. "We'll split him."

Everyone wanted her to come down tonight. As the man edged towards the stairs, Zed shook her head. They must think she's as thick as the rest. "Maybe later." She took off, heading straight up.

By the time she got back to the 19th floor, she couldn't hear their swearing anymore.

"Dan." She firmly planted herself in front of him.

Rat gave a start. "Don't call me that," he muttered. "Having enough problems telling the living from the dead."

"Rat?" She peered up at him. He was playing with the skin again, unhappy.

"What?"

"I'll pay you … another can of ham to follow me around for a day."

"Why do you want me to follow you?" He squinted at her.

"That's my business. You want the ham?"

He licked his lips. "The King Rat don't just give up a whole day for a can o' ham," he declared. "What else?"

"The ham and a porn DVD."

"Which one?" he asked suspiciously. "I heard you traded Stan one with just men."

Zed sighed. "Stan wanted one with just men. It's *Awesome Threesomes IV*. Here, look at the pictures." She dug the DVD out of her satchel and handed it over.

Rat's eyes danced across the front cover. He turned it over and looked at the pictures on the back. "Best Yet," he read, and licked his lips. "But where am I gonna watch it?" He handed the DVD back with reluctance.

"Trade with Gears to watch it there. He just got a new colour TV."

Rat looked at the DVD again. "Still not enough for a whole day; four hours."

"Nine hours."

"Fuck, didn't you hear me?" Rat yelled, leaning toward her. "Eight hours is a day. I said not a whole day."

"Twelve hours is a whole day, you mangy ferret!" Zed retorted.

"Yeah? Well, not to me ... five hours."

"Seven, and if you don't say yes, I'd rather hire Barry than talk any more to you!" Zed started putting the DVD back in her bag.

"Fuck, gimme the damn DVD." Rat pulled it from her hand. "And the ham," he demanded, his hand outstretched. Zed put it in his hand.

"Great." Zed had brightened. "I need two, three hours tonight and the rest tomorrow."

"You can't split it up," Rat protested.

"Why not?"

Rat thought for a minute. "It's not done," he finally said.

"Come on, we're going down to see Hammer." Zed ignored Rat and walked to the elevator.

Rat followed, reluctantly. They waited and waited and the elevator didn't come. But for once Zed didn't care; she wasn't going down the stairs again. The elevator, Lucky, stopped a foot above. The pool was drying in the corner.

"Get in." Zed pointed a finger toward the elevator.

"Why me first?"

"That's why I hired you," Zed explained, exasperated.

"Oh." Rat shuffled forward and peered to the right and left. "All clear." Zed climbed in and pushed the button marked G. Rat sniffed. "Smells."

"You're complaining?"

Rat sniffed his way into the corner and looked at the puddle lapping his shoes. "That's piss!"

"Yours?"

"No!"

"Then don't worry about it."

They rode down in silence, listening to the moans of the elevator cable. "What's 'repentance'?" Rat asked.

Zed thought. "Don't know, sounds familiar. Where'd you hear it?"

"The Father." Rat avoided her gaze. "He said my mother came back to bring me to 'repentance.' What do you think?"

"I don't know. What did the Father think?"

"He liked it, he wanted me to go to one of his meetings. He said everyone there had it."

"I don't know, but if the Father likes it, it can't be too exciting."

"Yeah." Rat looked a bit down at that thought.

In the lobby, Hammer was sitting watching the TV. He nodded her in, but glowered at Rat.

Zed stayed by the door. "He's with me."

Hammer thought it over. "By the door," he said finally, his nostrils twitching as Rat inched his way inside the room.

Zed pulled the book *The Thin Man* out of her bag and laid it on the shovel of Hammer's palm. Hammer's eyes lit up and he raised his free hand, wetting his thumb.

Zed kept her hand on the book. "I need some answers," she told him. "I'm not made out of books, you know."

Hammer looked at her, sizing her up. Zed tried to make her eyes like flint. "Three questions," he said.

"Three separate questions all fully answered," Zed rephrased.

Hammer nodded. Zed let go of the book and Hammer brought it up to his face, giving a short bark of laughter as he read the cover. He devoured the back, and then peeked inside the cover. His tongue was poking out and his thumb headed for the page when Zed cleared her throat. Hammer looked over the top of the book at her and frowned. He lowered it, keeping a finger in the book so he wouldn't lose his place, page one.

"So, who was in the lobby yesterday morning between seven-thirty and nine-thirty?"

Hammer growled. "Hammer," he said, starting the list, "Rat, Jenny, Norman, Barry, Burl, Gears...." He thought a bit more. "Quince." He gave a shrug.

Zed figured six probable for hauling the body, five if you discounted dead Quince, or six if Jenny had help. But that didn't answer the more important question: why move the body at all? Or an even more important question: why kill Charles and Pete?

"Did you see Charles before you found his body?"

Hammer thought again. His right hand came up to his forehead and he started giving it little taps, first one finger then two then all four: tap, tap tap, tap tap tap tap. "Night before.... Nine." He gave his head another series of taps, "Nine-thirty, at door, sticky hands." He looked toward the doorway. "Left mark." Hammer pointed out a dark smudge on the doorframe, knee height. It might have been part of a handprint.

"Where did he go then?"

Hammer jerked his thumb toward the entrance to the hallways. "Snivelling." He rolled his eyes.

In the hallways Charles could have met anyone, gone anywhere. When then did he end up in the water tank? One question left.

"You kill those children?" Rat's eyes bulged as his hands rose to cover his face.

Hammer nodded with a sheepish smile.

"You did?" Zed wondered what it was about them that caused Hammer to kill. Was it merely their small sticky nature? Hammer nodded again; he didn't look very sorry. "You killed Charles and Pete?"

Hammer's face broke into confused wrinkles, like a piece of paper being crinkled up. "Pete?"

"Bunny's kid, queer head."

Hammer shook his head.

"Killed on the 19th floor sometime tonight."

Hammer shook his head firmly. "No more," he said. "Kill no more." He thought before amending. "No more children." He turned his head and looked at Rat, lips a thin smile. Rat tried to step back, bumping against the wall. Hammer looked back at Zed. "Three," he said, with the slightest hint of glee. Then, leaning back in his chair, he took the book and, still looking at Zed, he deliberately wet his thumb and pulled the book open.

Zed could take a hint, especially one as broad as a fair-sized garbage bin. She gave Rat a head-jerk to go and headed for the elevator. It was waiting for them at the ground floor. They stopped to pick up Doper Cal on two and barrel-chested Pete on three. Both backed into a corner to try to distance themselves from Rat and his cloak of reeking filth. "Take a fucking bath," Pete pleaded. Rat growled.

"Fuck." Rat turned to Zed. "Why didn't you ask about dead bodies?"

"Too many questions."

"He did it," Rat hissed in her ear. "I know he did it; he killed them."

Zed looked over at Cal and Pete in the corner who were eyeing her curiously. "Yes, Rat," she said calmly, still looking at the two. "He killed them with his own hands, then jacked off using their dead bodies." She gave Cal and Pete a big smile. They huddled together.

"Just stay the fuck away from me, little girl," Pete said.

Zed slowly licked her lips and gave him a wink.

"I knew it. I knew it." Rat was singing to himself. "I'm so smart, I knew he did it." The rest of the message got through and he stopped and looked at Zed. "Fuck, he did what?"

"Exactly," Zed replied.

They reached the 10th floor and the doors opened. The two in the elevator slid out the door, keeping as far away from Zed as possible. Tom, still in his "Stoners are People Too" shirt, was standing in the foyer. "Is he open yet?" Cal asked, licking his lips.

"No! He's got some shit sign up, 'In Mourning.' Screw 'In Mourning!'" Cal and Pete's faces fell. They turned to the elevator, whose door still stood open. They looked down at Zed; she gave them a wolf-like smile worthy of Luc. They stayed where they were. Tom made a move forward, but Cal caught his arm and gave him a little shake of the head. The elevator doors closed.

Rat turned to Zed, his face confused. "Hammer's a fucking panter?"

Zed shook her head. If Rat couldn't keep up, well, that was just too bad.

They stopped on the 14th floor and Zed led Rat down to the Professor's door, giving it a single sharp knock. There was a shuffle and then an explosion of sound starting with a thud and things toppling and falling against each other. "Ghosts!" came the cry from behind the door. "Stay back, I've holy water. Carnaki! Save me!"

Rat looked at Zed, alarmed, but she just sighed. The door eventually opened, enough for one eye to look out. "Do you cry at the open door?"

"If you'd stop reading ghost stories," Zed told him, "then you wouldn't freak out."

"I never," came the petulant and subdued voice from behind the door. She stared at the eye. "Maybe one," he conceded.

"Come out, I need you."

"But they wander the halls, their spirits moaning their imprisonment. They languish and avenge themselves on whom they might. Listen, hear their wails."

Zed and Rat both tilted their heads. Nothing.

Rat poked Zed in the back. "Fuck him," he told her. "Let's go."

The eye moved to Rat. "It's Weasel!" the Professor exclaimed in a very different voice, high and excited; his eye moved back to Zed. "Look, my good friend Mole." He opened the door to reveal his face, hair askew, with a wide smile. "Come in, Mole, and I'll sing you a song

109

about the twelve ghosts I scared away, and how I'm the bravest Toad that ever lived."

Rat started forward and the Professor barked, "No Weasels in Toad Hall!"

Zed just shook her head; she should have known that you can't mix nuts. She reached out and grasped one of the Professor's large hands. It was cold. He looked down at her. "Parental unit?" he asked.

"I need you to come with me."

He thought a moment. "Curious, Curious George," he said, nodding. "And me without my yellow hat." He shut the door, then waved his hand three times back and forth. "Till all shall pass let this warding be," he intoned. "Okey-dokey."

She pulled the Professor toward the stairwell, stepped over the drunk, and started up the stairs.

"What's he for?" Rat asked.

"Wait and see." Zed would owe the Prof for this, but she'd find him a nice book, something with illustrations.

Zed had trouble pulling the Professor up floors 16 and 17. He kept trying to stop and examine the walls. "Strange texture, this," he murmured, "but things are always different in the centre of the earth."

At the landing of the 18th floor, there was a flash of a knife and the sound of someone yelling as a figure arose from the floor. "Gimme your drugs!" They all stopped, the knife waved back and forth between the three of them. "Gimme your drugs, man."

"Steve?" He'd looked bad in Luc's office, but now was barely recognizable.

Steve's face dripped with sweat and his hand quivered. "Zed, I'm out, man. You gotta help me. I've gone all day, all day...." He trailed off and shifted the knife toward the Professor, who had moved forward, his hand outstretched, murmuring, "The highwayman came riding, riding...."

Steve pointed his knife towards the Professor with his face to Zed, voice hoarse, eyes desperate. "Zed...?"

She shook her head. "Zed...?" It was like the cry of a child. Zed made her face hard, her eyes blank. She shook her head again.

"You can't go!" Steve stepped back and crouched. "I got to get something, I need...." He trailed off, watching, his knife shifting from one hand to another. "Give me something!"

Rat was coiled, ready. With a tap on the arm, Zed released him. Rat simply left the floor: a flying, screaming animal kicking the knife away before wrapping himself around Steve's head.

"Off! Off! Get off!" Steve shrieked as he thrashed on the floor, trying to dislodge Rat. Zed led the wide-eyed Professor by, who muttered a soft "...with a bullet in her breast."

Rat caught up with them at the 19th floor landing. He closed his eyes and smacked his lips. "Mmmm. I love a good scrap."

In Val's apartment, they found the Father talking to Burl and a clutch of old ladies. "...we'll form our own gang, a gang of righteousness, to protect righteousness and innocence," the Father was saying.

"Alone?" a woman asked.

"No, united, together in God's strength. And our first act is to protect this child's body until the authorities collect it."

"An all-night vigil?"

"Exactly."

Zed pipped up. "Yo, Father, can I check Pete out again?"

"Uh...." He looked over Rat and the Professor. "Sure."

As they tramped into the bathroom, Zed heard one of the ladies say, "How sweet, saying goodbye to her little friend." Zed rolled her eyes. Oh yeah, "little friend."

Once in the bathroom, the Professor let go of her hand as he turned around, his eyes drinking it all in. He picked up his foot and pressed down again, listening to the squishing sound. "Crime scene," he said with a big smile on his face. He turned to Zed and spoke in a stuffy British accent. "But Lady Southerton, if you were with Lord Acton in the Aviary, why are there no feathers among your attire? And where is the brooch your late husband left you? Why it is here ... under the body? Explain that away, if you will."

Zed shook her head, took his hand, and turned him back toward the bath. "How long ago did she die?" she asked him. She waited, hoping. The Professor seemed quite lucid today; he was almost understandable.

The Professor blinked, reached into his pocket, and proceeded to affix an invisible glass to his eye, then dipped his finger into the water and poked Pete's arm. The body rolled from side to side. He put his finger into the hole in her chest and prodded the skin. He bent down and felt the floor, felt the carpet around the bath, then proceeded to feel the wall, pushing and prodding the stained wallpaper. Going back to the tub, he looked around the taps, then checked in the overflow. Finishing, he stood and faced her, hands placed calmly behind his back. "It is simple, my dear Bartholomew," he stated in a nasal English accent, "if you would only apply yourself to observation. The body is rigid, hence rigor mortis has set in, the walls are dry, and the floor is wet. Simple observations tell us this child was killed but three hours ago, if my gauge of room temperature is correct. But this is ordinary." The Professor went on looking at her sternly. "A thing any beat officer might surmise. But have you noted the curious action of the blood?" They both turned to look at the bath.

"There is no blood." Zed said, confused.

"Exactly." He looked at her smugly. Zed was bewildered. The Professor sighed. "You see and yet you do not see." He gave a hard laugh. "A hole in her chest and no blood. Water, water, everywhere and no blood in sight." He looked at her and tapped his temple twice. "The skin was cut at least forty-five minutes after the death, when the blood had settled. It is simple, *n'est pas?*"

Zed nodded. That meant Pete was already dead before the séance had started. The Professor nodded again, then crouched down and twiddled two fingers in the water. "Watch out, Jeremy Potter!" he cried in a high voice. "Here comes that nasty old carp." And with a yelp, his two fingers leaped and dodged across the water, accompanied by "Ohh! Ahh!

Missed me that time!" The fingers got to the edge of the bathtub and did a merry dance; the Professor watched, delighted.

Zed turned and went into the main room, leaving the Professor to amuse himself for a while. Rat had cornered the Father who was shouting, "I didn't say you have to repent. I said you were ready for it, as I hope we all are."

"First I got it and now I don't," Rat said bitterly. He spied Zed and left the Father to stand beside her.

Rat looked past Zed into the bathroom. The Professor was crouched down by the tub, his hands over his eyes. Then he opened them with a cry and just as quickly closed his hands back up again. It seemed the Professor was playing Peek-a-Boo.

Rat quivered. "He did it," he hissed at Zed, eyebrows shaking in emphasis. "Look at him, he's as good as admitting it."

Zed looked. "What about Hammer?" Rat turned, spurning her.

Zed walked up to the Father and his group.

"You okay?" he asked.

She nodded. "Six," she told him.

"What?"

"Now you only owe me six."

She left him gaping and collected the Professor and Rat, heading them down the stairs to take the Prof home.

At 1406 the Professor stood, hand outstretched, and shouted, "Open, Sesame!" They waited. Nothing happened. The Prof tried again, his shout echoing in the hallway: "Open, Sesame!"

Zed turned the handle. The door opened under its own weight. The Professor looked around, pleased. "Magic door," he told them.

"Sure it is," Zed nodded. "I'll come by tomorrow." He smiled at her. "Go to bed," she told him, closing the door. "No reading." She heard a snicker as the door clicked shut.

"He did it," Rat told her as they continued down the stairs. "I know it, he did it."

"The Professor? Yeah, he was my number one choice too." Zed got sarcastic when she was tired.

"Fuck no, the Professor's screwy. I mean the Father," Rat nodded slowly. "He's a shifty one, never tells you things straight."

"Rat, you suspect everyone we meet."

"Not Steve." Rat defended himself. "Steve...?" He scratched his head to stimulate the blood flow to his brain.

At the ground floor Zed turned to Rat. "I'll look you up tomorrow."

"You live near here? Don't worry, you can tell me."

"Fuck off, Rat."

"All right already." He drifted off, muttering.

Zed waited a minute, making sure he was really gone before dropping down to her hidey-hole and to bed.

Chapter 6

Next morning, the Tower had a hangover, and it was raining to boot. It was a stay-indoors day, not the least because of a growing lake in the concrete depression outside the main doors; a good day for clean-up, with doors off hinges, blood and bile everywhere. But no one felt like cleaning and with Luc selling only liquor "for medicinal purposes," everyone was coming down with something, even if it was only hysteria.

Zed gave a heads-up for Rat in the lobby, but couldn't see him among the can-and-rag gang standing at the double doors staring forlornly into the rain. She'd look him up later. Right now she needed to work her trading magic and turn her new hoard of info into trading stock and even more info. First stop was Countessa to check if she was still interested in getting the dish on down below or whether she was getting it all for free from the dead.

On her way up, Zed stopped by on the 2nd floor to see if she could drum up some business. Christina was lying across the hallway, just inside the door. Armed with felt pens, she was turning her arm green, pausing every now and then to give the tip a lick. Now Zed wasn't up on all the science of it, but she was pretty sure that licking felt pens was bad; somewhere between clutching-your-stomach-as-blood-pours-out-of-your-nose bad and flopping-around-in-a-fit-frothing-at-the-mouth bad.

"Taste good?" Zed asked.

Christina eyeballed her before finishing greening her arm. Obviously, Zed thought, the brain damage has already taken effect. "Where's Ellen?"

Christina pointed to a door on the right before opening a brown felt pen and starting on her fingers.

Zed pushed the door open and looked inside. The living room was deserted. Squeaking springs and laughter from the bedroom told Zed that the two of them were at it again. She sighed. It was almost impossible to get them to think seriously when they were in this mood. She went to the open door and walked inside.

"Whee!" Teresa cried, flying into the air. Ellen was laughing, rolling about at the end of the bed. Teresa continued to jump up and down.

"Airplane! Airplane!" Ellen stuck her feet up for Teresa to jump on, but as Ellen was still laughing her legs gave way, dumping Teresa on the side of the bed. Teresa shrugged and took a hit of red from the bottle before returning to bounce up and down.

Ellen saw Zed in the doorway. "Forget it!" she called out, laughing. "It's our bed and it won't hold three."

Teresa stopped bouncing to elbow Ellen. "That's not what you said last month with you-know-who."

Ellen turned and gave her a punch in the ribs. "We weren't going to talk about that." Teresa's eyes widened at the punch and her tongue tip went up to explore the dimple above her lip before she burst into a flurry of punches. Ellen grabbed her and they started wrestling around the bed, Teresa hooting and screaming, "no tickling, no tickling!"

Zed felt like asking Christina for a lick of her pen. She watched the two of them rolling back and forth until they stopped in exhaustion, panting, Teresa holding Ellen down. Zed went over to Teresa, who had one hand containing Ellen and with the other was taking a drink from the bottle. "Need anything?"

"Naw, we're too sick. Right, Ellen? That's what Doctor Luc says, way too sick to get out of bed today."

Ellen snaked one hand toward Teresa's knee and started making feathery tickle motions. Teresa slapped the hand down. "We're okay," Teresa said. "If you see Christina tell her to drop by."

"She's in the hall."

"Super! Sweetheart?" Teresa yelled. "Can you bring Mommy some bread, cuz she's got the munchies."

Ellen's hand sneaked around Teresa to tickle the small of her back. Teresa jumped with a screech. "No tickling!" They rolled off, wrestling again. Zed headed for the door. When she looked behind her, Teresa was back on top of Ellen, shaking her head and saying, "No means no."

In the hallway, Christina had her shoe and sock off and was colouring her foot orange. Zed waited at the door to the stairwell until Christina licked the pen, her tongue a mix of blue, green, brown, and orange, much like the left side of her body. "Yum, yum," she said.

Zed had climbed two flights when she heard the singing; a baritone lead with a replying crowd.

Oh when the Saints   *Yes when the Saints*
Go marching in   *Go marching in*

A large group trod down the stairs, the Father at its head with Burl and Howard flanked behind.

"Victory!" the Father called to Zed. "They've picked up the body; we're seeing it off."

That's all he had time for until they all passed Zed.

Oh I want to be   *In that number...*
When the Saints   *go marching in.*

Everyone was nuts today, that's all Zed could figure, and not the usual bark-at-the-shoulder nuts, but just plain goofy.

Up on the 5th the smoke was pouring out of the burners and a line had already formed. Yup, goofy, Zed confirmed.

As Zed walked down the line, she noticed two new things: first was an armband some people were wearing: black with a white spot, and second was the eyes. They were the same type of people in line as yesterday, losers and loners, but she could see something different in their eyes; they believed. Exactly what they believed she didn't know, but there was no mistaking the look. She'd seen it in the Father's eyes often enough.

Don, the dork from last night, was standing guard again, wearing a dotted armband.

"Hey, Zed." He smiled at her, showing her he'd remembered her name. "Good séance last night," he nodded. "Countessa's got 'The Power.'"

An echo came from a dozen voices in line: "The Power."

Oooookay, Zed thought, *that was a little different.* "Let me through, Don, I've got business."

He shook his head. "Not on the list. You've got to wait in line."

"Not again." This just wasn't Zed's day. "I'm on it, Don, been on it for a *looong* time, and right now I got some trading to do, so step aside."

Don put his hand on her chest. "Not on the list."

She looked down at Don's hand and something inside just snapped. "First thing, Chuckles," she said, sweeping his hand aside and planting a kneepad into Don's nuts, "is you don't touch me, understand? You got to stop me, I get it, but you don't grab my fucking chest, right, Jolly O?" Don, whose face had turned white and greasy, nodded. "And now I want to see this bone-assed, slut-puppy list, this all-important, mother-licking, shit-cone of a list. Will you do that for me, Donny? Donski? Show me the list." Zed could admit it; sometimes she had a temper.

Don held out his arms. "Not on the list," he croaked.

"Show me the list."

"Not on it."

"Okay, you go and tell Countessa that I know about Charles and I got the straight dope, and tell her I got a shoe she wants, tell her it's a replacement for the one she smoked, she'll know what I mean. Go tell her that and then we'll see." Zed planted her fists on her hips. "I'll wait."

Don was massaging his nuts back to life. He paused and thought a moment, then shook his head. "Have to wait in line, not on the list."

He's forcing me to kill him, a voice inside her said through the red haze. *Anyone can see it.*

By the time Zed could see straight Don had backed up six feet, one hand covering his balls. "Sorry, Zed, you're just not –"

"*On the list!*" the people in line finished in unison.

"Don," Zed said, "there seems to be something you're trying to tell me."

"Yeah, Zed, you're –"

Zed held up her hand. "Let's not go there. Tell me about the armband instead."

A flurry of voices came from the line: "Countessa sees in the darkness," "Countessa holds the Power," "Countessa is the light," "Countessa bridges life and death."

"Sorry I asked." Zed felt a smile start deep inside. Now here was a market crying to be exploited. "I'm leaving," she warned Don, "but I'll be back."

Zed walked down the line, stopping when she saw Jenny, parakeet still gnawing on her ear. "Hey, Jen, you got the food offering for the dead?"

"Food offering?"

"Yeah, didn't you know?" Zed grinned inside as Jen started to freak. Oh yeah, this was a seller's market.

"No, I haven't got anything...." She felt around in her pockets. "All I've got is a half-pack and a pocket-knife. You think the dead smoke?"

"Nope." Jen looked glumly at the floor. "Hey, Jen, I've got this ham I was gonna offer, but now I have to take off...."

"Would you ... um, think of trading, Zed?"

"I dunno, I was planning on coming back."

"Please, Zed, please." Jenny was thrusting the smokes and knife into Zed's hands. "I know you'll find something else."

"All right, I'll do it, but you owe me." Zed dug out the canned ham.

"I do, Zed, I do."

"Later." Zed turned to go, then turned back as if remembering something. "I heard you were in the lobby yesterday morning, about nine o'clock. What was that about?"

"I was just meeting Gears; he was trading me a tin can to make a bird feeder for Juju here, isn't that right, Juju?"

"See anyone?"

"Naw, just Charles and Quince."

"Whatever, then. See ya, and good luck." Zed jerked a thumb at the line.

"See you, Zed. 'Countessa is the light.'"

"Uhh ... yeah, 'the light.'" Zed walked off whistling to herself. Looked like things were turning around.

Her mood lasted till the end of the line.

"Zed, love."

"Ivy?"

Zed approached and tried to hustle Ivy out of line. "Come on, let's go to your place for tea."

Ivy just smiled at her. "It's all right. I know you means well, but it's here I want to be."

Zed looked at Ivy in disbelief. "Why?"

"That Countessa, aye, she knows things, like about that girl killed, and there's a thing I wants to be knowing." She shrugged and her eyes twinkled. "So what if an old woman waits in a hall with this smoke and hocus-pocus, long as the message be true."

"As long as it's true," Zed pointed out, which just made Ivy nod as if Zed had agreed.

"But I've heard we be needing food for the dead?" Ivy frowned, "And me without any Welsh cakes."

Zed shook her head. It was unbelievable how fast some things travelled. "Trust me, Ivy, you don't need food for the dead."

Ivy winked. "You're a good gel, always in the know. You come see me later."

Zed gave her a nod and headed for the stairs, up to Luc's.

On the 11th-floor landing, a clutch of geezers played Pass the Bottle, a.k.a. Where Did My Life Go? Zed had almost wound through when a hand grabbed her wrist. She couldn't believe it. What? Was it "Touch Zed" day or something? She pivoted around, hand going for the blade, when Bucket Charlie let go.

"Something for an old vet?" he wheezed. "A cig?"

What's a vet? Zed wondered. "No."

"I could work for it. I'm useful, I can do things."

Zed was intrigued. "What things?"

Charlie chewed his lip, thinking hard. "You could hit me, and pay me for it, or cut me –" He watched her hand coming back out of her pocket. "– Long as it don't bleed too bad. We could roll someone in the stairs, get their stash. Or I could push someone down the stairs for you. I've done that." He held out his hand.

Zed shook her head. Charlie thought some more. "What else? I can make meth if you get me the ingredients. I can set fires. What else I done?" His face brightened. "I know, I could kill a cat for you."

"No, you can't!" The voice boomed through the hallway's metal door. It opened and Stu stuck his head inside; he was smiling. He peered around until he saw Charlie. "I warned you, didn't I?" Bucket Charlie's mouth was gritted in terror as he sat quivering in the corner. He had one hand outstretched to ward Stu off and the other in front of his face, his eyes peeping between his fingers.

"I warned you and I warned you." Stu was as happy as a kid unwrapping a present. He reached toward his shirt pocket, patting around. "Shit, where are my cigs?"

Charlie waited no longer. He leapt to his feet and with a high-pitched, drawn-out squeak ran down the stairs, the thudding of his feet giving counterpoint to the squeezed note.

Zed gave Stu a nod and walked past. Barry stood in the hall, hand on Steve's chest. Steve looked like puke; one lip was puffy and purple, his eyes sunken behind a veil of limp brown hair. "What you going to give me?" Barry asked, his eyes darting, but Steve just shook his head. Barry showed his crooked teeth. "Can't come in till you pay."

"Yo, Barry, want a porn DVD?" Zed asked.

"Porn DVD. Porn DVD, yeah, I want it. What you want for it? It's garbage, doesn't run anymore, give you a cig."

"Calm down, Barry, I haven't got it out yet." Zed walked forward rummaging in her bag, distracted, and bumped into Steve, throwing him off balance and pushing him into the office. "Oh wait, I forgot, traded it with Rat."

Barry snarled, his pupils shrinking to pinpricks as Steve stumbled past. One of Barry's hands grabbed Zed by the hair while his other went for his butterfly. Zed kicked at his nuts but missed, landing on his thigh. "Too fucking far," Barry told her, his teeth gleaming as he brought out the blade.

Zed threw the satchel at his head, using the strap to bounce it off and arc it around to hit his face again. Barry fell back against the wall, letting go of Zed to protect his face, but still thrusting with the knife. *This is it*, Zed told herself, *you've got to put him down.* She swung the satchel in half circles, hitting Barry on one side, then the other, ducking his thrusts. She wasn't damaging him, just distracting him, waiting for the break.

When it came, a thrust too wide, she went inside his reach and leapt onto his chest, legs wrapped while her hands clamped on his head, thumbs pushing down the eyeballs. *All the way*, Zed told herself, *don't go soft this time.* Barry was pushing her head back with the heels of his palm, keeping her just far enough away to save his eyes.

"Oh, how sweet," Luc said. "They're playing house."

"Not now," Zed told him, never breaking concentration. "I'm *busy*."

"He's *my* henchman."

Zed grunted as she made a last effort to dig into his eyes, but Barry was slowly forcing her head farther back, prying her off his chest. She let go, using the momentum to back-roll onto her feet. "Fine, fuck it."

Barry blinked his red eyes and started forward.

"Barry!"

Barry's face twitched in earnest as it pleaded with Luc to let the fury out.

"No, Barry."

Barry held up his hands, shook his head and stooped, picking up a kitten. He pocketed the knife and the kitten and strode out.

"I tell you," Luc told Zed, "watching the energy between you two, it's like being in love all over again." He held up his hands; one had a white bandage wrapped around the pinkie.

Luc glanced over at Steve. "Sorry, friend, was there something you wanted?"

"Wha?" Steve said.

Luc leaned back in his chair, his long tapered fingers stroking his chin. "I believe you are about to say, 'I got nothin', man, nothin', I know but I gotta have some, oh please, gimme something...' Yes?"

Steve nodded and sniffed, "I'll do anything, hire me, send me to beat up an old lady or something, anything man."

"Beat up an old lady, hmm." Luc tapped his chin with a manicured fingernail. "Not a great deal of call for that around here, truth. And when it does occur, I generally like to do it myself. I mean, if you can't have any fun what's the point of owning the place? And not to be critical –" He looked over Steve's twitching, quivering, sniffling frame, "– I rather doubt you're up to even an old-fashioned leg-breaking." Steve moaned and sank his head into the dark rich carpet at the foot of Luc's desk. Luc rose in his chair, watching Steve collapse into his carpet with concern. "Now before you starting oozing all sorts of bodily fluids into that carpet, I do have a proposition." Steve perked up. Luc opened one of his desk drawers and pulled out a medium bag of white powder. "I will give you this wonderful elixir, this magic carpet, yes, all this...." He swung it like a pendulum, Steve's eyes following every swing. "In just three hours, but –" Luc pulled the bag away and looked into Steve's eyes. "– you have to do it all."

"All? At once?" Steve looked at the bag; the powder sifted lazily back and forth as Luc swung the bag. "It'll kill me."

"Maybe," Luc said softly. "Maybe." He kept the bag out and it dangled from his fingers, rocking back and forth, twisting a half turn on each swing.

Steve turned his head, but his eyes, still watching the bag, betrayed him. He fell back into a sitting position on the floor. His trembling had subsided, and his breathing had slowed. He tried to swallow but couldn't. "Fuck you," he whimpered. "Fuck you."

Luc just sat there, his fingers twirling the bag, his face placid, serene.

Steve's hand rose to wipe the moisture that had beaded on his face. He just couldn't take his eyes off that bag. "I'll do it," he said at last, then his eyes fell to the floor.

"Would you do it now, all of it, right now?" Luc was curious. Without looking up, Steve nodded. Luc opened a drawer and pulled out a small black case and a candle lantern with a silver bowl on top. From the black case he extracted a syringe. "Roll up your sleeve," Luc ordered Steve, his eyes bright.

Steve looked up, scared. "Can't I smoke it? I gotta smoke it, I'll die if I shoot it, I swear."

Luc struck a match and held it to the candle. His voice was husky as he repeated, "Roll up your sleeve." He gave Steve a slow lingering look, like a lover, then he began to shake the powder into the metal cup.

"Man, let me sniff it, least then I got a chance. Please, man, just let me sniff it." Steve's eyes searched for Luc's and they met, and held there. Steve pressed forward and Luc changed not at all, a little smile, his teeth peeping through, his eyes lusting, doleful. Steve gave a slow, shuddering sigh and with his yellow fingers started to pluck at the sleeve of his soiled black sweatshirt. His fingers were trembling so badly it took a minute for him to fumble and pinch the sleeve past his elbow. He looked up at Luc, his face dead, but a crack in his voice. "Okay." Steve knelt before the desk, stretched out his arm, and closed his eyes. "All right, you bastard. Hit me."

Luc took the syringe and pulled the plunger back, filling it. He blew out the candle with a little smile. Steve turned his head, squeezing his eyes tight. Luc pushed out the air until a plume of liquid shot out. He lowered his hand to Steve's arm.

Zed watched this exchange with interest. She'd never seen this particular game of Luc's; it was mesmerizing. Luc looked over at her and winked, then pushed the syringe into Steve's arm. Steve didn't even twitch. Luc waited a few moments and pulled the syringe out. It was still full of heroin. He deftly put the syringe back into the black case and slid it back into the drawer.

Steve pulled his arm back and looked around the room. He slowly got to his feet, his sleeve still up. "I'm fucked," he said to no one in particular. "I can't even feel it. Wonder what that means?"

Luc reached into a drawer with his right hand and took out a smaller baggie of heroin. "Here," he said tossing it to the floor in front of Steve. "Take that. Use it ... at your own discretion."

Steve looked at the bag blankly, then gave a laugh. "More smack, just what I need." He turned toward the door, then looked back at the bag. "I don't feel anything," he said. "I'm so screwed, and I don't feel nothin' at all." And with a quick flick of the uncovered arm he picked up the bag and walked, a bit unsteady, out the door.

"And he'll still be back," Luc told Zed, watching Steve go.

"How long you think he'll last?"

"Until I release him," Luc said. "Shall we bet on it?" Zed shook her head. Luc was looking at her with a very pleased expression on his face, his cheeks flushed. "So careful do I gather them, one by one." He pulled out a clipboard and put it on the desk. His left hand reached for a pen, the pinkie finger white in its bandage.

"Nice hand," said Zed, making conversation.

Luc raised his left hand and turned it back and forth. "Admirable, I think." He put it back down. "Like to see my jewellery?"

Zed was shocked. Not surprised, shocked. Luc didn't do jewellery. Hats, yes, suits, yes, knives, yes, jewellery, no. Luc's hands were smooth, his fingers tapered, but nowhere on them was there a ring, or a bracelet on his wrist, or a chain round his neck.

"What jewellery?" Zed asked.

Luc reached into his silk shirt and pulled out a fine metal chain, drawing it up the neck until a small vial popped out. He pinched it between his finger and thumb and held it up for Zed to inspect. Inside the vial, floating in a yellow-green liquid, was a little lump, smooth at one end and ragged at the other. Luc gave the vial a shake and the lump gyrated in the liquid, turning. The dull surface became smooth and shiny as Zed recognized a fingernail turning toward her.

"Stu got it from the morgue for me," Luc said, beaming over the vial. "I may be in two parts, but I'm still together." He pulled the vial closer to his eyes. "Truth, I found the symbolic reunification to be soothing; this way I know what all parts of me are doing. I can be sure it's not off raising armies or becoming enshrined somewhere." He dropped the vial back down the front of his shirt. "Now that you are here, you can help me with the new betting pool." He lifted the clipboard.

"Another suicide?"

"No! And for once, I hope to go one day in this place without someone dying, especially if I am to get this tote done and the bets in. Now, my child, here we have the board on the kiddie snuffer." Luc raised one hand to the right, one to the left. "I envision a double board of both victims and perpetrators."

Zed nodded. "What's first?"

"Kiddies, I think, fewer, easier to limit … now there is Christina, number one." He wrote on the clipboard. "My last decent rider, except for Andy up on 15; I'll put him down as number two." Luc wrote again then looked up, musing. "You don't think Father and friends are trying to wipe out the racing a rider at a time?"

"I heard it was you put the hit on Pete."

"Really? Well that was quite forgetful of me, cutting off my ... nose to spite my face. So we'll put Jen down from 7. Anyone else?"

"There's some other kid down in Brat Alley, cries a lot."

"You mean that baby?" Luc scratched his forehead. "I suppose I could put it down. What's its name?"

Zed shrugged.

"Baby X. Now, should I put you down as a victim or as a perpetrator?"

"What does that mean?"

"Are you killing them or going to be killed?"

Zed looked at him, scornful. "Only kids get killed."

"Yes, my child, but to someone not as observant as me, you still look in the extremities of youth, lacking that –" His hands made an hourglass shape in the air, "– development."

Zed looked down at her grey coveralls. "I got tits."

"Ummm...."

"I do! Lots of guys go after me. Quince and Bob and them do all the time."

"Ummm...."

Zed frowned. "They don't count?"

"I'm afraid not."

While Zed didn't rate breasts, it was cruel to find them separating you from the adult world. To be lumped in with all the useless kids, it was sickening.

"I think you could have killed them," Luc said, trying to cheer her up.

"Thanks. But who will bet on me?"

"Lots of people, everyone knows you get around. Maybe you were wiping out future competition. I know Barry will bet on you, just for spite. Course, he'll bet more on you being the next victim."

Zed smiled at that. "So what are the odds?"

Luc looked down at the list of victims. "I haven't a clue." He leaned back in his chair, silent, his eyes gleaming. "Without odds this is a chump's game and I, Luc, don't do chump." He rubbed his chin. "But I know someone who does know." He gave Zed a wink. "Me? I don't know."

Zed smiled as she got it. "Countessa! Can you get in?"

"Oh, yes. I've got something on Countessa, a little word of power." He rose and put on his jacket. "You come for something?"

"I've got the skinny," she said. Luc cocked his eyebrow into a question. "About the dead kiddies."

"How much?" Luc asked.

Zed thought about what she had spent. "Two fifths of liquor, three joints, and a stack of books."

Luc closed an eye, evaluating her through the other one. "Perhaps," he said slowly. "You first."

"Pete was killed around ten o'clock last night." Zed gave the least significant piece of information.

"How much more do you have?" Luc asked.

"For the liquor, joints, and books, you get everything I know about Pete and a list of those who could have killed Charlie."

"How do you know who could have killed Charlie?" Luc asked, eyes narrowing.

"Cost you three more joints."

"Stop dicking me around," Luc warned her. "Is this everything?"

Zed nodded.

Luc got out the joints and two-fifths of rum and pushed them over before sitting on the corner of the desk. "I'll get you the books," he told her, "so give."

Zed cleared her throat. "Who first, Charlie or Pete?"

"Pete."

"She was drowned in the bath in Suicide Val's apartment."

"I know that."

"There was a chunk cut out of her chest, just like Charlie."

Luc was looking bored.

"But," Zed continued, "the chunk was cut out of her at least forty-five minutes after she died."

Luc frowned. "According to whom?"

"Something about no blood in the water," Zed said. Luc nodded. Zed took another breath. "And Charlie was removed from the water-tank, and I don't remember blood in that water either."

"How do you know Charlie was removed?"

"Sources."

"Hammer," he guessed.

She ignored that. "Charlie was taken and brought back sometime between seven-thirty and nine-thirty that morning. And the people in the lobby that morning were ... Norman, Barry, Burl, Quince, Jenny, Rat, and Gears."

"Quite a list." He watched Zed as she came up to the desk and started filling up her satchel. "That's it?"

"You got a list."

"A 'could-have' list."

"You want the killer's right hand? When I get it, it'll cost you more than dope and rum."

"Fair enough." Luc moved to the door. "Anything else?"

Zed nodded slowly. "I came to get my question."

"What is it?"

Zed watched him as she worded the question, waiting for him to squirm. "What were you doing last night when away from your office?"

Luc smiled. "I'm a suspect?"

Zed shrugged.

Luc opened the door. "Come on," he told Zed, "walk and talk." He punched past Barry, saying, "Lock up and meet me," and continued toward the elevators. Barry stuffed something in his inside jacket pocket that let out a squeak.

At the elevator Luc studied Zed; he stroked his chin. "What I was doing. That's my private affair, you understand."

Zed heard two words in her head: rip off.

"Don't give me that look. I gave my word, and I'll keep it. I'm just reminding you that my business is my business and if it gets out, you won't have to gamble on the next victim, yes?"

Zed nodded fervently.

Luc closed his eyes and then rubbed them with his right hand. "There is a place I go ... a retreat."

"A retreat?"

"Somewhere I can be alone. Surely you can understand that, the need to sometimes be alone."

Zed nodded; she did indeed.

Barry approached as the elevator doors opened. "We'll continue this later," Luc told her as they entered. "Lucky" was feeling frisky, shuddering and moaning all the way down.

"Who's on guard duty?" Luc asked Barry. Barry shrugged.

"Don," Zed told them.

"Dough boy?" Luc smiled. "Stopping seniors is about his limit."

Zed said nothing but felt her face getting hot.

"Barry, pay him off."

"With what?"

"I'm sure you'll find something."

The doors opened to a roll of scented smoke. "Shit," Barry said. Zed heartily agreed.

They exited and walked down the line, Luc leading with Barry and Zed on flank. Don saw them coming. He started backing up. "Luc, I don't know," he said, swallowing hard.

"Just a word in your ear, good man."

Don saw Zed and backed up further. "Hey Zed, you know I never meant nothing ... it was an accident, right, no need to get heavy."

Luc looked down at Zed with a grin. "You leave friends wherever you go, don't you?" He walked up to Don. "Don't worry, she's just along for the ride; I need a minute with Countessa."

A low growl rose from the line. Luc gave them a cool rake of the eye. The growl died. Luc touched his hat in salute and passed into the dark doorway. A second later Howard stumbled out. "But I'm not done yet!"

"You are now," Barry told him.

Howard looked from Barry to Don and back again. "But I'm not done."

Barry's hand slid into the jacket pocket. "But I am now," Howard amended, shuffling off.

They watched Howard go. Don turned to Barry. "You gotta pay, you know."

"Says who?" Barry demanded, hand back in his pocket.

"Luc," said Zed. Barry gave her a pus-filled stare. *Oh, blow it off the top*, Zed thought, it wasn't like she liked either of them, she just happened to hate Don less. Besides, if she really hated Barry, she'd have let him pay nothing and then told Luc.

Don smiled. "I heard Luc's selling cats now."

"Maybe."

"I used to have a cat. But it died recently, had an accident, off the roof." He glared at Barry who took out a stick of gum and popped it in his mouth.

"Yeah, so?"

"Sure'd like another cat." He stared at Barry.

Nobody said anything. Barry chewed his gum. Don kept staring.

"What?" Barry demanded. A meow came from inside his jacket. Don stared harder. "Fuck." Barry pulled out a black and white kitten that sneezed and blinked. "I was saving that one."

Don took it in his arms, giving it gentle pats. He mellowed right in front of Zed's eyes. Started talking to her about coming over to his place once he got off shift, they could watch his new TV. How he'd be able to see her on the inter-tower cable, how she could wave to him during the day.

Zed finally managed to escape, sidling down the line, wishing she could have the last five minutes of her life back.

"Back again, love?" Ivy called from the line. "Always popping here, popping there, just the thought of it tires me so."

"Sorry 'bout the water," Zed said, drifting over. "My source kind of –" she looked down the line toward Countessa's door, "– dried up."

"Don't worry none, I make out." Ivy said. "You come by for tea, mind, this afternoon." Zed nodded.

A sharp bark of laughter came from Countessa's door. Luc emerged, his eyes dancing. "Perfect!" he said. "Absolutely perfect!"

Barry came in close, disturbed by Luc's public display. "Boss?" Luc looked over and waved his hand; don't worry, everything's copacetic.

Luc was making his move and Zed turned to join him when Ivy tapped on her shoulder. "That be the slick one, Luc, yea, and his man too?"

"Luc and Barry, yes."

Ivy immediately stepped out of line. "'Tis God-sent," she muttered and blew by Zed, making a bee-line for them. Zed didn't know old ladies could move so quickly.

Ivy grasped Luc's arm with her soft hands. "Ah, ye be the hero of our building, you strong one, you and this ox of yours."

Luc looked down, astounded at anyone holding him.

Zed hurried up beside Ivy. "What are you doing? Let him go!"

Ivy ignored her. "Yes, you slick man, you saved us last night, and a tea I will make for you, you and your man."

"Zed, why is this ... woman hanging on to me?" Luc asked her.

"She's Ivy," Zed said. "She seems to want you to come to tea."

"Tea?"

"Aye, just two floors up, tea and Welsh cakes, a bit of the homeland, food for you growing boys, what strappers you are, lords of the land."

Luc had perked up at the word "lord." "You say we are to come to tea?"

"Aye, busy lads like you must be parched, you fighting devils, laying in to that madman last night and here running about the halls."

"'Fighting devils,' that's good, tell me more about the 'lord.'" Luc extended his arm, and Ivy removed her hands, sliding one of her arms inside of his.

"Boss? Tea?" Barry looked ill.

"Come along, Barry, learn to take the laurels of victory in good stride." Luc glided toward the elevator.

Zed caught up to them as they waited. Ivy turned to her. "Not you."

"Ivy?"

"There be times for grown-ups and times for little girls, and this be not your time."

"Yeah," Barry chimed in with a gleeful grin.

Zed was stunned. Ivy? Since when did Ivy blow her off?

Luc looked down. "Later," he told her. Zed kept standing there; she just couldn't believe it.

The elevator arrived. Ivy, Luc, and Barry entered. Zed lingered on the doorway. Ivy hissed at her through clenched teeth, "Not you." Zed recoiled and the doors closed.

Zed looked around. Don avoided her eye; everyone in line avoided her eye. Well, screw them, she thought, screw them. Next time she'd make Luc pay double and later she'd drop by Ivy's and suck every Welsh-cake she could and not bring her a drop of water to boot. Zed stomped off toward the stairwell. She'd go look up Gears and after that she'd get rich, she promised herself, off any poor sap she happened to run across.

Chapter 7

ZED STOMPED DOWNSTAIRS. Ivy wanted to freeze her out, fine, free country after all. Stomp, stomp, stomp. Everyone freezing her out, she couldn't care less. She didn't know why she stayed in this armpit. There were lots of places Zed could go, places that wanted her. Lots of them.

The word must have gotten out because on the way to Gears' she met no one, saw no one. It had to still be raining because the subparkade was starting to look like the inside of a nostril; moisture oozed down the cracks of walls and ceilings in green slime trails. A new stream headed to unknown depths.

Zed stepped over the stream to stop by Gears' door, listening to the voices within.

"Remember, O benign Buddha, those who live with attachments, cast your excess upon them." The Professor backed out of the door, genuflecting all the way.

"Chill," Gears told him.

"Meditations on climate, sage advice, O wise one," the Professor assured and then backed into Zed. "Agents of Fu-Manchu!" He spun around, spied Zed, and calmed down. "Hey, Dorothy, where's Toto?"

"What are you doing here?" Zed asked.

The Professor sniggered. "Secret." Then he muttered, "The book, the book, ah, for the cream of the creams, the rarest binding." He glared around, alarmed. "Shut up! Shut up!" He gave himself a thump in the chest.

Zed stepped back. On the plus, someone wanted to talk to her; on the minus, it was the Professor. "How'd you get down here?"

"Map." He held out a coloured map labelled *London Underground*.

"Good." Zed leaned forward to look closer at the map, but the Professor snatched it away. "I'll come see you later. Maybe have some books for you," she said.

At the word "books" the Professor started muttering again. "Books, books, the crop of muse, the pages so cream, the binding so...." Professor started slapping his head. "Shut up! O please just shut up!" The Prof's body gave a shudder and he turned to her with a cool look. "Righto Bingo, drop on by, anything for the old school...." He waved his hand airily. "Must be off, what, ho? Late for dinner, off to...." He plunged his finger at the map, then read where it had landed. "Golders Green." He turned and wandered off, holding his map in front of him.

Zed shook her head, clearing out that fog which invariably followed the Professor before popping her head round the door. Gears sat in a lotus position before a candle. He was naked from the waist up, long needles emerging from his shoulders, pecs, and back. Incense smouldered from the needle ends. "Gears?"

He held up a hand.

She sat down and watched the incense burn. Behind Gears' eyelids, there was rapid back and forth movement. Zed waited a few minutes and just when the incense was getting her high, Gears said, "Ha! That'll show you," and opened his eyes.

He looked over and smiled. "Thanks for chilling, just needed to show that pip-squeak Andrews where he can shove his chakra."

"Wha?"

Gears had stretched his arms, the long needles bobbing like cattails in the wind. "Just a little meditation by mail. Last week I get a letter from this Brit, Andrews, who thinks he's the King Meditator, thinks he can ascend more levels, see more past lives than anyone. I just accepted his challenge and blew him out of the Ether."

"Oh?"

"Yah, nothing like it, blow by a few newbies, alter your form a bit and they think you're the devil. You can chase them all over, really gets the juices going." Gears gave a big grin.

Zed pointed at one of the needles. "Doesn't that hurt?"

"Immensely. Neat, huh?" His face became a mask of pain before he flashed her another grin. "Nah, just giving you the gears. You want to try one?" He pulled out one of the needles from his left shoulder and extended it toward her.

She shook her head firmly.

Gears raised his eyebrows a bit but said nothing. He started pulling out the needles and putting them in a tall steel cup sitting by the candle. "I thought you were into everything, open to new experiences."

"Burning needles?"

"Just another of life's experiences, collect as we go, I say. I want all the experiences I can hold." Gears stripped the last of the needles from his back, stood up and stretched.

"What was the Prof here for?"

"Him? Oh, just a trade on something. What are you here for?"

"Armbands."

"Armbands?"

"Yeah, those black ones with the white dots, and headbands." Zed's hands rose to her forehead, outlining the headband.

"You work for the Countessa now?" Gears walked over to a workbench and slipped on the t-shirt lying there.

"Nah, freelance."

"Freelance or freebooter?" He gave Zed a wink. "I think I got some black cloth around here. How many you want?"

"Thirty."

"Thirty?" Gears furrowed his brow. "Yeah, I might be able to do that. All armbands?"

"Say, twenty armbands, ten headbands."

"And what's the juice?" Gears asked. Zed pulled out six joints and placed them on the workbench. Gears reached forward and picked one up, bringing it under his nose. "Ah! Tijuana Gold." He sighed. "That's one holy smoke. That's what I like about you, Zed, you look and you understand, fill the need, curb the lust. I ever tell you about when I was in Mexico after a five day binge, and the senorita in the restaurant just came up and gave me a glass of vodka and water?" Gears rubbed his head with a wistful look. "I was there trying that whole wanderlust, oblivion thing, Burroughs, Kerouac, crossing excess and purpose and seeing what my typewriter looked like, or where I would wake up...."

Zed sighed, another go-nowhere story. She sniffed the air. "Hey, you still got some stew. How much for a bowl?"

Gears looked over, blinking, trying to clear out the glory days of Mexican beaches and unlimited margaritas. "That's a new batch," he said shortly, clearly miffed at being cut off mid-ramble. "And it's already spoken for, part of Countessa's feast tonight."

"Feast?" Zed had heard nothing of this.

"Yeah, I got a sign about it, I was going to put it up when I take up Countessa's door."

"Countessa's door!" Zed was astounded. "Show me."

Gears shrugged, and led her through the curtain of car bumpers to a cleared work area. There it was, atop two simple wooden sawhorses, Countessa's door. Zed approached and ran her hand along the cheap oak veneer over particleboard. It wasn't a magnificent door, yet Zed knew she was touching a legend, something whispered about in laundry rooms and hallways. Many contended that Countessa never had a door, that it was this accident, combined with the dark, which granted her other-worldly powers. "You've had it? All this time?"

"Yeah. She asked me to store it for her."

"She's putting it back on?"

"Yeah, she wants to limit her hours, only see people a couple hours a day. She's going to announce her plans at the feast tonight." Gears looked over the door. "I got to take it up soon. I can do your armbands after that. They should be ready in, say, two hours, three tops."

Zed nodded and slouched through the door.

"Later, little dude," Gears called out, lighting one of the joints. Zed gave a limp wave. What now? She could look up Rat, try to find something on the kid snuffer. No, she'd drop by the lobby before hitting Countessa's.

The lobby was lined with the can-men, scroungers, and day-walkers watching the rain wash over their livelihood. The lake of water by the doors had grown out to the street and laterally extended farther than she could see. She drifted over to talk to Hammer, but spied Rat and his glowing forehead over by the far doorway.

She slid up beside him. Wet had only given depth to his odour. "Hey Rat, whatcha doing?"

"Nothin', fuck it," he told her, glum. "Rat wants to go scrounging."

"So?"

He pointed outside. "Can't fucking swim."

"Well, come with me, we'll go look up some stuff on Pete."

Rat didn't move, didn't stop staring out into the rain. "Can't."

"What do you mean, can't? You owe me, you owe me four hours."

He gave her a grin and with breath that would have curled her chest hair said, "Food truck."

Zed felt like smacking herself. She'd forgotten. "How long?"

"Hour, maybe less. The rest, fuckers, be here soon, gotta be by the door." He picked the red spot on his forehead, crusty with blisters.

Hammer was standing at the doorway to his bunker. "Rain," he told her as she approached. She nodded. "Truck day," he added grimly, eyes glaring at the stack of people along the walls and in front of the doors. He flexed and curled.

Zed paused. "Know anything about a feast?"

Hammer gave a negative jerk, never taking his eyes off the people lining the lobby.

Zed shrugged and pelted up the stairs to Countessa's: past the loungers in the stairwell, past the incense burners, past the Countessa groupies in the hall. She arrived just in time to see Gears fitting the door. Everyone stood in a semi-circle; close enough to see but far enough away to show they didn't want to see. A moan rose for every ring of the hammer on the door pins.

"Hey Zed, you get to see her yet?" Jenny was there with her parakeet.

Zed blinked to remember. Oh yeah, the food scam. "Naw, not likely to now, with the door and all."

"She'll still be Countessa, just not all the time."

"Sure." And Zed would still be Zed, 24/7.

Gears finished with the pins, unrolled a poster, and tacked it up on the door. Then, with a nod to Zed, he pushed the door closed.

"That's something, ain't it, really something," Jenny moaned, a tear in her eye.

People started to drift in, giving the door a touch before darting out again. Gears had blown off and Zed wasn't so keen on hanging with this sniff and blink fest. She came in to see the poster.

"Feast of the Dead – The living and the dead party down tonight! Drink the cup of all knowing, eat the flesh of ghosts – seven-thirty start, bring food offerings."

That seemed clear enough, though if the "Feast of the Dead" was anything like the séance, Zed figured on earplugs. She beat her way though the crowd to the stairs.

The Father stood by the stairwell door. "So what's the latest with the Countessa show?"

"Door's up," Zed told him. "Rest in trade."

"Hmmm," the Father said, scratching his head, "maybe I should trade, because walking fifty feet to find out just seems sooooo hard."

"Okay, okay, poster for 'Feast of the Dead,' tonight."

"Bread and circus." The Father smiled. "She knows her audience."

Yada yada yada, Zed thought. "Where's your gang?"

"Waiting for the Food Truck. Why aren't you there?"

"Wait ten seconds." She leapt down the stairs, two at time. "Going tonight?" she called back.

"In spirit," he replied and laughed.

Down in the lobby she had to push hard just to get the door open. Fortunately, the doorknob hit a kidney, which cleared some room. She looked at the bodies cramming the space: packed, racked, and stacked. Welcome to food day, where the motto was, "first come, only served."

She was late, too late. But Zed felt, with enough determination, you're never too late. She wriggled toward Hammer.

If wriggling through crowds ever became an Olympic sport, Zed was a gold contender. She crawled over knees, slithered by buttocks, over feet, under armpits, and through legs. She waited till they exhaled, till they scratched, till they tried to kick her; any little room or break and she'd inch forward. There is rude, there is bold, and then there's Zed.

She flopped into the billy club arc of space around Hammer. He looked down at her and grunted, "Truck day." His words radiated loathing.

"It's the rain," she told him, picking herself up. "And that lake keeps them in too."

A burst of laughter came from the crowd and Hammer's gaze burned into them, trying hard to make the offending heads spontaneously explode. The laughter died.

Zed was ready for round two. "You want anything?" she asked Hammer as she plotted her path.

"Chocolate." Hammer kept his eyes on the crowd. "Cheese."

"Aye, aye." Zed saluted and made a running dive into the mass.

She got to within three bodies from the door before she resorted to her final weapon: shoving people into their neighbours. When the arguments escalated, she wormed through.

As she was thrust against Rat, he turned and barked, "Fuck, find your own place." Seeing it was her, he started to smile, but then his face bunched up in suspicion. "What are you doing all the way up here? I had to wait, ya know."

"Trade you some info for a piece of chocolate." Zed had a policy of never giving answers, especially those which might piss people off.

"No." He looked at her from the corner of his eye. "What info?"

"It's happening tonight. It's big. And," she tempted him, "Father doesn't like it."

Rat scratched at his beard, freeing a cascade of debris. "Doesn't like it, or really doesn't like it?" It was an accepted truth that anything the Father really didn't like had to be worth trying at least once.

"Dunno, but I also got the word on Countessa's door."

"Countessa doesn't have a door."

"Well, maybe."

Rat started gnawing his lip over that one. He was rocked by a shove from behind and smashed an elbow in the general direction. "Dickwad," someone called out.

"Fuck, what?" Rat started swinging back and forth, searching. "Rat'll take you down." Hammer caught Rat's eye and gave him a four-hundred-watt stare. "Fuckers," Rat told Zed, giving it up. "So where am I going to get chocolate?"

"Truck."

Rat thought that over. "But I like chocolate."

Zed simply repeated, "Countessa's door."

"Fuck," Rat said. "What?"

"Countessa has a door and it's back on. Gears had it."

"Real?"

"Real. And she's got a party tonight, booze too. It's for the dead."

Rat frowned at that. "So can I go?" Before Zed could answer, Rat turned and screamed at the man behind him, "Stop fucking poking me!" He caught Hammer's eye and sank back down.

"You could crash," Zed offered.

"Yeah." Rat smiled, "I could fuckin crash all right, good at that ... wait!" He held up a hand as he opened the door. The smell of mouldy leaves and wet dogs slipped through. "Engine," he whispered to her.

Zed could hear it now, a growl with the low hum of tires on wet road. "It's coming," came the yell from the back, and everyone crushed forward.

"Ah shit!" Rat clawed at the doorframe as the weight of a hundred bodies pushed toward the rain. "It's another car!" he was screaming. "Honest!"

"I see it," came the cry, loud and clear. "The Food Truck, here at last." A cheer rose with a pushing, shoving stampede of bodies. Zed helped Rat try to hold the door, but two does not an army make. With the rasp of fingernails torn from metal, they were pushed free, carried forward by the crowd, right into the lake. Zed struggled as the water rose to her knees then thighs. "Come on," Rat called to her, pushing forward.

Zed looked up at him, trying to think of a good insult about long legs and short dicks when he grabbed her arm and dragged her up. They made it through the worst and out to the sidewalk, where the water was only a foot deep. Zed was already shivering. A space separated them from the crowd as people floundered in the high water.

With a grinding slam of gears it started down the street: the Food Truck. Old Ted was driving, high in the box above the Mac grill, his hairy forearms up on the wheel and his cap pulled low.

The Truck had two hands painted on the side, along with the phrase, *Feeding Each Other*. The Townies paid to have it driven out here every two weeks, filled with the bounty of dented cans and items just past their expiration date. It was both the back-patting outreach and the price the shops downtown were happy to pay to keep the Tower away, far, far away. There used to be a food shelter downtown until Rat and friends showed up and property prices started to fall. After that, they decided to deliver.

Ted was bringing it in hard and fast. Anything else and he would have twenty scroungers clamped to his sides like limpet mines. After all, the Food Truck came but once a fortnight. Zed gauged the truck's speed and sidled six feet further down the sidewalk, Rat following. It was all down to the first two minutes, as Zed well knew. After that, it was just bran flakes and jellied squash. Be first at the door, first with the hands, and Zed could live two weeks on what she got, and what she sold.

Rat was ready; Zed was ready. She could see Ted leaning back as he stomped on the brake. The truck started jerking, tires wet and sliding. Ted's face got that white frozen look of a guy who's sliding toward a stack of people in a one-tonne truck. *Well, that should thin out the competition*, Zed thought, till the crowd pushed her forward. She hit Rat and both of them staggered a foot into the street.

Rat turned, eyes blazing. "You fucking townie...."

Zed could see it all. The good news and the bad: good news was the truck was stopping shorter than she figured, bad news was she was still a couple feet the wrong side of a hood ornament. *Typical*, she thought, *my last moment and Rat's chewing on me.* So she fell, kicking out his legs.

Somehow, in the roar of the engine, and with half her head in the water, she could still hear Rat growling, "Oh, wanna scrap, you fucker?" Then the wave of water from the tires hit them.

Moments later, Zed sat up, sputtering. She immediately hit her head on an axle and sashayed back down before beginning to crawl toward the light. There was a hacking wet cough behind her. Turned out Rat had survived. They dragged themselves out from between the tires and pulled themselves up using the hot grill. Ted glared down on them, his teeth turning to powder if those cords on his jaws were any indication. Maybe he couldn't figure whether to hate or love them. Zed knew, because right now, she felt the same.

"Told you I can't fucking swim." Rat said when he caught her looking at him. He wiped his face, then turned and looked at the grill inches away. "*Fuuucckk,*" he said softly. He turned back to Zed. "That was close." He looked at her in awe, water dripping from her hair. "Why'd you do that?"

Zed shrugged. "You want some food or don't you?" she asked. Ted was fighting his way through to open up the gate; it was back to business as usual.

Rat looked at the grill again. "My fucking silver bullet." Then he joined her and they ran round to the back of the truck, fighting the crowd for the door.

The back of the truck slid up, and with a shout, everyone dove for it.

Rat held out his hand. "On my shoulders," he told Zed.

"What?"

"You fucking want in or not? Quick, on my shoulders," Rat told her.

Zed obeyed, seeing people pour into the truck like piranha on a cow.

"Ready?" Rat called, putting his hands under her feet.

"For what!" Zed cried, crouching lower.

"This!" And Rat gave her a heave. Zed's legs pushed off and she flew over the crowd, right toward the open gate. She splash-landed against those just climbing aboard. Jumping up from the complaining bodies she gave Rat a grin and a thumbs up. Showtime!

Zed had a technique: she let her mouth slow them down while her hands did the work.

"Heya, Sid, how's it going? Pretty rotten Truck Day or what, no? You want these 'tatos? Hey Jenny, how'd the food offering go? Can you pass me those fortune cookies wouldya, and a block of that cheese, yeah that one. Better give me a white and a yellow while you're at it, lots for everyone, eh? Take a look at these canned peaches, sweet or what?"

Sixty seconds of gab and Zed was cruising. While they grabbed the cheese for her, she took the bagels, the canned chili, the spaghetti, a pack of fig newtons, liquorice, two boxes of jello, and a packet of tea bags: a.k.a. all the good stuff. Let's face it, for every person who donated something anyone might want to eat, ten more gave the crap they bought when drunk, found when moving, or received second-hand from the old country. Hey, the demand for pig's tongue ain't what it used to be ... get my drift? Another sixty seconds and Zed had filled her bag. Good thing she'd brought a spare.

It was getting crowded and desperate. Zed went for a can of beans in tomato sauce. So did Anne, her face veiled in grey stringy hair. Zed was faster, getting her hand around the can first. Problem was, Anne was a sore loser. She stomped Zed's hand, can and all. It hurt. Zed had a technique for dealing with a situation like this. She called it "take down" because H.T.A.K.H.T.T.T.D.G.U.N.M. was too long to say. She waited till Anne tried to stomp again and swept her leg, then as Anne fell, she delivered an elbow on the larynx, hard. As Zed tucked away the can and went for a half-hidden bag of beef jerky, Anne thought about breathing and how nice it would be if she could do some soon ... real soon. Yup, good old Hurt Them And Keep Hurting Them Till They Don't Get Up No More.

"Yahoo!" Zed turned to see a flash of Rat flying through the air. He fell on the packed bodies and began his patented method of scrounging: he leapt onto a pile, shoved what he wanted into a bag around his waist, and then leapt onto the next pile, regardless of whoever was there; with a few well delivered bites, Rat always cleared a space. Zed caught up to him as he was shoving a hunk of old bologna into his bag.

"Good Truck Day," Zed called.

"Fucking-A!" he agreed while fighting with an old woman over a tin. He ripped it from her fingers. "Powdered milk!" he cried indignantly and threw it. The woman caught it on the rebound off her skull.

"Attention. Attention, please." Zed heard the call from the gate of the truck. She spared a glance. It was Don, headband and all.

"Doughboy wants us." Zed spied a packet of crackers and made a successful grab at it.

"So?" Rat was fighting with a young guy named Randall who had wild long brown hair, a squeaky voice, and missing front teeth. They were both clutching a bag of expired doughnuts. However much Rat pulled and punched, Randall refused to let go. "My doughnuts," he piped.

"You want your doughnuts?" Rat started to pound the doughnuts. "Have your fucking doughnuts." And he let the bag go. Randall swung the bag around and into Rat's head, exploding in a cloud of confection sugar. Guess Randall was pissed.

With a growl, Rat grabbed the largest item at hand, a bag of carrots, and lobbed it at Randall. The bag wrapped around Randall's neck, throwing him down.

"Attention," Don was still talking, "please leave the truck. Countessa needs the food." More and more people wearing headbands appeared beside Don.

Zed tried to grab a cereal box off the floor, but it had been stepped on and all the puffs inside fell out as she picked it up. "Don's back and he's *organized*."

"Screw organized," Rat told her. "They're the geek clique." He picked up a bag of potatoes and started swinging, moving toward the door of the truck. "Fuck, I love this." Rat sniffed and smiled, giving Bucket Charlie the full swinging weight of the potatoes onto his bald spot. Charlie's head flew forward, striking the steel wall of the truck before he collapsed to the ground. Zed and Rat quickly rolled him over and transferred the food from his bag into theirs. Hey, all's fair on Truck Day.

"Last call. Please leave quietly." Zed looked up at Don's voice. The gate of the truck was packed with the armband and headband gang and they all had that *look*, that "mind if I step closer before I detonate this C-4 taped all over my body" look. Zed went into an overdrive of grabbing.

The next two minutes were kind of hazy, but at the end, Don and friends owned the truck while Zed, Rat, and everyone else stood in the rain. The only thing Zed was sure of was that she didn't go quietly. Yeah!

The "one light" people were running a chain of food into the lobby: pairs of little old ladies and men slinging sacks of rice into a pile. There were at least seventy people and no matter which way Zed sliced it, it was impressive. Worse, regardless of the rain, the lake, the hard wet labour, they were smiling. Now that was scary.

Zed tried to console herself with her two bags of pure cream, but nobody likes to lose their parade, so she was in a bit of a snit. And seeing bags and cans of good, tradable stock flow past in someone else's hands, didn't help.

"You like rain?" she asked Rat.

"No."

"Then why're we in it?"

They waded back inside and leaned against the wall, sorting their bags. Rat handed over a small bar of chocolate before unwrapping another and popping it in his mouth. He chewed, he slurped, he sucked at his teeth.

"You're a slob, Rat, you know that? Everyone's staring over here, know why?"

"Cuz I got chocolate and they don't?"

"Yeah, probably, and because you eat louder than those 'one light' can chant."

She was referring to the crowd around the transferred pile. They were chanting, "One light. Feast of the Dead. One light. Countessa. One light." Then they broke up and started hauling everything up to the 5th floor.

Don came past, flanked by two headband-wearing toughs. Zed leapt up. "Don, yeah Donski, got some questions for you. Like about how I was thrown out of the truck."

Don retreated behind his goons and scooted for the staircase. The muscle stayed, giving her the eyeball.

Zed didn't have the energy for these two, so she contented herself with, "Small building, Don, small building." She turned around just in time to see Rat transferring a block of cheese from her sack to his. In two strides, her forearm was pushing his neck through the wall.

Rat tried to smile. "Truck Day, Zed. You know how it is."

"I sure do, so put it back." Rat put back the cheese and the tea. "All of it," Zed told him.

"Fuck, all right." Rat put the rest back then pulled out a whack of baloney and began to gnaw.

"And speaking of things you owe me, where's my four hours?"

"Screw the four hours," Rat told her. "And screw you and your precious bags." Rat drew a sleeve across his nose. He looked down at the bologna. Zed didn't move. Rat gave the hunk a few half-hearted nibbles before he sighed and gave up. "All right," he conceded. "When?"

"I got to get sorted and dry." Zed wiggled a finger in her ear, listening to the squishing sounds. "An hour, outside Gears'?"

Rat agreed. "You said he's got a DVD player?"

Zed nodded. She made a note to get there first. In a choice between helping her and watching oiled girl-on-girl action, she was pretty sure Rat wasn't picking the five-footer. She grabbed her bags and walked over to Hammer's bunker. He was sitting in his metal chair, watching Countessa's gang haul the food away. "Busy," he said, nodding at the scurrying.

She nodded and handed him the chocolate bar. He held it in his hand and looked at it, a boyish smile creeping into the corners of his cheeks. Putting it in his shirt pocket, he gave it a friendly pat. The cheese he took more matter of fact. Then he gave her a nod. "Bye!"

Yeah, right, try again, Zed thought. "So when did you see Pete last?" she asked.

"Pete?"

"Yeah, Pete. 'Member, we talked about this yesterday."

"Children." Hammer got that distant look in his eyes.

Not again! Zed thought. "Hello," she called, risking her life to wave a hand in front of Hammer's face. "Pete? You see her?"

Hammer's eyes lost the film and took on a sheen of water over steel.

"Good chocolate, huh?" Zed thought it a good time to remind him she was useful to him breathing, and with all limbs and digits attached.

He let out a low growl, like a bear looking for its first salmon after hibernation, then he turned and rubbed his broad forehead with two fingers. "Eight-thirty."

"Eight-thirty, you saw her here."

He shook his head, pointed to the TV facing him, bisected into four scenes. "You saw her in the cameras." He nodded, pointing to the camera that covered the stairwell between the 8th and 9th floor. "With Bunny?" Zed asked.

Hammer slowly shook his head. "Rat." With that statement, he sunk back in his chair and turned his head.

Zed survived by practicing the art of knowing when to walk away and when to run. Now was a time to walk.

Chapter 8

TEN MINUTES LATER AND Zed's bare feet were slapping cement, hoofing it up the stairs like a cat on fire. She had on her spare coveralls as everything else was drying. It was time for her to take care of unfinished business, like asking Rat not why he killed the kids, but why he was wasting her precious time by not telling or trading the info with her. But first she was going to Luc's, who still owed her some books and half an answer.

On her way up, she stepped over happy boozers and smiling stoners. And why not be happy? Luc was selling, the Food Truck had come, and there was a feast tonight. Life was sweet.

Stu was standing guard, leather collar up and hair freshly oiled, the spitting image of a hoodlum, a wayward youth, life spent in flophouses and poolhalls. Stu was filling time by throwing his knife into a silhouette carved into the opposite wall. Flick, bam, and a saunter over to pull it out. Flick, bam, saunter; flick, bam, saunter. My, how life goes by. The owner of the wall had come out, watching at his door. Zed could tell he wanted to say something, but he wouldn't. Stu looked over and threw a groin shot; flick, bam, saunter. Stu thought he was cool, Zed thought he was being a dick, but what can you say to a guy throwing a knife?

"Stu," Zed said, waiting until he threw so she could pass. "Stop being a dick."

He turned, leered, and threw it straight to the heart, not even looking.

"Show-off," she told him as she entered Luc's.

Stu chuckled.

Inside, the two chalkboards were down and Luc was working on the one nearest the door.

"I've come to collect," Zed told him.

"One moment, one moment."

Zed took a seat. One of the boards was "Snuffed," and the other was "Snuffers." Zed was proud to see she made both boards. The feeling went away fast as she checked her odds. 2:1 on getting snuffed! Sure, Christina was odds-on 7:8, with Jen at 3:5 and Baby X 2:3, but if there was one person who wasn't going down, it was Zed. That was just a fool's bet. She looked over at the other board and this just kept getting worse. "10:1! You gave me lousy 10:1!"

"Now, now, you know the game," Luc chided. "10:1 just gives you that edgy outsider chance which brings in the money. If I dropped you to 4:1 or 5:1, everyone would just bet on Hammer at 7:2 or Stu at 3:1 and I'm being generous with Stu because everyone knows Stu would kill anything."

"Yeah, but only for you," Zed countered. "You sure my attack on Barry and Don don't change the odds?"

Luc shook his head.

"You're sure that's 'edgy,' not 'pathetic,' right?"

"Definitely 'edgy.'"

"So how come you're up there at 9:2?" Zed wanted to know.

"I don't think I did it."

"That what Countessa told you?"

Luc just smiled and said nothing. Zed tried staring him down; she squinted, she scowled, she turned stony. Luc was very good at saying nothing.

"Fine," she said. "Leave it."

"Sure you don't want to scowl some more?"

She gave him a black look, hoping blood might start pouring out his eyes and ears. No luck. "I've come to collect. You owe me."

"Aren't you supposed to be tapping a baseball bat when you say that?"

Zed growled. Sitting in coveralls when your underwear is downstairs drying can make a person cranky.

"Okay, okay, I'll pay." Luc raised his hands in mock submission. "Books, right?" He got them out of his cabinet.

"And the question!"

"Question?"

"Yeah, about the R-E-T-E ... no, T-R...." Zed gave up. "About the retreat."

Luc glanced toward the door. "Sure, shout it around why don't you." He shook his head. "Meet me in the lobby in two hours. There's a special delivery coming and after that I can show you."

"Two hours. Fine. But you still owe me."

"I do?"

"Interest."

"You're sharking me? On information?"

"Wouldn't you?"

Luc tilted his head and gave her a professional once over. "Now that I consider it, I would. So what's the interest? A free line of speed?"

"Ha-ha. How about what the Countessa told you?"

"Whoa." Luc chuckled. "That question had pretty steep interest. What's that, one hundred percent interest?"

"Per day," Zed said with a smile.

"Dealer after my own heart." He pointed a finger at her. "Countessa told me who was doing the killing."

Zed was leaning forward. "Who?"

"Sorry, one day, one question. And I am definitely paying you off today. But tell you what. Give me the name of the next snuffee, and I give you the name of the snuffer."

"I'll think about it," Zed bluffed, packing the books away. "You know about the party?"

"Know? I'm catering. Looks like it will build up to quite the orgy."

"Orgy?"

"You know," Luc said, licking his lips, "the beast with two backs, the nine-limbed mambo."

Zed just looked puzzled.

"Squishy noises? The hotsy two-step? The down and dirty?"

Zed shook her head.

"Sex!" Luc called out in exasperation. "Sex, okay? They'll be screwing till their eyes fall out."

Now that's interesting, Zed thought. She gave a nod and started to go.

"A word," said Luc, "for that old biddy of yours."

"Ivy?"

"That's the one, plies everyone with hot flavoured water and talks continuously without breathing. At least that's what happened at the little soirée."

The one I wasn't invited to, Zed remembered fiercely.

"Well, she kept talking about family this and family that and the things one does for husbands and sons. Now, you and I know that most everyone here is without family, at least any who would speak to them. And while I don't mind it, it makes the boys edgy, somewhat irritable. So just pass on a word to the wise and tell her to choose her topics with care. And next time a little booze would go a long way too."

"I'll tell her."

"You want to lay anything before you go? How about $100 on you getting snuffed next?"

Zed grinned; that seemed a bit too win-win for Luc. "And how would I collect?"

"I'd hold it till you came back."

"I'm sure you would. See ya, two hours." She headed up the stairs to the Prof's to drop off the books.

The Prof's door was open, which was fine by Zed. She could really do without the usual hassle. Turned out, he already had a visitor.

The Professor was staring indignantly at Dean, the nurse/social worker who visited twice a month. Dean, in his white slacks, was saying, "I'm putting your pills over here on the table. Now, you'll take two a day, right?"

The Professor levelled a watery eye at him. "You can put me back in the hole, but I'll never break. I'm a British officer. Where is my copy of the Geneva Convention?"

"Just remember to take the pills."

The Professor caught sight of Zed. "Ha, ha! It be the fairie folk, come to take me to their magic land, where I shall be King! King!" he crowed at Dean.

And that was Zed's cue to exit. She'd come back when the Prof was making sense.

"And where are your wings?" the Prof demanded as she walked by.

Well, at least when he was making *more* sense. She stashed the books in a kitchen cupboard, intending to haul them out later to show him. She filled up a can with water and took it with her.

Dean caught her as she headed for the door. "I hope you didn't bring any more books. He should be encouraged to spend more time in *this* reality."

"Nope, just came for the water." She smiled the smile of the innocent. But Dean wasn't born yesterday, and she could tell he wasn't buying it.

"I don't fight midgets!" the Professor yelled, leaping to his feet. He glared at Dean. "Or Albinos. But I'll put paid to your bolshy underground, and if you've even touched Penelope Desmond, I'll thrash you to within an inch of reason."

"Exactly," Zed told him and zipped out. Good luck, Dean.

On the way up to Ivy's, Zed fished out the tea. It wasn't like Zed owed Ivy anything for that incident with Bobo, but this way she could clear the balances and get back to business.

Ivy's head popped out the door on the first tap. "Heard such a tiny knock, I never. For me? Tea? Oh you're a love."

"Here's some water." Zed handed over the can.

"Sit yourself down by the table while I brew the tea." Ivy held open the door.

Zed banged a heel against the wall. "I'd prefer not to."

"You'd prefer not to? What's this? Stroppy over tea? Don't be foolish."

Zed shrugged.

"Is it about the other day? That was nothing. Just a thing that needed doing." Ivy gave her a smile. "Nothing about you and me. Come on in."

Zed wouldn't meet her eyes. "I gotta go."

Ivy shook her head. "Well, you know your own mind, but don't be shy." Ivy looked down. "And I don't like the idea of you walking all but naked through half of God's creation. Wait." She pointed a finger at Zed. "Wait."

Things would be better this way, Zed convinced herself while waiting, strictly business, evens and trade for trades.

"For you." And before Zed could protest, Ivy had thrown a blue blanket across her shoulders. "Keep it."

"Ivy, I can't." She pulled the blanket off and held it out. "Here."

Ivy gave a smile that lit up her face, all sunshine and wrinkles. "I prefer not to." And she closed the door.

Ooooh, that Ivy! Some people just had to complicate life. Some people didn't know when they were well off. Zed was tempted to leave the blanket in the hall. That would teach her a lesson. Except someone would steal it and then Ivy'd think Zed still had it. Blankets were like gold dust, especially new, clean, blue ones. Zed ground her teeth and wrapped the blanket round her shoulders. She was just going to hold onto it long enough to give it back.

She stashed the blanket in her hole before she went to meet Rat. He'd gotten to Gears' first and was standing, glaring at the door and growling.

"So, how were the threesomes?" Zed picked her way around the glass, leaping over the stream swelled by rain.

"He won't let me in," Rat barked. "Says I disturb his fuckin' essence. Fuck his essence, I want lesbos!"

"Let me try." Zed gave the door a knock. There was no answer. Zed took that as an invitation.

Gears was at his workbench, an ancient sewing machine in front of him. He rocked his feet on the tread and the machine punched thread through holes, sewing another armband together. "Take off, my horny pal." He looked up. "Oh, it's you. It'll be another half-hour." He took a hit from an orange juice bottle.

"Cool, thanks."

"Half-hour." He dropped back to work.

Zed spotted the blow-off as it reversed over her. She nodded and closed the door. "Let's go," she told Rat.

"Lesbos?"

She gave him the negative. "Come on." She headed down the stairs to the next level.

"Where?"

"You're going to show me where you found the shoe."

"I do this and you forget the hours I owe?"

"No."

"Fuck." Seems it just wasn't Rat's day. So he led her down to a dark section in the corner.

Zed squatted onto her haunches, her eyes scanning the ground. Then she ran her fingers over it, slowly and carefully. In the darkest corner she picked up a small lump and stood up, walking back into the light.

"You haven't found a knife lying anywhere, Rat? A good cutting knife?"

"Me, find a knife?" He looked at her in disbelief, "Not without it still being attached to the fucking owner, I haven't. What you got?"

"Piece of meat." She turned it between her fingers.

"Fuck, I'm hungry." Rat snatched the bit of flesh and popped it into his mouth.

Zed stared at Rat. "You just ate the fucking evidence!"

"What evidence? I was hungry." He ran his tongue over his lips. "Nice, tasted a bit like chicken."

Well, Zed thought, *not everyone hates Charles.*

Rat had wandered over to the stream, watching it descend. "I thought about going down, you know, down, see how many levels. Maybe some good picking."

"You go?"

"Naw, too dark."

Zed said, "I thought you didn't mind the dark."

"Yeah, I don't mind the dark. But that, down there...." He nodded. "That's *dark*, like eyes ripped out of the sockets dark, and so quiet you can hear the voices."

"Voices?"

"I don't like it too quiet," Rat said firmly.

"Fine. Hey Rat, you kill anyone last night?"

Rat laughed. "No, you?"

"Just one. So what were you doing with Pete?" Rat looked blank so Zed reminded him. "You know, Bunny's kid."

"That townie leech! She was trying to steal from the Rat was what. So I put the hurting on her, but good."

"What she steal?"

"Fuck, I said 'trying,' didn't I? Nobody steals from King Rat. She was after my peaches."

"Peaches?"

Rat shrugged. "I was saving them."

"And you didn't cut her up?"

"No! A knife? On that runt? You think I'm some little girl, can't handle this with my hands?"

Zed glared. "Careful."

Rat cackled with laughter. "Little girl, like you, get it, I made a joke."

Zed's hand went to her coverall.

Rat laughed harder. "Whatcha doing? Getting your *knife*, little girl?"

Zed clenched her fists and waited while Rat held his sides, doubling over with laughter. As he turned to wipe his eyes, she kicked out his legs. It got easier with practice.

"Hee hee," Rat wheezed, looking up from the ground. "Okay, I deserved that, I admit it."

"Come on."

"I come with you and you forget what I owe, right?"

"No."

"Damn." Rat scrambled up and they headed back to Gears'.

"So Pete was alive when you left her."

"Alive and crawling."

"You see anyone after?" Zed asked.

"Cal and Ben P. were sharing a doobie in the stairs. That mean *they* killed her?" Rat was back to playing 'Name That Suspect.'

"Maybe, maybe not. Maybe you killed her and are covering up."

"Yeah, that makes sense." Rat puzzled over it. "Hey! Wait a minute...."

Zed gave Gears' door a rap.

"Done!" Gears called as he wrenched the door open. A joint hung loose from his lips. With one hand he gave Zed the armbands, with the other the headbands. "Done and done," he cried. "And I am off to Alice's Restaurant, to see the White Rabbit herself."

Zed and Rat looked at each other and shrugged. Rat pointed to the joint. "Can I take a toke?"

"All things to all people," Gears said solemnly and passed it over.

Rat took a long deep hit. "Ohhhh!" he sighed, smoke pouring out of his nose and the sides of his mouth, "yabba!"

"Oh Dabba!" Gears affirmed, taking the joint back and sucking down a hit. Zed just looked from one to the other as Gears and Rat gave each other a smile. "Do ba de do." They said together and broke into laughter.

"Come on," Zed said, grabbing Rat by the arm and dragging him out the door. Rat wistfully looked back at Gears lounging in the doorway. Gears smiled and took another hit.

"Come on, we're going to the lobby."

Rat asked, "If I go up to the lobby will you forget...?"

"No."

"Fuck, you always say that."

Up in the lobby, Zed saw Luc standing in the bunker, talking to Hammer.

"Shit." Luc was early. She ducked back into the stairwell, pushing Rat back. "Rat, you remember that party?"

"Fuckin'-A!"

"I heard it's going to be an orgy."

Rat licked his lips. "The Father didn't say that, did he? Cuz there was this time he talked about an orgy so I went and it was just a stripper, and she wouldn't let me touch her. Another time, the Father said it was an orgy, but it –"

"It wasn't the Father," she said, cutting him off. "It was Luc."

A shiver went through Rat at the thought of what *Luc* might consider an orgy.

"But you can't get in without a pass," Zed added.

Rat's mouth was open, his breathing rapid. He was just thinking about what might happen ... if only. "I need a pass," he told Zed, his voice hoarse.

"You still owe me," Zed reminded him.

"Zed. The Rat is underfucked. The Rat is so dry, he's in negative fucking. I *need* a pass."

"I can help you."

"Orgy?"

"But you gotta help me."

"You'll forget about the rest of the hours?" Rat wanted to know.

"Yes."

"Yes?" Rat blinked, making sure he wasn't dreaming.

Zed held up the armbands. "You sell these."

"Fuck selling. King Rat's a scrounger not a seller."

"These are the passes." Suddenly armbands held a whole new interest for Rat. "Can't get in without them," Zed told him.

"Why you selling them?"

Zed wanted to say, 'Cuz putzes like you will pay for them,' but replaced that with, "Cuz Countessa can't."

Rat nodded, accepting the twisted logic. "What do I get?"

"One armband for yourself and twenty-five percent of the take."

"And the time I owe?"

"Yeah, that too."

Rat's eyes shifted back and forth. "Two passes," he bargained.

"Rat, you've only got one body," Zed sighed.

He gnawed his lip in frustration as he pondered. "Thirty percent."

"Thirty percent," she agreed and handed the armbands over. She knew she'd be lucky to get half. But at least with Rat, you were dealing with a known element.

"Fucking!" Rat called out as he entered the lobby. "Get your fucking!" He headed toward the bunker. "Hey, Luc, want some ... never mind." Rat disappeared into the inter-walkways, singing the orgy's siren song.

Zed went over to the bunker to meet Luc.

"Later," Luc said to Hammer, who gave a slow affirmative nod. "You're late," Luc told Zed, moving toward the front door. "Luckily, so is she."

"She?"

Luc smiled and tapped his index finger on his nose. They both looked out the door over the lake, at the rain. It was pelting down like day twelve of the flood that wouldn't stop till they all glub-glubbed.

"Enter stage right," Luc said.

A brown station wagon had pulled up, depositing a woman in a pale blue dress with a green suitcase. She stood staring at the lake till her dress was soaked and clinging. The car took off.

The rain eventually drove her forward, wading through the water with her suitcase floating behind. She wrenched herself and the suitcase through the door to stand before Luc and Zed, water streaming off her. Behind the curtain of brown hair, Zed could see a scared face which might as well have been a sign saying, "Fresh Meat!"

Luc stepped forward. "My, my, what a day."

The woman stopped plucking at her clinging dress and looked at Luc over her black-rimmed glasses. "Are you the manager?" her voice trembled.

"Oh, no, I am far superior. I am Luc." He extended an immaculate hand.

"Ah...." The woman looked at the hand uncertainly before extending her own. "Mary."

"Yes, of course. Now don't worry, Mary. I know all about it, and I can get you settled right in. I see that...." His voice dropped to a conspiratorial whisper. "Mental Health," he told her with the faintest wink, "have handled things with their usual sensitivity."

"They really are very kind," Mary said, looking through the rain at where the car had stood. "I need to be with others, people. That's what Dr. Phillips said."

"I'm sure he did, along with 'transitioning' and 'therapeutic'?"

Mary gave a inquisitive nod. "Have you seen him too?"

"Not in person, but seeing as Dr. Phillips isn't here while so many of his patients are, I feel as if I know him. Let me escort you to your new accommodation." He led Mary to the elevator, leaving Zed to drag the suitcase.

The elevator came and Luc pushed the button for the 3rd floor. Mary looked from Luc to Zed, confused but silent.

When the elevator opened Luc led Mary down the hall to 304. He took a key from his pocket and opened the door with a flourish. With a slight bow, he presented the key to Mary. She took it in her fingers, toying with it.

"Who exactly are you?" Mary asked.

Luc gave her his #1 smile. "Just the local welcome wagon; I'm here to help. Anything you need, any problems you have, any medications you need, just come up and see me. I'm up on the 11th floor. Day or night, just ask for Luc. Or if you need any of those day-to-day trifles, then ask around for Zed here." He gestured to Zed, who had managed to drag the suitcase inside the door. Zed nodded at Mary. "I'm sure she will drop around from time to time to see how you are doing," Luc said.

"Uh … I…." Mary stood there with the key in her hand.

"You must be tired," Luc announced, looking down at her.

"I … I am." Mary retreated through the door.

"Just take a nap and you'll feel worlds better. Cheerio!" Luc gave a wave as he walked back to the elevator. They stepped inside as Mary peered out of the doorway after them.

"That first contact," Luc told Zed as he pushed the basement button, "is so important. Everyone needs a friend in a strange place."

"You're all heart," Zed agreed dryly.

"*Moi*? Did I not introduce you also?"

"That, or carry the luggage yourself."

"Please, you wound me." He gave a little laugh, got off at the lobby, and went down the stairs to the sub-basement, Zed following. He headed down the inter-stair Zed and Rat had used earlier. Zed lagged behind, wishing she had retrieved her shoes, wet or not.

Luc waited at the bottom and led her down into the darkened section. Zed stopped where the light ended. "I need light," she called, "for my feet."

"Among my other abilities," he told Zed, "I'm also psychic." He pulled out a sturdy black flashlight. "Luc calls for light." He flicked it on. "And there is light." He handed it over.

"If you're psychic, you should do readings, like Countessa."

"I'm going to pretend I didn't hear that." Luc led the way, whistling. He whistled the same note in endless and blurring variations until Zed began to believe it was not the same note, that somehow, when she hadn't noticed, he'd eased it up a half tone and started over.

"Just over here, my young reprobate." Luc led off to the right. "And remember, please, that if I hear of this around, we'll be having a 'chat.'"

"Come on, Luc. You know I don't give info for free."

"That's what worries me." They stopped before a metal door, brown and rusty at the edges. Luc dipped his bandaged hand into his pocket and fished out a key. He looked over as he slotted the key home. "Voilà!" The door went wide as Luc hit the lights.

Zed stepped into the room. "What does 'voilà' mean?" Her eyes darted about.

"Here it is."

It was a box of unpainted concrete, the joining seams running across the floor and up the walls. In the middle of the floor stood a small wooden desk and chair. An empty wastebasket stood by the desk while an unused pad of paper and three pens lay on top.

"Whoop-de-do," Zed muttered.

"Pardon?"

"This it?"

"None so humble, but still home. It's here I come to think." Zed watched as Luc struck several "thinking" poses: finger on his lips, finger on forehead, sitting on the corner of the desk, chin resting on fist.

Zed, no stranger to shaved deals, suspected faulty goods. If this is all there was, why was Luc so edgy over it? No, she was convinced that this room was a question vacuum, sucking down her legitimately paid-for question and giving garbage in return. "Nice room."

"Isn't it just. Well, I've got business waiting." Luc ushered Zed out, turned off the lights, and locked the door. "Remember to keep Luc's secret world a secret." He turned and led her back to the stairs up to the sub-parkade. "Coming?"

"I'll be along." She watched him leap up the steps and saunter away. Luc's secret world, my ass!

Zed reviewed current events: hours till the party, Rat out making trades for her, no new clues on the killers, and she was full of info that was either useless or untradable. Zed decided to scratch that itch she had about the sub-parkade. And what better day to do it than the day "uncle" Luc forgot to collect his new flashlight?

She followed the stream down. Where it would go, she would go. While the water was flowing now, it hadn't been during the Quince hunt. The rest of the floor and walls were dry, no mold or slime to show residual moisture. It was chilly but not clammy. Only the big rains must make the stream, Zed reasoned, leaking in from the roof of the sub-parkade. Maybe it emptied into the sewer or forgotten caves, maybe there would be tunnels, a whole city underground. Who knows?

She picked her way down, splashing her light on the faded graffiti of the walls. The floor was sprinkled with shards of glass, coated in dust, lights smashed long ago. She passed another inter-stair, the black entrance gaping. But Zed wasn't in a hurry to descend. It was just good to know there was another level to explore.

She had just passed a stripped-down car, all crusted axles and gaping holes, when she heard the whisper. On one hand, it was good news, it meant there was something worth exploring. On the other hand, it scared the bejesus out of her.

The whispering stopped. She advanced, it started. She waited. The whisper started again, but she kept waiting and soon enough it stopped, then started again. Against the advice of most of her brain and every horror film ever made, Zed turned off the flashlight.

She let her eyes adjust and looked around. Yup, there it was: a flickering glow at the next corner. Zed smiled. Someone was down here, which in her mind was a lot better than some*thing* being down here.

The whispers turned to murmurs by the next corner and Zed peered around to see a lantern downslope, flames dancing inside. A figure in black sat beside it.

The murmurs had become a humming and the head bobbed in time. Zed snuck up a foot at a time until she could scrutinize the bald spot on the back of the head. It looked familiar.

"Father?"

"Holy Moses!" the Father cried, falling down as he spun about. He lay panting, squinting into the dark.

Zed advanced into the light. "Hey, scared you, huh?"

"Not really," the Father gasped, one hand clutching his chest.

"What ya doing?"

"Thinking." He pulled himself back upright. "Or I was, back before my veins became packed with adrenaline."

"Where's the rest of your gang?"

"Getting ready for the party."

"Um." Zed tried being polite. "I don't know if they're invited."

"Don't worry," the Father told her, smiling. "I've had an invitation, not by the Countessa perhaps, but invited."

Zed gave him a grin. "You've changed."

"I suppose so. I guess I just hit a point where I wasn't going to sit still and watch it happen anymore. No matter the price. I can't say I'm sorry."

"I meant you've got a gang now, like Luc."

"Oh. That too. But not like Luc, I hope."

"Naw," Zed assured him. "You got all the losers."

The Father laughed. "They may surprise you." He looked down at her affectionately. "Zed, you ever think about what this place is doing to you?"

"Making me rich?"

"No, I mean, how you look at things."

Zed regarded him suspiciously. "You're not going to try to give me another bible, are you?"

"I'm just here to listen."

"For someone who listens, you sure try to give a lot of bibles."

The Father spread his hands. "Guilty."

"You still owe me." Zed got ready to go.

"Six, I remember. Where are you going?"

"Down. Been there?"

"Nope. This is as far as I go. See you."

"Ya, tonight." Zed headed down the slope.

"Wait. Tonight?" the Father called after her. "You're going tonight?"

Zed didn't wait. The Father was a nice guy, but Zed could stay talking all day and end up with nothing but bibles.

Zed hurried down the slope and around the corner. She turned off the light and waited. The glow from the lantern bounced faintly round the corner, then grew dim and disappeared altogether. Good. Exploring was something best done alone.

She turned on the flashlight and continued.

Zed wound her way down and down. At the landings were sliding doors, all padlocked. Some locks were rusted, others strangely new. Zed tried them all. No dice.

There was an inter-level stair and Zed passed it mid-point on each slope. She followed the stream, picking her way around rusted hunks of metal, an old shopping cart, pull-tab cans, and thick glass bottles. But mostly she picked her way through the dust; by the wall, it was like a shag carpet. She got the idea people didn't come down here much. She passed a burnt-out fifty-gallon drum and figured she knew why they steered clear: it was a dump.

Still she went down. A slope, a landing, turn and down, turn and down. She hadn't bothered to count on the way down, so she couldn't say for certain how far she'd come, but it was underground, way, way underground.

She passed another entrance for the inter-level stairs and walked on.

Something was different. She stopped and tried to figure it out, light playing on the far wall. The far wall? It wasn't a landing, just a wall, and for that matter, the floor wasn't sloped anymore, but that wasn't it. It was the dust. There wasn't any, at least not by the stream. She played her light back and followed the dust-free path till it met the inter-level stairs.

She turned around and headed toward the far wall. *Someone must come down here*, Zed decided, *and regular too.* Zed wanted to find out why. She followed the stream up to the wall where it disappeared under a brown door with a faded white sign: "Rec. Rm." She could hear the sound of falling water on the other side of the door.

Zed smiled. Here was a real secret: a path, a waterfall, and a secret door. She reached for the heavy-duty knob, then stopped. She had heard something. "Father?" she whispered. She used the flashlight to play back as far as the light would reach. "That you?" If it was, he didn't answer. The noise turned into a voice, indistinct, but growing closer. Zed flicked off her light and scampered into the corner, crouching, bum on heels, her head tucked behind her knees.

In the doorway halfway up the slope, a pin light appeared. Zed told herself: think small, think small, think small. The light bobbed and bounced, then made a large, round curve as the holder leapt the stream. The light advanced, right down the path to the door. The mystery path-maker had come a-calling.

In the last few feet before the door, the light reflected back, giving Zed a view of two pairs of legs. They stepped up to the door, between her and the hand holding the light, two people standing in profiles. Luc's trademark hat gave him away, while the crushed torpedo head of his follower was no less distinctive: Hammer. Luc opened the door and the sound of splashing water grew along with the putt-putt of an engine. "Hand me the little darling," Luc said and took the double armload with a grunt. "I think your work here is done," Luc told Hammer. "Usual payment, usual time, righty-o?"

Hammer grunted an affirmative and held out his hand, "Light."

"As I told you," Luc said. "Zed has mine, for now. I will return this one later."

Hammer's hand didn't move.

Luc recognized an immovable force. "Fine, just let me get some light in here." The light moved away, leaving Zed and Hammer in the darkness. She breathed lightly, listening to Hammer wheezing through his clogged nostrils. She tried to remain calm; her rational brain was waiting for the light to come back while the rest was waiting for Hammer's meaty fingers to grab her hair, a prelude to her head being ripped clean off. Luckily, Luc came back, *sans* package.

"Here's your precious flashlight," Luc said, handing it over. "I'm surprised you haven't named it."

"Mine," Hammer growled.

"Quite," said Luc. "Unimaginative, yet distinctive." He gave a wave of his fingers. "Well, mustn't keep you from your busy life."

Hammer grunted and trudged his way back up the slope.

Zed crept to the doorway and peeked around the corner. Luc was in the far corner of the room, his back to her as he leaned over a portable generator. The room was divided into two sections: closest to her was a deep-blue tiled pool, two-thirds full with water as the stream tumbled over a three-foot waterfall. The second part was a long hall with mirrors and a ballet barre on one wall; it was lined with rows of wooden chairs, benches, even pews, all facing a stage surmounted by a monstrous throne. The ceiling was high and decorated in blue with gold trim, mermaids and dolphins over the pool with bearded figures looking down. Along one wall were tables, stacked with candles twinkling brightly. The generator hummed steadily, and the two attached fans blew along with a heater. While Luc was occupied, Zed scurried round the pool and disappeared into the chairs, worming her way up between the legs.

The air was cold and dry, like the inside of a fridge. Yet it stank, a cloying mixture of scents: potpourri and rotting meat. Zed was reminded of a remark she heard one junkie exclaim to another: "Stop chewing that damn gum, man; your breath smells like you took a shit on a mint plant." It was something of the same horrible mix of sweet and foul that gagged Zed every time she took a breath.

But that, as Zed found out when she peeped up over the chairs, was the good news. In front of the throne stood a squat block of stone. And above that, suspended from the ceiling by chains, was the naked dead body of Bottomless Joe. His head lolled against his chest and a crude stitching ran up his torso and around his head. It seemed that Luc was still pissed at Joe.

Now that Zed's eyes had adjusted, she was wishing they hadn't. She could see what was making the stench: the bodies filling the chairs. Rotten corpses occupied row after row of chairs, cheekbones showing through the hanging flaps of skin, leg and arm bones where the flesh had been withered away; and their skin was shiny like dried leather, or squirming indistinctly below the surface, telling Zed that she didn't want to look too close.

Zed could recognize some of them: Quince and Brandy Bob, Valerie, Mabel and Sam and others. Those who had died over the last year, and who knew how many years before that.

This is bad, Zed told herself. And not just because this was the worst located Rec. Room in the history of apartment blocks. No, this time she had really entered the secret world of Luc, and it made her long for empty rooms and wooden desks. If she was found, she'd be joining this gang in about two seconds flat, the time it would take Luc to break her neck.

Zed could hear the long rasp of the zipper as Luc opened the black morgue bag he'd placed on the stage. "Out we come," Luc said, shucking the bag from the body. It was Pete, naked, with a thick stitching transcending her naked body from throat to groin. "Not a bad job," Luc conceded, running his hands over the stitching. He moved her over to a short triple row of chairs off to the right. "I think you'll go nicely in the choir." He pushed her into an empty seat in the second row. Pulling back, he rubbed against a small, wizened corpse, whose most notable features were the wisps of long red hair that splayed from the skin-wrapped skull.

Luc's brush caused the head, hair and all, to fall off into the decomposed lap of its neighbour. Luc sighed, picked up the head, dusted off its cheeks, and perched it atop the neck again. He smiled, stepped back, and surveyed the choir.

After a few seconds, he walked up onto the podium, taking off his jacket, which he placed on the seat of the throne.

He turned and walked to the altar, drawing out the black case she'd seen him use upstairs with Steve. He placed it on the altar and rolled up the sleeve of his right arm. Opening the case, Luc took out the syringe, still full of heroin from his mind-game with Steve. Luc closed his eyes.

"By the life you give me," Luc jabbed the needle into his arm, pushing the plunger home, "I bind you." He had time for two short breaths and a flash of teeth and then it hit. His eyes stretched wide, and his lips pulled back in a snarl. He dropped to his knees, his fingers digging into his head as he let out a scream: one long note, strong and piercing. He breathed and screamed again, same note, same despair, same anguish, and same madness. It began to trail off, turning into low laughter.

"Now that," Luc said, standing up to put away the syringe before taking out his blade, "is some high-grade smack." He pulled a sterile pad from his pocket and placed it on the stone. With a flick, he cut himself along the vein, his blood flowing red down his arm and pooling on the stone altar. "And by my blood, I bind you!" He slapped the pad into place, bending his arm up to hold it on. "I paid the price for you," he told his audience, "sold by lust and bought in blood, by the old contract." He chuckled and looked up to Bottomless Joe. "Even you, old dog, though your tax was a bit piecemeal." He pulled out the vial and smiled.

Zed had been worried before, but now she just wanted out. Luc was bad enough, but a Luc that took lethal doses of H and then laughed before claiming the dead, or perhaps the living, with blood, was someone she wanted nothing of.

Luc checked his arm. The bleeding had soaked the original bandage, so he replaced it with another, taping this one on with surgical tape. He wandered down the stairs to the main floor and slowly paced the aisles.

"Jacob, you old gambler. Susie, still giving tricks. Well, well, if it isn't Mabel. Another bottle of 'medicine'?" Luc chuckled. He stopped near the choir.

"I really dislike incomplete collections. Call me a perfectionist, but there it is." Luc reached out his hand and stroked Pete's cheek. "Little Charles should be here. What a cute pair you two would make. And he would have come, if only I had more time." Luc sighed. "At least you're one of mine, paid in full: amphetamines and betting slips." He bent over, looking under the drooping lid to the fixed, unblinking eye. "I get what I paid for. It's business." He turned to the red-haired head he had saved earlier. "Body and soul, you know, that's the deal."

He shook a finger at them. "You're just being unco-operative. But that's fine, I can wait." He pointed to the fans and generator. "See, every time it rains I keep you nice and toasty." He walked up to the podium and retrieved his jacket, easing it on over the bandage. "If there's anything else you need, you only have to ask." He packed away the syringe. "No? Like I said, I'll wait, and just keep adding while I wait." Leaning down, he retrieved the morgue bag, zipped it shut, then folded it and tucked it under his arm.

Luc was getting ready to leave and Zed was panicking, her heart thumping. Luc whistled a happy tune, puttering about on the edge of the podium. Zed raced through the possibilities: run for the door, likely seen: stay put, likely seen. Hide somewhere in the room, likely be locked in the dark with lots of dead people. There did not seem to be many choices. Luc started walking down the aisle. Zed gave up and just wormed her way to the middle and darkest part of the row. She could hear him approach, a step at time. When he got to her row, he stopped.

"Ohh, my favourite part," Luc said, and he started to blow out the candles, one by one. The room grew dim. Zed kept her eyes two rows ahead, focused on a pair of black legs ending in bone. The feet were on the floor, gravity separating them from the anklebones. Luc stopped and took a few deep breaths. "Whoa. Bit of hyperventilation." He took a couple more breaths before continuing.

The room was twilight and Zed couldn't see the detached feet anymore. She gripped the flashlight firm in her hand. It made her feel better. Above her Luc was counting, "Eight..." a gust, "Seven..." a gust, "six..." When he got to two, he said, "Well, you little fellows can come with me."

Zed heard a noise above her and then Luc's footsteps walking slowly away. Soon the click of his footsteps disappeared beneath the sound of the waterfall. She waited. Was that the click of the door she heard? Was he gone? It was very dark, but Zed tried not to think at all, she just took slow breaths, counted them. After twenty, she decided, just ten more and she would put on the light. When she reached the tenth breath, she pushed the button. Light, glorious light.

Zed threw her light around the pool room. It was empty. That was good. The door, however, was open and that was bad. Was he coming back? She grabbed her satchel; it was time to go. She moved in a crouch out from the chairs, past the candle rows, and towards the pool. She knew logically that crouching didn't make her safer, but it felt better so what the heck.

She was halfway round the pool when a tile cracked off underfoot, throwing her to her hands and knees. She watched as the flashlight, flying loose from her hand, bounced once, twice, and then flipped over into the pool. The gleam of light sank to the bottom of the pool. Shit! The gleam went out, the water must have gotten in. Double shit.

Okay, Zed told herself, *this is bad, but do-able.* She could edge round the pool, find the door, and go up endless ramps by touch. Pleasant, no, but possible.

So she took a breath and forced herself to stand. Arms out, she felt the brush of the wall on her right. Another breath and she started to move; edge around, edge around. She was doing it, it was okay, and she figured the door would be soon. Right on schedule, her fingers ran out of wall, just hit space. Then they hit something warm and firm: human flesh, live human flesh. And while she was trying to work that through she felt the force of two hands push into her chest. She was flying and she heard a scream. *Is that me?* she thought. *I don't scream.* And she hit the water, ice cold.

She dropped the satchel; it was dragging her down anyway, and pulled with her arms and kicked. Her head broke the surface and she screamed again. But as soon as she screamed, the cold hit her like a punch and she dropped under again. She clawed back to the top and sucked in a few breaths. Damn, it was cold. It seemed so hard to stay on the surface. She drifted below the spout and the torrent of cold water beat her down below. She was so cold and so tired. She struck up with her arms until she got her nose above the water. How could she be so heavy? Her head slipped under the water again and she kicked and struggled back up. "Hel..." she tried to call out. "He...." No, she wasn't going to call that; she wasn't going to cry out for help, like some newbie, she was Zed, dammit. Zed. Her head slipped under. And somewhere in the back of her mind a voice told her to not worry about it. Wasn't she tired, wasn't she cold, don't worry about it, the little voice was very calm and soothing. Screw that. She raised her energy and kicked again. "Fuck!" she cried, her head breaking the surface. "Fucker." The word was barely a whisper. Time to go to bed, the voice in her head told her, and she was just too tired to argue anymore. She turned her head and slipped below.

Chapter 9

ZED WAS DEAD. This was a relief to the brain stem which found, when things simply had to get done, Zed's brain a big distraction. There were still messages coming in from all over the body, way too many messages really. Still, there was this urgent one from the lungs and blood screaming something about oxygen. Brain stem knew how to deal with that, you hit the emergency eject. Before you could say "heave-ho," water was erupting from every orifice imaginable. The body, meanwhile, was going feral. It felt that if it could just get into that position where it had spent the first, and let's face it, the best months, somehow everything would be all right. But just as the knees were getting tucked under the chin, Zed's brain started churning, dropping her consciousness into the pool of fire which constitutes a full scale alert. Zed, caught between the panicked wailing of her brain and the screaming of her body, flopped around doing the funky chicken. She was dimly aware that there was light again, and she could feel someone's hands turning her over, but this was but one of so many sensations that the information rolled down the list from interesting to irrelevant.

With a wrench from her gut, she heaved up another pint and then took a long, shuddering breath. Now that the lungs were only mildly complaining, the other parts of her body started telling her the news. She was cold. Her hands and feet were so cold that they didn't even want to communicate anymore. "Ooooo," Zed moaned. It felt good to put some of her pain in words, or at least vowel sounds. "Ooooooooo."

"Shh." A damp hand stroked her brow. She could feel her head being lifted, which made her lungs protest with a new attack of coughing. Didn't matter, the head was up, and her feet lifted too. Lots of new sensations were coming in and Zed wished things would go a little slower. There was a metallic squeal as a door was opened, then the click of a switch. Zed opened her eyes and looked up at dusty tubes of neon. They grew nearer in jerks, then passed overhead. Someone was carrying her up stairs. That's nice, she thought, and shut her eyes again.

Opening her eyes, she remembered something she wanted to tell. "C … c … cold!" she informed the face above her, a face that looked vaguely familiar. The head nodded, wet hair stuck to the forehead. They continued up the stairs. Zed had her eyes open and was losing that strange drifting feeling. Her eyes watched the fingers curled around the bare skin of her shoulder. They were strong fingers, long and white: comfortable, familiar fingers. Her eyes travelled around the stairwell. It was dusty, the walls pitted concrete covered in black soot and old withered cobwebs. It was, Zed realized, quite a remarkable stairwell. Remarkable because it was not the inter-level stairway, nor the west stairway, or even the east stairway. She had never seen these stairs before. Odd, that. Her eyes fell to her shoulder and she realized she was staring at skin, bare-naked skin. She raised her head a little and then let it sink back with a moan; she was naked from head to toe.

There was a metallic screech and a long swoop and she was deposited, full body on concrete. The pale man from the elevator gave her a look over his shoulder as he hurried away. There was a square of light and him framed, then he was gone.

Zed looked around. She was lying by a sliding door, Gears' sliding door to be precise. Listening, she could hear the low murmur of conversation. She started slapping the metal with her open hand. "Open," slap, "The," slap, "Fucking," slap, "Door!"

"Open, Sesame," Gears' voice came through the door.

"I thought that the phrase only worked outside doors," a male voice commented.

"No, inside and out."

Zed gave another slap before sinking back down on the concrete. Her body was telling her that it was uncomfortable and wanted to move. She told it to go right ahead. That shut it up.

With a grind of the rollers, the door pulled back. "Whoa, it's a foundling," Gears said.

"No, it's Zed." The Father knelt beside her. "She's still breathing. Help me get her in."

"Of course she's breathing," Gears said. "Can't you see her quivering like that? I used to have a dog that would do that when he got excited."

"Less on the dog and more on the lifting," the Father suggested.

"Orders in the velvet glove, that's what it comes down to." Gears grabbed her feet and lifted. "I always knew you couldn't separate religion and authority. They say 'make your own choice,' but in the end it's 'do this, do that.'"

They brought her in and wrapped her in blankets, which smelled like motor oil and grease, but Zed wasn't feeling picky. The Father rubbed her arms and legs until the shivers went away.

"What happened?" the Father asked at last.

That was the tricky part. The Father had seen her going down. "Nothing," Zed replied.

"And did nothing take all your clothes? Zed, whatever happened, you don't have to be ashamed."

"Zed got porked?" Gears asked.

Great, Zed thought, *now they think I've been rolled and fricasseed.* "I fell into some water. Fell in. Lost my stuff while I was trying to swim."

"Swim?"

"I don't know," Zed said. "I remember going under, and next thing I know, I'm coughing up a lung."

The Father put a hand on her head. "Sounds like God was watching over you."

Gears laughed. "Classic, she loses everything and God likes her. You've almost got me converted."

"Is God pale with brown hair?" Zed asked.

Gears' head whipped around at the question and he studied her through narrowed eyes.

"Um," the Father said, scratching his chin, "everyone sees God in his own way, but generally no, not pale with brown hair. But trust me, God was with you."

"Sounds like someone was," Gears frowned. "Hey, where are you off to?" he asked the Father, who was opening the door.

"She's safe, she's recovering, and I've got, um, preparations to make."

"Oh, no. You've got that 'Let's all go out into the jungle and drink Kool-Aid' look."

"Where God leads, I must follow." He gave Zed a wink and slipped out.

Gears looked at the closed door. "That man is a walking advertisement for agnosticism."

"What's agnostisicm?" Zed asked, warming up at last.

"You," Gears told her.

"Oh." Zed frowned. "You ever hear anything about another stairwell?"

Gears looked down at her quickly, an odd look on his face, maybe angry, maybe cautious. "What makes you ask that?"

Zed may have been drowned, frozen, and naked, but she knew a defensive reaction when she saw it. She avoided the "And what makes you ask that?" and said, "Just curious about this place."

"You've turned into a real history buff." Gears kept his eyes locked on her.

"I'm into new experiences," she said, stealing one of his catch-phrases.

"Mmmm. Well, we should all experience the new. So you've wised up and started looking into the fabric of our realities." Gears leaned against the workbench with a grim smile. "You want to know what this was, this was Utopia, my little Heroditus, at least on paper.... Building of the Future, the low-income answer, a complex of buildings creating a community in the urban centre. Get it?"

"No." Gears was chanting out the usual gobbledy-gook.

"Then listen up. We are living the urban dream, leaving our dream apartments in our day-glo-coloured cars, amusing ourselves in the building's amusement and fitness centres, going to the adjoining clinic and starting our business in the low-cost, small business offices adjoining this building, dig?" He gave a staccato laugh.

"What clinic?"

"The one on paper. For you see, once this building was finished the city talked about cost, about resources, reanalysis, and reapportionment. They studied and debated and a couple decades later...." Gears' arms spread to take in the hanging bumpers and empty bed-racks. "Paradise."

"Oh." Zed was pretty warm by now and let the blanket fall off her shoulders. "And the stairwell?"

"I have no idea what you're talking about," he deadpanned.

Zed learned that you get more from sneak attacks than frontal assaults. She let that one lie. "So why do you still live here?"

"Family commitments."

Everything suddenly snapped together. "You're Ivy's son!" Her eyes gleamed. "Ivy was talking about family and –"

She was interrupted by peals of laughter. "Ivy? My mother?" He broke off laughing again.

Zed gave a stiff smile. Okay. She screwed up. Happens to everyone once in a while.

"Ivy, I'm home! I'm the son you never knew."

"Ha, ha. Can we do business? I need a new satchel."

Gears nodded, still laughing to himself as he turned to start poking through the boxes. "Hey, Ivy ... Mom!" He came back with a blue carry bag.

"Maybe, how much?"

Gears held up two fingers, setting his price in the currency of Gears' country, the joint. Thus all things translated into them: one DVD to the joint, one CD to the joint, two packs of cigs to the joint, etc.

Zed just raised her eyebrows. One of Gears' fingers wilted back down into his fist. She nodded. "How much for a –" Zed felt a flush coming on her face, "– knife?"

"Got a pocket job," Gears told her, "suitable for sociopathic boy scouts." He took from the drawer a hard, black, five-inch plug and tossed it over.

Zed pulled out the blade and tested it on her thumb. It was sharp enough. "How much?"

"Five?"

Zed snorted. That was outrageous. "Three."

Gears looked at the sliding door. "Long dark stairs out there," he mentioned, just in passing.

"It's a spare."

"Five."

"It's only a pocket knife."

He held up a hand, with thumb and fingers outstretched.

Zed sighed but nodded. She slung the bag over her shoulder, opened the knife blade, and held it ready in her right hand. The blanket was wrapped around her.

"The blanket is two," came the quiet voice.

She looked back. Gears was grinning, enjoying this. "I'm just borrowing it," she told him.

"I know. That's the price I'm quoting."

Zed laughed. Gears sure knew when it was a seller's market. She stepped out of the blanket and let it fall to the floor. "Later." And she was out the door. She didn't look back.

NAKED, PISSED, AND trembling, she made it. First she outfitted herself and then reviewed. Bad: she was out her best knife, all her backup clothes, trading stock from the Food Truck, and her clothes were damp. Good: she was alive, so screw the damp. She was alive and Rat was selling for her. Someone had elected Zed for snuffed #3, and that pissed her off. But she'd find them.

Chapter 10

ZED TRACKED RAT to the 7th floor. The screaming helped her narrow it down, not Rat's but his victims'; they all had the same "Help get this thing off of me" edge.

The screams died away as Zed came up the stairs. She'd have to get there quickly, sounded like Rat's playtime was over.

She pulled open the 7th floor door to find Rat crouched over Bucket Charlie's limp form. A blood-splatter and a red snail trail down the wall told the story. Rat, sporting a black headband, was prying a jug from Charlie's hand. Rat's bulging sack lay along the wall. Bucket Charlie's eyes were open, watching her approach, his nerve endings dead from chronic abuse.

"Betty done another batch, partner?" Zed stressed the last word.

"That's what I'm finding out." Rat uncorked the jug and took a swig. "Oh, baby." He gave a shiver. "Best drink this week."

Betty did batches of what she called "bathtub gin" and what the rest of the world might call enamel-and-paint stripper. But the main attraction was price; it was the cheapest around, even including Betty's cut to Luc.

"What you want?" Rat demanded, squinting at her.

"Sixty-seven percent."

"Deal's off," he growled.

Zed slowly nodded, appearing to think the idea over. But what she was thinking was, *why oh why did she have to lose her switch-blade now? She couldn't just step back and unfold her knife, what kind of surprise attack would that be?*

Zed finished her nod, reached down and grabbed Rat's hair, pulling his head back. She slipped out her knife and held the thin, closed blade against Rat's throat. She gave Charlie a quick look, telling him to keep his mouth shut.

"Shouldn't double cross someone while they're standing over you," Zed told Rat.

Rat took a slow swallow. "Remember that." His eyes caught hers. "What's up, partner?"

"Trying to decide what percentage to take," she said.

"Fifty percent?" Rat suggested, ever helpful.

She just stared at him. Rat closed his eyes as he forced the painful words out. "Sixty-seven percent?"

Zed gave him a thin-lipped smile and tightened her hold on his hair as she pushed the flat metal in.

Thinking his time had come, Rat bleated, "Fuck, take what you want."

Zed gave him a nod, tucked the knife away, and let go of his hair. "Sure thing, partner."

Rat rubbed his throat. "Always with the fucking busy hands. I don't like dealing with you."

"Cuz you can't rob me blind?"

"Yeah!" Rat's voice held back an "of course." "What are you laughing at?" he demanded, turning to Charlie, whose body was quivering on the floor, his face a grin.

"Nothing," Zed said firmly. "Nothing!" She glared at Charlie. His left eyelid dipped in a wink.

Zed stepped over Rat and pulled open the bag. It was a mishmash of everything under the sun: a radio, canned food, sunglasses, scarves, CDs, a DVD, some books, some odd utensils, a couple packs of cigarettes, two cigars, and a plug of tobacco.

Hunkering down, Zed pulled out the books, all the tobacco products, the CDs and the DVD.

Rat looked longingly at the growing pile at Zed's feet. "Hey, you're getting all the good stuff," he whined.

Zed picked up the DVD. "You really want *Bambi*?"

"Fuck, yes."

"You got a thing for deer?" Zed asked, reading the back.

"Fuck deer, that's about a woman with big jugs."

She pointed to the wide-eyed fawn on the cover. Rat rolled his eyes in disgust. Zed reached back into the bag and took a can.

"I've been saving that!" he told her, grabbing for it.

She pulled it out of his reach. "Eat a lot of ... artichokes?"

"You sure that's not anchovies?"

Zed shook her head.

Rat slumped back with a disappointed growl. Somedays, life was set against you.

Zed tucked the goodies in her bag before she looked back to Charlie. He had pushed himself into a sitting position. "I gotta job for you," she told him.

"Pushing people down stairs?" he asked, giving Rat surreptitious glances.

"Not yet." She turned to Rat. "Any more armbands?"

Rat looked her straight in the eye. "Fuck, no."

"Okay, partner, here's the deal. You give me the jug and you can keep the rest of the armbands."

"I don't fucking have no armbands," Rat told her as he handed over the jug. "And now I don't have no gin either."

"You can trade for more from Betty."

"But she's already got an armband."

Zed handed the jug to Charlie, who unscrewed and upended it in a single smooth motion. Zed grabbed his arm when he came up for air. "This is the job: you have to ask around and see if anyone's looking for me." *Or rather*, Zed thought to herself, *to see if anyone thinks they know where I should be – at the bottom of a pool.* Charlie's head bobbed in agreement.

"And the first person you ask," she told him, "is Luc."

Charlie blanched at that, but nodded. She took her hand off and he chugged it down.

"Fucker," Rat told him, mesmerized by the disappearing liquid.

Zed hitched her bag round her shoulder and gave Charlie the nod to follow her. "Later," she told Rat.

"Not if I'm fast enough."

Just then, the stairwell door opened, spilling in Don and a pack of One-Light goons.

"There he is," Don barked out, pointing at Rat, "the dog who tries to profit from Countessa's gifts. The scab who leeches from the dead."

"Wha?" Rat scrambled to his feet.

Zed so very much wanted to fall moaning at Don's feet, saying, "All I wanted was to see the Countessa, and after he took all I had, sob, sob, he said it still wasn't enough." But instead, she just stood silent.

"Come on," Don said, striding past Zed with the group following. "Let us go reason with him."

Rat sensed it was time to go and without a word he leapt up, grabbed his bag, and legged it.

At the sight of Rat's bag, the One-Light group let out a howl and ran in close pursuit.

"And that's our exit," Zed told Charlie, ducking into the stairwell. It was only four flights up to Luc's, but Zed had to stop for a breather. Her lungs were hurting something powerful. Getting drowned really sucked up the energy. At the 10th floor, Charlie was greeted by his stairwell cronies.

"Business," he told them, touching a finger to the side of his nose. Those conscious enough looked from Charlie to Zed and dug each other in the ribs. "Business, heh, heh."

"Just go," Zed told Charlie.

"I can't just walk in, what am I going in for?" Charlie asked. "I could trade some of your cigs for a fifth?"

"You could be looking for Stu for some more 'exchange,'" she countered.

Charlie shuddered at the name of Stu. "Just give me the plug and I'll see what I can get."

Zed fished out the plug and handed it over. Charlie opened the door and disappeared into the hallway. Zed looked down. The rummies of the stairs were all watching her. "What?" she demanded, staring them down. "What?"

They didn't say anything. She gave up and walked down the stairs, where Ben P. was rubbing his newly shaved head.

"Been having fun?" Zed asked, looking down at his arms.

"You've seen my babies." Ben's arms were a mass of bruising and track marks. "I got this thing, you know, for that white high tower, the H, which I can't really talk about except that, sure, my veins have collapsed, legs too, you know, and see this spot in my eye." He raised his head and pulled up a lid to show an angry red blotch. "Did a needle there last week, but can't do that too often, see, so I shoot up in my dick, but hey, who doesn't."

"Me," Zed told him.

"Yeah, but is that because you don't inject or because you're a girl, which I have heard rumours about." Ben licked his lips, his tongue tracing the cracks and crusts. "But I also heard you're like a boy, which I could kind of see, so can I check?" He reached a hand toward the coveralls.

"No." Zed stepped back.

"Okay, I understand. I mean, I'd probably do the same thing in your place."

"You're whacked, aren't you?" Zed asked.

"No, well, maybe. I mean, I took some meth, yeah, and some speed, yeah, and some tide-me-over white pills, so you know, whatever." He gave her a big-mouth grin.

"You know Cal?"

"Reefer, thinks he's hot stuff? Yeah, we hang, when I'm mellow. Why?"

"Whatever," Zed said.

"Yeah, exactly. Whatever."

Charlie descended the stairs holding three mini-bottles of Scotch. "Lookie, lookie."

"You ask?"

"Yeah. He just wants his flashlight. That make sense?"

Zed reached over and took two of the bottles. Too much sense. "Keep asking around and look me up later, and you'll get these back." She walked up the stairs, leaving Charlie and Ben P. blinking at each other.

Barry was guarding the door, his face splotchy and covered in sweat. He looked so bad Zed only gave him an elbow as she went by. He just moaned.

Mistress Anna was in front of the desk laying out her stack of bills for Luc. "I want forty dollars on Stu," she told him. "And ten dollars on you, for old times' sake." She leaned over and blew him a kiss.

Luc touched his hat. "Obliged."

"Now for snuffed," Mistress Anna continued. "An even spread on Christina and –" She caught sight of Zed waiting behind her. "Um, and on the fourth name down." Zed looked at the board. Hers was the fourth name down.

"Thirty dollars on Christina and thirty dollars on Zed," Luc intoned. He looked up and gave Zed a grin. "Always a pleasure." He ripped off a stub and passed it over. Mistress Anna tucked it demurely into the top of her brassiere.

"Good luck, honey," Mistress Anna told Zed as she left.

For life or death, Zed wondered. "Business good?"

"Business is great." Luc smiled. "The only thing that would top it off is if you went down and killed Christina. A bonus in it."

Zed shook her head.

"Keep it in mind. And there is a heap of money riding on you, so try to avoid stabbings, falls, and drownings."

Zed played it cool, her heart going rat-a-tat. "Why drowning?"

"The other two were found in water, remember." He looked her over. "Why are you so freaked?"

"I hate water."

"Since when?"

"Today."

"Good thing it's stopped raining then." Zed took a peek outside. He was right.

"So what is up, you look half dead?"

If that's a reference to his hobby, Zed thought, Luc is one sick dude. "I need some joints," she said, laying out the tobacco and the DVD.

"First, where's my flashlight?"

"Stolen. I'll pay for it." In a couple of days when the pool had drained, Zed would have to retrieve her things. Hopefully before Luc saw them.

"Stolen? From you?"

Zed shrugged.

"I'll take the DVD?" Luc looked it over. "*Bambi?* We're running out of the short stuff and you bring me *Bambi?*"

"You picked it, not me," Zed told him. "Gimme six for the tobacco."

He looked at the two crumpled packs of cigs and the two cigars. "Three, but only because I like you."

"How about five and I'll let you hate me."

"I'm almost starting to, four."

"Nope, I need five."

"Four." He gave that crooked smile, which meant he wasn't kidding anymore. Fine, she'd take what she could get. Zed nodded. Luc handed four over before putting one of the cigars in his mouth and lighting it up. After a few draws on the cigar, he blew a cascade of rings. "My profit, up in smoke."

There was a groan at the door and Barry's pasty face looked in. "I gotta lie down, I gotta lie down," he moaned before stumbling off. Luc was not amused.

"I'm going to make a new gang," he said, staring at the doorway. "I've just decided. I'm going back to the basics, displease me and you have to cut off a finger." He looked over at Zed. "You want a job in a growth industry?"

"I like my fingers."

"I'd make an exception for you."

"Aren't I a little small for thugging?"

"You'll grow into it," he assured her, waving his hand.

"*Luuucc*!" There was a slurred drunken call from the door.

Ellen staggered in, staring at Zed. "Luc?" She spied him at the desk. "There you are, you little devil." She tried to approach his desk, but mistimed the stop and fell over the desk, ending up in his lap. "Naughty, naughty," Ellen told him, wagging her finger at his nose as she tried to slither out from his lap. She succeeded and crumpled to the floor. "Wine," she cried from the floor, "gimme wine."

"You see why I need you?" Luc looked to Zed. "Five minutes and this is what happens. Be a darling and give her a few kicks in the ribs, won't you?"

Zed looked down at Ellen, who was mumbling to herself. "Bloody wine, want some wine." Zed shook her head.

"Naw," she told Luc. "But I can hire someone to do it for you."

"You're subcontracting a rib kick?"

Zed was spared answering by Ellen lurching off the floor and placing her hands on Luc's desk. "Wine," she told him. "Wine for the woman, wine for the song." She opened her mouth and let out a heart-stopping wail that staggered into "Blue Velvet."

"That's it!" Luc shouted over the song, standing up. "That is it." He walked around the desk and, grabbing Ellen by the hair, turned to the door and flung her out. There was a meaty thud as she hit the opposite wall. Luc pulled out a half bottle of red from his cabinet and disappeared into the hall. He returned moments later, the bottle gone. "Or she'll just come back," Luc explained, and blew another smoke ring.

Zed looked to the door. "I gotta go. Will I see you tonight?"

"A little too...." Luc's hands oscillated. "It would not do to be seen swigging from the neck of the bottle, no? But run along. Remember: kill all the children and there's a percentage in it for you."

"How much for just one?"

"First do it, then we talk."

Next stop was the Prof's. She had to drop off the books she owed. She threw her bag over her shoulder and headed up the stairs. After the Prof's, she'd hit Hammer to try prying some info out of him. While Hammer knew more about these deaths than he was telling, getting it out was going to be no picnic. But when it came to hiding information, Gears, Luc, and Countessa were up there on the list. Zed shook her head; she was starting to sound like Rat.

"And where are you rushing off to?" The words broke through Zed's thoughts.

"Ivy?"

"Only one of me. And where are you going so quick that you knock down strangers on the way?"

"The Professor's."

"Off to see that rude man and no time for tea?" Ivy rebuked, then turned to peer down as a stairwell door opened two floors below.

"Ivy?"

Ivy waved Zed quiet. "I'm after the slick one, and his man," she whispered.

"He's down in his office. I was just there. You want Barry or Stu?"

"Barry, aye. The one named like a town, not like a pot of potatoes. And how were they faring?"

"Fine, but Barry went to lie down."

"Ailing, was he?" Ivy was almost dancing about in her joy. "A little queasy." She gave a clap. "But nothing with that slick man?"

Zed shook her head.

Ivy held her chin. "Something needs doing there." She opened the door to the hallway and wandered off. "Must attend."

Great, Zed thought, *even Ivy's got a plan going on. Why don't I have a plan? I'll get to it, after I pay off the debts.* And, she reminded herself, if she was paying off debts, she'd better put Ivy's blanket on the list.

Up on the 16th, the Professor was already in the hall, hanging about. Well, more like lurking and accosting anyone who came by. "Your hand, your hand," the Professor screeched, dancing about her. "You must let me see your hand."

Before she could regret it, Zed held out her hand.

"Ha, ha, look at this love line." The Prof turned her hand to the light. "Hmm, double life line. Are you a vampire, by any chance?" He didn't wait for her answer but plunged on. "Your third finger is that of a man's, but the rest are children's. Wait and see, that's all I can advise."

Zed nodded and ducked into the Professor's. She unloaded the books and some basic food staples. She took his pills and two mysteries from the "read" box. The food/pill swap wasn't a verbal thing because the Prof had as much interest in food as in pills. But if it was around, he ate it. And, Zed figured, if he didn't eat, he wouldn't be around. And while the Prof didn't like his pills, a lot of Luc's customers did.

But something the Professor had said made a connection with Zed. A man's finger? It was right there, on the tip of her brain, when Steve's voice cut through her thoughts.

"Whoa, dude, what's with the hand grabbing?"

"Have you seen this line of influence? It's fire," the Prof responded. Zed thought she'd better get out there.

"Light, more light!" The Professor was twisting Steve's hand from side to side. "No, that's Goethe, the tree of life is green, no?"

Steve wore the same black t-shirt and as he peered through his hair at the Professor. "Man, whatever you're on," Steve said, "can I, like, have some?"

"Unusual love line, mmm." The Prof looked at Steve penetratingly. "Cigar? Knife? Sausage? Mother? Wizard of Oz?"

Steve pulled his hand out of the Professor's grasp. "I don't know what you are on about," he protested, backing up.

"Yup." Zed watched Steve edging away. "You really know how to charm them."

"His hand," the Professor protested in a pout. He frowned and retreated toward his door. "Watch the eyes and don't blink, that's when they get you," he advised Zed before sticking out his tongue and closing the door.

Zed just shook her head and loped after Steve. "Hey Steve, going tonight?"

Steve turned and waited for her. "Zed. Naw, I can't afford one of the armbands."

Zed looked at Steve. She felt oddly protective toward him. His face was looking better, the bruises from Rat's attack going, though he still hid it behind the hair. His eyes had a hint of glass, high but functional. "Anyone looking for me?" she asked.

Steve just shook his head. "No one said anything to me."

Zed gave her nose a tap. "You don't need an armband."

"What?"

She leaned toward Steve. "Go tonight, you won't need an armband."

"Yeah, you will, Rat was selling them." Steve nodded earnestly.

"Steve," Zed crooked her finger and twitched it toward her to get him to lean down. "Listen to me carefully; you don't need an armband tonight." She tapped her nose significantly. "Get it?"

"Ahhh!" Steve grinned and tapped his nose. "I don't need an armband." He stood and a puzzled expression spread across his face. "Why not?"

Zed sighed. "Just go tonight if you want, and if they ask, tell them you're a friend of mine."

"I am?"

"Just for tonight."

"Cool." Steve was standing taller already. He played with his hair, twisting it around his index finger. He asked shyly, "Does that mean I can hang with Luc?"

"You want to?"

"No." He licked his lips. "Maybe."

"Don't tell Luc you're a friend of mine." Zed didn't want to think what strange acts of humour that might produce from Luc.

"Oh." Steve was crestfallen.

Zed was starting to remember why she didn't have friends; they were a pain in the ass. "Just go," she told him and strode off, ignoring his goodbye wave.

As she approached the stairwell door, it opened and Burl came through. Seemed like you couldn't approach a door without someone blocking your way. Everyone was out and about, turning the hallways into highways.

Zed watched as Burl strode past purposefully. He stopped at a door halfway down the hall and gave it three raps before yelling, "God's will."

The door opened and a frowning female face looked out, grey hair tucked back. "I'm eating, dear."

"Father's called a meeting, my place."

The woman shuffled forward, revealing her shapeless, wildly-coloured muumuu. "Another? I'm eating, but I'll come in a bit."

"This is the big one," Burl told her. "Father's had a sign."

"He said that?"

Burl gave a shy smile. "Well, not in those words, but I can read between the lines."

"I'll be right up," she promised and closed the door, leaving Burl to stride on.

Zed was getting irritated. Used to be people would be despondent and lazy, you could depend on them. But now, everyone was a fanatic, running around yelling catch-phrases. From where she sat, only she and Gears were left of the independents. Gears? There was something she had been trying to remember about Gears.

Suddenly all the hair stood up on the back of Zed's neck, and she knew she needed to see Gears right now. Hammer could wait, but what she had to ask needed to be asked before Gears left for the feast. She made a run for the stairs.

Down in the sub-parkade, she reminded herself to calm down. Take a deep breath, she told herself, and look normal, act normal, everything is normal. She hammered on Gears' door.

"Hi ho?" The door slid back.

Zed held up the four joints. "Your payoff, you extortionist."

Gears took the joints with a smile. "Now, who taught you a word like that?" He retreated inside, Zed following. "Besides, I'm not an extortionist, I'm a profiteer; I ride the tides of fortune, and you still owe me two."

Zed took out five CDs and slapped them on the counter.

"It's only one a joint," Gears told her.

"I know. How about I buy a couple questions?"

"Sure." Gears gave a shrug.

"How come I was brought to your door?" *Let's not pussyfoot around*, thought Zed.

"Had to go somewhere."

"No, I remember. I was brought right ... to ... *your* ... door."

"What do you mean?"

"I mean, why not the lobby, why not anywhere else? Why did they think I would be safe with you?"

Gears smiled, not his spaced-and-all-peace smile but something a wolf would wear. "We care about you," he said softly, advancing. "Strange, but we do."

"We?" Zed backed up. Maybe that had been a bad line of questioning to start with.

Gears kept advancing, dropping his hand toward her. She went for her knife, folding blade be damned.

"Empty," Gears said, opening his hand toward her. She gave up on the knife. He lowered his hand with a strange smile, pushed back her bangs and looked into her eyes. "Can you even feel it, that desire, that life, so strong? Your aura is blue, through and through."

"Gears?" Zed backed away, only to find she was already pressed against the metal door.

Gears' finger traced across her forehead, cool and soft. She shivered. "You're so young," Gears sighed, "and you've felt so much, yet so little. I envy you, you know that?" He stopped, but didn't seem to want an answer, his finger dropping to her cheek. "All those intense experiences. I've never drowned, you know, I've felt the wind in my hair, a motorbike throbbing under me, but I've never died, never felt my life slip away, murdered." He rolled the last word out. "Delicious."

"Who...." Zed's throat had dried up. She tried again. "Who said I was drowned, or murdered?"

"Oops!" He brought his finger back and inhaled. "Ah, childhood with a garnish of dust." He stood straight. "Drowning, murder, I must have guessed." He stepped back. "You naked and shivering. The big bad killer around, drowning children. You lucky little devil."

Zed suspected that "luck" meant not in surviving but being chosen. "Did you kill me?"

"Murder you and then charge you for the privilege? No, not this time."

"You want me to murder you?"

"Yeah." Gears frowned. "But it wouldn't be the same. Where's the surprise, the terror? Naw, I'll wait for the real thing."

"Uh, okay." After that reaction, Zed wasn't keen to keep asking questions, but she didn't get to be Zed by acting shy. "Why was I brought to *your* door?"

"What?"

"Why does Countessa keep her door here? Why does she trust you? And why'd Countessa get your stew, your 'family recipe'? No one else, just her? And what's the family that keeps you here?" With every question Zed advanced, driving Gears back.

"I have no idea what you are talking about."

"I'll bet," Zed retorted, driving him back another step. "Then the Prof said something that got me thinking, an idea that answered some questions. Like, why you would ignore the man in the elevator? And why, when I was being carried, those hands looked familiar. It also explains how you just knew that I'd been drowned." She gave him a grin. "So where's Countessa? Where is he?"

Gears had a frozen face. "He?"

Zed wasn't sure what she had expected – something along the lines of a sobbing confession. "Now you know everything, sob, sob." But she and Gears just stared at each other. What now?

A bark of laughter from Gears' back room turned both their heads. Gears called out, nice and sarcastically, "Subtle, thanks, and perfect timing too."

"Oh, give it up," came Countessa's voice. "She got us, fair and square." Countessa swept out in black velvet skirts, a pale face now framed in black tresses and a silver necklace. "I was getting bored of Countessa anyway," she said. "But first I am going to have my party. If you've got to go, I figure to go with a bang."

At least the hands were familiar, Zed thought. She recognized Countessa's rings. "Did you save me?" Zed asked. "Kill me? Both?"

"Saved, darling, saved. Like my brother said, we like you. But as much as I'd love to catch up, I am out of time. The Feast is starting, and I prefer it to start with me." She turned to Gears. "Bring her along, we'll continue this up there." After peering out the door, Countessa swirled out.

Zed stared at where Countessa had been. "Brother?"

Gears wiggled his hand in a so-so gesture. "Depends on the day. Today, definitely sister. Stay put, I've got to fix the lights." Gears disappeared into his back room.

"If she wants to be hidden, then why wander around in jeans?" Zed called into the back.

"Because she's a busybody and not content to watch the in-house cable." Gears reappeared before Zed. "I'm done. She calls it the 'personal touch,' but I think she just can't resist running around in drag, even reverse drag."

"Oh?" Zed tried to work that out.

Gears went to the sliding door. "You heard her. You want to come?"

"Do panters live in the dark?"

"Great, then can we go? If you're sure you've gotten your CDs' worth?"

Zed followed, dazed with info overload, "Yeah, for now."

"Har-de-har." Gears locked up and strode past the inter-level stairs to a seamless beige wall. "Remember," he said, looking back at Zed, "I've never seen this, and neither have you."

"Seen what?" Zed asked as Gears ran his finger up the wall, suddenly pushing it in at the top. With a click a line appeared. Gears swung the door open to display a dusty stairwell lit by florescent tubes. "Oh, that."

"Yeah, that." Gears urged her inside and drew the door closed.

Chapter 11

ZED HAD NEVER BEEN to a Feast of the Dead before. She observed that the central elements seemed to be booze, stacks of food, billowing incense, half-lighting, and funky music.

"So where's the dead?" she asked Countessa.

"Coming."

Zed, Gears, and Countessa were sitting together on a couch pulled up to the doorway. They were covered by the darkness but with a clear view of the hallway and the elevator well. Zed could see everything people were doing and not a person could see her. She imagined how this voyeurism thing could be habit-forming.

"Those stairs are cool," Zed said. "They run up the whole building?"

Gears replied, "Yeah. It opens opposite to the elevators, but I welded that side shut and cut through the wall to this apartment. That's why the Countessa moved in here. But don't tell anyone about the stairs," he warned. "I like privacy, dig? If I catch you in them, I guess I would have to kill you, which would be a bummer."

"Brother...." Countessa warned.

"All right, I'd just maim you."

Well, Zed thought, *that'll keep me sleeping easy.*

"The wine ready, brother?"

"I'm going, I'm going." Gears headed out, dispersing bottles of red. He made enough trips that everyone had a bottle while people like Rat, Ellen, and Teresa clinked when they walked.

"Now we wait." Gears sank back into the couch.

"For what?" Zed wanted to know.

"Have some wine." A cup was pressed into her hands.

Zed didn't think that was such a smart idea.

"One sip, one question," Countessa said.

"Well said, sister."

"Why'd you call her sister?" Zed asked. Silence. She sighed and took a sip.

"I've never had a sister."

"And I've never been a sister."

"It's a new experience," they said together.

Zed took another sip. "But what if you don't like it?"

"A new experience isn't about liking or not liking. It's about something new and intense. Don't you ever get bored, Zed?"

"No." But she did get hungry. And Countessa's whole apartment smelled like one big barbecue. "Can you pass whatever's cooking?"

"Later." Zed felt some food pushed into her hands. She took a bite: cheese. Whoopie.

Out in the hall, things were loosening up. Except for the lack of patches and peg legs, it could have been a pirate convention: lots of swigging and singing. Zed recognized most people. Cal, Ben, and Tim were off in a corner sharing a toke. Rat was here, Don and his kitten, Teresa, Ellen, even Jenny with her parakeet. Luc and Hammer weren't, nor was Stu who was probably on door duty, but Barry was here, still looking pasty, but leering and ordering passers-by to bring him food. The Father and his gang weren't here, but Mistress Anna, Steve, and even comatose Bunny had made it.

"So where's the dead?" Zed asked again, taking a sip.

"Coming. Soon."

It must have been the wine, but Zed was having a difficult time telling the voices of Gears and the Countessa apart.

"Listen, they come now." The music was fading.

Zed listened and, sure enough, that whispering was there, at the ceiling, and growing till everyone had stopped and was staring up.

"The Feast," Countessa's hand emerged from the darkness holding a goblet of wine, her voice commanding attention, "of the Dead."

Everyone, including the voices at the ceiling, gave a shout. Gears had dragged Don away from his kitten and the two of them staggered out of the doorway with the platters of meat: chicken wings, kebabs, different meat steaks along with thin strips of meat. Platters of cheese, rolls, rice, and all varieties of canned goods followed.

The music came back up and it was chowtime. Miss Manners be damned, let's eat!

"Hungry?" Gears was back. He passed around a platter. Zed had a kebab, some turkey, and a couple slivers of the mystery meat. It was sweet and tasted a bit like chicken. Now, where had she heard that before? She concentrated on the eating because the best food was free food, and this was actually class food. So the next few minutes were devoted to mass mastication.

"Recovered," a soft voice asked, "from drowning?"

"Yes." Zed gritted her teeth for the next part. "Thank you. What do I owe?" Whew, that was over.

"Perhaps I owe you. A new experience, very intense."

"I'm evens if you are?" Zed was trying to be casual. "By the by, did you see anyone...?"

"No, just a shriek, which was you. Drink up, you're cheating."

Another drink and Zed was full, warm, and just wanted to close her eyes for a minute. The wine was hitting her and it had been a long day. A really, really, long day.

THE NEXT TIME ZED opened her eyes, the food was gone, the music throbbing, and empty bottles were stacked everywhere.

With the wine and the music, things had started to get rowdy. Zed had never seen so many naked people before. She watched Mistress Anna ride a man like a horse, lashing with her whip. Everyone had found a partner, or two, or twelve, and were doing things Zed had heard about, things she had never heard of, and a few things she wouldn't have imagined anatomically possible. But discounting gender and number of partners, everything resolved down to just a couple basics – lick everything and holes get filled.

"Looks like we have to clean the carpets."

"Looks like."

"Are they enjoying it?" Zed asked.

"Enjoy? They need it, want it, biologically require it, perhaps even like it, but no, take a look, you don't see a lot of happy people."

Zed pointed. "Rat's happy."

Rat was running around like a debauched monk, hair flying, tongue hanging out of an open grin. He leaped from partner to partner.

"He's making up for lost time."

"And he's only marginally human."

"Have some more wine," they both told Zed.

She took another drink. Everything was getting fuzzy and stretched. "What's with this swine ... I mean wine?"

"We drugged it."

"Drugged it?"

"An opiate, hallucinogen, pepper for taste, and a little special family secret."

"Your family has a lot of secrets," Zed observed.

"More than you'll know."

"Why drug it?" Zed wanted to know.

"To make people open to outside influence, possession, I suppose you could call it."

Outside, instead of mellowing out, the sex was just winding people up. Zed saw the flash of palms and heard the slaps, then the thud of fists.

"The Feast of the Dead."

"They have strong appetites."

"As we do."

"What a finale."

"*Yessssssss.*" The "s" drew out forever.

Zed needed to keep it together. Especially now that she'd figured out "The Feast of the Dead." Shit! Did she just say that out loud?

"Oooo, seems like someone's onto us." Was that Countessa or Gears?

"You kill them?" she asked.

"Not us, we just use what's made available."

"A new experience?" Zed wondered.

"So clever, yes, new and pleasant too. The books are right, nothing's sweeter than the breast."

Outside things had gotten vicious. Zed had seen violence before and thought herself immune; the snapping of bone she could accept, even seeing broken glass stuffed down someone's mouth was tolerable. But when she saw Teresa rip a chunk of Cal's cheek with her teeth, that was beyond "whatever."

Zed turned her head. She could have sworn she'd heard someone yell, "God wills." Looking around, she saw a phalanx burst from the stairwell, Burl and Howard at the head, the Father behind, mixed men and women surrounding him. The Father cupped his hands to his mouth. "Zed!" They were fighting forward, using bibles, bible cases, and crucifixes as clubs along with good old-fashioned fists, not a recommendation from the Gideon Society.

As for violence, the Father's gang was gasoline on the fire. The feast-goers stopped attacking each other and all turned to embrace these new foes.

"Zed!" the Father shouted while Burl backhanded Bucket Charlie into the wall.

"The Father's ruining the feast," Countessa complained.

"But it's new."

"Unpleasant, but not so new. Pagans have been rousted before."

That wine was definitely a bad idea. "So who killed the kids? I know you know."

"Sorry," they replied, "old experience. Luc beat you to it."

The Father called again. Zed gave up on Gears and Countessa and weaved towards the door.

"No, don't go."

"I feel concern over Zed, sister, in my chest, new and painful."

"Yes, me too. It's the anticipation; how exquisite."

"I imagine her being hurt. Oh! Can you feel it?"

"Yes, it's delightful, imagine her limp with vacant eyes, yes, oh yes!"

Gears and Countessa were so excited they didn't seem to mind Zed leaving, so Zed left them to it and, using the wall as a prop, headed toward the Father's gang.

"Zed! Zed!" He'd seen her, and Burl and Howard were pushing toward her, the rest of the followers fanned out behind. When one would fall, a group of older women would spring out from the stairwell door and drag the body back into the security of the stairs.

Howard had run into Mistress Anna who was screeching at him and lashing with her whip. He thrust his wooden bible case into her face and ran forward, smashing her head into the wall.

Howard only had a moment to savour victory when the irony of turnabout named Rat chopped at his legs, kicked him in the groin, and double-fisted him one to his head. The body was dragged into the stairs.

"Heh, heh, Rat wins again." Rat waggled his tongue. "Don't you fuckers learn, I'm King Rat and I can't be –"

Burl double-handed a mitre into the back of Rat's head. Pow, he was out.

"Come on," Burl told her. "Let's go." He guarded her body with his as they headed for the door.

"You didn't have to come for me." Getting saved twice in a day was doing bad things to her rep.

"I didn't." Burl backhanded Ellen and she charged with a bottle. "The Father did. Says he owes you."

"Damn right." She turned to tell him, but he wasn't there. Looking down she saw Burl slumped against the wall, head limp. She raised her eyes just in time to see Barry's crooked teeth.

"Been waiting for this." He grabbed her by the overalls, lifted her from the ground, and threw her across the hall. The wall knocked all the wind out of her, and she stayed on her knees only by willpower and desperation.

"Fuck, I feel like shit," Barry said as he sauntered over. "But I'll still do you, no worries." And he kicked her in the ribs, flipping her over.

Zed curled into a ball, writhing on the floor. In flashes she watched Barry fall, clutching his gut, then get back up. He weaved a little, but as his eyes dropped to her, he steadied himself, concentrating. His foot drew back and Zed got her arms up to protect her head, so he just started kicking her ribs and worked his way up. She was pretty sure she didn't give him the satisfaction of moaning, but her world was getting too dark and too red to know for sure.

Barry raised a boot to stomp on her head and hands when a fist caught him in a low uppercut, bouncing him off the wall and onto the floor. The Father looked down at Barry. "It is God's will that Zed should live. Who then are you to counter that?"

Barry rolled over onto his side and started spewing up black vomit.

"Thus the Lord takes care of his own," the Father intoned.

Barry moaned and vomited again.

Much as Zed wanted to rejoice at this, she was way too busy feeling like crap. She was sure this was making Gears and Countessa very excited. Her arm hung, dead weight. And, her ribs burned and all of this crappy potpourri fog was making her cough. She didn't even have enough energy to kick Barry's head.

The Father was carrying her, which she would allow this time, but only because he owed her. "And you still owe me," she mumbled into his ear while he tripped up a flailing Steve and stepped over him.

"How many do I still owe? Three, two?"

"Five, and you know it." Zed curled up against him. "But I'll call it four."

A scream behind made her look back. Barry had lurched up, clawing at his neck, black bile running from his mouth. His face was stretched and his hands pawed the air. Zed watched as he staggered, giving hoarse, birdlike cries. Then, with a sobbing gasp, his body shuddered and fell.

That's nice, Zed thought and drifted. Next thing she knew, she was lying on the stairwell landing, with Ivy looking down on her.

"Now what have you been getting into?" Ivy asked, head tilted to the side.

"She needs rest," came the Father's voice. "And she may have a cracked rib."

"Take her to my little room," Ivy said. "She can rest up there."

"Sounds like a plan."

"As for the hurting, there's nothing a good brew of tea can't make better," Ivy said, nodding. "Good strong tea."

Zed started laughing. Tea? What else?

"Don't worry," Ivy told her. "I'll make it good and strong."

Laughing had been a bad idea. A wave of pain rolled up from her ribs, and with the Father and Ivy looking down, she passed out.

Chapter 12

ZED WOKE WITH A groan, which was Ivy's signal to start the tea. While Ivy was in the kitchen, Zed took a peek at Barry's footwork. It was quite attractive, if black and red were your favourite colours. When she breathed, it burned, and when she ran her fingers over the swelling, she almost danced.

Ivy came with a cup. "Drink up, it'll do you a world of good."

"Okay." Zed took a sip. "Do you have any tape?"

"Tape?"

"Duct tape, packing tape?"

"Tape, to be sure, I've got tape." Ivy rose and scratched the back of her head. "Now where would that be?" She trotted off into the kitchen.

By the time Ivy returned, Zed was free of her coveralls and ready to go. "Oh dear, dear," Ivy exclaimed, handing over the tape. "You've a wild streak in you when it comes to decency." Ivy chuckled. "I was the same, though. There wasn't much I wouldn't do to expose my legs." She raised her skirt to show off her plump calf.

Zed nodded, gritted her teeth, and ripped the tape. Within ten minutes, she could breathe again and even raise her arm. She handed the tape back with a grin. "He ain't beat me yet."

Ivy looked down at her and nodded approval. "Who's that, love?"

"Barry."

"You should hear the news, then." Ivy clasped her hands to her chest. "That lackey of the slick man, feeling poorly wasn't he, and now he's passed on, poor thing." Ivy broke into laughter and a little dance.

"Barry's dead?" Ivy nodded, beaming. "Dead?"

"After bashing you about, there's nothing too bad for him," Ivy assured Zed.

It seemed to Zed that being dead was about as bad as it could get. Zed mulled over the news while she rose from the couch, holding the straps to her coverall. "Ivy, uh, do you have –"

"The loo is the door over there," Ivy pointed.

Loo? But she got the message and limped over.

Zed had just gotten comfortable when a pounding shook the whole apartment. Ivy pattered over to the front door and opened it. "Well, if you just aren't the mountain come to visit."

There was a low growl.

"They might grow the body big where you come from, but your speaking isn't much to write home about."

"Gas stove." Two words barked out in a gravel voice: Hammer.

"Course I've got a gas stove, everyone got a gas stove, what of it?" Zed could just imagine Ivy standing there with her hands on her hips, looking Hammer over.

"Inspection."

"Inspection?"

"Official," Hammer growled.

"Well, why didn't you say so like any sensible person?" Zed could hear Ivy shuffling out of the way, "'stead of this word and that, like some quiz show."

Zed sat, frozen, listening to Ivy pester Hammer about having a cuppa till he barked, "No." All the while there were sounds of metal on metal. This was odd, very odd.

Hammer finished and when he'd been sent safely out the door, Zed let herself out of the bathroom.

"Now there you are. I thought you'd been spirited away with the fairies." Ivy beamed at Zed. "But now that you're up, we can have a good catch-up."

Zed was swinging the bag over her shoulder. How could she explain it to Ivy? Zed was like a shark, move or die. "I've got to go get your blanket."

"Keep it," Ivy told her. "Don't you know a gift when it's given?"

"Well, I owe you for last night."

"Zed." Ivy cupped Zed's cheeks in her palms. "Do you know what a friend is?"

Yeah, Zed remembered, *pain in the ass, right?* "I owe you." She slipped to the door.

"I'll leave the door open," Ivy promised. "Come back when you've a need."

Everyone wants a piece of Zed, she thought as she headed for the stairs, but nobody's paying. She had a full plate of errands today: chase down some killers, visit Hammer about that stove business, maybe drop by that newbie, Mary, and make the rounds before people started fending for themselves. People may party, people may die, but business goes on and on. Mary first. She went down to the 2nd floor.

Pulling open the door, Zed stepped over Ellen, who was sprawled face up in the hall.

"Uhhhhhh," Ellen moaned. "Stop moving, stop moving, stop moving."

Teresa was slumped in her lawn chair further down the hall. "Stop shouting," she hissed.

"Ohhhhh!" Ellen moaned, sitting up. She pulled down her red-stained white tube top and prodded her arms, breast, and stomach. "I am so sore." She continued her personal examination. "And where the fuck are my panties?"

"How the hell should I know? And stop shouting ... please!" The last word was uttered with a guttural moan and eye pops. Teresa looked around with red eyes. "Must drink. First drink, then think."

"You remember last night?" Ellen asked, staggering to her chair.

"No. You?"

"No. Ow!" Ellen sat down, "But I think we must have gone to an S&M party."

"That would explain these cuts." Teresa examined her chest. "Christina? Christina, get Mommy her morning drinkie, and a band-aid?" No one came to the door.

Ellen noticed a bottle of red wine near the hall door. "Zed, anything in that?"

It was half full and a leftover of the drugged wine. "Half." She told Ellen.

Teresa was looking around. "You seen Christina?" she asked. Zed and Ellen shook their heads.

Ellen stared at the bottle with a tangible hunger, her tongue running along the back of her teeth. "Be an angel, Zed," she begged, "and pass that red beauty, and all of the solids too, if you got 'em."

Zed hoisted the bottle, then gave Ellen a long look. "What's in it for me?" It was great to be wanted.

"Anything, sweetheart, anything," Ellen said fervently. "But make it quick."

Zed considered for a few seconds; what exactly did these two have? "Got a knife? A blade?"

"No."

"CDs?"

"No."

"Books?"

"No." Ellen was getting desperate. "Come on, Zed. Anything, just hurry."

"Take it fuckin' later," Teresa said. "And give us breakfast now."

"I'll be back," she warned. Both the women nodded consent. Zed handed the bottle to Ellen.

Ellen upended it, coming down with a gasp. She handed the bottle to Teresa, who broke into a smile. "I don't remember much, but I bloody remember this. This is the fucking best wine I've ever had." Ellen nodded in agreement. "What about fucking snacks?" Teresa demanded. Zed took out a box of crackers split into two wrapped packs. She tossed Teresa a pack of crackers as she walked on by.

Teresa called after her, "You see Christina, you send her back." Teresa thought a moment, then added, "In an hour or two." Zed nodded.

Down at Mary's door, Zed gave three firm but friendly knocks. The door opened an inch. Zed tried giving one of Luc's smiles – the nice one. It opened another six inches. Sunlight didn't help, Mary had the same severe hair and bangs, same owlish glasses. "Hello?"

"Hey, Mary. Remember me?"

"Sort of."

"Here." Zed handed over the other packet of crackers. "You hungry, yes?"

"For me?"

"Could be," Zed told her. "I bring things around, remember, to trade." This was definitely slow motion trading. "You have anything you don't want?"

"Oh." Mary slowly closed the door.

After a long minute, she returned. "They gave me these, but I don't like them." She handed Zed a bag of jelly beans.

Jelly beans! This place was packed with sugar freaks and now she was holding the biggest stash in the Tower. "Yeah, they'll do," she told Mary. "You want anything else?"

"Can you get books? I like to read sometimes."

"Horror, mystery, crime, true crime, occult, ghost stories … conspiracy theories?" Zed rattled off the usual list.

"Do you get travel books? I like to read about far-away places."

"Travel books? Like true crime overseas? Historical mysteries?"

"No, just how people live."

Zed scratched her head. "Sure, lemme see what I can find. I'll drop by later, okay?" Zed gave a thumbs-up.

"It was very noisy last night...." Mary trailed off.

Zed laughed. "You think that's noisy, wait until the day the cheques come. Wait ... joke!" she shouted at the closing door. Too late. "Shit."

A male voice asked, "Why is it, wherever I go, you've been there first?"

"Maybe cuz you're so slow," she told Dean, the mental health nurse.

"You converted her to 'Zed's distribution scheme' yet?"

"In a day or two." Zed dug in her bag. "Want some artichokes?"

Dean gave a shudder. "Forbidden. Hey, what's with this?" He traced a finger down her bruising till he reached the tape.

She shrugged. "Tough night."

"Come on, don't give me that. Life's better than this. How about I report you to Social, then you'll get a check-up and a decent place to live? How's that sound?"

"No way," she told him. "If you don't want to trade, I got places to go."

"Just the medical check-up? No?" Dean sighed. "So what do you want to scam today?"

"Trade," Zed reminded him. "I want pain pills, but nothing that messes you up, okay? None of that sleepy shit."

"These for you?"

Zed said nothing.

Dean sighed and dug around in his pack. "You're just lucky that I'm dying for ... artichokes." Another shudder. "You ever been to a 'Medical Review and Disciplinary Board?'"

Zed shook her head.

"Funny, me neither. Let's see it stays that way." He took the can of artichokes and handed her the envelope. "One every four hours and you've never seen me, right? You need more, I'm at the Prof's tomorrow."

Zed nodded, opened the envelope, and chewed one down.

"One day you'll grow up and I'll stop being nice to you," Dean warned.

"You're being nice? Later." Zed gave a wave and took off, leaving Dean to convince Mary to open the door.

Down in the lobby things had returned to normal. The lake was just a scum-clogged puddle and the tinmen, dumpster-divers, and scroungers had all gone in search of portable treasure. Hammer had his boots up on the table, his hand folded on his stomach, watching the security camera. He gave her a look, then nodded her in.

As she got closer, Hammer noticed the bruising up her side and jerked his chin, telling her to come closer. He prodded the bruising with his finger and the corner of his lip twitched up. "Flower." He poked again. "Pretty."

Zed tucked away a note to hereafter stand outside of Hammer's reach, or anyone else who thought blood and torn muscles were flowers. She pulled the two books out of her bag. "Mystery." She said, showing him the first, then the second, "Murder."

Hammer reached a hand.

Zed kept them out of reach. "You give me some information, I give you the books?"

Hammer nodded. He waited, keeping a careful eye on the books.

"I know Barry's dead," she said, "but what happened to the body?"

Hammer gave his impression of an outcropping of granite.

Yup, she could tell that Hammer was just waiting to spill his guts. Ho boy! She took it as given that Barry had joined the 'choir.' "Been doing any body snatching lately?" she half-joked.

Hammer gave her his other impression, that of a frozen man with a really threatening look in his eyes.

Run or walk, she asked herself, *run away or walk?* "So, what can you tell me?" At this, Hammer's face started to thaw, his brow lifted a little, his cheeks rose, and his lip curled in a happy grimace. He put a single finger up to his lips. Taking his feet off the desk, he got up, lumbering out of the bunker and into the hallway. She followed him as he took a right and stopped at the first door, a very familiar door.

Zed had this déjà vu tingle. "You're shitting me, right?"

Hammer smirked and opened the door. The auxiliary water storage tank filled the room. He gave her a happy look and lifted off the metal lid. Christina floated inside.

Zed looked her over closely, making sure all the flesh on her chest was still intact. The brother-sister knife team hadn't found her yet.

Hammer closed the lid and shut the door. As he passed Zed on his way back, he plucked the two books from her hand. Back in the bunker he assumed the severe slouch of his reading position, tongue freshly moistened, thumb at the ready. It was a class-A trade for her, but she guessed Hammer had been waiting to tell someone, so why not her.

"Does anyone else know?" He shook his head a definite no.

"When?"

Hammer looked up from his contemplation of the covers. "Midnight, one o'clock." He shrugged.

"Who?"

He shook his head again. Zed found that hard to believe and opened her mouth to tell him so when Hammer levelled her with his fifty-megaton stare, the one that yelled, "Hammer busy now!" Sensible people walked away then while insensible ones writhed on the floor. Zed was sensible. She left Hammer and his thumb in peace.

Zed wound her way up to Luc's. The stairs and stairwells were crowded with people telling feast stories, at least what they could remember.

There was a group of four rummies passing the bottle on ten. "So then," one told the rest, "down goes Barry. Bam! Falling like a fucking tree."

"I heard that, once you die, all the blood goes to the dick and you get a raging hard-on."

"Hell," one of them piped up, "don't wait till you die, bud, try this technique I like to call ... masturbation. Same result, less side effects."

They all fell about laughing, which gave Zed the chance to push past.

"Hey Zed," one of them called. "Can I have the bottles?"

Zed looked close. It was Charlie, sporting a whopping shiner. "You find anything?" she asked.

"Naw, but I asked around, honest."

Zed had a rule that she disbelieved anyone who ended a statement with 'honest.' But she fished out a bottle. "You hear anything, look me up and I'll give you the other." She flipped it to him and continued up.

"Be careful!" he reproved her. "That's alcohol!" At the word "alcohol" the other three boozers perked up in expectation. Charlie looked around at them and muttered, "Ah, crap."

Up at Luc's, Stu was on hair patrol, his comb making sure each strand was stunning. Across Luc's door from Stu was barrel-chested Pete of the Quince hunt fame. Creepy Eddie and Tim were in line.

Creepy Eddie had his lip-gnawing and sexual tension working for him. Tim was decked out in full goth, including shades and trenchcoat. He was listening to his Walkman, probably a song about death.

Zed gave Stu the nod and headed in. She was stopped by an arm, a hairy arm.

"There's a line," Pete told her.

"Yeah?"

"You're third."

Zed looked to Stu who just smirked and returned to combing. She turned back to Pete and gave him a pitying smile. "It's your first day, isn't it?" She stepped back and waited. Pete clenched his jaw.

Pock-faced Jenny came out, parakeet at the ready, holding a tin of lacquer thinner in one hand and a plastic bag in the other. "Come on, Angel," she cooed to her parakeet, "let's go back to Mama's." The parakeet responded by taking a chunk out of her ear. Jenny didn't even twitch. She just gripped the lacquer thinner a little tighter and sidled off toward the stairs.

Luc sauntered to the door. "Everything going okay, boys?"

"Yes, sir, Mr. Luc," Pete barked out.

Luc sighed. "I'm not the army Pete, just an employer."

"Yes, sir, Mr. Luc."

Luc rolled his eyes, which fell on Zed. "You again? Killed anyone for me?"

"You really want me to tell you out here?"

"You're getting my blood all a-tingle. Come on in and tell me a story. I'll even let you sit on my lap." Luc gave her a wicked leer.

Creepy Eddie cleared his throat.

"Eddie, looks like you got a freebee, didn't you? Shall you come in so we can attend to your 'needs'?" Luc turned to Zed. "One moment, unless you'd like to...." Eddie looked willing.

"Next time."

"Really?" Eddie piped up, eager.

Zed unfolded her knife.

"Bring that too." Eddie was breathing heavy.

"Maybe you'd better just step inside," Luc suggested, escorting Eddie in.

The elevator made shrieking sounds, announcing its arrival. Everyone waiting turned to look.

"There is a place of skull where the red king lives!" a voice proclaimed as the doors shuddered open. The man in the black turtleneck was back, but no one seemed happy to see him. With the unerring ability to pick the person who liked him least, he approached Zed. "There lies the seed of blood and the womb of pain," he told her, wiping the sweat off his forehead.

"Speak on, prophet," Tim said, emerging from his headphones.

"Hey, Zed," Stu added, "all the guys dig you today."

Tim got a stare from the prophet. "Your body shall twist in the flames, and when you scream, death shall enter." He swerved toward Luc's door and goggled at Stu. "The Beast stalks the halls and sits in the bosom."

Pete and Stu looked at each other. Stu held his arm out, offering Pete first dibs. Pete inclined his head in thanks before crossing the hall to twist the prophet's arms up behind his back.

Pete held the prophet while Stu went into the elevator and started hitting buttons. He leaped out and together they threw the prophet through the closing doors.

Pete and Stu exchanged a high five and walked back with a cocky stride. They both had the "Isn't licensed violence great!" look on their face.

Eddie emerged from Luc's, giving Zed a suggestive gaze and a wink before heading toward the stairs.

"Not to worry," Luc called after him, "we'll get that pocket snake lively again. You're an inspiration to us all. Especially after last night." And Eddie was gone.

Zed walked in, saving a special sneer for Pete as she passed.

"Hey, I was next," Tim protested.

"Come in, come in. No need to be shy." Luc spread his arms wide. "Room for all in Luc's pleasure emporium."

Zed took her chair as Tim took out his wallet.

"Some coke," he asked Luc, putting down the money. "$100."

"Oooo, cocaine, I love dealing in cocaine." Luc looked from Tim to Zed. "Makes me so up-market." Luc pulled out a baggie, checked it on the scales, and handed it over along with a rolled cigarette.

"Just a speedball," he told Tim, who took the cig in puzzlement. "A Luc speciality, on the house." Tim smiled, nodded, pushed over the hundred and breezed out.

"Coke, meth, and heroin," Zed guessed.

"You're just trying to impress me so I'll make you an assistant because you blew the thugging job."

"No, you're just switching him to an addict. Pete is permanent?"

Luc steepled his fingers on the desk. "One always has to look toward the future. And why not Pete? He has a hair trigger, a capacity for violence, and he obeys orders."

"I thought you'd be pissed off, you know, over Barry."

"Don't get angry, get even. That's good business sense. And don't worry, I've dealt with it on the Q.T., as they say." He turned his palms up. "Now, what are you here for?"

"I've come to lay a bet, on the next kid." Zed's mind was thinking over what Luc had said. "Taken care of it?"

"I don't think so." Luc looked her over. "You got all the signs of knowing a sure thing and Luc doesn't take bets on sure things. I'll buy it, but won't bet it. What's your price?"

Zed aimed high. "$150, ten joints, and a bottle of the good stuff."

"Seventy-five and four joints."

"100, eight joints, and a bottle of the good stuff."

"100, fine. Six joints," Luc countered.

"Six joints and a bottle."

"Of the good stuff," he finished for her. "Which good stuff? Champagne, whiskey, brandy, cognac, port, sherry, wine?"

"Brandy," she told him. "Good stuff."

Luc went to the cabinet and pulled out a bottle. "Napoleon 1988 VSOP," he told her. She nodded as if she had a clue and he went to get the joints.

Hammer, Zed thought, *Hammer is acting for Luc.*

Luc put the joints and the $100 in her hand. "Who?" He demanded.

"Christina, in the water tank."

"Perfect." Luc flexed his hands. "Anyone know?"

"Just Hammer." Yes, Hammer, but then why hadn't Hammer killed Ivy this morning? Was it Ivy after all? Maybe it was something for later, like a bomb. And why hadn't Hammer told Luc about Christina? Too many fucking questions.

Luc had pulled down the tote boards and was rechalking. Everyone was getting long odds but Christina. Zed had gone up to 8:1.

Zed packed everything away. She had to talk to Ivy now. Ivy couldn't die yet; not when she still had to return that blanket. She was leaving now. "You kill her?" she asked Luc.

"Christina? No." Luc winked. "But thanks to you, I'm about to make a killing off her." He called out the door. "Stu!"

Zed was gone. She hit those stairs as fast as she could go. Even so, Stu passed her three flights down, taking the stairs four at a stride. Off to hide the body, Zed guessed.

Ivy's door was still ajar. "Ivy! Ivy!" Zed pounded on the door. It swung wide and the smell of gas poured out. This was bad. Zed dropped down into the fresh air. She could see Ivy's legs on the floor by the kitchen.

She hesitated. If Ivy killed Barry, then Ivy was already dead, for one way or another Luc would kill her. If not quiet, he'd kill her loud, loud enough to make a point. All that would happen if Zed went in there was that Luc would have two targets, not just one.

Zed shook her head. Damn that blanket. She never should have taken it.

She took a deep breath and crawled in. Zed grabbed Ivy's legs and started to pull.

Ivy might be tiny, but anyone's heavy when you try dragging them twenty-five feet while holding your breath.

Zed knew the door was close, but all she could see was red and flashes of white. Her ribs weren't too happy, either.

I can't do it, she screamed inside, *I've got to take a breath. One more pull and I'll take it; okay, just one more, no, this is the last one, I mean it.*

And then it exploded out and she lay there, head on Ivy's legs, just gasping. *Hey, I'm alive*, she thought. Looking around, she was just inside the door. Another breath and she dragged Ivy to the hallway.

Ivy's lips were blue, but she was breathing, shallow with long gasps, but breathing.

Zed knew in her bones that Hammer would be back. As soon as

they'd stashed the body, he'd come to shut off the gas. Why blow up a floor just for one old woman, no?

Ivy, Ivy, Ivy, Zed thought, looking down at her, *what exactly am I going to do about you?*

Chapter 13

WHILE ZED'S EYES WATCHED Ivy's breathing growing stronger and longer her brain was trying to figure a way out. Being a trader wasn't going to cover this: Luc wouldn't be satisfied with a couple packs of cigs. No, she had two choices. Get the blanket, throw it on Ivy, and sell her to Luc, or go to war. If it was war, then Zed's job was to survive. And to survive, she needed to be a stone cold player – no price too great, no stopping, no hesitation. If she went all the way to the wall without a flinch, she might make it out alive. But if she couldn't do it, she better just walk way.

See, Zed reminded herself, *pains in the ass, that's all they are.*

She gave Ivy a shake, which just caused a mumble. Zed shook her again, hard.

Ivy's eyes popped open and fixed on Zed. "Did I fall asleep again? You've come for tea?"

Zed didn't have time for this. She pulled Ivy up.

"What am I doing all sprawled here in the hall?" Ivy asked, using Zed's help to get to her feet.

Zed put one of Ivy's arms around her waist and with a hand behind

Ivy's back, she started moving them toward the stairs. "Listen to me. Luc knows. He sent Hammer to wreck your stove and kill you with gas."

"No." Ivy's face fell. She looked back to the open door and sniffed. "Must have made a mistake, that big lug, him with his chunky fingers."

"No mistake," Zed said. "We either go now, or they catch you. If they catch you, you die. You understand?"

"I'm not addled, just a little dizzy."

"Okay, if you are coming with me, we have to go down the stairs. Can you make it?"

"Course I can, don't you worry about me."

If only that was true, Zed thought. It was a slow journey. Ivy took the railing and Zed the outside, blocking Ivy from the traffic.

Jenny was sitting at the 4th floor, smoking a cig. "Move it, Jen," Zed warned.

"I was here first, so suck on that," Jen smirked.

Zed kicked her in the kidneys.

"Bitch," Jen sobbed, rolling on the landing in pain.

"Zed, that wasn't very nice," Ivy said. Zed just gave her a look. "All right love, I'm a-coming." Ivy continued past Jenny.

At the basement level, Zed took out her knife and opened the blade. "Here." She handed the knife to Ivy. "I'll be back in a minute."

Ivy took the knife. "Thank you, dear, but there's nothing to cut here."

"Just aim for the throat," Zed told her. "I'll be back in a minute."

Zed zipped over to her hidey-hole and loaded up: all the cash, the coke, and the cigs along with what she was already carrying. She had some ideas, maybe half a plan, which felt better than just running. She hoisted the bag. Carrying a stash like this was stupid: she'd be slow, she'd be seen, she'd get caught. But what else was there to do?

Ivy was right where Zed had left her. But so was Stu.

"You seem a good boy, a good boy," Ivy said to Stu. "What you want to work for someone like that? That slick man is no good for you."

Stu didn't look regretful at all. He looked happy. "Yes, ma'am," he said. "That's a nice knife. Where'd you get it?"

Zed, in hiding, was using all her mental powers to give Ivy a message: "Say nothing."

"Zed left it for me," Ivy told him. "But don't you worry about me, she be back soon enough."

Stu gave her a flash of tooth. "Indeed." He touched one finger to his forehead in salute, and started up the stairs. "I'm sure I'll be seeing you again."

Zed had learned two things: first, she had no telepathic powers, second, Luc hadn't put a kill-on-sight order for Ivy yet. But thanks to Ivy, now Luc would know Zed was helping her out.

Zed walked out and took the knife from Ivy's hand.

"Ah, you're back, so where we be off to now?" Ivy put a hand to her breast. "Isn't it exciting?"

Zed took a peek up the stairs, hoping Stu was close enough for a knife in the back. No luck, he was already out of sight.

"Come on." Zed led Ivy down the stairs to the sub-parkade. "You did kill Barry, I hope," Zed asked.

"And Luc," Ivy added. "I gave him a double dose, special. He must have a stomach like a goat."

"Double dose?"

"Of the poison. I poisoned the tea."

They were interrupted by a squeal of pleasure from the darkness below.

"Two, he, he, two!" A pale figure shuffled into the light, its blond hair wild and scraggly.

Zed sighed and gripped the knife. *Bring it on, panter*, she thought, *let's get this over with.*

Zed dropped down the stairs, then she and the panter danced; shuffle, stop, shuffle. Each waited for the other to make a move.

"That you, Eric?" Ivy's voice rang in the stairwell. "It is. Where've you been hiding yourself? Look at you," Ivy prattled on. "All pale and sickly. You need some feeding, you do. Just cause my boy's not around,

God rest him, no need to be a stranger."

Eric straightened from his crouch. "Hello, Mrs. Hughes." One hand went to scratch his ear.

"You should come up for a cuppa, Eric. You know what I always say."

"Cuppa never hurt no one," Eric intoned.

"That's the truth. But I can't chat now. Ha, thought you never hear me say that, did you? Zed and me, we're off on big things, big things." Ivy shuffled to the door. Eric stepped forward and opened it for her. "Thank you, Eric," she said to him with a smile. "You're such a sweet boy."

Eric blushed. "Thank you, Mrs. Hughes."

"Come on, Zed." Zed was just standing there staring from Eric to Ivy and back again. She hurried to catch up to Ivy before whatever affected Eric wore off.

"That was Eric."

"I know," responded Ivy.

"Eric, panter Eric, sex nutter Eric, will go after anyone anytime Eric!"

"I try to keep an open mind," Ivy said primly.

"Then why exactly did you poison Barry and Luc?"

"Because he killed my boy." At the last words Ivy's gaze grew wistful. "He killed my Quince, he killed my boy. That poor lad, hounded from his homeland, forced to live here, but that was enough for me, enough to see him." Her face turned stone cold. "Till that Luc kills him, my Quince who wouldn't touch a boy to harm him in his life. No not him, he didn't like boys, hated them, and that Luc goes and kills him." Zed was staring at Ivy. "And nothing was done," Ivy continued. "Nothing was done for my boy, so I did it, but that Luc," her brow crinkled in puzzlement, "what a stomach that man must have."

"Quince was your son?" Zed asked.

"Aye."

"So you decided to kill Luc and Barry."

"Aye, I asked around and I listened. They were the ones. Others might have helped, but they were the ones.

Finally things started to fall into place. Zed was sure Luc didn't know Ivy was after him, not that he'd care. "You don't know who killed Charles, or Pete?" she asked Ivy, just in case.

"Those poor children, no, but I wish I did."

I'll bet, Zed thought as they stopped in front of Gears' door. *Then there'd be another batch of "special" tea coming up.*

Gears was in, if the screaming version of "Puff the Magic Dragon" blasting through the walls was any indication. Zed pounded the door.

"Puff" died and a few seconds later the door slid open. "I have to tell you up front," Gears said, "breaking in on 'Puff' is way uncool, I mean, the song is only three minutes long."

"Emergency," Zed told him.

"Her?" He nodded at Ivy.

"Yup."

"Come in, then." Zed motioned to Ivy to stay outside. Gears looked Ivy over as he prepared to close the door. "Madam, I do not know if you appreciate the new experience. If you would be willing to overlook the minor difference in our physical but not spiritual ages, I must say that I consider you a juicy ripe plum from the garden of sexuality."

Ivy just looked him up and down then gave a laugh. "Oh, get away with you, you wild one, I don't go in for those types of chat-me-ups and shenanigans these days." But she turned and put her hands to her face all the same.

Gears bowed his head and slid the door closed. "That," he said to himself, "would have been a righteous new experience."

"I want you to hide her," she told him.

"Her? From who?" Gears looked at the door in disbelief.

Zed figured she might as well get it over with. "Luc."

"Luc? *The* Luc? He's after her?"

Zed nodded.

"Like, beat her up after her?" he asked. "Or like, want her body after her?"

Zed drew a finger across her throat.

Gears backed up and leaned on the workbench, his hands holding on to his head. "Whoa, that is heavy, very heavy."

"You mean you won't or you can't," she said bluntly.

"Course I can. It's just ... heavy." He gave his head a scratch. "How long?"

"Three days, maybe four." If Zed couldn't make a deal with Luc by then, they would just have to leave.

"It'll cost," Gears told her. "Three a day for the rent and $200 for the silence."

Zed handed him nine joints wrapped in two $100 bills.

"Shit, you're serious. What's she to you?" Gears nodded to the door.

"Business."

Gears looked sceptical. "So how much time do I get?"

"He's already looking."

"He doesn't know you're *here*, right? And he's not coming after me, right?"

"Yeah, he doesn't know. And you hide her so even I don't know, okay? I can only get to her through you, in person."

"I dig it."

"There's something else," Zed warned.

"Man, I almost hate to ask."

"I need something to go 'Boom!'"

"A gun? I don't do guns, because they have bad karma, bad mojo; cops come and it's a bad scene."

"No, not a gun, bombs."

"Bombs. Not a bomb, but bombs?"

Zed shrugged. "Yeah, you got anything?"

Gears gave a slow stare. "Normally I'd just walk but this must be fate, and you can't walk when fate calls. A while ago I helped out this draft dodger, 'cept he was a bit past the draft, know what I mean, already a soup of letters, AWOL, NCO and he left something he had lifted for payment. So I got some stuff, but just the stuff, no assembly." He told her.

"That's fine."

"And this isn't aimed at Luc because if you miss –"

"No, I'm not planning to kill anyone."

"But you want bombs?"

"Definitely."

"And you remember that buildings can fall down?" Gears asked.

"I remember."

Gears wiped his brow. "I must be nuts, doing this." He turned to face her. "$2500."

"I've got $1500."

"You've got $1500? Then why the hell are you still hanging around here? Go, fly, find the world." He saw she was serious. "$2000 in cash or trade."

"1800."

"Deal."

She counted out the $1500 in bills, wads, and pocket origami. She unpacked her cigs, her dope, her coke, and in the end, the brandy.

Gears went straight for the brandy. "This is good stuff."

"Enough?"

Gears kept his eyes on the brandy. "Close enough." He went into the back room, taking the bottle with him.

With a lever you could move anyone. Luc just needed a bigger lever. Zed shrugged. Looked like she was back to nickel and dimes after this for a while. But she still had fifty dollars or so left, she'd figure out assembly. It would work, it was do-able.

Gears returned with a small green gym bag. He placed it on the workbench, unzipped it, and motioned Zed over. "C-4 plastic explosive." He pointed to the three bright yellow bricks. "Detonators and wires." He held up the coils. "Plungers." He pointed to the boxes.

"Timers?" Zed looked into the bag.

"No timers."

"I need timers."

Gears slowly zipped up the bag. "This is what I got and this is what you paid for, take it or leave it."

Zed's mind screamed the first rule of business at her: big risks are for big losers. But sometimes, she reminded herself, big risks are all you fucking got. Besides, the first, first rule is that until you got something to trade, you ain't a trader. "I'll take it."

Gears handed her the gym bag. She shoved it into her bag and slung it over her shoulder. She paused at the door and looked back.

"Guess this is goodbye," Gears said. "*Finito*."

"Screw that," Zed told him. "Remember who you're talking to."

"Okay, later then." He gave her the peace sign. She gave him the finger.

Outside, Ivy was still waiting. Her face lit up at the sight of Zed. "Everything all right, love?"

Zed held one of Ivy's hands. "Ivy, the man inside, his name is Gears."

"Gears, now what kind of name is that?"

"Ivy!" Zed glared at her and continued. "He's going to hide you for a few days."

"Hide, me? Never." Ivy's chest had pushed out and she was glaring at Zed. "Me? Hide away?"

"Ivy." Zed gritted her teeth. "Do this," she added the forbidden word, "please."

Ivy's soft hand stroked Zed's cheek. "All right, but don't you go telling anyone Ivy Hughes went and hid. I never did, I'm just doing you a favour." And with that Ivy turned and marched inside. "I'm back, you randy young stud, and I hear you've a place for me."

Zed ran for the stairs. Time was against her and she had a lot to do. High on the list was to find a good hiding hole.

Eric lunged as she ran past him. She deflated him with a lisped, "You're welcome, Mrs. Hughes!" He retreated into the shadows in sullen silence.

The way Zed saw it, to make everything work out, all she had to do was: find timers, assemble and place the bombs, find a hiding place for a few days, and then make a deal with Luc. Problem was, Zed made her living by being someone everyone recognized. Which meant she had to find somewhere no one could see her or find her. Oh yeah, and she had to get this all done before Luc and Co. could get their shit together. Pipe dreams *awwwwaaaaaayyyyyyyy*!

Zed went to her hidey-hole again. She packed up the leather books, the booze, the blanket, and other portable items. The rest she hid around the room. It was a good hiding place, but then she'd never had a gang trying to find it. She just hoped there would be a few things left after they ransacked.

She had an idea about the timers and headed up to see Ellen and Teresa. On the 2nd floor, Ellen and Teresa were sacked out in their chairs.

"Booze run," Teresa called out, echoed by Ellen. "Booze run!"

"You still owe me," Zed reminded them. "Pay up first."

"What you want?" Teresa moaned, "Christina's hiding and we're dying here. You can have anything."

"Except the chairs," Ellen added.

"Yeah, except the chairs."

"How about clocks?" Zed asked.

"Take 'em!" Ellen shouted.

"We hate time, screw time!" Teresa added.

Zed took a scout through their place and found three mini mechanicals: yellow, black, and pink.

"We clear?" Teresa asked.

"Booze run!" Ellen moaned.

"Yeah, we're evens," Zed said.

"Zed," Teresa said, "if I try and leave this chair, my head will explode."

"Really?" Zed said.

They both nodded.

Zed thought about going up to Luc's for them ... for about a nano-second. "Naw, too busy today."

"Bitch!"

"Cunt!"

"Slag!"

"Ho!"

Zed laughed and took off for the stairs.

"Hey, bitch!" Teresa called after her. "Pink clock has never worked. Suck on that!"

Zed looked at the pink clock, shook it. Damn. Teresa was right. Oh well, she'd figure that out as she went along. Onward, onward, onward. She started to climb.

On the 14th floor she scoped the hall first before darting out to give the Professor's door four taps.

"Go away, Death," the Prof said through the door. "I recognize your knock."

"No, it's Zed."

"Who's Zed?"

"Me."

"Oh." There was a pause.

"Are you going to let me in?" Zed asked.

"I don't think so."

Enough playing, Zed decided. She reached out and turned the knob. As suspected, it was unlocked. The Professor shuffled back in surprise. "How'd you do that?"

Zed sighed and looked up. "Prof, I need you to make sense. I need fifty books. That's five-zero. One half mystery, one half travel. And a clock, too." Zed pulled out the leather triplicates and unwrapped them. "You understand?"

The Professor's eyes lit up and he took the books from her, rubbing them against his cheek. "Leather, softest of the soft. Rare, cream of cream? Children's leather?" he asked.

Zed finally figured out what Prof had been doing at Gears'. "I hope not!" She wasn't keen on the dead, but that was a bit much. "No, normal leather. We have a deal?"

The Prof was stroking the books. "Mine."

"I'll take that as yes," Zed said. "Prof, where's a clock? Clock?"

"Tempus fugit?"

"Clock."

"Waits for no man."

Zed rubbed her eyes. Where were the normal people? In other buildings? "*Bbbrrriiiinnnnnnnggggggg!*" she shouted.

The Professor scrabbled around on the floor. "Wake up!" he screamed, thrusting a small brass clock into her face.

One down. "Mysteries?"

"I will not be blackmailed," he stated, then turned and rushed to the wall of bookcases, running his finger up and down the rows of spines, muttering to himself and pulling out the occasional book. "Give him the Mickey, Mickey Finn ... Lord Wimsey, Nayland Smith, and Campion go to dinner, but who buys? ... 39 steps, bosh!" Behind him grew a pile of mysteries. He turned suddenly and grabbed the last one he had put on the pile and returned it to the bookshelf. "Not yet, my little Dick Donovan!"

"Travel Books?" Zed primed, as he reached the end of the bookshelves.

"Eh?" He paused, puzzled.

"Travel books!" Zed shouted, happy. She started packing the mysteries away.

"Travel, travel." The Professor returned to the bookshelves, pulling here and there. "Mottle my lizard indeed, Patagonia, roosters and trains, roads of iron, roads of silk." He turned, his arms full.

"Halle-freakin-lujah," Zed said.

"Religion?" He went back to the shelves. "Witchfind this, General."

"No, no," Zed called him back. "No religion."

"Atheist?"

"Whatever." She scooped the books into her bag. "I got to go."

"Waiting for Godot?"

"Uh, sure." She waved goodbye and let herself out, heading back down to the 2nd floor, secure knowing there was at least one person who wouldn't give her away, or even remember her name.

Back on the 2nd floor, the hallway was empty: Ellen and Teresa had been forced to do a booze run for themselves. The plan was coming together perfectly. Or luck. Zed would take what she could get.

She gave Mary's door a knock and waited for the eyeball. "Hey, Mary. It's me, Zed, remember?"

"Zed?"

"I came back. I brought you travel books." Zed reached into the bag and brought out *The Flame Trees of Thika*. Zed looked over the cover. "It's about Africa," she added in a tempting voice, putting it up toward the crack in the door.

Mary's hand reached out and brought the book up to her glasses. "Looks good," she said, but with hesitation.

"I've got more," Zed told her, dragging out *Patagonia Express, Jaguars are Ripping my Flesh*, and *Road of Silk and Iron*.

Mary's face broke into a shy smile. She reached up and pushed her glasses firmly to the bridge of her nose before choosing *Road of Silk and Iron*. She read the cover, her hand trembling with excitement. "I like reading about other places."

Gotcha! Zed thought to herself. "I've got lots here for you," Zed told her as she plunked down the bag. Mary opened the door to reach for the bag, but Zed's hand covered it first. "A little thing from you," Zed added. "Just want to stay with you for a bit."

Mary froze mid-reach, "Stay … with me?"

"Yah, all the travel books and you just let me hang in a corner for a little while, just for a night, two tops." Zed worked at keeping each word casual.

"I ... people, people make me nervous." Mary looked at Zed with a pleading look. It seemed that even the thought was making Mary nervous.

"I keep to myself," Zed assured her. "Besides...." She started taking the travel books out of her bag, one at a time, nice and slow, flashing the titles to Mary and then stacking them on the floor.

Everybody has a "thing," some object or hobby or interest which, once excited, can outweigh even the strongest logic or reason. Zed didn't need to understand it, she just had to identify and supply it. And by the time she had pulled eight of the books out of her bag, she recognized that particular gleam in Mary's eye. These books were Mary's "thing" and even now Zed knew that particular itch was starting to grow. That itch wasn't just having the books as much as the fear that here were all of those particular books sharing the same time and place as Mary and she might not have them. Zed kept pulling the books out, showing them to Mary and stacking them. When the stack hit fourteen she started to worry about what the magic number would be. When she pulled out the twentieth book, she felt in her bones that Mary just was too scared, too much a newbie, and maybe there was no magic number.

Zed pulled out the twenty-second book when Mary whispered, "Mine."

Zed paused "What?"

"Mine," Mary told Zed as she pulled the books toward her and put her arms protectively around the pile.

"Course they are," Zed reassured her holding back a smile. "Just a day or two, right?"

Mary looked up, distracted from the pile, and nodded agreement.

"I'll be back in a bit, okay?" Zed pulled out the last three travel books and showed Mary. "And when you open the door, you get these too." You got to keep back a sweetener for when the mood changes.

Mary nodded and Zed could see she was fair dealing, at least for now.

Zed picked up the blue bag, considerably lighter, and slung it over her shoulder. She left Mary to it and walked to the stairs with a spring in her step. All right, all right. Zed loved it when a plan came together. One last stop and she was home free.

She dropped down to the lobby and pulled open the door. Big mistake. Pete was fifteen feet away staring at her with a stupid "That really her?" expression on his face.

When you can't escape, fight; but when you can't fight, run. Zed ran. "Zed!" Pete bellowed, blurring into action.

Great, now *he knows my name*, she thought.

She hit the 2nd floor before she heard the lobby door bang open below and Pete pound up the stairs. She was worried, sure, but she wasn't panicked. After all, she might be small, but nobody could slide, squirm, and fly around this building like she could. Of course, she usually didn't try while hauling half a bag full of books, which was going to really cut down on her endurance. Still, already a hazy plan was coming together.

She sprinted up the stairs, passing the 4th floor. "Clear, clear!" she shouted, pushing through the incense up to the 5th floor. She pulled open the door and ran down the hall. "*Move it!* Move, fuck." She saw a flash of a line and Don and was by. Her chest was killing her. Was she getting soft? Was it internal bleeding? The books weren't that heavy. She decided to blame the incense.

"Zed!" Pete had seen her, but she was out the opposite stairwell banging the door shut behind her.

Pete would have to figure up or down; she might gain some seconds on that. She leapt up the stairs to seven, racing to make the door before Pete could reach the stairwell to hear her.

She made it; home stretch. Staggering and wheezing, she limped down the hall and pushed open Ivy's door, collapsing inside. She lay, trying to slow her heart, her breathing, so she could listen. Had they seen her? She counted the seconds, ten, twenty, it'd be anytime now. She heard a noise. It was from the wrong direction: Ivy's bedroom.

Had Luc sent someone to wait here? It seemed a bit too indirect for him. She couldn't smell the gas anymore, but with her love of oxygen and all she decided to crawl anyway. She made her way to the source of the noise, just beyond the open bedroom door. Inside, a hunched form stood, slid open a drawer, and started rummaging through the clothes.

"I should have known," Zed said.

"Wha?" Rat turned, a blue scarf in his hands.

Zed stood up and stepped inside and closed the door. "What are you doing here?" she whispered.

"What are you?" Rat whispered back. He frowned and straightened. "Why are we whispering?"

Zed cocked an ear for the hallway. She figured that Pete would notice in one, maybe two floors that she wasn't there. How long until he worked his way back?

"I want to make a deal," she told him. "You scavenge in the front and if anyone asks, you haven't seen me."

"Why?"

"Because that's the deal."

Rat lolled his head and stuck his tongue in his cheek. "What's in it for me?"

"I saved your life, remember?"

"Oh yeah!" Rat's eyes looked left, remembering. "What else?"

"What?"

"What else do I get?"

Nothing ever came easy, did it? She dug into her bag. "You get these, but then you can't scavenge more than five things."

"Jelly b –!" Rat shouted before Zed clamped a hand over his mouth and beard.

"Five items, we have a deal?" she hissed.

His eyes travelled from the jelly beans to her face, to the door, and back to her face again. He gave a slow negative.

"What?" she whispered, loosening her hand.

"I get to scrounge twenty more things."

"It's jelly beans!" she hissed. "Jelly beans!"

He looked over her shoulder at the door. With a panicked heartbeat, she gave a quick look; it was still closed. "I smell fear, Zed," he told her in a smug tone. "I don't think you've got a lot of time to deal."

"Next time, I'll let the truck run over you," she told him, heartfelt. "Seven, and no food."

"Fifteen."

"Ten."

"Twelve. Was that a step I heard?" he asked with a grin.

"Ten," she told him, reaching for a side table, sweeping up an orange lamp and yanking the cord out of the wall, "or I brain you and take my chances."

Rat grinned, his eyes quivering in violent anticipation. He smacked his lips. "You don't want to fuck with the Rat," he told her, then gnashed his teeth against each other.

"I'm not an old woman and I'm not a junkie," she said, raising the lamp up for a head swing. "Ten, all right?"

Rat's limbs were twitching, urging him on, but his eyes kept darting to the lamp. "Fuck, all right. I thought you were my friend," he whined.

"That's why I didn't use the knife." She threw him the beans. "Now get out there."

"Fucking women," Rat muttered, yanking open the door to the living room. "Bust in on a scrounge and they think they own the place." He wandered into the kitchen, banging open drawers and slamming them closed, muttering away. Zed eased herself into the closet, sitting atop of Ivy's shoes, her bags pulled to her chest. She left the door open a sliver, just enough to see out to the living room.

"Gotcha!" Pete came hurtling into the living room after throwing open the front door with a bang.

"Get your fuckin' hands off me," Rat yelled between grunts and pants as he writhed in Pete's grasp.

"Zed?" Pete struggled to hold Rat still for a good look.

"I fucking look like Zed?" Rat asked with a gasp as he broke free. He paced back and forth, eyeing Pete up while patting down his long hair and beard. "Fucking people breaking in on a fucking scrounge." Rat was quivering, biting out each word. "Zed have a beard, fucker? I some little girl, fucker?"

Pete backed up. "Sorry, little man, honest mistake. You seen Zed?"

"Little?" Rat was frozen staring. "Little? Oh, you sad fuck." He shook his head. "Hey, fuck-brain, I'm not Zed, get it, fuck-wonder? Zed not here! Zed run!" Rat jerked his arm back and forth in an angry pantomime. "Run by, go bye-bye, into stairs." He pointed to the opposite stairwell. "Zed gone. So run, fuck, run."

Pete had listened, his chest and fists tightening. As Rat leaned forward to finish, Pete introduced his fist to Rat's head. Rat flew into the couch and slumped to the floor. "Yeah, I get it!" Pete turned and walked out.

Zed counted forty breaths before moving, then she crawled to the front door. Rat was rubbing the side of his head. "Fucker called me little," he complained as she crawled by.

The hallway was clear. Zed took a moment to feel like crap. But that's what pills are for. *Moment's over*, she told herself as she chewed another pill down. She caught her breath, raised herself up, and crept to the stairwell. Empty. She headed down the stairs, back to the lobby.

"Zed, hey, Zed." Zed flinched. She really wasn't keen on hearing her name today. But it was only Bucket Charlie. "I heard Pete and Stu are looking for you."

"'Kay." She dug out the last little bottle and handed it over. "I got another job for you." She pulled out a fifth of whiskey, making Charlie's eyes light up.

"Anything," he promised.

"You tell anyone looking for me that you saw me running towards downtown. Can you do it?"

"Sure." He reached for the bottle.

"Say it back to me."

"I saw you running towards downtown."

"Good." She handed over the whiskey, watching as he opened it in less than two seconds. She took out her knife and showed it to him. "And if you don't, I'll come get my whiskey back."

"But I'll have drunk it," Charlie told her, eyeing the knife.

She looked at his belly. "I know."

Charlie started to shake. "I'll tell them, Zed, I'll tell them downtown."

"Good." She put away the knife and continued down to the lobby. This time she checked before opening the door. Empty. She scuttled over to the bunker.

"Hammer." He looked up from his mystery at her, then went back to the book.

"Hammer, there's more, see?" She was holding out two of the mysteries from her bag. "Trade?" Hammer looked at the mysteries in her hand, back to the one open before him, frowned, and nodded her in.

Zed gave the lobby a quick scan, then plucked out the green gym bag and placed it atop the TV table. Drawing back the zipper, she plunged her hands in, returning with a block of C-4 in each hand. Hammer's feet hit the floor as his body sprang to attention, his eyes focused. He leaned forward and took the C-4 blocks from her, his fingers squeezing and caressing them like oversized bath soap. He brought them to his nose for a long inhale. "Mmmm." His eyes glistened, happy and dreamy.

Zed pulled down the side of the bag, showing him the wires and plungers. "I want them timed," she told him, "but I could only get these." She pulled out the three alarm clocks.

Hammer dropped the C-4 into his lap and took the black alarm clock. After scrutinizing the face, he pried off the back. Bringing the clock up to his eye, he squinted at the gears. He looked over and gave Zed a grunt and a nod.

"Who?" he asked, scowling at her.

"First, how much?" Zed countered. "For assembly and ... placement."

Hammer pulled the gym bag into his lap. He rooted among the wires and detonators before giving Zed an easy shrug that said, "piece of cake."

"Mysteries, eight," he told her.

"Total?"

"Each."

Zed nodded and unpacked the blue bag, making three stacks of eight books each. "Okay."

Hammer surveyed the mound of mysteries, then turned to focus on Zed, face set, total business. "Tell me."

"I know what you did at Ivy's this morning."

Hammer's gaze dropped on her like hot tar. "So?"

"I want you to do the same, only to three empty apartments. First the gas, then the explosions two hours later."

Hammer shook his head. "Thirty minutes."

"Why?"

Hammer rolled his eyes. Amateur hour was irritating him. "Too much gas."

"Okay, whatever. I want them set for tomorrow, ten p.m. But don't set them until a couple hours before, okay?"

Hammer twitched, more amateur hour. "Luc know?"

"No, and that's part of the deal, you don't tell anyone. And unless I tell you in person, you don't stop."

Hammer's brow creased. It was obvious the thought of stopping had never occurred to him.

Well, there it was. Either Zed was broke with a lever against Luc, or she was broke. But as Luc would say, that's why they call it gambling.

"You owe," Hammer told her. He held her, weighed and measured in his eyes.

"Eight each, I paid."

Hammer held up two fingers. "Bombs." He lowered a finger. "Luc."

"No," said Zed. "One deal, not two, all the same."

Hammer gave a slow shake of the head. "Bombs paid." He looked her over. "Luc."

"You want books?"

He shook his head.

"I got some money. Drugs? Chocolate?"

Hammer shook no.

"So what do you want?"

Hammer put his hand on her cheek. It was big and hard. He could snap her like a lizard. His hand moved, neither fast nor slow, just casual, down, inside her coveralls. She stayed still, very, very still. Down it travelled until it reached her crotch, where he gave her a tweak before pulling his arm up and out. "You. Want you," he told her.

Zed was pretty sure he wasn't asking for her conversation. Surprise, surprise, at the end of the day it all boils down to dicks and chicks.

So how hard core am I? Zed asked herself.

She eased her arms out and shucked the coveralls off. "One hole, one time," she told him, showing she'd learned something from the feast. "Final deal."

Hammer's breathing rasped through his nose. "One time, one hole." His lids drooped, "Later."

"When?" Zed demanded.

"After tomorrow."

Well, that made good business sense, just bad emotional sense. "You tell Luc and you get nothing," Zed warned, climbing back into her coveralls. "Tomorrow," she reminded.

"Ten p.m.," Hammer agreed. And stared.

That kinda creeped Zed out. Leering would have been better. Anything but that totally focused stare. She grabbed her bag and left. What was the point of saying anything? They both knew they'd be seeing each other again.

The 2nd floor hall was still empty. Maybe Luc had invited Ellen and Teresa to a slumber party. Zed leaned up against Mary's door. God, she was tired. But she'd won, hadn't she?

She knocked. Mary came and Zed disappeared inside.

Chapter 14

BY MORNING, ZED WAS cranky, that irritability of having an itch you can't scratch until it makes you want to start slapping people. Thing is, Zed had a plan: cool out for a day, get an intermediary, and make a deal trading Luc's empire for their lives. If she'd had an extra bomb, she'd have set if off to show she was serious, but since she didn't, she'd just have to make do. What wasn't in the plan was what happens to a going-eighteen-hours-a-day-evaluating-checking-the-odds-and-making-three-deals-by-daybreak trader when she was forced to sit still. Being trapped sucked. Being quiet sucked. But what sucked big time was not being in the game. Zed almost looked forward to the occasional pounding on the door where Stu would ask if Mary had seen Zed or Ivy. Mary just peered out over her glasses and asked in that innocuous voice, "Who's Zed? Ivy?" After playing "pass-the-peanut" with that question four or five times, Stu gave up and went to pound on other doors.

Except for when Mary read out loud a few lines from one of the books which had enraptured her, there was nothing for Zed to do but sit next to the door and listen to Ellen and Teresa bitch or look out the window at the scroungers fighting down below.

It was morning and Zed was hungry. She watched the canmen shamble through the fog toward downtown. She was still hungry. And in pain. She took one of the pills and ate the last of Mary's salt crackers. Didn't help the hunger. Made it worse. The stomach liked what she sent and it wanted more.

"Please stop," Mary asked, looking over from the table.

Zed was bewildered.

"That walking up and down you do, it's very distracting."

"Don't you ever do anything?" Zed asked.

"I told you before," Mary said, "I read, I write in my journal, I write in my dream diary, and on Tuesdays I see Carl."

"The therapist," Zed added for her. This had become familiar. "But don't you ever want to do something different?"

Mary turned her head to the side and contemplated it for a minute. "No." She went back to her book.

Zed started pacing again. Mary lasted another three pages. "Zed?"

"I'm hungry," Zed complained. "And when I'm hungry, I get some food. Are you hungry?"

Mary thought that over too. "Not really."

"No wonder you got rid of the jelly beans," Zed retorted. "But since I can't go, can you go get some food, please?"

"I don't like to go out," Mary said, a furrow breaking her smooth brow. "Besides," she said softly, "I don't have any money. And that Mental Health Nurse will bring some food tomorrow." Having covered all angles, Mary gave a little quiver and subsided into her book.

Zed growled then paced. And paced. Went to the window and looked out. Went to the door and listened. And went back to pacing. "I have some food," she told Mary. "You want to go get it?"

Mary frowned. "Will you sit still if I get it?" she asked with resentful doubt in her voice.

Zed nodded.

"Will you eat very, very quietly?"

Zed nodded more slowly. What was wrong with this lady?

Mary thought a little more. "No." She went back to her book.

See what happens when you got nothing to trade, Zed reminded herself. But then again, maybe she did.

Zed started pacing again, but this time humming a two-note variation, a trick Barry used to annoy her with. She held each note an erratic time, from a few seconds to a minute before switching over. Now there was something to trade: quiet for food.

The skin around Mary's eyes and lips tightened, but she kept on reading. Within half an hour she pushed her glasses up on her nose and stood.

"I'll be quiet," Zed promised. "All day. Just go to 712 and get the food, okay? You don't have to talk to anyone, you just go up, get the food, and come down."

Mary sighed again and drifted toward the door. She opened it a crack and peered out. She looked back to Zed, "And you'll be still and not make noise from now on?"

"You get the food and it's a deal."

Mary looked out the crack again and opened the door a few inches. She waited. The world did not try to dive in the door at her, so she slipped out.

Zed went back to pacing, breaking every so often to listen at the door. This was her new game: waiting for Mary. The game went on a long time.

"I met a friend of yours," Mary said as she pushed the door open holding a jug of orange juice and a block of cheese. "Very rude."

What? "Who? What'd they look like? Did they follow you back?"

"He wouldn't leave me alone," Mary said. "But I ran away." She handed over the food.

Zed ripped into the cheese. "That's good. Who was it?"

The door swung open and a familiar stench rolled in. "Me," Rat said, stepping in. "I was curious about this fuckin' newbie. Not much of a scrounger, too focused."

"Take off, Rat. You've never seen me." Zed pasted a smile on. "I just saw a townie do a car-dump, just two blocks from here."

Rat stood eyeing her. "Fuck it."

"That," Mary said, retreating behind the table for safety, "is your friend?" She held her nose.

"I wonder," Zed said. "Hey, Rat, you my friend?"

"Sure I am," Rat replied. That's when Zed knew; he hadn't said, "Fuck, what?" or "Yeah, I'm fucking warm all over." Nope, Rat had sold her out.

"You bastard." She went for her knife.

He leapt on her, pinning her arms to her side, his beard crushed against her face. "I got her, I fucking got her!"

Zed tried a knee in the groin, but Rat blocked it with his thigh; he was no stranger to dirty fighting. Zed's options were limited; she tried stomping on his foot, sweeping his legs, and head-butting, but all of them were no goes. All she had left was the neck bite, but she'd have to go through Rat's beard first. And that smelled like quite the meal.

She was spared the sacrifice by the arrival of Pete and Stu. They held her between them while Rat scavenged the knife off Zed.

"I'll be back for you," she promised Rat. "And next time, I'll kick you under the truck."

"It was a good deal," Rat told her. "H for a year, all three hundred days. You'd have done the same."

Would she? Zed wondered as Pete and Stu hauled her between them. Not a regular customer, she decided, and not for H.

They hustled her down to the elevators and pushed the button. While they waited, Zed remembered a trick one of the "care-givers" had told her. She stretched her hands and placed one on Pete's and one on Stu's thigh, then slid them along, slowly flexing till she got to the groin.

"Zed!" Pete grabbed her hand and pushed it away while Stu just groaned and said, "More baby, more."

Zed was not, however, trying to buy sexual favours. But as the woman told her, once you get to the groin, everything else relaxes. Zed dropped with a twist and found out it was true. She was free.

She scrabbled over Pete's feet, heard Stu curse, but her eyes and mind were ahead; get down that hall and away. She barely heard the "close but no banana" as Pete's fist hit the side of her head.

"WAKEY, WAKEY," A playful voice called, combined along with the ball of someone's thumb being drawn across her brow. Zed groaned. Her head felt like it had been split open and left to dry. She blinked her eyes to see Luc peering down at her. "It's been 100 years, beauty," he said. Stu was there too. Behind them was a glass sliding door and beyond that a white gauze curtain, which she assumed blocked her view of Luc's desk and cabinet. She felt a slight breeze brush through her hair and the sun beating down on her.

Luc held out his hand. "I told you she'd live." Stu looked at Zed with disgust, but dug a ten out of his pocket and slapped it in Luc's hand.

Looking about, Zed found that she was in a wooden box frame, like a bed frame, propped upright against Luc's balcony. Like an X, two two-by-fours crossed the frame and Zed had been tied to them. An X and a box and Zed pinned like a bug in the middle.

"Not bad, no?" Luc came over and ran his hands over the smooth sides of the two-by-fours. "I, too, was a carpenter's son." He looked down at her expectantly, but whatever reaction she gave was not the right one because he looked up to the sky, his hand held out in exasperation. "No one ever gets that."

"You want me to laugh, boss?"

"If you have to ask," Luc told Stu, "then the answer's no."

Zed cleared her throat and they both turned to look at her. "Think I'll be going now," she said. Luc and Stu looked at each other and broke into laughter.

"She doesn't get it, does she, boss?"

Luc inclined his head toward Stu. "She does, but that's the difference. No moaning in the carpet, no loud denials." He turned back to Zed. "It's a pleasure to be working with a professional."

Zed could tell Luc thought it was a compliment, but Zed would rather be on the other end of the torturer/tortured relationship.

"So I'm afraid you won't be leaving just yet," Luc continued. "At least not until –"

"You cough up the old bag!" Stu yelled into her face, stepping forward.

"Stu?" Luc's eyebrows had fallen. "I thought we already chatted over this verbal initiative of yours."

Stu backed up to the edge of the balcony, his hands protectively wrapped around his neck. "Sorry, boss, but I had to walk around this building for six hours last night." He turned and yelled at Zed, "Six hours!"

"Perhaps you are tired?" Luc suggested.

Stu was confused.

"You would like to go inside and rest for a few minutes?" Luc pointed to the open glass door. Stu lowered his head and slunk inside.

Luc watched until Stu disappeared behind the white curtain before turning back to Zed. "Now, let's get to business."

"Fine. That fifty dollars which you probably stole from me if you untie an arm."

Luc raised his fist to cover his mouth and gave a single polite cough. "Let's start again. Would you like to deal for your life and comfort?"

"Sure, here's my deal," Zed told him.

Luc cupped a hand to his ear. "My ear the eastern harbour, your words the spice ships of Alexandria."

Zed just stared.

"My best material," he lamented. "Fine. Speak!"

"You let me go, you forget Ivy, Ivy forgets you, and we all go back to the way it was."

"Except for Barry," Luc reminded.

"But nobody liked him."

"That's not the point. He died, in public. I have to respond."

"Choose somebody else," Zed suggested. She reviewed her "hate" list. "Pick Rat."

"Ha ha. I like it. But no, let me recap: I have you. I don't want you, I want this 'Ivy' person, so I can set her on fire and throw her off my balcony. Now, I'm going to let her off easy because she's old and probably can't take torture. But because I don't have the woman, I'll have to start on you. And you can take torture. Any problems?"

"One," Zed told him. "I left some packages in safe-keeping and if you don't let me go, I'll take this building down. You get me but you lose the rest."

"Um...." He stood back, his fingers squeezing his chin, thinking it over. "No." He came back to Zed and his hand went up to her tied-down left hand. His finger traced the arm back to her shoulder and, using his thumb and the first two fingers, he gave the bruise on her shoulder a vicious squeeze. Zed gasped.

"Zed, I like you but this is how it is: I don't care about the building, I don't care if your threat is real or not. If you tell me where she is, I'll let you go – whatever shape you're in. I think of you as my child. Perhaps somehow, you are, but it won't stop me for a second." He reached down and ripped the tape off her ribs. "Do you believe me?"

Zed did believe him. A part of her was afraid because she did not want to watch herself being chopped up, or survive what might happen. But another part reminded her that this is when you find out what kind of dealer you are. And Zed lived by the rules. The rules were all she had.

"Take it to the wall," she told him.

Luc considered her. He sighed. "That was refreshing." He smiled at her and when he looked at her, his eyes were unmasked, afire. They blazed with passion and excitement. "Looks like we've got a date then. And if you live past tomorrow, forget about thugging, because you're

245

made for better things." He turned and called through the door, "Stu."

Stu bounced through the doorway. "Seems she doesn't want to play," Luc told him. "Could you entertain her while I go work up something special for later?" Luc walked inside.

Stu came over to her and leaned down so he was looking at her eye to eye. "I'll save your face for last," he told her, then straightened up and pulled his packet of cigs out of his pocket. He flipped open the top and drew one out, long and white. A flick of the lighter and Stu took a couple long drags, getting the end nice and hot. Then he took it between his thumb and forefinger. "This might sting," he told her as it approached her right shoulder.

It did, it stung like mad. Zed jerked. He pressed it in, lightly, enough to burn, but not enough to snuff the cigarette out. Then it was back to his lips to stoke it red-hot again. The smell of burnt flesh flared in Zed's nostrils. She could feel it, white and raw and far away. Stu lowered the cigarette again, his eyes drinking in her expressions, her every twitch and jerk. The cigarette burned in and she arched, stretching against her bonds. Stu laughed, his face alive with pleasure.

Charlie did this, Zed told herself, biting her lip. Charlie did it all the time and she was tougher than Charlie. And she'd be tougher than Stu too.

So the time passed. Zed wasn't sure how long Stu worked on her, but he went through eight cigarettes, on her shoulders, her upper back, her arms, legs, and even her neck. But she didn't cry out, and after trying ten or more times, she even managed to stop flinching that second before the hot tip of the cigarette bit in. Her body hated her, it wailed inside her mind to scream, to cry, to plead with Stu to stop. But she just concentrated on looking Stu in the eye and making her face as bland as possible.

Luc entered through the open glass door, with Pete and Hammer trailing after him. "So, lackey number one, how goes the work?"

Stu straightened up, reached down, and put out his lit cigarette on her collarbone before throwing the butt off the balcony. "She's a tough nut," he said with the tinge of joy in his voice.

"I expected nothing less," Luc assured both Stu and Zed. Stu retreated and Luc came over to stand by Zed. "Nice day?" he asked her.

"Known better." She licked her lips, tasting the salty blood from where she had bit through during Stu's early attempts.

"Play time's over," he told her, his voice light and gay but his face serious. "You need to tell me where she is."

"Screw –"

Luc's hand covered her mouth. "I don't think I want to hear what comes next." He nodded to Stu and Pete. "I'll attend to this myself." They retreated inside, leaving Hammer.

"Last chance," Luc told her. Zed just glared.

Luc nodded to Hammer, who advanced holding what looked like an oversized power-drill, only instead of the drill point, there was just a hole. Hammer looked down at Zed's burns and the corner of his mouth twitched. He held the drill high on her wrist while his other hand held her hand firm and taut. He looked toward Luc and nodded.

Luc had been watching Zed. "You don't know what it is, do you?" he asked. "Well, where's the fun in that? That, my tortured chum –" He nodded toward the instrument in Hammer's hand. "– is a nail gun, an instrument which shoots nails out at high speed, right into wood, hey –" He watched Zed turn to look at the nail gun again, her arm pulling and twisting against Hammer's grip. "No, no," Luc admonished her. "You don't want to be doing that. Our good friend here has it positioned to miss your bones and major arteries. Isn't that good of him? But if you twist all over the place, then who knows what will happen? So just lie back, all right?"

Zed lay her head down. O fuck, o fuck, o fuck, o fuck.

Hammer looked back and Luc nodded to him. Hammer squinted, checked the target, and squeezed.

The small "phut" sound the nail gun made was completely drowned out by Zed's scream. The nail had ripped right through a nerve. The pain just rolled down, pouring into her mind and flooding through her, taking every refuge possible: she writhed, she flopped, she screamed. Zed's scream died away and her body slumped, drained.

Luc checked the work. "You set the pressure too high," he chided Hammer. "It's gone right through. Now you'll have to do it again."

Hammer growled but adjusted a knob at the base of the gun. He brought it to her wrist, an inch further up.

Zed couldn't swallow, couldn't speak, couldn't seem to do anything but watch Hammer bring it down.

Hammer squeezed the trigger. Same scream, same funky-chicken dance. Zed tried to find a place in her mind to hide, but the pain just kept bringing her back.

Luc inspected. "Perfect." He pulled out a blade and cut the ropes binding that wrist. "No need for these now."

Hammer stood with the gun, waiting. "Deal?" Zed croaked toward him. "How much to cap Luc?" Luc and Hammer shared a smile. "I'm serious." But what Zed really wanted to know was, Hammer, have you sold me out?

"Once more, my good man." Luc nodded to Hammer. Hammer advanced and grabbed Zed's other wrist, holding it firm and flat, then sighted the gun. Zed was trembling all over. She could feel the burning of bile in her throat. She couldn't face it again, she just couldn't. "Come, come," Luc said, bending down to catch her eye. "One little word and we'll ply that nail out, sweet as rain."

Zed was awash with fear. She could feel it sweeping over her in waves, running up and down her limbs, paralyzing her. That was good, because if she could have spoken, she would have. Luc shook his head, then gave Hammer the nod. A pause and then, "phut!"

Zed screamed again, harsh and raw. She couldn't control it, she just screamed. By the time her lungs had exhausted themselves and she hung limp from the nails, she could feel the clammy grip of her coveralls stuck to her legs, and the moisture, still running down her thighs and legs, dripping from her ankles.

"Don't worry, Zed," Luc told her encouragingly as he bent over to cut the ropes on her other wrist. "Happens to the best of them. The old bod tends to get a bit shook up under pressure and all, lets go of things at the wrong moments, nothing personal about it. Stu, can you get me a towel?"

Hammer stood back, watching her. Zed lifted her head, then let it sag back down. "Die?" Hammer asked Luc.

"Her? Oh no, doesn't know the word 'die,' do you?" Luc chuckled. "That's one I'm trying to teach her, that and some other words: surrender, quit, inform."

Hammer grunted. Zed lifted her head and caught Hammer staring. He saw her and gave a slow nod. She almost started crying. He hadn't told. She was sure of it. Survive, that was the key. Scream, writhe, wet herself, who cares. Just survive.

Hammer looked to Luc who waved him out. Hammer went out, passing Stu who was coming in, towel in hand. Luc pointed to the growing puddle under Zed and Stu threw the towel over it, careful to avoid any contact himself. "Boss," he said, turning his back to Zed to address Luc. "We've had some ... complaints, about the noise."

"Which you dealt with?"

"Yeah, but the Father out there is talking big. He says he knows it's Zed and he wants her."

"Anyone can walk across the street and see it's Zed up here. As to getting her, he has to stand in line like everyone else."

"He said if you don't let her go, he'll come after you."

"Really?" Luc said. "What an extraordinary statement. Let's invite him in." Luc followed Stu into the office.

Though she couldn't see, Zed could hear everything.

"Have a seat," Luc said.

"I've come for Zed."

"Afraid she's rather tied up right now. No, scratch that, more like nailed down."

"You listen to me," the Father's voice was low and commanding. "God may tolerate you, but I won't. Not in this. Either you let Zed go or kill me now, because I will come for you, today."

"Strong words for a man who drops his hands when he fights," Luc said. "But seriously, if I thought you were a threat, I'd kill you. But I don't. Regardless of what you've done, you're a non-violent man. And between a gang of religious zealots who may be able to beat up doped-out drunks and my two guys, I bet on my two guys. Drop by anytime."

"This isn't over."

"Throw him out, boys," Luc said, "and don't spare the horses."

They left her there for the afternoon and she listened to drug deals, pimping, bets, and a bit of loan sharking. It sounded so normal, she almost expected to hear herself walk in.

Business tailed off late in the afternoon.

Stu reappeared in the doorway, carrying Luc's office chair. Putting it down, he went and got the second chair, placing it by the first before dropping into it. He pulled out his knife, looked at her, raised his eyebrow, and gave his wrist a flick. Zed, reminded of the outline on the plaster wall, flinched. Stu laughed and showed her the knife, hilt in his palm, blade trapped between his fingers. Luc, now wearing his grey jacket, strolled out onto the balcony, shot Zed a glance, and continued to his chair. "How are things with you?" he asked as he sat down.

"Hanging," Zed croaked out. "Business good?"

"Phenomenal, particularly the last two days. After you took my suggestion to heart and dropped out of sight, the money on your being snuffed grew exponentially."

"Christina?" Zed asked. "When?"

"When am I going to unveil the body?" Luc's index finger rubbed the side of his brow. "Difficult question that, do I keep the body hidden and pocket all the cash or do I 'find' it to keep the game going?" He pursed his lips, his hands templing under his chin. "I think she'll be 'found' tomorrow, all things considered. But right now, my problem is what to do with you."

"Let me go?" Zed suggested.

"No. Let me rephrase that, the question is how best to get you to divulge the hiding place of Ivy."

Zed licked her cracked and cut lips. "Just don't give me anything to drink," she said.

"Oh," Luc said, sitting up, his eyes big and goggling at her. "Do tell, Bre'r Rabbit, you say you don't want to go in that briar patch?" He laughed, but shook his head at Zed's disappointed expression. "You aren't staying with me today," he told her. "Let's just say that I do not follow or react to any suggestions you might make."

"Why don't you spike her a few more times, Boss?" Stu asked, having watched the exchange with bewildered irritation. "Then she'll spill it."

"Spill it?" Luc said, looking at Stu with an expression one would give a peacock who had just landed in your lap. "Really, Stu, you are a fount of archaic expressions. Do you think we should 'squeeze her,' use my 'knuckle duster,' or threaten her with a 'swim with the fishes'?" Stu slouched lower in his seat, avoiding Luc's eye. "In my experience," Luc continued, "after two nails, they'll either tell you everything or nothing. We did three and she hasn't budged. You could 'spike' her a dozen times, it wouldn't matter." Stu looked from Luc to Zed and back again, trying to tell Luc that this was a challenge he was willing to take. Luc sighed, "No, we'll have to break her, so first we wear her down."

Zed wanted to tell him that it really wasn't necessary, but knew that no matter what she said, they would continue until they got what they wanted, or until ten o'clock came. Time was her only saviour. The Father was nice, but she agreed with Luc, no rescue from that quarter.

"Want me to pound her? Give her a 'chat'?" Stu was eager, very eager.

"I think Barry tried that two days ago," Luc commented. "Did it work?"

"I could break some fingers, file down her teeth, rip out toenails?"

Luc thought about that. "No ... just more of the same. Besides, I want her to be able to function after this. And the toenails, just not enough, she could take that."

Stu and Luc studied her, silent. Zed watched the shadows of evening lengthen into the grey world of dusk.

Luc spoke out of the grey. "I'll bleed her." He nodded to himself and repeated it, "Definitely, bleed her." He stood and eased himself out of his jacket, handing it to Stu. "Get a couple buckets of water, cold," he told Stu. "And some salt, or vinegar."

Stu rose and disappeared inside, with Luc on his heels. Zed heard the clang as the metal door of the cabinet was opened, then closed. Luc returned with a big, thick knife in his hand. "Not for you." He said to Zed at the widening of her eyes. He reached over and cut her coverall straps. Then, blade out, he ran it down the sides, shucking the coveralls like a corn cob.

He gave the cracked ribs a slap.

"Ah," Zed moaned.

He winked at her. "Stings, don't it?" Luc stepped back and drew his long double-bladed knife from its harnessed holster. He stood over her, knife in his hands, turning his head this way and that, like a painter surveying an empty canvas, preparing his work.

Stu staggered through the door, a bucket slopping in each hand. He put them down and wheezed out, "Salt," before exiting.

"Now we're starting," Luc said, putting the knife back and rolling up his sleeves. He lifted up the bucket, and with a heave, sent the water in a wall toward Zed.

It was cold: wake-me up, skin-contracting, heart-pounding cold. "That's what I like to see," Luc said, drawing out his blade. "All that nice, tight skin." He put the blade to her breast bone and with a flick of his wrist, made a three-inch-long cut to the right. Zed gasped. It was like an iceberg; freezing stings, rough, and about ten times as bad as you thought it would be. "I know," Luc said, his face kind and soft. "It's really something when you're cut by a good blade, none of the hack and slash, but a sweet kiss. You'll bleed and weaken, and that's what I need.

The cold will help." He touched her skin and his hand felt burning hot. "I'd better hurry, before you start to shake."

With one hand holding her neck and upper chest, Luc started to work, flick, flick, flick: each a cut. He worked to the left, long cuts followed by short ones, then back to the right, and finally a long, slow one, right across the belly. He stepped back, looked down, and gave a reproachful snort. "Forgot the most important part." He came back and flicked little diagonal cuts all across her upper chest, smiling and nodding. Holstering his knife, he picked up the second bucket and threw it over her.

Zed had started to shiver uncontrollably. The wind was picking up the water on her skin and freezing her to the bone. Halfway through Luc's work, Stu had turned on the lights and returned with the salt. Luc picked up two handfuls and turned toward her. He saw her face cringe as he approached. "Last chance," he called out. "Will you tell?" She shook her head. He applied the salt in a block, rubbing it into the cuts with both hands, his strong palms pushing her twisting, cringing, writhing body. He stepped back beside Stu and surveyed her. Zed just hung and let the tears stream out. God, she hurt. Broken ribs, nails, cuts, and now she was freezing, literally. It just wasn't her day.

"Nice, Boss. What you call it?"

"Rain over Mount Fuji," Luc said with pride. "With the salt, she'll have it forever. It's not woodblock, but I do what I can." Stu nodded and they both contemplated it. Zed looked down, but it was just a blur of cuts.

"Zed!" Luc cried in exasperation, "you're moving too much, the blood is covering the picture." He poured the left-over water from one bucket into the remains of the other and sent a litre or two over her.

"Nice." Stu nodded.

"I like the dichotomy," Luc told him, preening to an audience. "The traditional view, traditional theme, very Hukio-e, but with the freshness of the medium."

The darkness had descended. Zed didn't know what time it was, but she knew she had survived. She was going to see it through to the end. "You won't take me," she croaked out.

"Beg pardon?"

Zed tried to make some saliva, failed, decided to swallow anyway. "You won't take me." Her voice was clearer, "Won't take me below."

"Below?" Luc was looking wary.

"Below. Pete below, Joe below." She looked to Stu. "Barry's down there too, and you'll be there soon."

Stu was staring at Zed in confusion.

"Ask him where Barry is," Zed told him.

"Boss?"

Luc's voice was calm, but dangerously edged. "Stu, go guard the door."

"Boss?"

Luc turned and shouted at him, "Go ... guard ... the ... *door!*" Stu leapt through the door, scrambling through the office to the safety of the hallway.

Luc turned back to face her and for the second time Zed saw the true face of Luc. His lips were pulled back and while Zed had often seen his tight-lipped smile, here was the unrestrained gleam of sharp canines. "You," he breathed out, approaching her. "So many secrets." He grabbed her head with both hands, raising her face toward him, his fingers pressing into her neck. He gazed down at her face, his pupils dilating wide, until all Zed could see was his black orbs. "Don't you know," he whispered, "why you're not like the rest?" He lowered his head and pressed his lips to hers, his tongue flicking out, licking the blood from her cut lip.

In the background came sounds of shouting, filtering in from the hallway. Zed could hear the Father calling her name and Stu shouting for Luc. Yet she couldn't tear her eyes from Luc's black irises. "You're part of me," he whispered to her. He broke away, eyes dilating back to pinpoints, public face slamming back on. "Must excuse me." He entered the office.

"I can't hold them back." She heard Pete's panicked voice.

"Then close the door," Luc replied.

It must have worked because soon she could hear the pounding on the door. She watched the sun set.

"Anyone have a gun?" Pete called out.

"We don't use guns," came Luc's withering reply. "They have no style."

Pete responded with frightened hysterical laughter. "You got a sword then?"

There was the squeak of the metal cabinet. "Here, try the bowie knife," Luc said.

The banging on the door had turned rhythmic and regular, with a solid boom. She could faintly hear, "Back, back ... now ... *boom* ... back, back ... now ... *boom!*"

"The door's going to bust!" Pete wailed.

"I'm aware of that," Luc said calmly. "So when I give the word, we throw the door open, okay?"

There was a "Yes, boss!" from Stu and a sniffle of agreement from Pete. The door took another resounding boom and Luc yelled, "Now."

Zed wished she could see it because all she heard was a few seconds of silence as she imagined the two groups staring at each other. "We lose, you win," Luc finally said. "So, Father, would you like to come inside and talk about this?"

"No!" he retorted. "Just let her go!"

"Okay, I'll rephrase: you come and talk and she walks, you attack and she dies."

A confused murmur rose from the crowd; the Father was silent. "All right!" the Father called. "But if I go in there, your two henchmen stay out here."

"Fine," Luc agreed, followed by an outraged squawk from Pete. "Let's go talk on the balcony," Luc suggested. "After all, that's where the chairs are."

"Oh, Zed." The Father was there, draping a jacket over her. "Why are you just sitting there?" he demanded of Luc, who had taken a seat and was watching. "Help me."

"Sit down, Father, she'll keep for a minute or two, won't you, Zed?"

"Screw you," Zed told him.

"See, lots of life left in her. No, what really made me curious was why you want to free her so badly after you failed to drown her. Is it envy?"

"I should have known you'd misunderstand." The Father sat down. "I did it for them, always for them."

"You see," Luc explained, "I knew it was you, I just couldn't figure out why. Is it sexual?"

"No!" The Father rubbed his forehead, a sure sign of frustration. "It was when I saw Charles, a child with no future, no hope, and he was watching you, imitating you."

"And you offered them...?"

"Hope."

"So death equals hope?"

"I will be the killer, they won't. I will take anything, and they will be innocent. I accept that others hate me, that even God would turn his face. But then Zed...."

"I am finding this hard to follow," Luc complained. "I'm still trying to get how you saw Pete as 'innocent.' Okay, so what's with Zed?"

"God brought her back. That's when I knew God was still watching over me, taking some and turning back others."

"Countessa saved me," Zed said. She was trying to clear things up.

"Yes," the Father responded, "but by whose hand?"

Luc and Zed stared at each other. In this they were united: the Father was one strange dude.

"Okay, I'm confused," Luc confessed. "Why was Zed saved?"

"I drowned her," the Father said.

"You drowned her?" Luc turned to Zed. "You were a victim and didn't tell me? You really have been busy." He turned back to the Father. "Shoddy workmanship on that one, friend."

"I'm done explaining. I came, I talked, now she walks." The Father stood, a grey outline in the dusk.

Luc shrugged, "If she wants to go."

"That's your whole plan: confront Zed with the truth and have her recoil in horror?"

"Not at all," Luc chuckled. "This is more of a catch and release game. I get the pleasure of hunting her all over again. And as a bonus, she gets an education on the limitations of good people."

"I think Zed will surprise you one day. She knows far more about the mix of good and evil than you think."

"Zed has surprised me, several times, just today. My, aren't you getting possessive."

"You tortured her, what kind of claim is that?"

"Ummm...." Zed moaned to get their attention.

"That was business." Luc's eyes twinkled. "All right, a bit of pleasure too. But what's testing without me?"

"Hey!" They both turned to stare at Zed. "Done?"

"We'll continue this later," the Father promised Luc before hurrying over to Zed.

"You know where I am, same cast, same balcony tomorrow, that okay?"

The Father and Zed both growled.

"I'll get you free in just a minute." The Father looked into her eyes. "You still trust me?"

"You still feel like killing me?"

"Absolutely not."

"That's okay then, call it evens." Zed licked her chapped lips. "What time is it?"

"What?" The Father had been examining her arms to try and free her.

"Time, what's the time?"

"Just turning ten o'clock, why?"

Zed dropped her head and smiled. "You'd better hurry."

Chapter 15

ZED WAS A LITTLE DELIRIOUS. Taking out the nails had pushed her over the thin edge. They'd fiddled around with the pliers long enough. "Pull … them … fucking … out!" They took a few chunks of flesh, but they got them out. As the second nail came free, her moan turned to a flipped-out giggle.

"I won!" she crowed at Luc, who watched in the doorway. She could feel Howard and the Father stiffen, but she'd never pretended to be a good winner.

She lay wrapped in towels, giggling. She knew it was just a buzz from the pain. Deep down, she was kinda pissed off, because she was sure it was ten o'clock and nothing had happened. That meant Hammer conned her. But on the bright side, she wouldn't have to pay.

But watched pots and all that; just as she finished damning Hammer, she felt the building shudder. All right, here we go. A split second later, an explosion of light and sound rolled up from below. Everyone crowded onto the balcony, looking down at the flames billowing out of the third floor. While they thought this was the main show, Zed knew it was just coming attractions and busied herself worming into the corner by the door. As she caterpillared over Luc's shoes, he looked down. "Hey, no blood on the leather," he complained.

Even more people pressed out onto the balconies. "Bad move," Zed said, and pulled the towel over her head.

Another explosion blew out Valerie's apartment, up on the 19th. *Don't look up*, Zed mentally projected to the people on the balcony, just *don't*. They looked up.

Well, so much for no one getting hurt, she thought as the glass rained down. Turned out the building wasn't equipped with safety glass, but the good old sheet and shard.

Zed watched as people hunched, held up hands, and pulled up collars to ward off the rain. But this was a different rain and shards punched through hands, embedded in arms and backs, cutting scalps and necks.

The Father turned, blood running down his face from the cuts on his head and cheeks. "Luc!" His face was throttled in rage, veins bulging. "Luc." Those not screaming and writhing turned to stare at Luc.

"Nothing about 'God's will' now, I notice," Luc said.

The Father pointed an accusing finger. "You."

And with classic timing the last bomb went off, directly below them.

The force drove them to their knees as a sheet of flame ripped past the balcony – a choking blast of heat. Luc's glass shattered, flooding the balcony with jagged fragments. Zed could hear herself laughing while she watched Luc's hand grow white on the doorframe.

As the smoke curled up over the balcony, those who could stand, rose, their faces ugly, fists clenched as they gathered, eyes fixed on Luc. Luc looked them over and gave them his smile. "Love to oblige," he raised his hands in defence. "But it's not me, couldn't have been."

Logically, he was right. But mobs don't worry about logic, to them the formula was simple – they had threatened Luc and now he was retaliating. The crowd slowly advanced, people reaching into pockets for knives or ripping off pieces of cloth to wrap up a suitable shard of glass.

The consensus seemed to be that two could play at retaliation.

"I'm a victim here," Luc told them. "Just like you." The crowd just kept advancing. Luc stepped back into the office, his hands dropping to his knives. "Boys!" he called. "I think we've got a situation here."

"Boss, Pete took off!" Stu called back.

There was a pause: a little well of silence and then, like a frightened, enraged mob in a burning building, they attacked, the Father in the fore calling, "Responsibility. Time to take responsibility."

That kinda ticked Zed off. I mean this was a thing going on between her and Luc and while it was nice for the Father to clear off old debts, there was no call for him to be stealing the show.

She got Howard to carry her to Luc's desk before he too ran into the hall, chasing Luc.

Zed found her bag and chowed down on pain pills. She put the fifty dollars in her boots and pulled them on. Thanks to Luc, her coveralls were toast, so this would have to do.

Ben P. stuck his head in, "Hey, cool, you are a girl." He winked and cocked a finger. "Our little secret, yeah? Hey, nice scars." He checked out her torso. "Course, that'll be a bitch when your tits come out more, I mean, wow, way to fuck those suckers up, but maybe you'll get little ones, heh?"

"Pass me the coat," she told him, pointing to the one thing untouched in the room, Luc's coat rack. His blue silk jacket swung peacefully in the breeze from the freshly ventilated windows.

"Yeah, sure." Ben handed it over. "You wanna come out to the hall? There is a class-A ass-kicking going on and dig this, the building is on fire. Is that wild or what?"

Zed climbed into the coat, grabbed a knife, and jumped off the desk. She joined Ben P. in the hall. He was right, it was wild. Someone had opened the stair door and now the wall, paint, siding, baseboards, and ceiling were merrily burning. The top foot near the ceiling was a black haze of smoke, and visibility wasn't too hot at ground level either. But all this was secondary to the wild-'n'-wooly knife fight going on.

Zed's eyes followed the trail of bodies to a mixed mob of dissatisfied customers, One-Lighters, and the Father's Gang. They all pushed forward, intent on a simple plan: kill Stu and Luc.

Luc and Stu stood shoulder to shoulder, knives out. They covered the hall, but were being slowly pushed back. The mob had numbers, but Luc and Stu had skill; it was a series of lunges and dashes into Luc's knives. No one spoke, just the crackle of flames and the gasps of the crowd.

Looking at it, Zed realized it was a stalemate. Luc and Stu could run out of hall, or the crowd could run out of bodies, but unless someone did something suicidal, it was fixed. And she doubted that Luc would be the suicidal one.

"Bummer, bummer, what a bummer," Zed heard. Steve was sitting down holding his arm.

"You attacked him?" Zed asked, nodding toward Luc.

"Attack?" Steve stared at her with dazed, spaced out eyes. "I came for another hit, but it's like everyone's buying today." Steve shook his head. "I'm like having this really bad trip right now, there's like yelling and fire and all sorts of crap." He looked at her and sniffed. "I just need a few uppers to get everything right."

A howl brought Zed's head up. Howard had made a lunge and gotten a Stu special, knife to the ribs, for his effort. Leaping up and off of Howard, Charlie flew through the air, arms extended. Stu brought up his knife in time to slice Charlie from sternum to groin, but not until Charlie had slammed a shard of glass in Stu's eye.

Stu dropped, Stu flopped, and most of all Stu screamed. Luc stayed on, defending his henchman with an unusual loyalty. But the crowd had numbers and he was driven back. The way they hacked Stu up, it seemed that Charlie wasn't the only one with a grudge. Zed watched Stu till he stopped twitching. She was disappointed. If one person in the world needed burning, it was Stu.

Anyone in a knife fight facing 40:1 odds would have been mincemeat in seconds. Luc wasn't anyone. He weaved, dancing and blocking, his hands flicking everywhere; a cut, a slash, a near decapitation. But he was taking licks too and his coat hung in bloody tatters. Only his hat, at a jaunty tilt, seemed unaffected.

They backed him to the far stairwell. He back-kicked the door open and the smoke billowed in. Taking advantage of his break in concentration, Jenny spun in, getting a knife in the shoulder. She gripped it hard, teeth bared, and ripped it from Luc's hand as she sunk to the floor. There was a pause then, a breath; Luc was down to a single blade. Everyone watched Luc, but Luc looked up over them and met Zed's eyes as she stood on the edge of the crowd.

"Just in time. I've mislaid my knife," Luc called, blocking Tim's attack and cutting through his black t-shirt to score on his ribs. "You selling?"

"What's the trade?" Zed asked.

"Right now, I'm open to offers." He jammed his knife into an attacker's neck, then, wrenching it free, kicked the body back into the crowd. "You mind?" he yelled at them. "I'm dealing here."

Zed laughed. Tomorrow he'd probably skin her for a new lampshade, but she couldn't help but smile. "One knife, express." She reversed her knife, holding the blade with her thumb. Sure, she'd smiled, but that didn't stop her wanting him dead. She pulled back her arm and let it fly, full bore, spinning on toward his head.

He blocked a cut, then plucked her knife out of the air. Zed sighed. She knew that'd be too easy.

"Obliged." With the knife he drew his chain off his neck and spun it through the air to her. "My marker. We'll talk later. And bring the jacket. This one's seen better days."

Zed grabbed the vial as it flew by. Luc's pinkie tip rolled in its prison. She looked back up. "What's this?"

The crowd had surged again, pushing him back into the flames licking up from the stairwell. "My marker," he yelled. "You've got your piece, now step aside, there's others in line."

Sure enough, there were plenty in line. The crowd smelled blood, a special kind of blood too, untouchable. They were close and they knew it, and everyone really, really wanted to see Luc fall.

Luc's eyes flicked to the fire. "Good old flame," he said. The crowd pushed him into the doorframe; cutting or burning, either would do for them.

"Luc's not for killing," he told them as they made a rush. "Old Luc will never die." His body fell back, disappearing into the smoke. "Remember," he called to Zed and then he was gone, swallowed up in the flames.

They all stared, expecting Luc to leap out, to rise up, maybe even fly out, but all that came out was smoke. And there was plenty of that already. The hall was so thick with it you couldn't see the ceiling. That was it. Luc had fallen.

With Luc gone, the crowd fell apart, everyone freaking out in their own way. Zed could hear sirens coming from downtown as she watched people running up and down the hall, in and out of the rooms, everyone wanting a way out. What they found was grim. The stairs by Luc's office were a holocaust. Fire had taken the whole end of the floor. There was fire below and burning debris falling from above.

"To the balconies!" someone cried. "We'll climb down."

"Too high!" Jenny wailed, blood streaming down her shoulder as she limped by. "Too high!"

"We can't go down."

"Try the other stairs."

"Oooo!" screamed one of the One-Lighters. "We'll die, we'll all die."

The crowd was moaning and some were sobbing. "We won't die!" came a voice, forceful and strong. "We won't die!"

"Father?"

The Father crouched in the centre of the hall, the smoke thick above him. He looked over at Zed and nodded. "While we can't go down," he told the crowd, whose faces turned to him, desperate for any hope, "we can go up. Up to the roof, where there's clear air and safety.

"Roof's all concrete," a voice agreed. "We'll be safe there."

"What about that explosion above?"

"It was over this stairwell, so we'll take the far one," the Father explained.

"But that's the one Luc disappeared into."

"He's either gone or barbecued." The Father made it plain. "Either way, I'll go first. Those who are healthy have to help the injured. And stay low. There'll be smoke, but don't be scared, God will see us through, no fears. We'll get going and stay together and we'll get there." He leaned and took an injured woman over his shoulder. "Come on, get up, we're going." He turned and led them, still crouched, to the open stairwell.

The Father waited a few seconds until the bulk of the group was behind him. He looked over the crowd to Burl. "Bring her," he told him, looking over at Zed. Burl nodded.

The Father's eyes swept the crowd, his eye contact comforting, reassuring them. "Stay low," he said. And then he was through the door, disappearing up the stairs. The crowd followed, two and three at a time.

"No!" Zed yelled, "don't go."

"Don't worry," Burl told her. "I'll take you."

"You idiot," she said. "Stu locked the roof, remember."

Burl frowned, watching the crowd push through the door. "That was three days ago." He advanced. "Come on."

"No way." Zed backed up toward the elevator bay. "There's another set of stairs, we'll take them. I just have to find the door."

Burl crouched. "Zed, you're in pain, you're not making sense. Come on, I'm just trying to help."

Zed backed up past Stu, pulling a knife out of his body as she passed. "I'm not going."

Burl just kept coming. Zed drew back her arm and threw. She had better luck this time. Burl was a not a bad guy, but she didn't want to die just to suit him. She reached for a shard of glass. Burl pulled the knife from his bicep and watched the line of blood pour out. He stood up and dropped his hands. "Okay, you win. I'll tell the Father you'll see him later." He tossed the knife at her feet, then turned and ran for the door, disappearing into the smoke.

Zed didn't have time for goodbyes. She was on her knees, tracing her fingernails along the wall, feeling for the crack. *Come on*, she told herself while coughing on the smoke, *you've been in tougher spots*. Just find that door.

It took a while, long enough for the smoke to make her cough a fit that she thought might never stop. Still, she found it. Her nails traced the crack in the wall. She'd remembered how Gears opened it: a switch at the top. Problem, she was too fucking short. She looked around, her mind racing full speed and going nowhere. What could she do? Look for a chair. That was it. The groan of the elevator distracted her.

A short figure in black pants and a black turtleneck leapt out. "Fire and brimstone!" the prophet yelled, happy to be right at last. "For the sky was black as ashes and fire fell from the sky, such were the signs." He spotted Zed and walked over to her, oblivious that his head was almost obscured in smoke. "Such have the mighty fallen, and the end is nigh, for I have eaten the little book and it is bitter, it tastes of soot and sulphur."

"Help me?" she asked. He ignored her and wandered toward Luc's office and the flames.

That's it, Zed figured as she lay on the floor trying to suck clean air through the carpet, she'd run out of time. No time to search, no time to run around, it was game over. She could make a break for the stairs or try a repeat of Bottomless Joe's big leap. She didn't like her choices.

Zed had decided to risk the jump when a voice intruded. "Hey, Zed." It was Steve again, crawling toward her. "Did you know, I think the building's on fire."

"No kidding."

"Hey, we're still friends, right?" Steve gave her a grin. "I mean, it's okay if I hang with you?"

And here it was, a way out. If only she could get through to what Steve had left of a mind. "Hey, friend." She guided his hand to the wall. "You feel this crack?"

Steve giggled. "Yeah."

"Okay buddy, follow it all the way up and then push in. You got that?"

Steve looked up. "But it's smoky up there."

"You want to hang or not?"

"Okay." And twenty seconds later the door swung open, cool clear air rushing out.

Zed crawled in and found the light switch. "Come on," she told Steve. "We're outta here."

He had a huge grin. "Hey, I just realized, Luc's door is wide open and all his stuff is in there."

"Steve, don't be an idiot, you'd fry like chicken."

"Naw, just think of the H – like, for free." He turned toward the office.

"Steve, hey, friend, come on." Zed extended her hand.

"Don't worry," he called back as he crawled down the hall. "I'll be back."

"Steve!" But he was gone and Zed knew he was never coming back. Still, she left the door open.

The further Zed descended, the clearer the air became. She counted the flights down until she had reached the sub-parkade. She ran out and over to Gears' door, sliding it open.

"If I wasn't stone cold," Gears said, "I would definitely say this was acid blues."

Zed blinked, her eyes adjusting to the dark of Gears' back room. Gears was reclined on a sofa, a TV on the table in front of him. Lying in his arms on the couch was the black-skirted, short-haired figure of Countessa. The scenes of fire broadcast from the in-house security cameras flickered unnoticed as Gears and Countessa stared at Zed. "Really, Zed, have you ever tried knocking?" Countessa asked, turning her back to Zed and leaning up to give her brother a kiss. He wrapped his hands in hers and slowly started plucking the rings off her fingers.

Zed frowned. "Aren't you brothers?"

"Zed, there is a fine line between an innocent and a prude," Gears told her, breaking off the kiss. "Besides, there's something very erotic about fire, it's built into our tribal patterns, so why fight it?"

"Lots of room," Countessa offered, arching a look at Zed and patting the cushions on the couch.

"Er, not now," Zed said. "Where's Ivy? Oh, and I need some gasoline."

"Class. Only you, Zed, could sell gas at a fire." Gears laughed. "I like what you've done with the building, very stylish. Your chest isn't too bad either."

"Ivy," she reminded.

"Just a second." He pushed Countessa back from sucking on his nipples. Gears reached into his back pocket and pulled out a key. He flipped it toward Zed, "E-4," he told her. "Second level from the bottom. There's gas in the back room."

Zed ran into the back and found the five gallon can by smell. She grabbed a flashlight on the way out.

Zed came out to find Countessa crawling up Gears' body. "Being Countessa's boring. I wanna be someone new."

"Okay." Gears wrapped the Countessa's hands around his neck, "Brother?"

"No, still sister, I think." She leaned in and kissed his neck, working her way up to his ear.

Ick alert, Zed told herself as she dug the fifty from her boot and threw it down. She took off down the parkades, checking door numbers on the way down. Sure enough, she found E-4, on the floor before the bottom.

It wasn't much of a room, just a single bulb hanging from the ceiling, four grey walls and a cot. But Ivy was there, alive, wrapped in a blanket. She looked tired, but she smiled when she saw Zed, her eyes widening. "You and your wanton ways," she sighed, shaking her head, but with a twinkle that said she was kidding. "I never seen a girl who could lose clothes so quick."

Zed ran across to her, putting a finger up to her lips. "Luc's just down a bit," she told her.

"That slick devil? What's he want?" Ivy demanded.

"To kill you."

"Oooo! The nerve, the nerve of some people," Ivy wailed, outraged. Her eyes narrowed as she examined Zed's chest. "What's this? What's this?"

Zed closed her hands over Ivy's. "Not now. The building's on fire."

"Is it? Well, I never." Ivy sniffed the air. "Can't smell nothing."

"It is, and we have to go," Zed told her. "But first I've got to go do some business with Luc. So if I'm not back in ten minutes, you go ahead."

"And leave you behind?" Ivy was offended. "Never."

"I'll be coming." Zed ignored Ivy's frown and reminded her. "Ten minutes." Then she slipped out the door.

Did she have a plan? Well, sorta. She had an intention, that she should survive and that Luc should never bother her again.

Halfway down the last slope, she stopped and slipped off the jacket, draping it over an arm. In the other, she dragged the five-gallon can.

The door to the rec room was open and as Zed edged past the pool, she pointed the light. Yep, there was her stuff, still at the bottom.

In Luc's little kingdom, everything was pretty much the same: charnel house smell, rows of dead bodies, Bottomless Joe still hanging, and even Luc up on the podium putting on bandages.

Zed walked up the middle row halfway, Luc's vial bouncing against her naked chest. She stopped and put down the gas.

Luc raised his head. "I can't offer you much," he sang out and gestured to his burnt skin, "but feel free to help yourself to a bit of jerky."

Zed's eyes roved over the place. She spotted a new face in the choir: Christine slumped in the front row. "You couldn't wait?"

"I know." Luc raised his hand to his forehead. "I have no defence, it's just I was so short of altos." He levered himself up by his elbows. Now that he was standing, Zed could see that his pants had burned away and his legs were a red and black mass of scorched muscles and oozing burns. "I was wondering if you were coming."

"We've still got some business to take care of." Zed advanced far enough to throw the jacket.

Luc caught it and pulled off the tatters of his grey jacket before sliding on the blue one. "There you go again," he said, "what a turn of phrase. Aren't I supposed to be tied up and you tapping a baseball bat against your leg when you say that?"

"Okay!"

"Ha, ha." He looked over her naked body. "Is this supposed to tempt me?"

She looked down at her skin and her boots. "No, you cut my clothes, remember?"

"Oh, right. You want a nice silk suit to replace it?" He tipped the brim of the Panama hat. "Maybe a hat?"

"Naw, who wants to look like you?"

"Everyone. They all want it, but only I've got it. So what's your pleasure?" He staggered over to the steps and started down. On the second step he tumbled, his tortured legs refusing to work. He rolled to the bottom. Zed waited while he dragged himself upright. "You hold the marker. What's your price?"

"First." Zed went over and grabbed a candle, tipping the wax off. "I just want to know. Why couldn't you make a deal with me?"

"Oh, I'm sorry? Feeling guilty we blew up the building, are we?"

"No, all I'm saying is you could have left me alone." Zed unscrewed the cap on the gas.

"And you could've given me the woman, but you didn't, and I didn't, and that's who we are. I would have paid, though."

"I owed her, unfinished business."

"Must have been some debt," Luc observed, lurching over to sit with the choir. He rested his hand on Christina's shoulder.

"A blanket," Zed admitted.

"Blanket." Luc looked out from under the shadow of his brim.

"Sometimes, when I think I've got you all worked out, you pull something like this. I like it. So, you ready to deal or what? I'm offering, in exchange for my own little pinkie, a position as my assistant, not lackey, not thug, but the brains behind the brawn."

"You mean all this –" Zed swept an arm over the rows of rotting corpses. "– can be mine?"

"Certainly. They don't look like much now, but they've got potential. Besides, I've markers on all of them. They'll be coming back, sooner or later." He broke off into racking coughs. He pulled out a white handkerchief to cover his mouth. It was red when the coughing was over. "Red? My blood's red? Well, that is a severe disappointment."

"I think I'll pass," Zed told him.

"Okay, final offer. I'll throw in Barry." He pointed to a corpse in the second row. Barry leered, slack-jawed and looking gamy. "He's yours to own outright. But hurry, it's a time-limited offer. Look around, Countessa's out, the Father's gone, the followers dispersed, ready to be led, to be gently nudged back into the tracks. With the two of us, why stop at the Tower? The whole downtown has been begging for us for years. Either way, Luc's still here. What about you?"

"I'll pass. You know something? You wiped me out, down to the last can of peaches. I'm bust. I'll be back to running crackers. But not for you."

"Oh, ho, I see it," Luc smiled and rubbed his hands together. "It's revenge you want, and this is the old shootout. Tower not big enough for the both of us, eh? Where's your knife?"

"You think I'd win with knives? No. I'm not here to try and kill you. I'm cleaning you out." And with that, she kicked over the can, letting the gas run out in a slow moving wave.

"Hey," Luc struggled to his feet, a knife in his hand. "That's not funny. You really, really don't know what you are doing."

"It's just business," Zed told him.

"Now don't go sticking your head where your body can't follow," he warned. "You just tell me what you want for my marker and we leave it at that."

"Now *you* don't get it. I'm cleaning you out, marker and all." Zed twisted off the lid to the vial with one hand and upended it, swallowing everything in a single salty gulp. Ugh, she never wanted to do that again. "Tastes like chicken," she choked out.

"Fuck." Luc was well and truly pissed off.

Zed ducked to escape the knife that came flying end over end. It clipped her arm, but it wasn't deep, just another bleeder. As she ducked, the candle slipped, and now she could feel it sliding from her hand. Shit, shit, shit. She let it go and leaped for the door. Next time, she told herself, stand away from the can.

Her boots were smoldering and her legs singed, but before she could think about it, she was standing by the pool, watching as the chairs caught fire, and the bodies on them popped and snapped like hot dogs on the grill. And above it all, a single scream of rage.

The scream died out and she watched as the fire spread, sending up a gagging smell. She didn't see Luc for the longest time, then spotted him dragging himself up the stairs with his hands. He reached the podium and slumped, his eyes on her.

"Fucked. So continue this later then?" he yelled, before breaking into another coughing fit. And then he gave a salute.

Zed's hand raised before she could even think. He was smiling at her. Even with the blood and burns and everything he had done to her, there was something about him. She found herself grinning. "You're a bastard!" she yelled.

"You know," he said, propping himself up on an elbow, ignoring the flames already devouring his new jacket, "I think you're right."

Waves of thick oily smoke rose between them and the next time Zed saw Luc he was pulling himself into his great chair.

The pain came now, as the anger drained out of her. She threw one of the small candles at him, but it missed and hit the stairs instead. "Why?" she yelled.

He turned to sit, his body slumping to one side. "Why what?" he shouted.

"Why ... fuck, why don't you die?"

He laughed then, long and loud, his laughter ringing around the high roof, now choked with smoke. And that's the only answer she got because Luc didn't move again or respond to any of her shouts. The fire rose up from the dead like a wall, until it even engulfed Bottomless Joe and blocked her from seeing that lounging figure, in his white hat and burnt remnants of a grey suit.

ZED TURNED AND RAN. She paused at the rec room door, but didn't bother turning around. Screw it. Screw everything. Ivy was at the top of the slope, waiting.

"Business done?" Ivy asked, holding out a blanket.

Zed accepted the blanket. "I thought I told you to go already."

"I'm sorry, I can't hear very well." Ivy's eyes shone. "Being so old and all."

"So can we go?"

"My, look at the fire." Ivy was watching the smoke and flickering light coming from the rec room door. "It seems to just follow you around."

Zed couldn't decide whether to laugh or sigh, so she did both, a sort of choking noise. "Long day," she told Ivy and herded her toward the stairs.

Ivy wasn't a quick mover. Zed had lots of time to think things out. She didn't want to move on, but she had to see how much would be left – not that the die-hard junkies wouldn't be staying. Burnt-out buildings were familiar ground to them. But they traded low.

"Now, love," Ivy broke into her thoughts, "you'll come live with me. It's no bother. With my Quince gone, you're the closest I got to family, and I like having family about." She rubbed Zed's back. "Hold on, young colt, these bones aren't made for leaping up stairs."

Zed looked to Ivy who looked up at her with a kind and lonesome face. "It's no bother," Ivy repeated. "After all you've done for me." Ivy hesitated, then added, "Been to me." Zed held out a hand and led Ivy up the stairs.

They opened the door at the lobby and the smoke was down on them like a wall, hard and choking. They couldn't see more than a few feet, yet wafts of fresh air kept blowing toward them, so they followed the drafts.

A creature in a black mask and covered in yellow loomed from out of the smoke. "Got two." Zed was blinded by the beam of light in her face. "Alive, repeat, two alive, coming out." A hand rose and pulled off the mask, pushing it over Ivy's face. "Breathe in. You're going to be all right."

The fireman took the middle and moved them forward. He pushed the mask in Zed's face and she breathed. It was cold and dry air, and it made her remember the air the first time she explored underground. Wonder and fear.

They emerged through the front doors. The street was littered with fire trucks, ambulances, police, hoses, watchers, lights. A fireman rushed past and another approached, taking Ivy's arm and herding her toward the ambulances. "Get your hands off me, you big slab of muscle!" Ivy protested, but she went.

Once clear of the fire hoses, Zed stopped and looked back at the building. Flames had broken out through most of the windows of the first twelve floors and were still working their way up. The outside of the building was stained black from the flames that licked the walls and the smoke bleeding upward from every window, joining up in a black tower above the building. A fireman came up. "Come on, we'll get you checked out."

I think not, Zed figured. She was working on an escape plan when she heard her name being called. She turned and Dean, the social worker, was leaping over hoses running toward her. He nodded to the fireman.

"Social Services." The fireman gave a shrug and turned to go. Dean dropped to a crouch, his hand moving up to sweep back her bangs. "I heard on the radio and I came down. God, look at the place. But you made it!" He grinned at her, the relief evident in his voice. "You made it." He waited to see if she had anything to say, but she didn't. Nothing even to trade. He stood and put his hands on her shoulders, leading her between the fire trucks, past the lights. "You know, you can't go back there," he told her, then looked back at the building and laughed. "Of course you know. But don't worry," he said, "I'm going to pull some strings. I know this family. They'll take you in. They're really nice – two kids your age and everything. It'll be a shock at first, but give it a chance. I know you'll have them milked dry in no time." Dean rushed on. His hand, on her shoulder, gave her a squeeze. Zed stopped and looked up at the 19th floor and the roof. Both were empty, only smoke.

She tried not to think about them up there, jammed in the stairs, up at the door. She'd told them it was locked. The Father would be strong, calming people down. Burl, Howard, Jenny, and the rest. *Idiots*, she told herself. *They were idiots.* She stared around her, wondering who could be left. She spotted Mary, travel book in hand, trying to hide behind an ambulance.

"Zed, you seen Christina?" It was Ellen. She was strapped to a gurney, waiting by an ambulance, covered in black soot.

Zed slipped out from under Dean's hand and walked over to the gurney. "Where's Teresa?" Zed asked, ignoring the question.

Ellen gave a hook of the thumb to the ambulance. "She's already inside." She wrinkled her nose. "I overheard them, they're taking us to detox."

"Bleah!" Zed agreed, sticking out her tongue.

"You haven't got anything on you, have you?" Ellen asked. "Booze, pills?" Zed shook her head and Ellen lay back down. "Just hoping."

She overheard a deep gravel voice barking out a word. It came from behind the ambulance so Zed left Ellen and crept around the ambulance. She dropped to her knees, peeping around the tire. She was right. It was

Hammer and he was standing, his blue shirt only mildly stained in soot, talking to the police.

"Priest," he barked out. "Petrol bombs, Molotovs, throwing," he told the man in blue, who wrote it all down. "Religious fanatics, attacking," he finished. The man in blue nodded. They walked off together toward a dispensary truck.

Oh yeah, she remembered, watching Hammer's back, *unfinished business*. She ducked in the shadow of a fire truck and edged along, angling for the Tower's entrance. She let a crew of fire fighters run past with a hose, then slipped in behind them.

She was fine till they hit the cleared area before the doors. The lights made it a shadeless wonder, not a single spot to hide.

"Wait." She heard the yell and took off, heading right for the double doors. "Grab that kid."

Ha, too slow, she thought as she dove through the doors, her body crawling forward as it hit the floor. She was headed for the bunker because the way she figured it, she owed Hammer twice, once for the bombs and once for the nails.

She quickly crawled to Hammer's bunker. Inside, she reached up and felt the table, only the surveillance TVs. Nothing on the floor but trash and some of Hammer's ripped, cast-off pages. Damn. It must be in one of the storage cupboards. *Let it go*, the sensible part of her shouted. *Is it worth dying for a chance at vengeance? Business*, the other part of her said. *It's business.*

She crawled out of the bunker and down into the alleyways off the lobby. She counted with her left hand, one door, two doors, three. Using only her touch, she felt around inside until she found it. She wrapped it in the blanket, hugging it to her chest. She crawled on, a quick left and through the door, and she was outside again, in that small, tucked-away exit where she had watched Luc sway the mob only a few days before.

As she looked out over the lights, she saw Dean pulling and shouting at the fire chief. The lights were on full. She'd never make it back.

"Fly, fly, my pretties!" came the scream from above as a bundle hit the ground with a thwack. Zed hoped it wasn't more cats. Another thud, then another, and to the shrieks of, "You're free, you're free!" A steady rain of objects started to fall. The spotlight moved up the building till it caught the Prof heaving books off his balcony for all he was worth. He was a regular catapult. "Nero! Fish Street Baker! They're after you again. Run, run."

"Sir, calm down," a voice from a bullhorn said. And Zed took the Prof's advice, running through the space, leaping over hoses until she slid to a stop beside an ambulance. Thanks again, Prof.

"Sir, we're setting up a net, just calm down."

Zed grabbed the nail gun in one hand and let the blanket drape over her. *Last thing*, she told herself, *and then you can rest.*

Zed positioned herself behind the chief, waiting to catch Dean's eye.

"Zed!" he rushed over, his hand falling on her head. "Don't do things like that. I've only got so much adrenaline, you know. You don't want to go in a foster home, just say no next time."

"No, it's cool."

"It's really not going to be that bad," he reassured her. "Ready?"

She swallowed and nodded. "Okay, but I want to thank someone first." She kept her voice steady. "That man, over there, he saved me." She pointed at Hammer standing by the concession truck sipping a coffee.

Dean looked down at her, smiled with understanding, and nodded. "Sure."

"When we get to him," Zed asked, "can you lift me up so I can –" Zed's face pinched as she tasted ashes. "– hug him?"

Dean nodded and with his hand resting on her they walked over to Hammer. Coming up behind Hammer, Dean grabbed Zed round the waist and hoisted her up. Zed felt sick when she heard Dean say, "Mister, I thing Zed has something she wants to tell you."

Hammer turned and Zed caught a surprised glint in his eye as she wrapped an arm around him. "Zed?" He grunted.

Dropping the blanket, she brought the nail gun in close. "No," she hissed into Hammer's ear, "it's flowers." And with the squeeze of her finger, Zed sent a nail ripping into Hammer's skull. She moved the nail gun an inch and pressed the trigger again, just for good measure.

Hammer stood, his eyes open, the edges of two nails protruding through his short speckled hair. Then, stiff-legged, he toppled backwards. At the first "phut," Dean's hands had dropped away, so she clung to Hammer and rode him down.

Zed scrambled backward, thumbing off the belt and ripping open Hammer's trousers. She felt the body twitch under her, so she guessed he wasn't dead quite yet. She pulled out his dick and found out that the boozer's fable was just that, fable; dying men don't always get hard.

She ignored the sounds around her, the calls of her name. She was Zed: she didn't take shit from no one and she never backed down on a deal. One hole, one time. So she shut her eyes and stuck the dick in her mouth.

IN THE BACK OF the police van, Zed watched through the metal mesh as Ellen's gurney was slammed into the ambulance and driven away. She watched Dean as he rounded up Mary and shepherded her into his car, giving guilty glances toward the van. She was watching the fire trucks now. A runty-shaped fireman caught her eye as he slipped out of the shadows and tried on helmets off the back of the truck. After finding one he liked, he slipped into a jacket and grabbed an axe. "Hee, hee," she heard, as the fireman stepped into the light, revealing his grey beard and twitchy eyes.

"Rat!" Zed pounded on the back of the van, shoving her fingers through the mesh. "Hey, Rat!" He turned and growled, shaking the axe at her. "Shut the fuck up," he told her, then slid around the fire truck and followed its shadow to the next one, where he unscrewed some of the brass and secreted it in his jacket pockets. Zed watched until he passed out of her range of vision.

She didn't know where they'd be taking her. Did it matter? She'd have to start over, but she'd done that before. She folded up her single asset, the blanket, and checked herself out with her fingers and eyes. There was a cracked rib, shoulders, arms and legs covered with burns, her chest covered in cuts, and holes through her wrists.

They looked good, she decided. They gave her character.

Okay, first book and I've got to figure out who gets the dedication. I suppose it could be a writer; there was the one I bet a case of wine with on who would finish their novel first. Except he turned out to be a pretty nasty alcoholic. The last I heard of him was at a writers retreat when he banged on my door at two a.m. screaming that he was going to break in and kill me, "you fuck-cunt," if I didn't hand over the bottle of port he had seen in my luggage. So, not him, and I'm still owed a case of wine from someone.

Relatives are always a good stand-by for this sort of thing. Except that most of them wouldn't stand in the same room with me in case I sneezed and infected them with confusing yet strangely satisfying homo-erotic nocturnal dreams. I wish my Great Great Aunt were still alive for dedications. I found her life very inspirational; she ran away in her teens to join the circus (more precisely, the circus master), and after outliving four husbands by the time she was eighty-five, used her fortune on hiring gigolos to service her.

First Love, Teachers, or Mentors: yeah, they would all do. Too bad one stole all my money and used it for cocaine. Another told me that I would probably end up as a whore in a Central American country. The third made it clear that I was deeply, deeply disturbed and exuded something pornographic, not the sex, just the sordid firth of it all.

So, to every person out there who knows that "What doesn't kill you makes you stronger" is not only total crap but far more likely to make you limp or ache when it is about to rain. Or to every person who realizes that the scars of facing the enemy and the scars which are self-inflicted look pretty much the same. And especially to every person out there for whom doing what you love is a giant scream saying, "I exist, I exist, I exist!" – Well, I agree. This book is dedicated to you.

– *E.M.*

I was conceived in the summer of '69 thanks to a road trip, a late summer heat wave, deficiency of birth control, and an air-conditioned movie theatre showing Zeffirelli's *Romeo and Juliet*. My earliest memories were of watching National Film Board experimental films in our basement and falling in love with my babysitter, Shandora, who lived next door with her many, many cats.

While growing up my secret dream was to become an orphan. Every book from *Anne of Green Gables* to *Pippi Longstocking* demonstrated that to have a life of excitement, adventure, and envy to all, you either had to be plucky with an incurable disease, or an orphan.

I've lived in three countries, travelled through four continents, and I came back to the West Coast because I like it the best. So until community petitions or restraining orders say otherwise, my partner and I could be living in a neighbourhood near you.

— E.M.

Publisher's note:
An essay about the writing and themes of Zed *is available by*
email from the publisher upon request. info@arsenalpulp.com